PRAISE FOR GUY IN REAL LIFE

"Brezenoff successfully immerses readers in the characters' progression from awkward acquaintances to adorably besotted teens. In addition to alternating between their perspectives, he also spends time within both the digital and analog RPGs, exploring sexism and gender stereotypes, while highlighting the way that both types of games are often driven by a novelistic kind of storytelling. An idiosyncratic romance that offers plenty of cultural food for thought."
—*Publishers Weekly*

"Virtual worlds collide with 'real' life in this dead-on depiction of teen gaming culture. Demons, warriors, and orcs abound, but it's the reality that bites hardest. I suppose Steve Brezenoff will have to grow up one of these days and forget what it was like to be sixteen, but let's hope it doesn't happen too soon—at least not to the part of him that can write a book like *Guy in Real Life*." —Pete Hautman, National Book Award–winning author of *Godless*

"*Guy in Real Life* is a fascinating, original take on the spaces that exist between who we are and who we hope to be. Virtually everyone will love this book." —John Corey Whaley, Printz Award–winning author of *Where Things Come Back*

"Brezenoff's writing is intelligent, engaging, and insightful. He understands that even the smallest detail informs who people become." —*VOYA*

"In a first-person narration that alternates between the boy in black and the girl dungeon master, Brezenoff conjures a wry, wise, and deeply sympathetic portrait of the exquisite, excruciating thrill of falling in love. This is not the teen love story you've read a thousand times before." —*Kirkus Reviews* (starred review)

ALSO BY **STEVE BREZENOFF**

Brooklyn, Burning
The Absolute Value of -1

GUY IN REAL LIFE

STEVE BREZENOFF

Balzer + Bray

An Imprint of HarperCollins*Publishers*

Balzer + Bray is an imprint of HarperCollins Publishers.

Guy in Real Life
Copyright © 2014 by Steve Brezenoff

Library of Congress Cataloging-in-Publication Data
Brezenoff, Steven.
Guy in real life / Steve Brezenoff. — First edition.
pages   cm
Summary: "The lives of two Minnesota teenagers are intertwined
through the world of role-playing games"— Provided by publisher.
ISBN 978-0-06-226684-2
[1. Love—Fiction.   2. Video games—Fiction.   3. Fantasy games—
Fiction.   4. Role playing—Fiction.   5. Minnesota—Fiction.]   I. Title.
PZ7.B7576Gu   2014   2013021584
[Fic]—dc23   CIP
                                                                 AC

Typography by Ray Shappell

15 16 17 18 19   PC/RRDH   10 9 8 7 6 5 4 3 2 1
❖
First paperback edition, 2015

To Etta Ruth, my girl

It is to be all made of fantasy,

All made of passion, and all made of wishes;

All adoration, duty, and observance,

All humbleness, all patience, and impatience,

All purity, all trial, all obeisance.

As You Like It, Act V, Scene II

LEVEL ONE

CHAPTER 1

LESH TUNGSTEN
<DRUNK AND STUPID>

"This is not my life."

Everything is spinning on the curb in front of Vic B's bar. I shouldn't have been drinking. I knew that beforehand. I knew that as I drank. I know that now, sitting on said curb, with my head on my knees and a puddle of chunky vom next to my feet. It smells like bile and the banh mi I had before the concert. But on the last Saturday before school starts up again, with What Dwells Within, the best quasi-local metal band there is, playing within walking distance of my house, should I be expected to stay home? Of course not. And with school about to start, me entering my sophomore year, should I be expected to pass up vodka drinks when I'm given the opportunity to demonstrate my badassedness? Probably, but when seniors are pushing me up to the bar, that's pretty much not going to happen.

The music has stopped now. It was thumping hardcore until

a moment ago, I think. It might have been the echo bouncing around in my empty head for the last few minutes, though. I missed the encore, I guess. Sucks.

But the spinning is the worst part, because the rest of that little Vietnamese sandwich is about to come up. A hand slaps the top of my head a few times and I groan.

"You missed the encore, Lesh." It's Greg—Greg Deel, my best friend, too-constant companion, and all around PITA. We're identical in a lot of ways: black trench coats, supernaturally black hair, black jeans, black tennis shoes. Greg's mom says we also constantly wear black faces—this is right before she tries to tickle us like we're both five, hoping our surly exterior will crack. It doesn't.

But he's also about a foot shorter than me, and he still has big fat baby cheeks, where mine are kind of bony and require semiregular shaving. At the bar, he got ignored and would have even with the best fake ID around. But I got served half the time I tried, and that's enough that I ended up feeling like this at the end of the night, and he ended up feeling like the newborn babe he so resembles, which means he can torment me while he makes sure I get home alive. It's lucky we both live about a ten-minute walk from the bar, in the part of Saint Paul that has nasty hole-in-the-wall bars that book metal bands when they're not serving hardcore alkies and women with eye patches.

"What'd they play?" I try to say, but it comes up like "whuu," before turning Technicolor.

Greg jumps back about five feet. "Dude, you almost got my shoes." He sticks a bottle of water in my face. I manage a thank-you, unscrew the top, and pour about half of it on my head. For some reason I'm burning up—I mean, sweating like mad. The idea of putting the water into my body is unpleasant, but on my head, it's actually quite nice.

Greg grabs the bottle back. "Hey, don't waste it," he says, and I manage to ask what the encore was. Anyone other than Greg probably would have still found me unintelligible. "'Where Are You Now, Isaiah?' It pretty much melted everyone's goddamn face."

That's their best song. It never fails to get the crowd going insane—except the members of the crowd who have had to give up waiting for the bathroom to sprint outside and puke in the gutter between parked cars, in plain sight on goddamn University Avenue, across from the twenty-four-hour grocery store where half the neighborhood shops every Sunday after freaking church. "Come on, get up," Greg says. He grabs my wrists and pulls me to my feet. Then we stagger along University to the first corner and north into the neighborhood. We could have walked a little more on the main drag, but staggering on University after two a.m. is a bad idea, generally. If you don't get beat up and mugged or spotted by the police, you still have to walk past the first gay bar in the Twin Cities, and then they whistle at you from the little gated smoking area. That's always a little uncomfortable, to put it mildly, but with Greg's arm around my waist—to keep me from walking into the street or falling right over—it'd be unbearable.

"That girl was looking for you," Greg says. My head spins a little as it looks for a picture, a still or animated image, of the girl in question. I remember ogling a girl with pink streaks and three rings in her bottom lip. I remember talking to one with lots of black eye makeup and leather bands on her wrists. Metal spikes.

"What girl?" I mumble.

"Man, how much did you drink?" Greg says. He shakes his head, and we stumble a little as he turns me onto Thomas Avenue.

"Why are we taking Thomas?" I say.

Greg ignores me and goes on about the mystery girl. "She had black lipstick. Her name was Kiki."

An image—a pink image with a black cat—flashes across my hazed-over eyeballs. "Skirt?"

"That's her," Greg says. He gives me an extra stabilizing shove and stops. It turns out I can stand on my own, and we walk on, no longer embracing. "Anyway, she was worried about you."

"Huh," I say. "Does she go to Central?"

Greg shrugs. "Didn't ask. Didn't recognize her, though."

We get to the corner with a stoplight—Hamline Avenue. Greg cuts diagonal through the intersection, and I hobble after him. No cars around this late, but the Super USA is open. It's the sketchiest convenience store for two miles in any direction. My mother won't go in there at noon on a Sunday. That's Midway, and that's our neighborhood.

"Thirsty," I say. Greg's already got a big bottle of water by the time I walk into the store, and he's at the counter dropping two bills. I barely enjoy the cool convenience-store air before it's time to go back outside. I take a swig—a long one—from Greg's bottle as we get back to the sidewalk. I guess I've forgotten I'm still a little drunk—okay, bombed—because the bottle is upside down and still to my lips, so I'm looking up at the overcast night sky when we reach the corner again. That's why I'm not watching where I'm going, and though Greg is saying things like, "Watch where you're going," I still don't watch where I'm going.

Which is when the bike hits me. The bottle of water is the first casualty: I don't just drop it; I fling it, screaming, toward a row of hedges on the retaining wall next to me, and its contents fly in every direction like a sprinkler's spew. It lands in someone's backyard.

Second casualty: me. I collapse as I finish my scream, and my back slams against the aforementioned retaining wall. I feel the rocky face scrape up my back as I slide. Somehow my head hits gently. I don't think I'm bleeding.

Third casualty: the biker. She careens off my stupid form, off the sidewalk—and why the hell is she riding on the sidewalk?—and drops from the high curb with a thud and a rattle. Her handlebar basket dumps its contents, and then her seat dumps her, right into the gutter.

She says, "Ow," and Greg runs over. She pulls off her helmet and lets her long, blond hair fall out. Don't get the wrong idea. I'm not giving you the old "helmet comes off, blond hair shakes and falls in waves on the gorgeous girl" routine. This is more like white blond, first of all, rather than golden, and it falls not in waves, but in a matted bunch of twists and clumps and messy flyaways—like actual corn silk, when you can't get those last few strands off the ear.

"You okay?" Greg says, but she pulls away when he grabs her elbow and gets up on her own. She's shaky, and it's an awkward move with her helmet still in one hand. When she sees the contents of her basket—a now-empty tote bag and a bunch of spiral notebooks—spread across the pavement, she freaks.

"Graham cracker crust!" she shouts, or something equally censored and ridiculous. I can't be sure. I can't even be sure she's really standing there. Under the flickering white light of the lamp in the Super USA parking lot, she looks like an angel, as imagined in the movies of the 1920s. I reach back and put my hand on the back of my head, and it's a little damp. Maybe it *is* bleeding. The world is spinning as bad as it was twenty minutes before—before I lost my supper in the gutter. I'm about to lose it again, no doubt about it, so the stupidest thing I can do is try to stand up to help this biker girl pick up her books and papers. When I reach the pile, though, I'm still on all fours.

"Just leave it," she says, and she isn't angry—which, good,

because honestly, it was her fault. Side*walk*. But she's on all fours now too, and Greg is picking up her bike, in the middle of the street, and my head—which you'll remember is still spinning and is also bleeding, and it's probably the loss of blood that has me in this sort of state—clunks right into hers, and despite all that white-blond hair, there's very little cushioning, so our bowling-ball bonkers straight-up echo with the collision. Anyway, mine does.

"Ow!" we both say. "Shit!" we both almost say, and I do, but she manages to take a sharp left and spit out "Shark attack," and I don't know what that even means. We're both on our knees, rubbing our heads, and Greg is standing in the middle of Hamline Avenue holding this girl's bike. When she stands, her face crinkled in pain and confusion and anger, the light from the Super USA parking lot seems to ignite her white-blond hair, its frizz and flyaways like lightning. By the time she mounts her bike, her sleekly muscled arms bare and stiff and her helmet back on her head, strapped under her chin and everything, I'm not even sure she's real.

She's about to pedal off when I spot a spiral notebook in a puddle near the curb—she must have missed it. I grab it and call to her, "Wait!" and I hold it up, me still on one knee in the gutter, her above me under the otherworldly light of the parking lot lamppost, and between us—in both our hands—is this notebook, its cover wet and full of ink, so ink runs in wild shades of purple and pink and blue, like a young bruise. But the art—it's a drawing of a gnarly forest, and a swirling

9

sky, and an icy mountain range, and over it all a huge beast with twisted horns and torn batlike wings. It's something out of an epic fantasy, and it's ruined.

"Thank you," she says, frowning at me, her eyes narrow and scornful. Then she shoves the wet notebook into her bag, pushes hard on the pedals, and creaks away.

CHAPTER 2

SVETLANA ALLEGHENY
<BRUISED AND BATTERED>

Quel imbécile! Quel imbécile ivre!

I can hardly ride now because my right knee is starting to bruise and I can feel it throb every time I pedal, and there's a big dent in the front fork of my bike. I love this bike, and I love the notebooks in my tote bag, the notebooks swollen with black and blue ink, a summer's worth of work, a summer's worth of imagination and dirty fingernails and a wicked callus on my right middle finger.

I should have flipped that idiot my middle finger!

Then again, he fished my precious green notebook out of an oily puddle of heaven-knows-what in the gutter outside a Super USA.

The poor green notebook—the very bible of the new semester, which starts in two days, thank you—is destroyed, soaked pages wrinkling and running ink into each other, in that pale and sort of cool-looking way that they do. And cool or not, I'd rather have my green notebook, unharmed. I have also made three copies of the green notebook, and thankfully they are safe at home in my desk drawer. I'd *still* rather have my *original* green notebook, unharmed.

They'd adored the green one—the Central High School Gaming Club, I mean. It was the only one I passed around tonight, to the eager and variant hands of the other members. There are only five of us, and it's been us five, and only us five, since Roan joined her freshman year, my sophomore year. As of Tuesday, I'll be a senior. So will Abraham, Reggie, and Cole. Roan's our baby, just a junior this year, and a year younger than the rest of her class. She skipped a grade—ages ago, back in elementary school—and she's in the Central High honors program. I swear, if she wanted, she could ask the principal if it would be okay if she just spent six and a half hours every day in the media center, studying on her own, and he'd probably pat her head and say, "Sure, Roan. I can't wait to hear about what you discover."

Abraham gaped at my artwork and detailed stats on each new creature—stunned into swearing, like always. He flipped through the pages of the green notebook with his right hand and pushed back his greasy dark-brown hair from his forehead with his left, revealing—and no doubt worsening—the acne problem his bangs usually hide (and probably cause). "Holy fork," he said. "Holy fork, Lana. This is forking ridiculous."

I am not big into swearing. I have censored Abraham's speech.

"It really is, Svet," said Roan. "You've gotten so, so good." No one else—no one—calls me Svet, but Roan has been forever. We lived on the same block as little kids, she as a toddler, chasing me around the backyards, me as a preschooler, happily teaching her what being a big kid was all about. My parents moved us—clear across town, into a different elementary school's territory, and to the huge and gorgeous and Frank Lloyd Wright-y and probably on the National Register of Historic Places house that had been my granddad's—when I was ten, but Roan is a persistent and wonderful child and wouldn't let me slip away, and our friendship with me. Is it any surprise that she joined the Gaming Club on the first day of her freshman year?

Reggie doffed his fedora when it came his turn to examine my summer's work. Upon seeing the very first page—the one of the feline-faced abominable snowman, something of a tree-sized, man-shaped lynx, prowling across the ragged and snowy cliffs, guarding the entrance of his treasure cave; I was especially proud of that drawing—his jaw dropped into a big, openmouthed grin, and his eyes went wide. I swear, I thought he'd cry when he started shaking his head slowly, like he was my grandmother and I'd just finished my doctorate or something. "This is amazing, Lana," he said, his words clipped and strained. He held up the drawing so I could see it too. Then he asked, narrowing his eyes, in a dark whisper, "We're going to fight this thing?"

I shrugged. "If you live that long," I said.

Cole grinned and let his head fall onto Reggie's shoulder. I wasn't sure if he was impressed or sleepy.

"Is he the end boss?" Abraham said, leaning forward. His bangs fell in front of his eyes, and he shook them away with a jerk of his head.

Abraham never fully closes his mouth. It makes him look sort of stupid, though we all know he's an übergenius. The rest of our class, though, makes their own assumptions.

I looked at the ceiling and feigned innocence. "How would I know?"

I'm the dungeon master, that's how. But I wasn't talking. My adventurers would discover the campaign as intended: as they went, deep in dungeons, roaming thick forests of eternal night, in the hidden chambers under innocent-looking village taverns. Between you and me, though, no. This beast of the snowy peaks was not the end boss. He was merely a diversion—albeit a diversion that could rip a low-level fighter's arm off at the shoulder and use it to pick the bits of the rest of the party out of his teeth after he'd finished eating.

It had only been an unofficial meeting, of course. Officially, the Central High Gaming Club couldn't meet without our faculty adviser, and never outside our assigned room in the school. But we're excited little campers, or anyway I am, and I just couldn't wait till our first official meeting on Wednesday to show the club my new monster manual. I should have waited, though. I should have kept my green notebook deep in my desk drawer, where it would have been safe from drunken, dirty boys in black.

I grit my teeth as I cross University Avenue and pedal hard up the hill toward my neighborhood, on the other side of the interstate, where people don't wander the streets at two in the morning, drunk and stupid, knocking innocent girls off their bikes and their most prized possessions into oily puddles in the gutter. As I pass the police station, I even think about stopping to report the drunken disorderlies—who, by the way, couldn't have been much older than me. One of them looked like he was twelve, if I'm feeling generous, so the other probably was too. He likely had some sort of hormonal imbalance that made him taller and hairier than his age should naturally. Maybe it comes from drinking so much.

The wind is nice now. It's rushing down the front of my dress and over the nearly invisible hair on my arms and into the vents of my helmet, cooling me off. It's always at this point—after climbing up from University to reach Marshall and then again over the bridge toward Summit—that I realize I've been biking hard, and I begin to sweat. This old bike isn't exactly an efficient machine. I love it, don't get me wrong. But it was built for comfort and a ladylike riding position. I can happily bike in a dress or long skirt when I want, which is always, and not worry about grease stains on the hems or pieces of cloth getting caught up in the chain. But I won't get anywhere quickly or easily, because I'm sitting straight up and the bike itself weighs as much as me.

I take Grand Avenue, which is weird. It's usually so crowded with traffic and delivery trucks and people walking and shopping and sipping coffee from one of the several thousand coffee shops within a mile of my house. Now the storefronts are dark. The streets are nearly empty. Even the bars are closed, thanks to Saint Paul's reasonable last call. I wonder briefly where those two boys in black had been drinking—probably some dank basement apartment where someone was cooking meth.

I take a deep breath, try to relax away my anger, as I turn off Grand and slide into the cool, quiet darkness of my neighborhood. It's only a few more blocks, over cobblestones, so I slip onto the sidewalk and coast the rest of the way. I never get tired of admiring the houses on this part of the ride, even ours. From the outside, they're stunning—each a picture-perfect example of one or another major era in American architecture. Ours is a two-and-a-half-story house from the Prairie School, immaculately cared for and boasting all its original wood detail. It's gorgeous. Still, I don't love it. I doubt I'll ever love it.

I hop off when I reach our driveway and enter the garage through the side door to put away my bike. Inside, the house is dark, and with my tote—which is still damp—on my shoulder, I move through the dark kitchen and into the front hall. It's a grand thing, with parquet floors and a Tiffany chandelier. Just off it is Dad's den—we all use it now and then, but it's got his records and his liquor cabinet and two leather couches that make me want to barf—and I don't let myself glance inside. I never do after dark: it's cavernous and empty, high ceilings and huge windows on the far side letting in moonlight and heebie-jeebies. It's like living in a Gothic horror, but with tackier furniture.

I climb the two flights to my attic bedroom, ducking as I go in. I never planned to be so tall that I'd have to, but there it is. It's still worth it, though. Having the highest bedroom in a house—and a whole story to myself—has its obvious advantages. Plus, since my darling parents see the attic bedroom as rather a bonus space, I'm allowed to do whatever I like in it, decor-wise, from eclectic wispy drapes in all the little windows, to painting the cantilevered ceilings with murals in shining, glittery paint. I have room up here for a drafting table, a small desk for my laptop, and another for my sewing machine. There's even a half bathroom. If the rest of the house were somehow destroyed, I'd still be okay up here. I might miss the kitchen.

I should probably get a small fridge up here. It will come in handy in college anyway, right?

But now I'm exhausted. It's nearly three, and my body is sore from biking halfway across Saint Paul, so I get ready for bed, put Berlioz's *"Marche au supplice"* on the iPod system on my nightstand, and slip under the gossamer canopy over my sliver of a bed along the wall. My eyes are closed, and my mind is taking me back to the snowy peak as the accused is climbing the scaffolding to his beheading in the symphony. Before I drift off, though, little eight-year-old feet sound from the steps, and I can picture Henrietta on the stairs, in her cotton pajamas, maybe with her stuffed sea monster tucked under her arm, climbing the steps to my bedroom. She's probably stopped in my open doorway now, watching me, wondering if I've fallen asleep yet. She probably holds a lock of her long white-blond hair—our only common trait, our parents like to say—stroking it slowly in the self-assured way that she does.

"Are you okay?" she whispers into my artificially starlit room.

"Yes," I say.

"You were out late."

"Mmhm."

She's still there. Her footsteps do not retreat. So I ask, "Are you okay, Henny?"

"Mmhm," she says. A few seconds pass. "Good night."

"Good night."

I'm asleep before I'm aware of her footsteps on the stairs—for all I know, she falls asleep in the bundle of throws on the beanbag chair in the corner; it's happened before. But I'm somewhere else now, at the top of the snow-covered mountains, high above the village, facing the entrance to the treasure cave. The giant feline monster has already been killed, and his body lies across the cave mouth, his black-red blood staining the snow. I must climb his body to reach the entrance, so I begin to, but his fur is still warm, and so soft and thick, and I find I want to curl up in it to sleep.

CHAPTER 3

LESH TUNGSTEN
<SHOULD BE SLEEPING>

Greg is a gamer of the finest order. I've played console games—who hasn't?—but Greg is far beyond anything most people would consider healthy. His pasty skin, dark, greasy hair, and T-shirts that honor the obscure and well-known alike from the realm of gamer-geekdom are all clear indicators of this aspect of Greg's life. We get along because (A) we have been best friends since the age of four, and (B) because when we were eleven, I told him I wouldn't be his friend anymore if he kept throwing game-related tantrums or brag sessions. He slips up now and then, but it's never been so bad that I've had to separate myself from his being, which is a good thing, since he lives on my block and neither of our parents are likely to move anytime soon.

Here's the upshot: for the last two years, Greg has been deep in an MMORPG—a massively multiplayer online role-playing game, that is. He hardly plays anything else, and his homework, aside from math, and his social life would have suffered if they weren't already in barely working order. As it is, when we hang out at his place, he has the game going the whole time, even if it's just so his "toons"—that's what he calls the characters he controls—are just fishing or learning to sew.

Yes, really. Fishing and sewing. These are things your toons too could excel at in this magical fantasyland of dragons and heroes and voluptuous elven women.

My parents and Greg's have a longtime and ongoing understanding that the boys can sleep in either house, no notice, period, so as I'm in no condition to go home, I crash at his place. Yeah, it is on the close-to-sunrise side of three a.m. when I crawl into a sleeping bag, so why not walk home and sneak in? Because sneaking into a hundred-year-old house with creaky floors and creaky stairs and a light-sleeping dad is pretty much impossible.

Greg's house isn't much bigger than ours, so when I crash, I crash in a sleeping bag on his bedroom floor. So you won't blame me, I think, for snapping at Greg as he sits in the desk chair several millimeters from my prone form, flicks on his desktop computer's huge display, and logs into that damn MMO. (You can just say MMO; the RPG part usually gets left out. I don't know who decides these things.)

"What the hell are you doing?" I close my eyes tight against the bright images flashing across the display and throw my arm across my face. "Turn it off!"

Greg is already in deep pose: his back forms an admirable

hunch, and his face is much too close to the screen. His jaw hangs open, just a bit, and sometimes he forgets to breathe. "I'm just going to check my auctions."

This game has its own economy. Greg has explained it to me on numerous occasions, but never while I was listening. In fact, the moment he starts to explain anything about the game, I stop listening.

"Nice," he whispers, practically begging for me to ask him what exactly is nice. I don't, of course, because I don't actually care what's nice, but he explains anyway. "I sold that world drop for almost a thousand gold."

"Wonderful," I say, which is dumb. It just eggs him on to get any kind of reaction. He's a lot like a toddler in that way.

"My stacks of elementium aren't moving at all," he goes on. "Some dink has cornered the market at way too low a price. Moron."

"Shut," I say. "Up."

He does shut up, aside from some whispers under his breath, and now and then I hear the computerized sound effects of sword on sword and spells being cast. In ten minutes, though, I'm dead to the world and soaring on the slowly spinning and tumbling—finally not entirely unpleasant—vodka ride. I don't know when Greg leaves his fantasyland and gets into bed himself, but when his mom taps gently on the door, it's the bright morning of the next day—Sunday—and Greg is snoring, completely covered by his crazy black quilt, the one his mom made from a few years' worth of retired geek T-shirts.

Okay, that's pretty cool. Obviously the kid is my best friend, and I don't hate him as much as I'm making it seem. Let's move on.

"Come on down for pancakes, you two," his mom says.

The words hit my skull like a heavy dinner plate. In my mind, the plate is covered with ten-inch flapjacks, swimming in butter and syrup, maybe slices of banana and granola crumbles. I groan and Greg's mom shuffles away, calling as she goes, "They'll get cold."

Is anything more vomitable than cold, untouched pancakes? Probably, but I won't try to figure out what, at least not while I'm feeling like this.

Greg rolls over. "Pancakes?" he says in a dry voice pitched about an octave lower than normal.

I manage to sit up and put my head in both hands. "Where's the water?" I say, thinking for an instant of the big plastic bottle we bought. Then the rest of the movie starts to play: the bottle soaring through the air over the row of shrubs next to the sidewalk, and I rewind a little more, and the bottle is slipping from my hands and I'm shouting, and a little farther, and the girl in the long skirt on the old-fashioned three-speed barrels into me—or I walk into her.

"Crap," I say, and Greg agrees. "What time is it?"

His head is back under the quilt, but one arm pops out and grabs his phone, pulls it back under the covers. "Almost ten," he mumbles. "Mom was feeling charitable this morning, I guess. She probably heard us come in."

But I'm barely listening, really, because I'm remembering when the helmet came off, and maybe I'm a little fuzzy in the head—I definitely am, really—but it's a beautiful picture, and my hand goes back to my head when I remember the bonk we had, like two coconuts passing in the night.

"I'm going home," I say, but I don't move. The very thought of standing up creates a heavy void in my gut.

"No pancakes?" Greg says.

"The next person who says 'pancakes' will die," I say.

Of course, from Greg comes: "Pancakes pancakes pancakes . . ."

On and on he goes, so I find my sneakers—heavy, black, and ragged enough that the brand is indiscernible; spoiler alert: they're from Target—and pull them on. I've slept in my jeans and everything else, so—sucking my tongue and wishing that water bottle hadn't flown away—I head out.

"Call me later," Greg says. "After you recuperate."

I salute as I close the bedroom door behind me. Greg's mom is at the bottom of the steps.

"Morning, Elizabeth," I say to her smiling, in-on-the-joke face. My own face must be pale and pallid, betraying my hangover—and like Greg said, she probably heard us come in. "I think I'm going to skip breakfast this morning."

She nods slowly. "A good idea." From behind her back, she pulls a glass of water cold enough that its outside is fogged and wet. "Here."

I say thanks with the glass already at my lips and down the

whole thing in one go. When I pull it away again and hand the slippery glass back to Ms. Deel, I'm woozy a minute and the cold water sits in my stomach like a cannonball. But it passes, and then I want another glass.

She thumbs over her shoulder toward the front door. "Git."

"On my way," I say, and I can feel her watching me leave when I pull the door closed behind me. The morning is cool and drizzly, so I pull on the hood of my sweatshirt and duck my head for the half-block walk.

No one's home when I get there, which is nothing new. I'm an only child, for one thing, and for another my folks work whenever they can. My dad works for himself; my mom works at Target. If they give her hours—especially weekend hours—she takes them.

The only evidence of parentals is hanging from my bedroom door, suspended by a wrinkled piece of cellophane tape. The handwriting is Mom's—specifically, angry Mom's, because the ink is dark and the letters angular. It says:

Do NOT leave this house today AT ALL.

Translation: she spoke to Elizabeth Deel, and I'm grounded. Now I get to decide if I'll actually obey the note. I mean, it's just a note. I tear it from the door—the tape holds and the note rips—and crumple it in my fist, then toss it toward my wastebasket. The shot's wide, and the way I feel, I'm not going anywhere anyway. I hit play on my laptop—it's been paused all

24

night—and Whitechapel bursts from my tiny desk speakers in mid-blast-beat. Then I sit on the edge of my bed and let myself roll back and to the left, listening to the rain get heavier on the skylight above the bed—the one Dad installed so I would feel like I wasn't sleeping in the attic, which I am—and I'm asleep.

CHAPTER 4

SVETLANA ALLEGHENY
<BAD DAUGHTERS>

It's raining the next morning, and I'm sitting at my sewing desk, penciling an embroidery design onto a new tote, listening to the rain on my window and Björk on my iPod system. The drunken disorderlies stained my favorite bag, and I'd been looking for an excuse to start a new one anyway. I found this new gold hologram thread that's going to look amazing on a green tote I've been saving. I'm thinking of a huge tree, with a short fat trunk and a giant leafy canopy. If I get the details right, it will look positively epic. But as I'm starting, there are fast heavy steps on the stairs, and now Dad stands in the low doorway of my room, bending at the neck and shoulders just a little, like the roof might fall on him. "So," he says.

"So," I say. I move my embroidery to my lap and turn slightly, not quite to face my dad and the door, but enough so he can see I'm busy. I'm not going to put it aside unless this turns out to be an actual conversation, rather than an imprecise, indelicate prod, my dad's specialty. I'm also not going to turn down the music, even though the track is "Pluto," which my dad once spent fifteen minutes deriding as the most grating piece of supposed music he'd ever been exposed to.

"Whatcha workin' on up here?" Dad says, though a monkey would have known by the pencil in my hand, the bag on my lap, and the golden spool of thread on the desk, which is to say nothing of the activity wheel hanging on the door at the bottom of the attic steps, which exists for the sole purpose of avoiding conversations like this one. Before I started, I turned it to "embroidering" and then hurried back upstairs. It's possible my activity wheel is too subtle for my family, because it never seems to keep them away.

"I'm just training for the krav maga demonstration," I say. I even smile.

"What?" Dad's a very swift cookie at times.

"Did you need something?" I ask, to maybe help him through the thick undergrowth of my bewitching conversational style.

"Oh," Dad says, standing straight up from his doorjamb-lean. "Just wanted to let you know we're heading out."

"Where?"

This is a running gag in my house, which is putting it in a nice way, since it often ends in blowout fights, with Mom, Dad, and Hen at the bottom of the main steps and shouting up at me, and me at the top of the attic steps, shrieking down at them to mind their own business. Businesses. Whatever.

The gag starts like this:

"We told you, Lana," Dad would say. "Why, your mom and I have been talking about it all morning/for days/all summer/since Christmas."

"Refresh my memory," I'd say without thought, or, often enough, even looking up from my embroidery/drawing/map/miniature/book.

At this point, Dad would remind me about the beach day/camping trip/picnic/hang gliding that everyone in the family was about to pile into the family SUV for, the activity that I had allegedly agreed to do as well—which makes *perfect* sense, if you've been paying attention at all, because I'm frequently so amped for outdoor activities like sewing, reading, and creating role-playing games. Oh wait. Those aren't outdoor activities, are they?

Anyway, that's when the fighting starts. I insist no one ever told me about any such activity, and that I certainly didn't agree to join in, and then: *J'en ai ras le bol!* Soon I'm slamming doors, and the family is once again just the three of them as they set off without me.

On this particular morning, as it has been for months now, the activity is a Thunder game—that's a local professional soccer team with which my parents, for some reason I've never been able to discern, are utterly obsessed. Remember Hen's stuffed sea monster? That's official merchandise. The team's mascot is the Loch Ness monster, Nessie, because they play at the National Sports Center, or NSC. If you say it fast, it almost makes sense.

From downstairs, Mom—in her bellowing falsetto—insists this will be our last opportunity for the whole family to get to a game until next summer. "The weather won't be so inviting for long!" I wish you could hear her say that. In a previous life she was an opera singer who could never get a part. I'd put money on it. But more to the point: how inviting is a rainy day? I swear, I sometimes think the rest of the Alleghenys actually enjoy torturing themselves in this manner, and that the rain pittering on them the whole time adds to the appeal.

Of course, all I can reply is, "Good! I don't want any more opportunities." And I don't. No shady, drunken weirdos with painted faces, smoke bombs, Dad screaming at the ref. It's miserable. Dad sighs and stomps back downstairs.

He mumbles something to Mom and Hen, probably already dressed and waiting at the bottom of the main stairs. That's when Hen comes tearing up the main steps, a last resort. They're not giving up this time. I hear her tennies squeaking on the steps the whole way up, and I go to my open doorway to see her little blond head appear at the bottom of the attic steps. My sister is valiant, and I respect and love her for it, but it's still pretty annoying.

"Lana." She stares at me.

"I'm not coming," I say.

More staring.

"I'm not coming, Henny," I say. "I don't like soccer. I don't like going to games. I don't like cheering and shouting and I don't like Fry and his tiny trumpet."

"Mom and Dad do," she says. "I do."

"Then have fun."

"It's more fun with all of us," Hen says. And I'm this close. "I'll protect you from the tiny trumpet. And I'll share my nachos."

I sigh, because I'm going, and I lean a little farther through the doorway and shout over Hen's little towhead, "I have to get dressed."

I hear delighted murmuring and quickly add, "And brush my teeth! Don't rush me!"

CHAPTER 5

LESH TUNGSTEN
<ASLEEP AT MIDDAY>

It's dark and humid, but cool. The air smells like springwater and compost. Something brushes against my leg, and I wave it away. It's a moth—a huge moth, bright green, the color of sunlight filtered through a forest canopy, and I crane my neck looking up, and that's what it is. The moth flutters higher and higher, closer to the treetops, lush with huge, translucent green leaves. It disappears as it climbs, blended in with greenery. I'm walking now, next to a narrow, quiet stream, as clear as filtered water, bubbling over broad, flat, copper-colored rocks, glittering with silver and gold specks. It makes the water look even cleaner, more delicious. I am going to kneel and take a handful to my mouth when the thing brushes against my leg again, and I go to brush it away, but this time it's no moth. It's a cat, a big one, and it's batting at me with its paw, the claws still withdrawn, and our eyes meet—its like gold coins with black slivers, mine no doubt huge with fear—and in that instant it opens its mouth and lets loose a deep and shattering roar. The world around flashes bloodred, and the ice-capped mountains in the far distance seem to erupt. Above it all, bigger than the world itself, soars a demon shaped like a man, but with gnarly horns and huge leathery wings. He bellows—a visceral, animal roar, like violence and death and horror itself have been twisted into a thunderous boom, and the cat raises its paw again. I grab for my leg, where it is poised to strike.

My phone is vibrating in my pocket. I can't even open my eyes, but I pull the thing out and slide a thumb across the face. "Hello?" It's a whisper.

"Dude." Greg. "You were supposed to call."

"I feel asleep," I say. "I think."

Weird dream, too, I add in my head, but Greg talks on. "So what's up?" he says. "Wanna do something?"

"What'd you have in mind?" I say, which is my typical response in this conversation, but then add, "I'm grounded."

"Snap," Greg says. I hear the world-entrance *bong!* of his MMO.

"Well, you're busy, so . . ."

"Not really," he says, but even his tone has changed, and I can see him, with the phone cradled between his ear and shoulder, his posture becoming unhealthy, his left hand forming a claw over the keyboard, his right on the mouse. This is called dual wielding. He's gone.

"Right," I say, ready to end the call.

"Wait a minute," he says, and he's back. Like, super back. He's focused and psyched about something. I begin to worry. "If you're stuck inside anyway . . ."

"Whoa, whoa," I say, sitting up. "I can see where you're going with this, and we've been down this road, too, too many times."

"What else are you gonna do?" Greg says, and I respect that he's remaining calm, and even not immersed in the game at the moment. I can picture him, having taken the phone in his opposite hand—maybe he's even up from the desk.

I wonder how the pancakes were. "How were the pancakes?"

Greg ignores the question, and it was meant to distract. It failed.

"Look," Greg says. He's back at the computer now. I can hear him typing, but it doesn't sound game-related. He's tabbed out, then. I groan, get to my feet, and switch on my own display. My computer isn't half the machine Greg's is, but it works. "I'm sending you a link."

At the same moment, an IM window pops up. "I see it," I say, and click the link. "What the hell is this?" A download window has appeared.

"Just tell it to save to the desktop, okay?" Greg says.

I sigh and close the window. "I'm. Not. Playing. The Stupid. Game." Then I click end call. The IM window beeps and flashes, Greg pleading his case. After a few minutes he gives up, and I hit the kitchen because I'm suddenly ravenous. But here's the problem, and it comes to me as the big glass of orange juice is tipped back at my mouth and a pancake-wrapped breakfast sausage is weighing down my gut. It really is amazing how hungry I can be after a night like that, even if it did take a night's sleep and a power nap to get there.

But I was saying: here's the problem. Greg's right: I am grounded, and for some reason, I'm curious. I can't explain it—if I could rationalize this, believe me, I would—but with that orange juice at my lips, and the deep yellow of the drink itself shallowing in the upturned glass before my eyes, visions swim through my mind. They're from the dream, obviously. I'm not that dense. But why the dream? Why did it linger, too?

I place the empty glass in the sink and hurry back to my room. I close the door and lock it and glance at the clock: it's almost three. Then I click that link again, and this time I tell it where to stick it, by which I mean I tell it to save the file on the desktop. I lean back in my desk chair, with my hands folded behind my head, and I can smell that forest, and I can see, when I close my eyes, a huge translucent moth, fluttering against the bright-green forest canopy.

This is what Greg didn't tell me: downloading an entire MMO—even the free starter version—takes a very, very long time. By the time the growing green progress bar hits fifty percent, both my parents are home. Mom's loudly banging around in the kitchen, and Dad's showering away a day's worth of sweat and sawdust. In a few minutes I'll have to face the music, but at the moment, Greg is blowing up chat.

> **Me:** <<What.>>
> **Him:** <<You installed it, didn't you?>>
> **Me:** <<How the hell could you know that?>>
> **Him:** <<I connected to your wifi and it was mad slow.>>
> **Me:** <<I am going to change the password. I am changing the password right now.>>
> **Him:** <<Sure you are. Anyway so you did?>>
> **Me:** <<Obv but it's not done yet. And my mom is knocking on the door. GTG.>>

I hide everything on the screen but the desktop and unlock my door, then retreat to the safety of my bed.

"Hi," I say when she steps inside and leans on the jamb, arms crossed, face cross.

She stares.

"I'm sorry?" I say.

The white noise coming through the floor suddenly goes quiet, and the shower curtain rattles loudly on its metal hooks and rod.

"He'll be up in a minute, so I'm giving you a chance for this to be slightly better than the worst day of your life," Mom says. "Tell me everything, and we'll see."

I sit up on the bed and plant my hands on its edge. "I just said I'm sorry."

"I'm not looking for sorry," she says, and she moves to my

desk and sits in my chair, turns it toward my bed. "I'm looking for the narrative."

"The narrative," I say, and I close my eyes and run my hands through my hair. I haven't showered. "The narrative is me and Greg went—"

"Greg and I," Mom says.

"—to Vic's last night and I had two tiny drinks. Two."

"Tiny drinks," Mom says, and I nod, and she sighs. She looks at the clock next to my bed. It's almost seven. "Did you eat dinner?"

I shake my head. "Hardly left my room. I think I had breakfast."

Mom stands when Dad shows up in the doorway. "Well?" he says.

I glance at Mom, who is no help. "I'm sorry," I say, not meeting his eyes.

"You're goddamn right you're sorry," he says. "And you're going to be sorrier, because you're done with staying out at all, and you're sure as hell done with going to concerts at bars. Anywhere there's liquor. You're done."

"Oh, come on," I say.

"Come on?" he snaps. "I spoke to Elizabeth Deel myself this morning. She said she heard you stumble in. She heard you puke in their bathroom."

I puked?

"And this morning you were hungover—" He swivels his tensed neck to Mom. "How much did he drink? Did he say how much he drank?"

Mom sighs again and rubs her face. "He said two—"

"Ha!" Dad says. "He had at least four, am I right?"

I look at the ceiling.

"All right, I'm done," Dad says in his thin, aggravated, out-of-patience voice. "Grounded. Forever. School. Home. That's it."

"What?" And I'm on my feet, and he's heading for the door.

"You heard me," he says. "Dinnertime."

I stand in the doorway and call after him as he heads down the narrow steep stairs. "This is completely unfair. It's one time. One time! And you cannot tell me you didn't drink when you were out seeing Metallica or whoever."

Dad stops at the bottom and looks up the stairs at me. Mom is behind me now with a hand on my back. It's meant to soothe, but also to warn: I should stop arguing now.

"What I did has nothing to do with this, first of all," Dad says, and his voice is straining like a wildcat in a canvas bag. "But since you bring it up, yes. I did. I also never went to college, and barely finished high school, and I work sixty hours a week building garages for men who did. Wanna follow that path?"

The discussion has taken an unfair turn. Even I can see that. So I clam up and stare at the ceiling. He decides he's won and walks off, repeating over his shoulder, "Dinnertime."

"Come on," Mom says. "I got extra fries. And I'll talk to him."

"Thanks," I say, and we head downstairs. The spread on the dining room table is straight from the deli counter at Target. An extra hour on the clock and a juicy employee discount trump hurrying home to cook.

CHAPTER 6

SVETLANA ALLEGHENY
<HUDDLED AND WET>

It's raining. *Il pleut comme vache qui pisse.* We all knew it was raining, but we climbed into Dad's giant house of a truck-car and took the longish drive up I-35 to picturesque Blaine, Minnesota. In the back, we put pounds of bratwurst, a bag of rolls, and the folding canopy.

So now, here we are: Mom and Dad in their violently fluttering blue-and-yellow ponchos, gathered near the communal grill with the other hardcore fans, their various meated foods scorching away, stinking up the parking lot; Henrietta, under the canopy with me, a thick and ragged novel in her dirty little hands, pages flipping not from the wind, but from her preternatural reading speed; and me, my own blue-and-yellow poncho up over my head, my knees against my chest, and my arms around my knees, and muttering to myself, "This is not my life. This is not my life."

A slap in the back and I spin, my eyes burning with rage as my blue-and-yellow hood flips back.

"Hey, blondie." It's Fry Dannon, the single other "fanatic" of high school age (specifically and unfortunately Central High School), the son of my parents' good friends, and the only person stupid enough to approach me and offer conversation. He's got on an official Thunder-merch jersey—it's got a number on the chest and the sponsor's name on the shoulder. It's probably got a name on the back, too. Hopefully I'll get a look at that— at least it would mean he was walking away. "Excited?"

"What do you think?"

He throws his head back and laughs. Then, from behind his back, he produces the littlest trumpet I've ever seen—and I've seen plenty, because Fry brings one to every game. He must have a collection, and his choices get smaller every time.

"My newest," he says. "It's a piccolo, obviously, from 1920. Check it out."

He takes a deep breath, and I hurry to pull my hands out from under my poncho to cover my ears. I barely have myself protected before his blaring and shrill "Charge!" music blasts across the Twin Cities' northern suburbs. Thunder claps and the gaggle of Dark Clouds—that's what this group of thirty or so fanatics call themselves—cheer.

The thunder—you will recall, that is the name of the team— at the end of Fry's "Charge!" instigation was pretty amazing. But still. Let's not encourage the boy.

"You're the greatest, Fry," my sister says, her voice as flat as ever, her eyes still on the page, and then the next page. "Now could you please go blow that thing someplace else?"

Fry leans down so his body blocks the little light Hen is reading by. "This is a soccer game," he says. "Not a reading . . . um . . . game."

She smirks up at him, draws back her foot, kicks his shin. It definitely hurts, but he laughs as he hobbles off.

Henrietta faces me. "That boy is in love with you, Lana."

I nod at her.

"You should tell him you're not interested," she says. "Otherwise he'll just bug you forever." Then she goes back to reading.

And I huddle up into a ball again under my poncho, wallowing in the misery of a rainy day, a soccer game, beer-drunk parents, grilling meats, and love-life advice from an eight-year-old.

"This is not my life. This is not my life. This is not my life."

With my eyes closed, under the poncho, and the sound of heavy rain drumming the top of the canopy, I let my mind wander back down I-35, right into Saint Paul, along Lexington Avenue, over and around three-story Victorians, and little Mission bungalows, into our house, up to the low-ceiling third story, under the dormer on the south wall, where my drawing desk is, and my notebook sits open. As my spirit approaches it, the pages flip like the leaves of a witch's most magical tome, and the blue and black and red and green inks of my four-color pen—my tool of creation—leap and leak from the pages, filling the attic with first grass, then thicker growth, then six-inch-tall pixies, then a spotted wildcat, skulking between the thick trunks of wise old trees, then a centaur, stopping at the stream running toward the stairs, and he leans over to take a drink of the moonlight-colored water.

I sigh and smile, because I'm not under my poncho anymore. I'm not at that soccer game's tailgate extravaganza. I'm not even in my wonderful attic bedroom.

I'm in that forest oasis, my hand on the centaur's velvety haunches, my toes in the cool babbling stream. I sit down on its edge and let it run over my calves for a moment. Then I lie back in the grass, and the dew soaks through my dress. Soon my hair is drenched. Thunder claps somewhere far off, and the centaur is spooked, and he gallops off. The wildcat, crouched beside me and lapping up the water, stiffens, and when the lightning cracks across the sky, lighting up the forest, he bolts too. I sit up. I am soaked to the skin.

Fry stands in front of me, holding my poncho, which he has obviously tugged from my very person. The canopy is gone; I look around and spot Mom and Dad and Hen—each shouldering a bag of food and drink—heading for the stadium entrance. They probably called my name ten times and finally gave me up for lost in a dream. It sort of happens a lot.

Fry's stupid grin is bigger than the whole outdoors, but with crookeder teeth. "Finally," he says. "I thought you were dead under there."

I stick out my jaw and grab for my poncho, but he pulls it away. "Your family went in without you," he says, the poncho now behind his back. "I was gallant enough to wait, though."

"I'm thrilled," I say, crossing my arms, mostly because I'm freezing my stupid, narcoleptic butt off. "Just give me the poncho, please, so I can catch up with them."

"Not so fast," Fry says. He looks at me, hard, as he taps his chin with a crooked index finger, diabolical. "If you want your poncho back, you have to make me a promise first."

"Well?" I say.

"Tuesday, in school," he said, bringing the poncho out from behind his back, "have lunch with me."

I clench my teeth, grab the poncho with my left hand, and suddenly he's a boy in black. I mean, not literally, but all my anger at that rude drunk jerk just surges into my right arm. So I punch Fry in the stomach. Then I stomp across the puddling short grass around the parking lot toward the ticket collector, listening to him groan, no doubt on his knees in the mud, behind me.

I'll spend the next two and change hours in the back row of the bleachers—in the crazies section—with my poncho over my head and a plastic tray of nachos congealing on my knees, feeling like the biggest rhymes-with-witch in Mean Town.

CHAPTER 7

LESH TUNGSTEN
<GROUNDED FOR GOOD>

I wasn't going anywhere anyway, most likely. I mean, it's Sunday night. Who goes out on Sunday night anyway? Sure, tomorrow is Labor Day, and the next day is the first of school, so ideally I should be doing something, as a last hurrah for summer.

Okay, fine. This blows.

I'm in my room, lying on my back on my bed, staring at the flickering light fixture in the middle of the ceiling and ignoring the incessant *bong!* of Greg trying to get my attention in chat. But I know what he wants, and my feet are cold—like, shivering, like a groom's get. I know exactly what I'm in for when I get up and reply to Greg and enter his pixelated world. And I know I'm grounded until the stars fall from the sky. Those two things add up to a lot of time with Greg, in his world. The good news is Mom did talk to Dad, and rather than a forever grounding, I've got two weeks.

I sigh. I sigh again. I pick up the old copy of *Metal Hammer* on the nightstand. It's got Lamb of God on the cover. I've read every word in this thing probably five times each, so I toss it aside, sigh again, and roll to my feet.

Me: <<What.>>
Him: <<Finally. What were you doing??>>
Me: <<Wallowing in self-pity. I'm very grounded.>>
Him: <<Perfect! Let's chat in-game, then, since you have nowhere to go.>>
Me: <<You're a dick.>>
Him: <<I know. Pick up the phone.>>

My cell is vibrating on the desk, next to my computer, so I slide into the desk chair and hit the speaker. "What."

"Log in," Greg says. He's probably slipping on his gaming headset, leaning over his gaming keyboard, and stroking his gaming mouse. "Let's get you started."

So I do. The fact is, he's right. I'm stuck here, in this bedroom, really, for the next several lifetimes. If the best escape I can get is into a magical wonderland of spells and demons and elves with great bouncing bosoms, things could be worse.

"All right, I'm in," I say, staring at a green muscular giant, gaping at me, breathing heavily, and holding a big ax. He is, bar none, the ugliest humanoid I've ever seen.

"That's an orc," Greg explains.

"I can read."

"Good job!" he says, thick with sarcasm. This is Greg's

territory, you see, and when you're in Greg's territory you get the worst kind of Greg: know-it-all, intellectual bully, all-around unbearable Greg. This is why we don't traditionally game together. But nobody ever said being grounded would be easy. I persevere.

"Okay, now choose warrior," he says, and waits for me to find the place to click, which eventually I do. "Then pick a name."

"Wait, a warrior?" I say, looking at the ax man again, ugly and mean and probably smelly. When they invent games in smell 3D—or whatever—I predict anything with orcs in it will suffer a severe loss in market share. "I don't want to be a warrior. I want to cast spells, raise the dead, bring the fury of hellfire down from above. You know, warlock stuff."

I click on the warlock now, and though the orc dude is still the ugliest living thing in God's creation, he's now wearing a dress and has a little imp next to him, tossing fireballs.

Greg laughs—gives me a short "Ha-ha!" like Nelson from *The Simpsons*. "You can't handle a warlock, Tung."

"Why not?"

"It's complicated," he says. "But the short version is: you're a noob. Noobs roll warriors. In fact, noobs usually roll human warriors, but luckily I'm here to make sure you don't roll a human."

"What's wrong with a human?"

"First of all," he says, sighing, "they're boring. Second, wrong faction. They're the good guys. Boring, nice, clean, and gay."

"Gay?"

45

"Gay." Greg clears his throat. I can hear his fingers some-times slapping at his keyboard over there. He's probably already in the game, playing one of his über-leveled toons while I pitter away my time on the character-creation screen. "So did you pick a name yet?"

"Oh, right," I say, and click into the little name box. The cursor flashes, waiting for inspiration to strike.

"Don't overthink it," Greg says. "You'll just come up with something gay."

"Lesh," I say, and I type it in.

"Taken," Greg says.

"How do you know?" I ask just as the alert comes back: Name Unavailable.

"Dude, anything remotely like a real word or name is taken," Greg says, "and there are serious Deadheads who play this game. Hence, Lesh is taken."

I should explain. I was named for the bassist of the Grateful Dead, Phil Lesh. It's a weird name, yes, but I'm glad I wasn't burdened with Phil instead. Phil Tungsten sounds like some-one's weird uncle, who maybe works as a postal clerk and collects Civil War miniatures. Lesh Tungsten, though, sounds like the lead guitarist of a death metal band, and that's all right by me.

"Tungsten," I try.

"Taken," Greg says, and again he's right, which is getting old already. A whole grounding in this magical world with know-it-all Greg Deel is sounding worse all the time.

"What would you suggest?" I ask.

"Just let it randomize for you."

I click the appropriate button and am offered a name.

"Kugnar?"

"Sounds good to me," Greg says, letting his impatience come through as loud and clear as possible. "Just freaking start, loser."

"I did," I say. I watch the screen and click up the volume a little. A quasi-British narrator speaks over sweeping footage of a clay-red landscape. "It's a movie."

"Hit escape," Greg says, "and skip it, unless you're a dork."

I roll my eyes and watch the short cut scene. The narrator explains the orcs' history, and soon the point of view dives to eye level. Now I'm in control of the newest member of the orc army: Kugnar the warrior.

"See the guy in front of you?"

"The one with the exclamation point on his head?"

"That's the one," Greg says. "Go talk to him."

"Um," I say, scanning the keyboard, as though the directional keys will glow or something and tell me how to use them. I shake the mouse, and the cursor flies back and forth on the screen. I click on the guy with the golden bang on his head. Nothing happens. "How?"

"Lord," Greg says. "Let's start with basics. Form your left hand into a claw and hover it over *W*, *A*, *S*, and *D*."

I obey, and Greg goes on to explain how to move, how to interact, and how to attack something or pick something up.

"So, you getting the hang of it?" Greg asks after a few minutes.

"Easy," I say, and then I don't say, *And this is what you do for hours at a time?* I don't get it. At all. But it's not even eight, and I'm definitely not showing my face downstairs tonight. So fine. I'll crawl into this disgusting monster's skin for a while and see how it feels.

"I'll leave you to it then," Greg says. "I have a guild raid in like five minutes."

"Peace," I say, and hang up.

CHAPTER 8

KUGNAR
<YOUNG WARRIORS>

Meat. Blood, thunder, and meat.

The sky fire is low and hot, and the ground is dry and orange. Dust fills the air and stings his eyes and his lungs. He grunts and tests the weight of his ax. It is a good day to die.

"I am Kugnar!" he shouts.

The orc before him nods gravely. He rambles on about honor and blood and thunder and the great orc god. Kugnar is sweating profusely now. He grunts loud and kicks the earth with his heavily shod foot.

The orc before him flexes. His leathery skin ripples under the low sun. "Kill six pigs," he says. "I will give you some new boots."

Kugnar raises his ax and lets loose a deafening guttural battle cry. He runs off, just a few loping steps from the village, and then stops. In every direction—besides behind him, where the huts and leather tents of the village squat around the great brazier at the center—the landscape is the same: a dusty, red-rock field, leading to a great mountain range in the long distance. Here and there, Kugnar sees something move, but as he tries to catch it with his eye, it vanishes into the waves of heat off the parched ground.

"Where are the pigs?" he shouts. No one replies.

"WHERE ARE THE PIGS?!" he shouts again, louder this time, in all caps and everything. He waits. Again, there is no reply.

Kugnar grunts. This time the sound from the back of his throat has an irritated air, and he runs farther from the village. His boots slam the earth as he jogs. His shoulders and hips rock and twist. He is not the picture of grace. He is the picture of fearsome death come to town.

"A pig!" he says. "Smash pig!"

Kugnar raises his ax and brings it down. He misses, even though the pig did not move. Perhaps he needs more practice. Now, though, the pig is angry, and it turns to face him. Though it is small, and its tusks hardly appear a match for Kugnar's mighty ax, the pig is a worthy opponent. Kugnar withstands a terrible strike—presumably to his ankle or maybe knee—and his health begins to falter. As quickly as he can, he raises his ax once more. This time the strike is a powerful one. The pig limps briefly and attacks again.

Kugnar is thrown back. He is bleeding badly now. With a great shout, he raises his ax one last time and, with a flourish and a spin, brings it down on the pig's already bloody head. The beast lets out a plaintive wail, and it falls to the dusty ground, dead. Kugnar catches his breath as he gropes the decimated corpse. He takes the pig's tusks and a good chunk of pig meat.

It is a good day to kill, as well.

"I have killed many pigs this day," Kugnar says, standing once again before the quest-giver in the center of the village. His gear is battered. His knees and ankles are badly bruised and bloody. His small bag is bulging with pig meat.

The quest-giver, seated cross-legged before the brazier, hands the young warrior a pair of boots and then nods slowly, and Kugnar is overcome with light and honor. He swells with pride and flexes his great and muscular chest, for he has reached level two.

"Only forty-eight to go," says a voice near Kugnar's head, and he grunts.

Kugnar stands beside the raging fire in the center of the village. His quest log is weakly populated: he must kill several humans and collect several pieces of fruit. The great warrior—swollen of chest and pride—sighs. Other new orcs—some warriors, some warlocks—are nearby, and they move quickly in and out of his field of vision. There is great purpose in their bearing, or sometimes there is great jumping up and down and spinning in circles.

Kugnar watches the other orcs, but he cannot speak to them unless they speak first to him; his is a trial account. So alone, he jogs afield of the village once again and raises his ax, for the human scouts will not be tolerated, and their end will be bloody. None presents a greater challenge than the tame little piggies, and soon a great many human corpses litter the landscape. Kugnar growls and glows with pride as he hits level three.

But he is not satisfied, and he slaughters now without thought, without remorse, and without reason. Human scouts, despite valiant effort, are no match. His ax is bloody, and his head is light with the intoxicating smell of death. There is great honor today in the fields around his village. Level four.

As the rush and light of honor flood his body, and then recede, his great shoulders sag. He sighs—it sounds like a wild boar exhaling through a pile of its own feces—and plods back to the village for his rewards. They are insignificant. He feels no sense of honor, nor of accomplishment at their receipt. He turns and faces the human—the one who controls him—and intones, "Bored now."

CHAPTER 9

LESH TUNGSTEN
<TURNCOATS>

I lean back in my chair to stretch. The crick in my neck is a surprise, and when I check the time, it's a surprise too. I've been playing this game for almost an hour.

"How the hell . . . ?" I mutter to no one in particular. Then I tab out—that is, hit Alt-Tab to switch to a different program—and find Greg in chat.

Me: <<Hey>>
Him: <<still raiding. sup?>>
Me: <<Bored. Quests are boring. Game is boring.>>
Him: <<O.o>>

Greg loves the owl faces.

Me: <<The MMO part is there. The RPG part, not really. It's just clicking and running.>>
Him: <<later we can argue. raiding now.>>

I tab back over, and there's my big dumb orc, sitting in the middle of the little orc village, level four, halfway to five, and I just don't care. I have no empathy for this green monstrosity, no affection. I have no desire to navigate through this hellish environment for his sake.

I log out and click "Create New Character." Maybe I can try some other race—that's what they call the different species you can play. Maybe species isn't the right word, though. And now I'm wondering if they can breed, because isn't that one way of defining species—something that can breed and create fertile offspring? And that's what I'm thinking about—fertility and breeding—when I click over to the elf race. Suddenly breeding among these pixelated characters doesn't sound so strange.

She's staring at me, with glowing, silver eyes. She smiles, and bounces on her toes, so her breasts bounce too. It's not unappealing. It's in fact tingly. I'm a little uncomfortable. I begin to randomize her appearance now—a feature I hadn't bothered trying with the foul-smelling (I'm sure) orc—and her hair goes short, then very long, then green, then purple. Her face comes alive with bright tattoos of leaves and hawks and butterflies and then, most perfect, no tattoo at all. My heart races, my head goes light, as I watch her change on the display, coming closer to something familiar, something magical. Her hair is very long now, and one more click, and it's shimmering and silvery white.

My breath catches in my throat, because this is *her*.

I'll grant you, it's not her. This is an elf, and as such seven feet tall (to scale) and with ears that wouldn't seem out of place on a Mr. Spock wannabe at a Star Trek convention. Also: voluptuous—like, 1950s Hollywood voluptuous. Betty and Marilyn.

But to me, it's her. It's the girl on the bike—and off the bike, on the street, glaring at me and remounting to ride off into the night. I wonder if the big light in the Super USA parking lot shined a magical white light over her blond hair and alabaster skin, because something other than the vodka was messing with my brain last night.

So I click in the name field, and the cursor flashes at me, and I freeze, because I still don't know her name, and if she doesn't have a name, she can't play. Besides, the elves are on the opposite faction from the orcs, and that won't fly with Greg, so I hit Alt-F4, the game closes, and I flop onto my bed again. School starts tomorrow, anyway.

LEVEL FOUR

CHAPTER 10

LESH TUNGSTEN
<SOPHOMORE SLACKERS>

Greg is sitting at my feet, leaning against my neighbor's locker, our respective class schedules side by side on his knees. With the stubby dirty index finger of each hand, he runs down the papers, comparing our days.

"This is very bad," he says.

"It's what I told you," I say, unspooling a bit of clear tape and affixing a slightly wrinkled photo of Salt the Wound I tore from an issue of *Kerrang!* magazine. It looks good under the chained-up skull from the original cover of *Killing Is My Business*—the cardboard jacket of the vinyl copy I stole from my dad's collection. I pretty much usurped his entire vinyl and CD collection—and record player—on the same day he joined the digital era and got an iPod. Anyway, this is called establishing cred. "If you're going to take honors math, we're going to have different schedules."

"Yeah, but this is nuts," he says. "We're not even on the same lunch."

"Nope," I say, and I'm a little relieved. Maybe tenth grade is a good one to start fresh. Double digits and everything. "I'm skej A, you're skej C." Schedule, that is. "Look on the bright side: at least you don't have to have lunch before eleven every stupid morning."

He shrugs. "Yeah."

I stand back and look at the inside of my open locker door. "What do you think?"

Greg glances up. "Looks good."

I slam it closed. Satisfying.

Greg stands with a little groan. "First class, three minutes."

I nod and slap his hand. "Peace."

"Tonight we get you to level twenty, bro."

Can't wait.

He heads off toward the science wing, and I slip into the nearest room, math for the slow-witted.

I can practically count his shuffling and squeaking steps; I'm that familiar with his gait. And after five minutes, for the first time in years, Greg and I are more than seventy-five yards apart.

As a member of skej A, I am expected to eat lunch at ten forty-five a.m. This is pure madness, and I will remind my mother of this when she insists I eat breakfast tomorrow morning. As it is, I can probably force something down, and I line up for the privilege.

"Ohmygosh."

It's from behind me. It's on my neck. The voice is secret

and soft, and it smells of cucumbers and strawberries. I turn around, and the cafeteria—which is huge and wide and high-ceilinged and was certainly there a moment ago—is gone, because now it's just her eyes, and her sneer, and the smell of her shampoo.

"Hi," I say, and I think my mouth stays open. Flies are getting in. "You go here too, huh?"

She narrows her eyes.

"I'm sorry," I try, "about the other night. I was—"

"Drunk," she finishes. "I guessed that."

"Right," I say, turning back around. She's too tall and shiny. "Sorry. I don't usually do that. Drink, I mean. At all, really."

She's quiet now, and I suppose that's the end of it.

I stare at the glass-covered offerings of the lunch line today. Baked beans. Dry, cracking chicken swimming in butterlike fluid. Green, yellow, and orange vegetables. As I get closer, the air grows thick with their mixed steams. It's revolting. But down at the far end, in the very last steam table tray, next to a smallish vat of red sauce, are golden little dumplings, the skins of which bubble with the evidence of having been deep in the fryer.

Pizza rolls it is.

She sighs behind me, and for an instant the air is all cool and clean before the foody steam reclaims the back of my neck and the underside of my nose.

"I got grounded," I say, not turning around, not sure I even want her to hear me.

"Good," she says, and if I can just keep her talking, the

whole building will fill up with that scent. It would be a great service to all mankind.

For the good of everyone, I push on. "It wasn't *just* my fault."

"Ha!"

A sharp exhale and toss of her hair. It's a delicious shotgun of body wash across the back of my head. I'm slain.

"You're not supposed to bike on the sidewalk," I say, and I'm smiling a little, I realize, but still not looking at her, still just shuffling along the line. Soon I'll reach the pizza rolls and have to order.

"Says who? It's not against the law."

It actually might be. I know it is in some places, anyway, but I don't say so.

She's not feeling nearly as charitable, I guess, and my sense that she is somehow special—a magical girl I want to be next to—begins to fade when she grabs my shoulder and spins me around. "But do you know what is?" she says. "Drinking when you're underage."

Yup. Definitely not magical.

I nod. "Too true."

And that's the end of that. I turn back and step up to the pizza rolls, and nod at the woman behind the glass. She serves 'em up and I grab the plate, drop it onto my heretofore empty tray with a thud and a rattle, ceramic on plastic on hollow metal tubes.

I type in my PIN at the register and step off the line, face the quickly filling cafeteria. Sure, I'm relieved to be apart from

Greg for a few hours, but the fact is, facing a crowded cafeteria on your own is less than ideal, spiritually and emotionally. I home in on a sparsely populated spot in the corner, apart from the gathering reunions and preternaturally comfortable seniors at the big window, who seem to me like extras on a miserable teen TV show. I sit and fish in my pocket for my phone and headphones. Lunch alone is all right, I tell myself, as long as you've got your music.

I take the chair in the deepest corner, facing the line, and by the time I'm sitting, unfolding pizza rolls so their molten interiors can cool and congeal, she's leaving the line too, standing there at the exit, scanning the thickening crowd. When she gets bumped by some guy leaving the line behind her and almost tosses her tray, I jump in my chair a little.

Now that's empathy. Maybe she is a little magical.

CHAPTER 11

SVETLANA ALLEGHENY
<TROLL HATERS>

"Whoops!" says Fry. "Sorry, blondie." He cackles a little, because though we've determined—with a little help from my preadolescent sister, sure—that he's in love with me, he still flirts like a seven-year-old, shoving lizards in my shirt and hoping for some sort of reaction.

He comes up next to me, immune to my glares, and says, "So, where are we sitting?"

"I have both my hands on this tray, Fry," I say through my teeth, "so I cannot hit you this time. Be thankful."

He laughs again and gives me a little shove—it's meant to be playful, I suppose. It's not, and somehow my eyes fall on the boy in black, deep in the corner of the cafeteria, hiding in his hood and headphones, but watching us, me and Fry. I shake my head slowly at him, and the corners of my mouth go up—why? He looks away.

"I'm not eating with you, Fry," I say.

"You'd rather eat by yourself?" he says, and of course I would, but I think this is one of those things where even answering—no matter how thick with snark and distaste—will inevitably be interpreted as flirting, and just lead to further aggravation, so I simply walk away, toward the corner, because in spite of everything, the boy in black is the only person in this cacophony I even recognize. That is, apart from Fry and other admittedly recognizable faces I'd still prefer to avoid. I have known many of these children a long time, after all, and have developed a mental list of those to whom I'd prefer solitude.

If I'm honest, it's most of them.

Besides, there are very few empty seats, and several of them are adjacent to the boy in black—these metal boys are intimidating, especially tall ones with facial hair, and the freshmen at his table have given him a wide berth. I've never spoken to one of these metal boys, aside from a few moments ago on the lunch line. It could be a fascinating anthropological study. Plus, maybe I'm not done berating him.

I take the seat opposite him, next to a freshman-looking boy who shifts away from me about three inches in a squeaky shuffle of his plastic blue chair, as if I might bite him or—maybe worse yet—talk to him.

The boy in black is staring at his pizza rolls, peeling each one and then marveling at the steam it produces. See? Fascinating. When I pick up a single pea between my thumb and index finger, he looks at me, his face still pointed down at the steaming inside-out tiny pizzas, so I can see all the whites in his eyes' southern hemispheres, laced with red. It gives me an idea for my next embroidery project.

"What," he says. No question mark. Such inflection would shatter his black exterior.

"There's nowhere else to sit," I say, and he checks the room to confirm my excuse. It's mostly true. I eat the pea and stop watching him so he'll stop watching me. I'm about to tell him about the green notebook, the one fanned open on the windowsill in my bathroom, so he'll feel positively miserable—just because he's fascinating doesn't mean I don't want him to squirm a little—when he looks over my shoulder and spots Fry. He nods toward him.

"That dude is coming over here," he says, and I don't bother looking over my shoulder.

"He won't have a seat," I say, and then quickly add, "How do you do that?"

"What?"

"Talk in a normal voice with headphones on," I say. "I always talk super loud, like a dummy."

"Practice," he says, and he starts rerolling his pizza rolls. His bangs, which are of course black—probably unnaturally black, I decide—fall over his eyes, and he shakes them back. It's an effeminate little move, and kind of childlike—reminds me of Henny when she reads. When one roll is closed, he takes a bite. Flakes of crust stick to his bottom lip, and his tongue pokes out to grab them and pull them in, with the congealed cheese and sauce.

"Good?" I say, and he shrugs. "How can you hear me?"

"It's not on," he says. "It's just a prop right now."

Translation: *Leave me alone*, and this is when Fry sits down, two seats over, between the freshman boy and a girl with a still-closed paper bag in front of her, and her phone in both little hands, thumbing away. I bet she won't eat.

Fry leans close to the freshman—I can see his sniveling little grin in my peripheral vision—and in a moment the freshman is getting up with his tray and swapping seats. Fry is next to me, and once again it's on.

He's got the special—the hot meal: an aged chicken breast in butteresque sauce. Also, mashed potatoes. He did not accept the little bowl of peas and corn and carrots. I glance at my own tray, and there it is: a lonely little bowl of peas and corn and carrots, because it is all I was willing to accept from behind the foggy sneeze guard. I feel myself shudder, imagining that Fry probably takes our respective lunches as an indication of how well we complement each other.

Fry's food stinks. The boy in black's food isn't tempting either, but at least it smells vaguely nice. I mean, I was five once. I ate pizza rolls too. So the smell has a certain nostalgic quality, perhaps of life pre-Henny, even, in our small house up in Como, on the same block as Roan, when I was the growing-like-a-weed White Queen of the block.

"Hi, blondie," Fry says. Does he ever stop smiling? "Wasn't it nice of Gordy to give up his seat so we could sit together?"

I don't answer, but my heart is racing, not with heated

passion—so obviously—but because in my head I'm working out what I can say. I'm thinking about Henny's advice—heaven help me—and trying to find the words. I'm trying to find the words I can spit at him if I swivel suddenly in my seat and open with a fierce and sharp "Listen, Fry," but nothing comes to me . . . nothing but "Listen, Fry," which on its own would be less than effective.

The boy in black looks at me and shakes his head, then adjusts his headphones as if they're really on. Lucky jerk. I wish I had some headphones.

I should probably get some. I'm not dying to be one of the kids who walk around in headphones all day, always looking all put-upon, but hey, I like music. I like being left alone. Fry is still talking, or talking again, and now he's got meat in his mouth, shoved over to one side, shoved into his cheek like he's a chipmunk—a very loud and annoying chipmunk—and he's got potatoes in there too. There's mashed potato shoved into his cheek with all this dry chicken and he's talking, so little droplets of butter are escaping every time he tries for a *P* or *F* sound, or generally anything with a dental or labial stop. It's making me ill, and even if I had just the thing to say, I couldn't get it out now. I can feel my face going green, if faces actually do that, and my head going light. An episode is approaching. My days are rife with episodes.

I'm staring at the boy in black now, envious of his headphones, because he certainly can't hear the chewing and spitting. I wonder if he'd care. Probably not.

He's staring back, and I'm feeling woozy. He pulls off his headphones and lets them hang around his neck. "You okay?" he says, I think, but it's like he's lip-synching, because I don't hear any of it. I just hear a moist chomping at my left ear. Almost unconsciously, I shrug on that side, and then shake my head at the boy in black, because I'm not okay. I'm not at all okay. I'm not okay in the biggest way.

He looks at Fry, his face going hard, and his front teeth are on his lower lip for an instant, like he probably said the F word, among others, and I squint at him, trying to make out the words. I can't. He seems like he might get up. He glances at me, and I get the vaguest sense of motion to my left: Fry's tray is leaving. I hope for an instant that Fry will follow it. He does.

"Hey, are you okay or what?" the boy in black says again, and this time I nod a little. "What the hell was that all about?" I can hear him now, like through an old radio picking up signals from another era, but I just shake my head: a little *I don't know*, and a little *Don't ask*.

The blood in my veins is rushing back where it belongs, from wherever it gets to during an episode. The skin on the palms of my hands and on the top of my head is tingling—pins and needles, jabbing at light speed against me, micrometers apart. Tiny incessant pricks.

Just like Fry.

I giggle, and the boy looks at me again, and I look back, and now it's my turn to say it. "I'm sorry."

He just stares. I go on. "Sorry about that. He . . . I don't like him. But his family is friends with mine, or something, and he's always around. He usually has a tiny trumpet. And I think he's in love with me or something. It's all very . . ."

He's still staring.

"It's all very uncomfortable."

He nods. "Well, he went away. I don't think he'll come back soon. That was pretty freaky."

Freaky. Of course. What else? Because I'm freaky.

"Anyway, sorry," I say, and poke my fork into three peas, so there's one on each tine, and then pull them off and into my mouth. I like the feel of the plastic fork—the rough, biodegradable kind—as it scrapes through my teeth.

"Don't worry about it," he says, and I guess it's over, because there's a long silence. He keeps eating his reassembled pizza rolls, and I continue to work on my little bowl of yellow and green and orange. They're cold now; have you noticed how quickly bright steamed little veggies get cold? It's astonishing. With enough salt, they're tolerable little pebbles that go to mush in my mouth.

"Does that happen a lot?" he asks, timing the question as well as the servers at Green Mill, who always come up to the table to ask how everything is at the exact moment that everyone in my family has just shoveled a forkful of something into their mouths and therefore can only nod awkwardly and mumble something unintelligible.

Which is my first instinct: an urgent and rushed, headshaking, pea-filled: "No!" At his smirk, I regain composure and grab a napkin, quickly wipe my mouth, and then cover the speck of green that's landed on my tray. I'm Fry all over again, aren't I?

"No." I push my tray an inch or so away—finished—and add, "Well, sometimes. I zone out sometimes, like, when the situation calls for it."

"Like narcolepsy?" he says. "Do you pass out?" He doesn't speak with the excited interest of a ten-year-old boy meeting a circus freak, but with the disinterested frigidity of a scientist—kind of like Henny, actually.

I shrug. "I have," I say. "I have passed out. But I don't usually. One time I fell off a ladder." His eyes go wide, or as wide as they seem to be able to. He's like Jughead: his eyes seem mostly closed, most of the time. But it's true: one time I was on a ladder, at the old house, helping Dad clean the gutters. I had on his extra pair of work gloves—heavy and thick and crusty, and sort of baggy, despite my long fingers. When I reached a little too far for a sodden bunch of leaves, the ladder shook. It was fine. Mom was down there with both hands on it, holding it pretty steady. But I swooned, and then went deaf, and the world went fuzzy and white. Then I fell off, right backward, right on Mom. No one was hurt.

"I'm Svetlana," I say, on the off chance we're polite, mature individuals.

"Hi," he says, and he briefly wrestles with decorum, I guess. "Um, I'm Lesh."

I nearly say, "Les?" to clarify, but I don't, because maybe

71

he has a weird lisp and I'd be calling attention to it, and besides, are guys really named Les nowadays? He said Lesh. Lesh. I say it back to feel it in my teeth on the sides of my mouth. I say it again.

"Okay," he says. "Yes, Lesh."

"Sorry," again. "I guess I'll see you." And I'm up, with my tray, on the way to the bus window.

CHAPTER 12

LESH TUNGSTEN
<BREATHLESS BOYS IN BLACK>

I walk home alone. I walk home alone because I don't want to see Greg. I just want to whisper her name to myself for ten blocks and change. I just want to whisper her name to myself until it's the same as breathing. I want to whisper her name to myself until I hear it in the sound of my breath and the rustle of the leaves in the trees, until I hear it in the sound of late-summer rain on the roof over my bed.

I whisper it to myself to the rhythm of the music in my head-phones, with each inhale, with each exhale, with each stride.

I whisper it to myself with the key in the lock, and my feet on the steep steps to my room, and my socks shushing on the thick rug, and then I say it out loud—right out loud, in my ugly voice—as I open the character-creation screen and type it into the name field.

CHAPTER 13

SVVETLANA
\<ALLURING AND ALONE\>

The air hums. It is the life of the tree, and of the trees within the tree, and of the water—the rain and the pools, glowing with moonlight, and the water even within the plants. It is the heartbeat of the cats and the boars and the timid deer. It is the prattling eight-legged steps of the spiders in the cave to the north. It is the gentle wind circling around and up and down the great tree in the center of the forest.

Svvetlana opens her eyes. Life surges around her, and she must catch her breath. Before her is an elf man, and he presses his palms together gently and bows. She closes her eyes to him and opens them again, in the manner of a gentle curtsy. He speaks of the power of life, and he tells her, "Kill six pigs."

"Really?" she says, for she—a holy elf woman, practically bubbling over with light and goodness—did not expect to have to do exactly what the heathen, animalistic, violent orcs had to do. Still, she complies, and, spotting a small pig not far off—it is the color of young dandelions, speckled with black, and stands out strongly against the deep greens of the forest—raises her hands to cast a spell.

Holy light bursts from the heavens, and it comes down upon the pig, which rushes at her, its tusks flashing in the soft moonlight.

"Ah!" she screams as it strikes her ankles and the tops of her feet. She thumps it with her staff—a simple, narrow length of strong wood—and it falters briefly, but strikes again. "Ah!"

Svvetlana closes her eyes and sheathes her staff across her back. She summons the life force of her heart and mind, and the bright energy of the woods and the water and the sun and the moon in the sky. It is holy, and it blasts from the sky and destroys the pig. With a squeal, the beast falls to its side. It looks so peaceful now, so timid. Svvetlana kneels beside it and says a prayer, and then digs through the corpse. She pulls away a piece of meat and a pair of frayed cloth gloves, which she supposes it had eaten.

They'd fit quite well and with ten armor points are better than nothing, so she slips them on. Then she stands, wields her staff, and eyes the horizon for another squat, rambling, dandelion-colored shape among the deep green grass so that she might kill it.

Svvetlana sits on the stone edge of a pool. Its water shines in the green-and-silver moonlight, filtered through the thick foliage all around. She has reached level four—the same level as a new orc, halfway across the world—and she is catching her breath, drinking water from a leather pouch and reading through her quest log: only one remains, and soon her quests will take her out of the safety of these novices' woods and into the wide, wild world. Already she's mastered two spells: one that destroys, and another that heals.

"Wanna group?"

Svvetlana stands. Before her is another elf—a man. He carries a simple wooden staff—actually three small staffs, held together at their ends with bands and twine—and a small bow. At his side is a black-and-white cat—something like a small, oddly colored tiger. He has very long blue hair, tied in braids that fall down on either side of his face. In the back, his hair is tied into a small, upright ponytail. But his eyes—so golden and bright, they even cast a golden light over her face. The light warms her, and she moves closer.

He smiles, and his cat sniffs at Svvetlana's sandals, then presses its nose against her knee. Svvetlana reaches down with her free hand and rubs its head.

"My cat likes you," the hunter says, for that is his class, and the cat is the devoted partner in his trials. He is a bit taller than Svvetlana, and when she looks into his face, the light from a wisp—a glowing spirit of the woods—catches her eye.

"So wanna group?" the hunter says again.

"Okay," Svvetlana says. "What are you doing?"

"Leveling as quick as possible," the hunter says. He runs off, and his cat follows. Svvetlana hurries to catch up. "My friend has a level-forty paladin. He's going to meet us."

"Okay, cool," says Svvetlana. Together, the two elves and

the black-and-white tiger gallop through the tall dewy grass toward a dark cave mouth at the edge of the clearing.

"Wait here," the hunter says. He stops, and his cat circles his legs before settling into a lazy stretch to lie down.

Svvetlana stops nearby.

"Is this your first toon?" the hunter asks.

Svvetlana blinks twice and shakes her head. "Yeah, pretty much," she says.

"We'll make sure you don't get lost."

"Thanks." She turns in a slow circle and spots a fawn. With one finger, she lets loose a blast of holy light from the heavens and strikes it down.

The hunter laughs. He and his cat slaughter a handful of fawns, squirrels, and huge moths. The silence makes Svvetlana edgy, and briefly she considers leaving the hunter's side, leaving the forest outright. Finally, though, he speaks. "I have three 50s on a different server."

She falters an instant and says, "Wow."

He smiles at her, and a moment later—atop a long-haired, big-horned ram—a dwarf arrives. "Ready, bitches?" he says as he dismounts.

He doesn't wait for a response. He simply joins their group, charges into the cave, and lets loose. At his feet, the stone ground seems to burst into flames. Svvetlana can only watch as the ironclad dwarf destroys giant spider after giant spider. She can barely raise her hands to cast a spell before their enemies are dead before them.

The hunter laughs. "We'll be level 15 in no time," he says. "Then he'll take us on some dungeon runs."

"Okay," Svvetlana says. She's hesitant to say more, unsure of herself, unsure of how a lady of her station is expected to behave.

"We'll get you some good gear."

Svvetlana nods, and she goes back to watching the dwarf. He's stopped at the top of a long outcropping of rock deep inside the cool, moist cave.

"Go turn in the quest and get the next one," he says.

The hunter and his cat head for the exit, and the young priestess follows. When they reach the quest-giver again, Svvetlana's body fills with light, and she nearly bursts with pride. She's leveling furiously now. These two, she realizes, will take her to the ends of the world if she lets them.

"Girls are always healers," the hunter says. He is running behind her as they head back to the cave, and Svvetlana begins to wonder: *Is he behind me just because, or is he watching my . . .*

No, she thinks. *He couldn't possibly be.*

"What's your name?" he asks. "Is it really Svvetlana?"

She doesn't respond, not right away. She just stops running—maybe he'll pass her. But he stops too, and she turns to face him.

"So how old are you?" he asks.

CHAPTER 14

LESH TUNGSTEN
<TEASERS>

"Aw, crap," I mutter, and I lean back in my desk chair and check the clock: nearly eleven. I'm slightly troubled by how long I've been playing, and by the little bit of first-night homework I still haven't touched. I'm more troubled, though, because: "This dude thinks I'm an actual girl."

I get up, crack my neck and back and knuckles, all of which have seized up something fierce, and lean over the keyboard to check the chat window.

The hunter, Stebbins, has typed: **<<So how old are you?>>**

"Christ, and he wants to hook up, apparently." I glance at my door—it is somehow ajar—so I stretch a little and close it with my foot. Then I drop back into the chair and groan. Of course, I could explain right now—*I'm a sixteen-year-old boy in Minnesota*—but then I'd be on my own again, more than likely—that is, if this hunter and his high-level friend are indeed only helping me out because my avatar has a bouncy rack and great legs.

Not that I blame them.

I decide to play it safe, and so I say nearly nothing at all: **<<Don't perv out on me>>**, I tap out, and everyone is happy. It's not the truth, and it's not a lie. It's simply a warning: *We can group, and you can have your ogling fun, but don't expect reciprocation.*

The paladin—still inside the cave and waiting for us to get back with our new quests—laughs in party chat. **<<Nice try, Stebbins.>>**

That seems to be the end of it—at least for now. I sag in my chair a bit and follow Stebbins into the cave. For some reason, this is easier when I know he's not behind me, watching my gossamer priestess robes flutter around back there. Anyway, it's just until I get the hang of the game—the dungeons, being a priestess and a healer. For now, I'll hang with these guys. I'll stay friendly, but I'll keep my distance, and no one will get the wrong idea.

So I'll be a tease. Great.

CHAPTER 15

SVETLANA ALLEGHENY
<RAPUNZELS>

"Lana!"

I've been hiding in my room since I got home from school. It worked okay for a couple hours, but Henny has been calling up to me for the last thirty seconds. It started with my mom, but she only tried once. Then Henny took up the job, calling first from the bottom of the main steps, and then thumping her way upstairs to the top of the main steps to shout again.

"Lana!"

I heard her exasperated, precocious *soupir grand*, and then her little impossibly heavy feet tramping across the second floor to the bottom of my steps—my steep, uncarpeted, creaky, and narrow steps. "Lana!" It's sharp that time. I slip into my bed and pull the cover over me and hold my breath. I'm certain I'm still, undoubtedly asleep to an outside observer, when Henny reaches my room. She's probably kneeling on the second-to-top step, sticking her head into the attic, craning to see my desk, finding it empty, crawling into my room, just a few feet, and finding my bed, seeing the lump behind the canopy that is me.

She pokes my hip. She pokes my shoulder. She pokes my head.

"Lana," she says, finally quietly. "Lana, I know you're awake. Get up and come downstairs. The Dannons are here."

"Oh no," I say, because I can just see them all, standing on our front stoop, huddled against the rain—is it raining?—their pale, drooping faces and big, white, worried eyes. "Fry told us Lana wasn't feeling well at school," they're probably saying. "We just had to come and see how she's doing."

"Tell them I died," I say, and I roll closer to the wall and pull the duvet on tighter. It's so warm and nice in here. All I can smell is the lavender laundry detergent and my own breath.

Henny doesn't reply at once. She's thinking it over.

I peek out. "Will you?"

"Okay," and she plods back to the steps and down. She can't be halfway down the main steps when I hear her announce like the town crier, "She died!"

There are gasps (not at my death, which they wouldn't have believed, but at my audacity and sacrilege in saying I'd died) and mumbles and aggravated masculine sighs, and then more feet—two of them unfamiliar, on the steps, and before I can jump up to leap from the window, which would be preferable, he's in my room.

"Wow, you are sick," Fry says, and he sits at my desk and

leans his elbows on his knees—settled in and prepared for some real talk. Ha!

I sit up cross-legged, with the duvet still over my lap and around my shoulders and up over my head, but so I can see and he can see my face—shadowed slightly, I hope. "I'm fine, Fry. I'm not sick. I wasn't sick. I was never sick."

He sits up, aghast and astonished. "You sure looked sick to me," he says, and he's desperate for a good snicker. I can tell. I don't like him, but I know him like the underside of my down comforter. He's been around longer, actually, but he's nowhere near as pleasant to be with. The point is, I know what he's thinking before he does. And I know when he wants to go all hyena. This is one of those times. "Your face went totally white."

"My face *is* totally white," I say.

"Whiter than normal," he says. He's sneering—that lecherous smile he's got is at about seventy percent. And I think about what Henny said, and I know why: it's because I've let this go on—I continue to let this go on. Fry believes my genuine disdain for his person is some kind of playful sparring, like we're characters in a romantic comedy from the 1980s, and I am right now continuing to let this go on.

I pull the comforter more tightly around my shoulders and curve my back. I am a cozy potato bug. "Fry," I say.

"Who was that guy who cursed me out?" he asks.

He cursed him out? The boy in black cursed him out?

"No one," I say, which is about as close as I can get to a straight answer without giving an actual straight answer.

"Whoever he is, he's a jerk," says Fry.

I nod under my goose-feather fortress. "I know," I say, and I start again: "Fry."

"I was just worried, Lana," Fry says, and I can't even accuse him of interrupting, since I have no idea how to continue anyway. Besides, he called me Lana instead of blondie. He must sense this won't end well. "I mean, you really looked sick. If you could've seen your face . . . it was scary. I thought you were going to puke or have a seizure or something. Are you epileptic?"

I shake my head, staring through the little breathing and seeing gap in my hood at the wall behind Fry. The anxiety is coming back—it's the false starts, and the sensory memory, I think. It's miserable. It's nauseating.

"Yeah," he says. "I guess I would have known if you were epileptic."

"You have to go," I say.

He stands. "Okay," he says, and I know I haven't said enough.

"Fry, I mean you have to leave me alone," I say, I think a little firmer, but the world is getting fuzzy, so I fall onto my side, with the comforter still up over my head, and look at him shifted ninety degrees. "I think you're pretty annoying. I don't want to hang out with you. I don't want you to hit on me anymore."

"Hit on you," he says, not quite a question. Barely alive, even.

"Right." I roll over to face the wall, waiting for his foot-steps on the steps. I wait and wait. I'm breathing better, but still no footsteps.

"Is that it?" he says, because he's still here, of course, otherwise: footsteps. And I don't know how to answer. What does he mean? I haven't dumped him; that wouldn't make sense. So is what *what*? "What about what happened the other day?"

"When I punched you in the stomach?"

"Tell me that wasn't flirting."

"That was assault," I say.

He's quiet. Another minute, and finally footsteps. Heavy ones. On the steps, on the second floor, on the main steps. The front door is opening and opening and closing. And it's opening again and closing again.

I can breathe and I can see, and I can sit up and I can throw off the comforter and I can walk to the top of the steps and listen to the brief silence before it collapses under six excited feet rumbling up the stairs and across the second floor and toward me. I have some explaining to do.

Henny and I sit on the back deck. It's chilly—it's still summer, according to astronomers, but we all know it's autumn now. This season always makes me think of Roan—I suppose because of her color palette. I'll see her tomorrow, because the Gaming Club will finally meet, the first of our semiweekly official meetings for the next nine months. I couldn't be more thrilled.

"That was pretty cold, Lana," says Henny. "Cold, cold, cold."

Thrilled besides that. My parents tore into me, with Henny kneeling before the top step to my room, arms crossed and disinterested mug set to moderate. How could I be so cruel to the poor boy, my parents wanted to know. He was positively crushed, my mother pointed out. Do you know how long we've been friends with the Dannons, my father demanded rhetorically.

It ended with the two of them turning to leave, and snapping at Henny, "Hen! Don't eavesdrop!" which I felt was entirely unfair, because it's not like she was hiding in a closet or hanging from the eaves. She was kneeling in plain sight. She'd clambered up the steps with them, and only a person blind, deaf, and with no sensory perception whatsoever would have missed her. That doesn't count as eavesdropping.

The parental units banged around in the kitchen, probably planning to serve something Hen and I hate and preparing it with the volume of the ill-mooded, so I took Henny's hand and my quilt of knitted squares in every color of yarn I had lying around, and we walked down to the deck off the second-floor TV room, and now we're huddled on the cold wood bench, looking at the backyard, and beyond that the river and Pickerel Lake and Dakota County, and somewhere out there is Iowa. The stars are giving it their all, though the lights from two downtowns don't make it a fair fight.

"I had to," I say. "You told me I had to."

Hen doesn't answer. She sniffles. She sniffles against the air, which is getting colder by the minute. She sniffles because it's ragweed season, and she belongs inside, where the air filters work double time to keep her sinuses healthy and to keep at bay the red in her eyes. She sniffles mostly, though, because that's her thing, and she knows it. I'm the fainter, and she's the sniffles and coughs. When there's a bump in the road, it's her place to sniffle.

"At least it's over," I say. I shiver once, and Henny drops her arm around my shoulders—or she tries to. It's an awkward position, since I'm practically twice her height. I huddle in closer, and she's nodding.

"He probably won't be nice to you anymore," she says.

"He was never nice to me," I insist. "That's not being nice."

"Sort of it is," Hen says. "He talks to you and smiles at you. That's something."

"No, it isn't. It's lecherousness."

"What's that mean?" Hen asks, so I take a deep breath and let it out, then lean back till my head is against the back of the house. "Like a leech? A bloodsucking leech?" She derives some pleasure from saying such things: using the word "sucking" in an allowable context. I can feel her cheek against my arm as she grins and says it again: "A bloodsucking leech."

"Not at all," I say, "or quite a lot, actually."

"Never mind," she says. "I think I know. Context says so much."

I nod, because it does, and Hen goes on, "Anyway, you had to do it. And Mom and Dad will get over it."

I shrug. "Season's over anyway, right?" It's a joke, but not. If they can't count on seeing the Dannons at Thunder games, avoiding them till this blows over is a safe plan.

But Hen shakes her towhead. "Play-offs, we're in them."

"We?"

She ignores it, which is fine. I've said it before, I'll say it again, and it's a silly if valid point: Hen and the parentals are not members of the team, and using the multiple first-person pronoun to imply they are is downright insane. But fine. I rolled my d10 for charisma, hoping for a digression distraction, and needed an eight. I got a two.

"So they'll see the Dannons again," I say. "Soon?"

"Soonish," Hen says. "And you will too. Because you have a ticket."

"That doesn't mean I'll go."

"We'll see," says my intolerable little sister.

"Why is this door open?" It's Dad, poking his angry giant face through the open sliding door to call us to dinner. Hen and I stare back but don't reply. "Dinner. Right now."

He pulls his head back and—astonishingly—closes the door. I get that he wants the door closed at all times except the precise millisecond at which a human form requires passage through what would otherwise be a wall or window, but to call us inside and then close the door before we come in is pure hostile madness.

"Dad's still angry," Hen says. She's very helpful in addition to being intolerable. We stand up, and now her arm has to slip down to my waist. Her hand falls on my far hip, and I pull the door open for her, and we step inside.

"Go ahead," I say. She waits a moment, and then stomps off. One of her socks—the green one, as they don't match, and the other is red; very Christmas, or traffic-lighty—is slipping off as she goes. I watch her a minute, then close the sliding door and lock it and lean on it. The air inside smells of onions and boiled carrots and yeast, which means we're having carrot bisque, which looks and tastes like vomited baby food, and those rolls that pop out of a tube.

My parents have funny ways of exacting revenge.

CHAPTER 16

LESH TUNGSTEN
<ALPHA DOGS>

"Where were you last night?" Greg says as our palms make contact on the sidewalk in front of Central High. It's Wednesday morning, and I'm tired and sore. The crick in my neck is a thumping ache now.

"What are you—" I start, because he knows I'm grounded, and we didn't plan to meet anywhere, but then I stop, because we did, at least vaguely. "I forgot. Sorry." I forgot the tiniest, briefest hint of an inkling of the suggestion that we'd meet in the game and level my ugly-ass warrior.

He shrugs as we head inside. "No biggie."

"You should've IM'd," I say, and then regret it, because maybe he did.

"You weren't on. I texted."

My hand instinctively goes to my hip pocket, like I could read his text and respond through time. Had I been so lost in his ridiculous world that I hadn't even opened a browser? Checked my phone?

"I fell asleep early," I say, and the lies have begun, because I am not about to admit that I spent the night—right through till nearly one in the morning—pretending to be an elven girl, bombarded with untoward comments from a ingratiating hunter and foul-mouthed dwarf just to help me level. "Anyway, tonight for sure." It's a promise I intend to keep. In the clear, cold light of Wednesday morning, my behavior last night seems even to me a perverted step off the rails. I vow silently to keep my interest in Svetlana Allegheny (her last name was easy to find; how many Svetlanas do you think there are at Central High School?) on a purely appropriate level. No more of this online impersonation junk.

Anyway, Greg thinks about it. Checks his mental calendar for other online commitments, I assume, and finds none. "All right. Enjoy skej A." We slap five again and he's off. I'm getting used to this. I pull my headphones back up and find my locker.

She sits with me again at lunch.

Maybe she had been planning to—who knows. But just in case, I had exited the cafeteria line and grabbed the same seat as the day before. With a little maneuvering of freshmen, I arranged things so that the seat opposite me—Svetlana's seat—was empty, and when she came out of the line, carefully carrying her tray of food, looking out over the sea of eaters, her chin high and her shoulders back, I caught her eye. It worked.

I'm not getting used to this, but I pull the headphones clear off this time. Not even the mime of solitude today. I'll try talking. I'll try talking like a guy who can smile and be around people made of silvery light without pulling his cape across his face and hissing like the undead cat from *Pet Sematary*.

"Do you mind?" she asks when her tray is across from me. Its edge touches the edge of mine. I shake my head. So much for being able to talk.

"More pizza?" she continues.

I look at the food in front of me. It is pizza—the rectangular kind, with pale yellow cheese, no demonstrable sauce, and a thick, undercooked, and freezer-burned crust. But it's not more pizza. "More?" I manage to croak.

"You had pizza yesterday," and now she's sitting. She's got the pasta side—penne with veggies—but no meat. She's probably vegetarian. She picks up a noodle with her fingers and eats it.

"I had pizza *rolls*," I point out, "but fine. Yeah. More pizza."

She eats another noodle, still regarding my pizza. When noodle number two is gone, she finally picks up a fork to grab a plank of carrot. It doesn't look delicious.

"So," I say.

She shrugs, like I'd actually said something, and then it's silent for a while, as I take bite after bite of rectangular pizza, being extra careful about chewing with my lips closed, and she moves her fork in slow circles around her plate and pasta.

Finally she says, "I told that boy off last night. Fry. The one you sent running. He said you cursed him out." She leans forward when she talks, like we're conspirators. She sits back and shifts in her chair then, and her head falls to one side, and she shifts again, and she switches the fork to her other hand and puts the first hand on her bottle of water but doesn't take a sip. It's making me thirsty, how much she's not taking a sip.

"I didn't curse him out exactly," I say. "I cursed, and when I cursed I was talking to him. But I didn't curse him out."

She shrugs one shoulder again, lifts her body, and folds her leg underneath her butt. I wish for a second that I could get a better look at that, because her skirt is heavy and thick, like it must weigh thirty pounds. I can't imagine how she bothers to walk, never mind constantly change position in her chair. When she pulls off her green button-up sweater, I look back at my pizza. It's gone. I've eaten two crappy slices of pizza just to keep something in my mouth and hands. My fingers are greasy, and as smoothly as I can, I rub them across the thighs of my jeans. *Say hello to yesterday's pizza-roll grease.*

The boy—Fry, I mean—is watching us. He's sitting at the table closest to the lunch line, but he's not eating. He's just sitting, and there's an open textbook in front of him on the table. He's not even being subtle. Svetlana has her back to him. She probably doesn't know he's there, spying on us.

"He's right over there," I say, and quickly add, "Don't look, probably."

"Fry is?" she says, and she looks. Quickly, sure, but it's not like he would miss it. *"Incroyable."*

"Did you go out or hook up or something?" I say, because I

don't know this girl at all and that's the kind of thing that can only be taken well. I'm being sarcastic.

She's sickened at the thought, I hope. Her face twists and her tongue pokes out between her teeth and down-turned mouth. I even laugh.

"He's just a family friend. He's a member of my social circle against my will and entirely contrary to my wishes."

I nod. "Noted."

She eats something and lets herself sag in her chair a little. My overheated little brain is cataloging her moves at a furious rate now. It's unhealthy. A moment passes and she's bolt upright again. She pushes her tray to the side—Gordy the freshman has finished his lunch and adjourned—and leans over to her tote bag, pushing her longer-by-the-second white-blond hair behind her ears as she does. I see the arch of her back and her hair as it falls from her ears again—she could do with some elf leporine (I looked it up) ears to hold it in place—and the spot on her lower back where her orange T-shirt should reach the top of her skirt, but doesn't quite.

Look away. Look away.

I'm desperate for anything to say, anything to do with my hands. If I had more pizza, I'd eat it. I consider eating her pasta, but then she pops back up. She's holding a spiral notebook in both hands, and she lays it on the table with a slap.

"Homework?" I say, but then I glimpse the cover. "Whoa, what is that?"

Our eyes meet, and hers are beaming. Her smile is beaming.

Her hair falls from her ears and settles on her lean, broad shoulders like a silver shawl. A magical silver shawl. She's a priestess, there's no doubt. She's pure magic.

The cover of this notebook—once probably on the shelf at my mom's Target, on sale for ninety-nine cents—is now more amazing and wondrous than any spiral notebook from Target should ever expect to be. She's filled it with ink—blue and red and green and black—in a not-quite-abstract explosion of swirls that shine like heavily laid ink does. They form a dragon, soaring across the center of the page, over a frosty mountain range, at its feet a small medieval-looking village. I'm standing now— I didn't mean to get up—and leaning across the table, twisting my body to get a better look. "Holy crap. You made that?"

She nods and tucks her hair again. It falls right out. I nearly try to retuck it for her.

"I knew it," she said. "I totally knew you'd like dragons."

I squint at her and sit back. My heart thumps once against my ribs, because no, I'm not into dragons. Who's into dragons at sixteen? But the game—the game is full of dragons, and she can't know about me and the game. She can't ever know.

"So . . . just so we're straight," I say, "you don't hate me any-more. That right?"

She shrugs and isn't smiling or looking at me. "I'm not big on hating," she says, and after a beat, "generally."

"There's Fry."

"I don't even hate him, really," she says, and she's rooting around in that bag again. I wish I hadn't sat back down. I could still be leaning over the table. I could still be in the perfect position to see her leaning over.

"But I want to show you something," she says, sitting upright again. And she drops this thing onto the table—this severely damaged spiral notebook, with its cover in tatters, its pages matted and warped at the edges, its spiral backbone bent and misshapen, no longer connected to the pages at the top and bottom of the spine.

I'm no dummy. I can see why you might think I am, but I'm really not. So I know right away what this mess is. I shrink in my seat and groan.

"Don't worry," she says. "I'm not going to make a big thing of it. I meant to. I put it in my bag this morning with the intention of shoving it in your face."

"So what's stopping you?" I ask all casual, but inside I'm anything but casual because that means Svetlana, first thing this morning, was thinking about sitting at lunch *with me*.

She shakes her head and holds my gaze, narrows her eyes even. "I wanted to," she says. "I wanted to pull out this notebook—this symbol of all my summer's hard work—and I wanted to reignite the fire in my belly. The fire in my belly I felt when I was biking home the other night, after the incident."

The incident.

"The fire in my belly when I spent the entire next day in a supremely foul mood."

She drags the word "foul" so it takes a full second to say. To intone. She's Shakespearean or something all of a sudden.

I bet she drives the English teachers positively wild with academic lust.

"The fire in my belly when I punched Fry in the gut at the Thunder game."

Too many questions to process now. My jaw drops. I intend to speak. Nothing comes out, and her fuguelike state is over. Another shrug, another tuck of the hair, and our staring contest ends. "Anyway, it didn't work. I think you're okay."

"Thanks."

"You shouldn't drink, though," she adds, as if I didn't know. "Because when you do, bad things happen to me and my stuff."

I let a short little laugh out and then catch something in the corner of my eye. It's Fry. He's walking toward us. Svetlana catches me watching and turns in her seat.

"This doesn't look good," I say. "I should bail."

"Don't you dare," she snaps, flipping back to face me. Fry is at our table in an instant.

"Hi, Lana," he says, and I already feel like a moron, because here I am thinking her name—the one people call her—is Svetlana, when obviously anyone who has known her for any length of time calls her Lana.

I should also explain that first of all, the name "Lana" is undoubtedly taken on every server in the game. Even "Svetlana" was taken. Hence the two *v*'s. Plus, changing your toon's name is not free. It's, like, twenty bucks.

"Hello," she says, and now she's back to poking pasta.

"About yesterday . . . ," Fry says, but he can't really get this confrontation off the ground. He sees me watching him and maybe remembers he's a senior and I'm not. "What are you looking at?"

I look away, back at the green messed-up notebook, but I try to smirk. I'm not the omega in this situation. He is. I'm not sure he's accepted that yet.

"Fry, don't start," Svetlana says. I'm still calling her Svetlana in my head. I think I'll stick with it. It's more magical than Lana, and it won't require a twenty-dollar payment. And I like the feel of the V on my bottom lip. I glance at her and there's her bottom lip. She pulls it between her teeth—a nervous little tic, maybe—but I want to bite it. I suddenly can't wait to get home and in the game, where I can be with her in private.

That sounds more lecherous than it is.

"What am I starting?" Fry says, because this spat isn't going to wait around while I daydream about silver-haired Svvetlana. He's smiling at her, but I can see he's angry, and getting desperate. His haunches are starting to fluff. His tail is dropping. If we corner him, he'll probably snap. Might take a finger. "I'm just saying hi."

Svetlana wiggles her plastic fork till a single piece of penne slides onto one of the fork fingers. Then she goes after a second.

"Fine," Fry says. "Fine, be completely insane. We won't talk anymore at all. Sound good?"

She's got the second finger loaded up. There's a third one—obviously—but I don't think she can fit another noodle in the gap. It's not big enough.

Fry's still waiting for her to respond, but she's still wiggling her fork at a slippery little penne. It's not going to work.

I glance up at the boy. He looks back, so I shrug. That doesn't go over well, probably because I'm still smirking—I look all alpha, like I've won some noncompetition we're having over Svetlana's love (if only)—and the cornered stray dog with his tail down finally lifts his lips in a snarl and snaps.

Fry grabs the fork from Svetlana's slender hand—it's ink-stained; I hadn't noticed, but of course it is—and throws it at the wall of windows behind me. The noodles stick to the glass. That can't have been very satisfying, because next he pushes my tray—laden only with my empty pizza plate and unopened milk—onto my lap. It lands hard, and I stand and jump back, sending my chair slamming into the metal-covered heating system under the windows.

"Are you serious?" I say, but he just stares at me before stomping off, slamming with a grunt through the cafeteria's double doors to the stairway. The plastic pizza plate is still finishing its tightening spin on the floor at my feet, like a quarter does when it's nearly done spinning on the tabletop. It's one of Greg's annoying habits: spinning nickels and quarters on the desk in front of his keyboard during even the tiniest moment of downtime.

Svetlana looks up at me, her mouth open a little, and then pulls in the bottom lip again. She can't be real.

I'm waiting for her to speak. I'm waiting for her to explain how Fry can be real too, how a little late-night bike mishap could lead to cafeteria assault that I should rightfully have nothing to do with. My timeline has crossed with Svetlana's—and with it Svvetlana's—and they're both magical, so it can't be an accident. I'm beginning to think single-*v* Svetlana is the more magical of the two, no matter what spells the priestess masters.

Her lips part again, and she says, "I need a new fork."

CHAPTER 17

SVETLANA ALLEGHENY
<DUNGEON MASTERS>

Pretty sure I won't be eating lunch with Lesh again. It's not like people find it a thrilling prospect to be harassed by the stalking nemeses of girls they hardly know and have had lunch with by accident twice.

I'm not sure how I feel about this. On the one hand, I hardly know him, either, and it's not like he's an obvious choice for a friend (or whatever). He's younger than I am, and he dresses like a teenage funeral director. On the other hand . . . I don't know. He's gotten rid of Fry twice now. And he clearly liked my notebook—I don't know the last time someone who wasn't a Gaming Club member even got to *see* one of my notebooks.

I'm staggering numbly down the English hallway, and now and then I have to violently shrug my right shoulder to keep my tote bag on there. It's too heavy, but when I remember why—five copies of my hand-drawn, meticulously articulated monster manual and one pristine copy of the green notebook (for the dungeon master's eyes only), full of maps and monster notes and encounters—I smile. In less than three hours, I'll be with the club, and I can forget about Fry's insanity and Lesh's dark eyelashes.

Dark eyelashes? Where did that come from?

I slip into Dr. Serrano's poetry class and into my desk, and then find the anthology sandwiched between monster manuals and my DM's screen. Among the spiral notebooks, one has a swirling drawing, all in blue ink, of a rough-wave ocean crashing against tall cliffs. Very Nordic. That's my poetry notebook, the only academic notebook I have that doesn't make me want to crawl back into bed.

I'm still flipping to the page marked on the board—it's the poem we read last night, by Longfellow—when Serrano calls on Atticus Bernstein to give his thoughts on the reading.

Poor boy. With a name like Atticus, every word he utters ought to be inspired and wise, spoken with a voice that compels all within earshot to sit up and listen. I wonder how disappointed Atticus's parents must be. Such a noble and lofty name full of great expectations, and they end up with a heavyset boy with a prominent brow and underdeveloped frontal lobe who says "um" a lot and scratches himself in the cafeteria.

His response is neither inspired nor wise. It is predictable and vapid. I'll not bother transcribing it for you.

Dr. Serrano crosses his arms and leans one shoulder against the whiteboard. He smiles and nods and doesn't say a word.

"Um . . . ," says Atticus. "Dr. Serrano? Was I right?"

Serrano stands up straight and looks out over the sea of young and oblivious faces.

"Answer him, learners," Dr. Serrano says. "Is he right?"

Eyes go down. Some people look around, to see who might dare speak up. Finally I take a deep breath and raise my hand. I love this poem, and I want Serrano to know it. He doesn't look at me, though. He just points and says, "Go."

"He is right," I say, and the Cro-Magnon walking literary reference smiles. But then I go on: "Strictly speaking. But saying this poem is about life and death and everything is like saying— I don't know—that *Romeo and Juliet* is a little love story."

"Explain," Dr. Serrano says. He sits at his desk and holds his hands like a steeple.

I sit up a little straighter and clear my throat. My ears are getting hot now, but I press on. "It's a technical poem," I say. "Longfellow got every word, every repetition, every sound, just exactly right." My words begin to come faster—too fast—as I go on. I'm speaking and spinning out of control. Just let me stay awake. "You feel the draw and release of the current in your stomach as you read, because that's the rhythm of the poem, and that's what the alliteration of the piece makes you feel. You feel the waves move up and down, and the tide go in and come out. You feel the horses ready to run. You feel the earth itself breathe in and out. In and out. In and out."

I try to catch my breath, to slow down a little, but I can't. "Longfellow makes you feel the rhythm of life and death," I add quickly, glancing at Atticus. The words tumble out of me, like dice from a cup. "We're each of us the traveler. Those are our footprints in the sand. It'll all be wiped away."

Now my face is hot. I'm out of breath, and I know the class is watching me now, turning in their seats, so I drop my eyes and shrug—*No big thing*—but it's no good, because I've just been short of breath, repeating "in and out, in and out." I pick at the corner of my notebook, staring at the art on its cover—the drawing I'd made after reading and rereading this poem—and wish desperately I were there, tossing in those waves. A boy snickers, and my face gets even hotter, a little tingly. I don't know if I can hold on.

"Anything else?" Serrano says, snapping me out of it, just enough, and finally looking at me.

"I kind of think that even if you didn't understand English, just listening to this poem, you'd get it." I can speak more slowly, but my voice is quiet now, barely a whisper. "You'd feel the tide rise and fall."

Serrano is standing over my desk now, smiling down at me. "Good," he says, very quietly. "Good."

Then he bursts into life and in three long strides is back at the whiteboard on the longest wall of the classroom. "Svetlana has led us beautifully into why I chose this poem for your first reading assignment: it's short."

The class chuckles, and the tension—if it existed in the room outside of my own thundering chest—is broken. I glance out the window. The big maples that line Lexington Avenue are still green, but they're thinking about turning. I can tell.

"But seriously," Serrano says, grabbing a marker. "I want to talk about form now, and that is the heart of what Svetlana has shown us. Form isn't just a vessel. It's not a paper cup that we fill up with a poem, a liquid poem that would fill a glass vase or a gravy boat just as well. It's a part of the poem itself."

I pull my eyes back to watch him write, and I cross my ankles and prop up my chin with both fists.

A good afternoon puts me on air. I'm not walking anymore when the final bell rings and releases me into the normally stifling hallways of Central. I'm not prancing, skipping, sashaying, either. I'm floating. I'm like a windborne seed, up near the ceiling, curving mindlessly toward the English wing, toward room 3212. No one sees me, no one notices—no one would predict I'll land in that linoleum room on that linoleum floor among those linoleum desks, and I'll somehow take root and blossom.

Cheesy, I know. It's the mood I'm in, and I suppose I'd better shake it, because a good DM can't be cheesy and cheerful. She has to be ruthless, cold, and utterly certain in every choice, every calculated obstacle and predictable misstep the party will make. I am not their opponent, and I am not their ally. I am their god.

Cheery-and-cheesy mood shaken, I step into 3212 and grin. I let my tote slide down my arm and catch the handles as they reach my hand. "Hi, Ms. Grimmish." Classics, Latin, Shakespeare, Elizabethan Playwrights . . . if there's an elective for those of us who were born in the wrong era—never mind the wrong year or decade—Ms. Grimmish teaches it.

She pulls off her glasses, lets them hang from the chain of fake pearls they live on, and clucks her tongue. Then she throws out her arms, like the big desk at the front of 3212 is actually center stage at the Globe Theatre. "She arrives!" She bellows it.

I turn as the chairs scrape at the back of the room, pushed back from the table, and Roan and Reggie stand up. Cole hardly shifts. He uncrosses his arms and grabs a pen to twirl. More oddly, he's not sitting next to Reggie. He's directly across from Roan, on a short side of the table, and Abraham is seated in the gaping canyon that separates Cole and Reggie.

Abraham leans back and makes a point of checking the clock behind Ms. Grimmish. "Did you get lost on the way here, Allegheny?" he says, folding his hands behind his head.

Roan hurries to join Reggie and Abraham on their long side of the table, facing the room, and mounts an empty seat on her knees. She leans eagerly across the table, her arms and fingers stretched as far and wide as they'll go, like she's a lion waking up with a grin. Her tangle of orange hair is her mane, and the freckles across her nose and mouth are the dried blood from her pre-doze kill and feast.

"Finally!" she says, and she drums the table with her fingers. "Let's go, let's go."

"Am I that late?" I say, glancing at the clock. I'm not.

Reggie sits down and shakes his green velvet bag—his dice

bag. "We're excited." Cole scoots his chair over, around the corner of the table to join the adventuring party—a slight little shuffle, void of enthusiasm, and I make a mental note to check with Roan later. Something's off between Reggie and Cole, and that cannot be good.

I grab my seat facing them—a key aspect of dungeon mastering is the solitude of tremendous power—and dump the contents of my tote bag across the big table. Reggie and Abraham grab for the duplicates I'd made, Cole casually takes his, but Roan pauses and stares: there's the mangled green notebook.

"Whoa," she says, reaching for it, touching it like it's a wounded eagle. "Svet, what happened?" She takes the cover between her thumb and first finger and lifts it, just a little, just gingerly. "Oh my gosh."

I slide down in my seat. I nod and frown. I lean forward and take the wounded eagle from Roan's careful fingers, and I flip through the warped pages, with an absent mind checking again for the few spots of unharmed ink therein. But it's all for show. It's all because these four—these misanthropic, misplaced, mismatched, mistreated four—will know how much this should upset me, and I don't want them to know (not yet; maybe not ever) that I've already forgiven Lesh.

Lesh the miscreant, Lesh my lunch friend, Lesh, who sent Fry packing.

"The other night," I say, "I fell off my bike."

Blink. Blink.

"The other night," I try again, "I hit a boy with my bike."

"Oh my gosh, who?" "Was he hurt?"

"The other night," I try one more time, "some drunk guy knocked my bike over and the green notebook landed in a puddle."

"Should we kill him?" Roan says, leaning farther yet across the table.

"Ms. Garnet," Ms. Grimmish bellows kindly from the front of the room. "Climb in the playground, if you please, not in my classroom."

"Sorry, Ms. G," she calls back, and settles down a bit. She still leans farther across the table than decorum typically allows. She's an easy girl to forgive, though, and Ms. Grimmish is satisfied.

"Who was it?" Cole says. His voice is flat, disinterested. Bored.

"A sophomore," I say, and then I follow it up with a lie that I should know better than to attempt: "I don't know his name. It doesn't matter. He's a miscreant."

"What's he look like?" Abraham says. Now even he's leaning forward, and this isn't, so far, how I intended our first meeting of the year to go.

"Guys, forget it," I say, and I shuffle some papers and start to unfold my screen. "I thought you were excited to start this campaign."

"Fork the campaign," says Abraham.

"Mr. Polsen!" says Ms. Grimmish. "Language!"

"Sorry!" he calls back, and then he says it again, super quiet: "Fork the campaign. I wanna know who this jerk is."

"It doesn't matter," I say, and I grab the duplicate green folder and hold it up. "See? A perfect copy. It's safe. The material is safe. Your campaign will move along brilliantly."

He sags back. Reggie shrugs. Roan drums the table with both hands. "Agreed," she says. "Let's start."

"Good," I say. "Got your character sheets?"

And Cole stands up. For the first time, I notice he is without bag, without notebook, without anything.

"Guys, I'm quitting the club," he says, and he looks at Reggie, who is not looking at him. "Sorry."

He walks toward the door at the front and Ms. Grimmish hops up from her desk and puts out an arm to gently stop him. At the back of the room, we're all straining to see and hear, but it's just whispers and mumbles. He moves for the door again.

"Mr. Andersen," Grimmish says louder, "if you leave, membership falls to four."

"Oh, sugar," says Abraham, sort of.

And the door opens, and Cole goes out, and for a moment we hear the after-hours murmur of liberated students moving through the halls or speaking to each other in their own club meetings before the door clicks closed again, bringing our sad silence back to us.

Lucky jerks. They all have five—probably way more than five—members. But now we have only four, which means we don't get a faculty adviser. We don't get room 3212. We don't get extracurricular credit.

We get nothing. We get future meetings in the Garnets' basement. And we all know better than to think we'll find a fifth member, some random geek that heretofore we'd never uttered a word to, roaming the halls of Central with a secret affinity for role-playing. We've been down the road of recruitment before. It never ends well.

Roan lets her head fall forward onto the table and rolls it back and forth, her hair rolling with it. She's set her little section of the table on fire.

Reggie's eyebrows are way up, deflecting blame. We won't talk about it now—there's no point—but obviously he dumped Cole, and Cole therefore dumped us.

Abraham drops heavily into his chair and lets his head bang into the wall behind him. "We," he says, "are forked."

CHAPTER 18

LESH TUNGSTEN
<MALL RATS>

Greg is not my only friend. Our circle will probably change over the year—that happens, thank god—but for now it's got a few other guys, and a few other girls. They're generally not important, especially as I'm grounded for the rest of my life. Anyway, one of them is Fio, short for Fiorello. He's the most obnoxious guy you've ever heard of, but it's made him one of the most notorious (which is at least widely known, if not well liked) guys in the grade.

Greg's hanging around my locker with Fio when I show up after the last bell. I'm not really in the mood for either of them, but if I have to walk home with Greg, I'll bear it. He's going that way anyway. Fio, however, is never interested in a casual walk. He's got something ridiculous in mind.

Something about Fio: he leaves the fly of his jeans open all day, every day. Don't ask him why, because he'll just say, "It needs air," and then stare at you. He's challenging you, but you'll never know if it's to a fight or a make-out session. The point is he's uncomfortable to be around.

Still, I can't help checking: today's no different. His fly's open to the extreme. He's got some fabric from his underwear pulled out the toothy opening.

"Hey, Tung," says Fio as I slap five with Greg to say hello. "We're going to MOA with Cheese and Weiner."

These are people. Both are seniors, both are deeply metal. I don't even know Cheese's real name. I do know they are the two biggest potheads at Central.

I shake my head and open my locker. "I'm grounded." Who knows if I'd break the grounding? The fact is I don't want to go anyway.

Fio laughs at that, and Greg says, "I told you."

"Tung, bro," Fio says, grinning, "your idiot parents aren't home."

I'm shuffling books in my locker. I let the insult slide, not because he frightens me, but because I don't actually care. My parents are, occasionally, total idiots.

"How the hell do you know?" I ask instead of defending them.

"I know because your dad is never home," he says, "because he's always building garages. Am I right?"

I shrug, shoulder my backpack, and slam my locker.

"So your dad's building a garage," Fio goes on, and then he glances at Greg and finishes, "and your mom is probably pitching someone's tent."

Greg laughs it up. I just shake my head. "Whatever. Have fun."

"You should come," Greg tries. "You'll be home by six."

"No, you won't," Fio says. "You'll be *stoned* by six. You'll be getting head from Jelly by eight."

Jelly is a person too—a female person, often seen in the company of Cheese and Weiner. I doubt very much she deserves the rep she has, but that doesn't mean she doesn't look good in tight black jeans, and it doesn't mean Fio's not-so-vague prediction isn't both appealing and positively terrifying. I'm glad my jeans are, as always, mad baggy.

"Can't do it." I turn my back on them and head toward the door.

"Okay, faggot," says Fio, and Greg laughs.

The wit, it's astonishing. And I'm starting to talk in my head like Svetlana talks out loud. I better get home and slip into her skin and an extra *v.* I walk faster.

Greg is after me like a shot. "Tung," he says, grabbing my arm. He's quieter now, speaking so I can hear him and Fio can't. We're about to have a friend moment.

"Dude, I can't," I say.

"You can," Greg insists. "And forget Fio. He's just being normal Fio. You'll be home before your mom. I promise. Come on."

I look past him at Fio, who is standing with Cheese and Weiner now. Actually, they're standing near him, laughing, while he rubs the front of his body against a locker a few down from mine. I suppose he might know whose it is. I suppose it doesn't matter.

"I don't know," I say. Fio is moaning now, ecstatically, "Oh, Jelly . . . Jelly," and I'd rather just go home. I'd rather just go home, whisper Svetlana's name to myself—one or two *v*'s, doesn't matter—and run her around fantasyland.

But this is Greg, and he looks so pathetic, out here in the real world, away from the glow of his computer screen. His posture is about the same, but he isn't a master of dual-wielding epic blades of agility. So I nod, just once, and say, "All right."

He smiles.

"But no joke: I have to be home by six thirty at the latest. If we're driving out there with Weiner, we'll reek. I'll have to shower and get my clothes in the wash before my mom gets home."

"Fine, fine," he says. "So you and me will take the bus back, okay? Whenever you want."

"Okay."

Weiner knows every spot along Hamline Avenue where his mile-long Oldsmobile can get air. There are more than you might think, as long as you're willing to drive twice the speed limit through intersections with school crossings. Weiner is willing.

The windows are closed, and all three seniors—in the front seat—are smoking cigarettes. They're also passing a joint. In the back, it's me, Greg, and Fio, in that order, and I can't open my window because Weiner keeps the windows locked at all times. There's a story. I'm told someone heaved a full beer bottle through a store window once. That's the short version.

"Yo, can I get a hit off that?" Fio says, leaning left and forward, so he's shouting right at Jelly's ear. She's not answering, and the music—Lamb of God—is loud enough that Fio thinks she can't hear him. But from where I'm sitting, I can see her rolling her eyes. They're huge, or maybe they just look that way because of the makeup. It's black and all around them, and under her right eye it seems to drip down to the corner of her mouth. I can't tell if she looks ridiculous or sexy as hell. Probably both.

As for me and Greg, we don't want any. We're not stupid; we know someday we're pretty much going to have to get high, and—if these three wasters are a good sampling—we'll probably like it a lot. But for now, and at least for today, we'll both be happy putting in our appearance at this little warped tour and getting home before our folks.

We hit Highway 5 like a four-door 1991 rusty POS out of hell, and then blast onto 494 toward the Mall of America. Weiner is doing ninety, easy, and has to slam on the brakes pretty good when he reaches the exit for the mall. We all jerk forward. Weiner puts out his arm to stop Jelly from going through the windshield.

"Spaz," says Jelly, and I love her for it. None of the guys in this car—except maybe Greg—take crap from anyone. If a senior jock stepped up to Fio in the hall, he'd go ballistic. I've seen Weiner toss a kid against a locker, scream like a maniac, and then strut off quietly. Scary. Last year, two then-seniors said something about Cheese's dead mother. He shouldered both of them into a stairwell, so they fell on their butts when they tripped backward on the bottom step. One of them knocked his head on a step and went to the emergency room. Got ten stitches. But when Jelly tells us off, there's no question: she can, and she will.

Weiner heads to the top floor of the parking ramp on the west side. It's close to the food court, first of all, and second, no normal people ever park that high up except during the holiday rush when they don't have a choice. We pile out, three cigarettes spark, and we strut across the lot. Jelly walks fast, and she picks Cheese to hold by the arm. The rest of us hang back, watch her ass, and take it slow. Greg and I wear the same long black coat, open, so it flaps behind us like we're both Blade the vampire hunter. *It's all role-playing,* I think as we walk.

Jelly and Cheese—they'd make a good sandwich—are already inside. Weiner flicks his cigarette off the ramp as we reach the door. Jelly's boots on the mall floor are like thunder. I'm watching her feet, her butt. I watch her lips—deep, dark red: bloodred—when she shouts back at Cheese. I don't even know what she says. I don't even care. She's the sexiest woman alive.

When the seniors get in line for tacos, me and Greg and Fio silently agree on burgers and line up there instead.

"I'm telling you, Tung," says Fio. "She'd definitely put out for you."

I'm watching her, and I'm thinking about Svetlana at the

same time. I'm putting them next to each other on a video screen in my brain. I'm lining them up, like a cop: I think Jelly's a little shorter, but it's close. Her hair is blacker than mine, blacker than a raven's heart. Svetlana's hair I've said enough about. Jelly's mean, brusque, quiet, angry, and stoned. Svetlana is none of those things. She is sparkling light; she is shimmering sobriety. She smells like strawberries and honey. She talks too much and too fast.

I suddenly want to get close enough to Jelly to check her scent. It's probably hot sauce.

So which one should I be lusting after? Jelly, obviously. While I'm standing there, waiting for my combo meal and staring at her, it occurs to me I can't be into Svetlana anyway, because the two asshats I'm standing with right now wouldn't let me.

We eat. Jelly laughs at a joke I make about Fio. Fio pretends to jump from the food court onto the floor of the amusement park two stories down. A mall cop gets in his face, so the rest of us bail on the food court. Cheese and Weiner announce they have to meet someone, and Jelly joins them, so when they head off, me and Greg find the bus. I'm home by five, and I remember I don't have to lust after Svetlana. It's not about lust. It's about crawling into her skin again, and I spend the rest of the evening—with limited interruptions from Greg, Mom, and Dad—running around the land of imagination with a hunter called Stebbins and paladin called Dewey. And while I'm there, I am sparkling light, shimmering sobriety, and I smell like strawberries and honey.

CHAPTER 19

SVVETLANA
<WET AND WILD>

The elves step out of the blazing-hot sun of the wide, rolling desert and into the cool shade of the cave mouth. The priestess Svvetlana sits down and takes a long pull from a skin of water gathered from the dew-fed pools of her homeland. It fills her with light and brightens her spirit.

"Can you spare some?" says the hunter Stebbins. He sits next to her, and his cat curls up at her feet. It's becoming a habit with these three—to sit and refresh together. Svvetlana is beginning to feel that the hunting cat is her companion as well as the hunter's himself. She passes the skin and leans back. A moment later, the paladin Dewey jogs into the cave. He'd been finishing off a huge group of angry centaurs.

"Remember the rules, you two dorks," he says as he cracks his knuckles and then pulls out his hammer and shield. "Stay back. Don't aggro. Don't pull. Don't do anything."

"We know," says the hunter. The priestess is silent, as she

usually is. She just stands up and casts a buff on the party to increase everyone's stamina.

"Pulling," says Dewey, and with a great battle cry, he charges into the cave itself. Before long, he is standing in the midst of a dozen or more angry druids. They are bringing down upon him blow after blow of sword and staff and balls of fire and lightning. They cast upon him poisons and curses and spells to weaken him and slow him and fill him with dread, but they are meager foes to his vast skills and strength, and he is not affected. With each swing of his club, with each stomp on the earth, with each strike of his shield, another foe falls.

"Onward!" he shouts, and he runs deeper into the cave. Svvetlana, far behind, begins to understand the complexity of the task ahead of them. This is no simple cave; it is an underground world, with its own rivers and lakes and mountains, each section more dangerous than the last. Around every turn are monsters of every imaginable shape and design. There are druids—elves much like her, but with evil in their hearts—vipers that tower over even her and the hunter, great monstrosities of stone and earth, taller still, and even plants that walk like animals and fire thorns and poison that threaten her very life. If not for the powerful paladin leading the priestess and the hunter, they'd be doomed.

It's a long journey to the heart of the cave, with its convoluted system of land bridges and tunnels and underground water passages. They must swim and jump and climb—and fighting, always fighting. The paladin, at the front of the small group in his gleaming golden armor, bearing his lion-faced shield of silver and huge stones of topaz and sapphire, attacks dozens at one go. The earth at his feet glows with the fire of justice. His foes collapse. They flee. They cast desperately, and to no avail.

Svvetlana and Stebbins—the cat has been dismissed, for it will be of no help—stay well behind, watching, gathering experience and gold from the fallen enemies. The trio finally reaches the first boss of the cave. He is a powerful druid, imbued with the animalistic magic of all druids, his beast of choice: the viper. The paladin bellows, his hammer high, and charges the fiend.

In a flash, a viper approaches from each side.

"Watch out!" Svvetlana calls, alarmed at the sudden addition of these two beasts. As she calls out, the druid himself transforms as well, into a viper even greater and more powerful than any they've fought so far. His skin is a lurid blend of red and green, shimmering in the sickly blue light of the fume-lanterns that flank his worship circle at the top of the path. His neck swells and contracts in the threatening manner of the lowly cobra. On a creature a hundred times a cobra's size, this is far more intimidating.

The priestess moves closer to the hunter and says at his ear, "Will he be okay?"

"Of course," Stebbins replies. He puts an arm around her shoulders and gives them a squeeze. "He's done this a hundred times."

Then he draws his bow and sets an arrow on the string. "Watch this."

"Careful," the priestess warns. "He asked us not to get involved."

"Don't worry," says the hunter. "I can't do enough damage to pull his aggro." And he lets the arrow fly. It strikes the boss in the center of his reptilian belly, but Stebbins was right. It's as if the druid didn't even notice. His attacks continue to fall upon the paladin's golden armor, and to no avail.

Svvetlana grins and calls down holy power from the makers. It channels through her body, filling her with lightness and joy, and then blasts from her outstretched fingertips. It collides with the giant viper, causing critical damage. Still, it is nothing compared to the damage done by the very earth the druid stands on, glowing under the paladin's runic power.

She closes her eyes and focuses now on the paladin himself. Though she has trained as a healer, the priestess has had little opportunity to practice this selfless art. Now, as the paladin fights valiantly against these three colubrine monsters, she takes the chance. She presses her palms together, clasps her fingers, and mutters an ancient prayer. Her chest swells, and when she opens her eyes again, they are lit from within, silver and gold. The light blasts from her every pore, from her eyes and mouth, from the ends of her silver hair, and it blasts across the rocky, wet ground, surges into the paladin's very being, and heals him of his minor wounds.

Suddenly the two secondary vipers pull up and find her

with their red beady eyes. They slither quickly on the slick ground, hissing and spitting. In an instant, they are upon her.

"What did you do?" Dewey shouts as he runs after them, but the boss—still with a few tricks of his own—paralyzes the paladin with a blast of venomous spit. He is unable to assist.

Stebbins is at the priestess's side, but with no pet to help him, he can do very little. The two vipers tear at Svvetlana's body. They dig fangs into her shoulders. They spit poison into her wounds. They tangle around her long, muscular legs with their slithery tails, and she drops to the ground.

"I'm coming," the paladin shouts as he falls upon the two secondary vipers, but he is too late. Svvetlana is weak and near death. One strike will undoubtedly—

"Ahh!" she cries, and she is dead.

"Crap," says Stebbins.

"Why don't people listen?" says the paladin. He casts a vicious area attack, killing the two vipers. Then he turns back to the boss. In seconds, the giant viper lies dead. He loots the body, finds nothing of value to anyone in the party, and then walks to Svvetlana's prone corpse.

"I should make you walk," he says.

"Don't be a jerk," Stebbins says. He is down on one knee beside the fallen elf girl. "It was my fault."

"Why?" says the paladin. "Did you cast a heal on the tank and aggro the adds? No. She did."

"I told her it was okay to join in," Stebbins says. He closes his eyes and bows his head, and he mutters a prayer to the elf goddess. "Protect her soul," he says, and the paladin laughs.

"Moron."

"Just resurrect her," Stebbins says, "so we can keep going."

"She has to promise not to cast anything else," says the paladin. He sits down next to the elf girl and pulls a bottle of wine from his sack. "We have a long way to go."

"She promises," the hunter says on the priestess's behalf.

"Let her say it."

"She's dead."

The paladin sighs. "Good thing she's so hot, or I'd kick her in a second." He stands, lowers his head, and begins to cast a spell of resurrection. The earth at his feet glows with his great power. But the spell never finishes. The cast simply continues.

"Hello?" Stebbins says. "Dewey, wtf?"

There is no response. The cast simply goes on, never finishing, for several tedious minutes, until the paladin himself vanishes.

"He's gone," the hunter says. "Look, you'll have to resurrect yourself at the graveyard, Svvet. I'll meet you there."

Somehow, the soul of the fallen elf—perhaps because of the hunter's words of prayer—can understand these instructions. An instant later, Svvetlana wakes. She is lying in the grass, surrounded by tall stones. Each, she realizes, represents the burial site of a fallen elf, and each glows with a tiny light—the evidence of an elven soul within.

She is groggy and dizzy. She sits up and shakes her head, hoping to clear it. This just makes her dizzier, and she has to lean over to throw up. With the help of the nearest stone, she climbs to her feet.

It is dark here, and wet. This is not the desert they'd traveled through to find the cave entrance. They must have traveled very far underground if this is the nearest graveyard.

"I hope Stebbins can find me," she says, "for I've no idea where I am." But she begins to walk, glancing now and then at the very incomplete map of this region she keeps in her pack. She's never been here before, so the only location on the map she's familiar with is the graveyard itself. Then it begins to rain.

It's as if the sea itself has flipped upside down above the earth, and it falls down upon her in heavy sheets. She is soaked through her enchanted gowns to her very skin. Her meager sandals and the sliver of silver she wears as a crown, though powerful in granting her intellect and spirit, offer little protection against the elements. She runs from tree to tree, desperate for cover, not bothering to check her map or even look up to search the horizon for a familiar landmark.

She huddles against a tree, an ancient ally of her people, and peers out into the weather, hoping for any sign of her friend the hunter. When a figure appears in the mist, running across the grassy plain, her heart soars and she stands up and waves.

"I'm here!" she calls out. "Stebbins, I'm here!"

He doesn't see her. Desperate for aid, she casts a simple healing spell on herself, knowing it will make her figure glow brightly, helping her to stand out in the grim weather. It works. The figure stops, and a moment later, it's running toward her.

Smiling, Svvetlana steps out from the shelter of the tree. She walks out to meet Stebbins halfway, but soon stops. His gait is wrong. He doesn't run with the strength and poise of an elf hunter. And shouldn't he have summoned his pet, out on his own as he is now?

No, this isn't Stebbins. This isn't any elf, nor any human, and it's certainly not a dwarf.

"Undead," she says aloud in a sacred whisper. The forsaken clan of the opposing faction.

And just as the fear sinks into her chest and she casts a protective spell upon herself, the figure vanishes, for this is no hunter, either: it is a rogue, it's seen her, and now it's prowling nearby. She is vulnerable. She is alone. She is afraid.

Her spell will protect her for only a few more seconds. Then the bubble of protective holy power will fade, and she will be helpless. She fixes her grip on her staff. She takes a deep breath to keep her soul and mind clear and ready to defend herself. It's not enough. When the sky flashes lightning, the rogue appears on her right. She turns, but he is faster—much faster—and his dagger sinks into her back. She tries to call out, but the world is black. She is still on her feet, but unable to move, unable to see, unable to cast even the simplest defensive spell.

His fist connects with her nose—she can feel that much—and she falls to her knees in muddying grass. "Please stop," she says, but the undead fiend laughs. He steps quickly and lightly around her prone form, kicking her, stabbing her, blinding her with powders and poisons.

"You're a long way from home, little elf girl," the rogue says in his unliving voice, gravelly but wet, thick with blood and phlegm and viscera. The undead are known to eat their victims after killing them, Svvetlana remembers.

Something growls. Is it the rogue? She cannot see to know. Do the undead growl as well as laugh when they kill? She rolls onto her stomach to try to push herself up, and lightning strikes again. A black figure, lower to the ground even than she, leaps over her, knocking the rogue to the wet earth. Svvetlana squints against the still-falling rain and cannot believe her eyes, still foggy from the rogue's blinding powder.

A striped cat has the rogue pinned on his back, and it strikes once, twice, three times with its claw, leaving long bloody marks on the face and chest of the forsaken rogue. Svvetlana sits up. This is no wild tiger and stroke of luck. This is Stebbins's cat. She searches the horizon and finds a tall figure fifty yards out. She watches as the figure raises its weapon and lets loose a flurry of arrows, attack after attack. Each strikes the rogue expertly, filling him not only with physical damage and pain, but with the poisons and soul-destroying curses in which hunters specialize.

The rogue climbs to his feet, somehow, and runs off, using his preternatural speed. When he is a few yards away, he vanishes completely, near death. He'll run a good distance off, Svvetlana knows, and bandage and heal. But with Stebbins and his pet with her now, she knows the rogue won't try another attack.

Stebbins runs to her, his heavily booted feet sending up splashes of new puddles as he comes.

"Thank you," Svvetlana says as she takes the hunter's hand and climbs to her feet. "I was dead for sure."

"I'm just glad I got here in time," Stebbins says. He is standing close to her—too close, perhaps, but Svvetlana doesn't back away.

"I owe you, I guess," the priestess says, and she drops her gaze. If she stares too long into his big, golden eyes, she knows what could happen.

"No," he says, and she can hear the smile in his voice. His cat pushes between them, rubs its face against Svvetlana's knees and thighs. Stebbins's hand is on her cheek now. "You don't owe me. You never owe me. I'd die a hundred deaths to save your life just one time, Svvet."

"Stop," she says, but her voice is quiet and shy. She knows he won't stop—and she even hopes he won't.

The hunter bends just a little, so their faces are closer still, and she gives in and looks up at him. He times the kiss just right, and their lips are together. She can taste the rain and his sweat and blood on their lips. His arms are around her. Hers hang limp at her sides.

"Svvet," Stebbins says.

"I have to go," says the priestess, cutting him off, and she turns and runs into the shadows of the wood. In a moment, she is gone.

CHAPTER 20

LESH TUNGSTEN
<GLOWERS IN THE ATTIC>

Svetlana skipped lunch yesterday, I guess. She was probably feeling all awkward about it, since Wednesday's lunch was a fiasco. I don't blame her. I wouldn't exactly be fired up about the possibility of another clash with Fry either.

That doesn't mean I didn't show up on Thursday morning and do my best to keep Svetlana's seat empty till she got there. A tiny part of me was relieved, I think, when she didn't come. Wednesday afternoon at the mall had been an epiphany— that's what she'd probably call it. I realized something, is the point, staring at Jelly and goofing off with the dirtbags I normally associate with: Svetlana is way, way better than me.

So I'm all kinds of shocked when, on Friday at lunch, I hear a little cough and look up to find a tray right at my eye level. It bears a bowl of brown rice under a heap of broccoli and sliced chicken and smelling of garlic and soy sauce. "You didn't save me a seat," she says, and she's not vegetarian.

I pull my headphones off and push my seat back a little. "Oh, well. You didn't show up yesterday," I say. "I didn't know . . ." I stop myself before I sound like a moron—right—and shove over a little from the corner, knocking my neighbor's plastic chair a bit. He shuffles too to make room.

"Thanks," Svetlana says, and she puts her tray next to mine and pulls a chair over from against the heater. She wields her chopsticks like it's the most natural thing in the world and, after a mouthful of rice, says, "I took lunch in the library yesterday. It's a thing I do, sometimes, to get some drawing done or to do some work."

The drawing—I'd almost forgotten. It's more evidence that she of talent and uniqueness and bright blond hair and eyes like deep wells of cool water, and I of dank attic bedroom strewn with metal magazines and mall trips of fast food and Jelly ogling and general misanthropy, are about the stupidest pair anyone could imagine. And that's to say nothing of the fact I could never see myself choosing the library, and productivity, over the cafeteria for lunchtime.

"Did you come up with anything?" I ask. "Any new drawings?"

She nods as she shovels more rice into her mouth. This is the first time I've seen her enjoy food. It's kind of startling. "Do you want to see?"

"Yes," I say, and she's already laying down her chopsticks, side by side, with their tips hanging over the edge of her tray. She leans to the tote bag beside her chair and pulls out a spiral

129

notebook and flips past drawing after drawing—a blur of black and blue and red ink—so I can hardly catch a glimpse of each beast, elf, dragon, and so many other things I couldn't possibly name, until she reaches the freshest ink close to the back of the book. She puts it on the table and turns it a little to give me a better look.

"*Voilà*," she says, and not like your aunt says it either, unless your aunt is a sophisticated French actress from the 1960s whose breath makes you feel faint—in a good way. I'm not so sure I care at all that she's better than me, as long as she keeps saying things in French.

But the picture. Today it's a cat—a huge cat, but lithe and low to the ground. She's given it swirling stripes and saber fangs, one immaculate and deadly, the other snapped and rough. "That's amazing," I say, tempted to run my fingers over the shining blue ink. I resist. I can only imagine her French-infused anger if my greasy fingers—fried chicken today, if you're wondering—smudged this masterpiece. "It's almost like it's moving."

"Really?" she says, completely pleased.

I nod. "Totally. I don't know how you do that."

She smiles as she turns the picture back toward herself, maybe to try to figure out for herself how she does that, and I have to admire the background—more of the icy landscape; they must be part of a series—from a funny angle. "Thanks," she says, quiet and modest, and she tucks her hair behind her ear.

We're quiet a minute as she puts away her notebook—"I'd

die if any garlic sauce splattered on it"—and I just listen to the hum of the cafeteria as it rises and falls and watch Svetlana maneuver her chopsticks between the bowl and her mouth. She isn't watching me; she's looking around, half interested.

"I can't imagine what's keeping that red-eyed troll," she says. "Fry?"

She nods and hums as she finishes chewing a larger-than-average floret. "It's weird to get through an entire lunch without him coming over here to bug us," she says, and it's like a switch flicks off. I'm hyperaware now of how vulgar it is to eat fried chicken with my hands, tearing the flesh from the bone with my teeth like a caveman. Every moment that ticks by, as though I can hear the whirring clock at the far end of the room, is a silent eternity in which I have nothing to say. It's as if without Fry—without his boorish approach—I have no idea how to act with or what to say to this girl.

My epiphany is right: she's better than me—better than us—and for the rest of lunch, though she tosses a couple comments at me, I can hardly think of a thing to say.

CHAPTER 21

SVETLANA ALLEGHENY
<STARVING ARTISTS>

Well, that was weird.

This time two days ago, I was sure I'd seen the last of—or anyway, chatted the last with—Lesh Tungsten. (I managed to find out his last name. Oddly, there are no other Leshes at Central, and I bet that's the only time anyone has pluralized "Lesh.") Two days of Fry would have likely driven away better friends than he. Yet there he was, right in his spot, just where I'd left him. He hadn't given up on me; why had I given up on him?

For that matter, why did I take Thursday off from the cafeteria? Was it anxiety at the possibility of discovering that Lesh would, upon seeing me exit the food line, recoil and quickly invite every random passerby to fill the plastic chairs within fifty yards of his person because that's what it might take to keep me away from him?

Not to put too fine a point on it: yes.

Still. A half hour in the library with a four-color ballpoint and my notebooks was good for my soul. I made some decisions about the campaign—how I might edit it quickly so that our Gaming Club, such as it was, might still dive in, albeit with a smaller party.

I can't believe I mentioned Fry, I think as I shrug my shoulder to keep my heavy tote from sliding off it. Well, I didn't actually say his name. I called him a red-eyed troll. Lesh drew his own conclusions—and, of course, retreated into his black-brick wall. I can't blame him. He probably hardly talks at all. I should be prepared to take it upon myself to initiate conversation. How hard can it be?

I reach Dr. Serrano's room and find my seat. Class hasn't started quite yet, but Serrano is already busy getting some key points on the board: "iambic pentameter" and "a-b-a-b-c-d-c-d-e-f-e-f-g-g." *Spoiler alert, Dr. Serrano.* I dig into my tote bag, all ready to open to the next blank page in my poetry notebook and write "Shakespearean sonnets" at the top with the date, but my hand instead finds a different notebook—the one I showed Lesh at lunch today. I flip quickly to the newest drawing, of the prowling huntress, her stripes designed to hide her better in the swirling mist of the frigid mountains, and hunch over the notebook so no one else can see it. *Is it as good as he said? Maybe it is.*

My face warms again and my tummy twists, like they had in the cafeteria. I can picture his face—his eyes wide; they're so often half closed—and his elbows anxious, propping him up and forward on the table beside me, to get a closer look. I must have blushed. I blush too easily. I'm probably blushing right now.

So I close the notebook quickly and, as the bell rings to start the class, swap it for my poetry notebook, with its swirling ocean scene on the cover. I wonder what Lesh would think of that drawing, and I suddenly want to show him all my drawings—every one, for every encounter and every campaign. I want to give him a copy of my bestiary just to watch him flip the pages.

"'Shall I compare thee to a summer's day?'" Dr. Serrano says at the front of the room, both hands on the windowsill, staring out over I-94. "'Thou art more lovely and more temperate.'"

CHAPTER 22

SVETLANA ALLEGHENY
<FLOWERS IN THE ATTIC>

"Lana!"

I'm busy. It would help to say that out loud, you're probably thinking, instead of muttering somewhere between my brain and my teeth, which are clamped tight in concentration because getting just the right gossamer glimmer in the black center of this giant eye is pretty tricky. I'm doing it by hand, with the skirt on my lap, and with a needle and shining thread, and I can't be bothered right now by—

"Lana!" It's Dad this time. First he sends Mom. Then he takes a crack. Next Henny will pitter-patter her way up here. But I'm not budging, I'm not peeping, I'm not answering—I'm not reacting at all to this beckon until the stitches I'm working on are done.

I can hear her little feet now, and you probably think I'm being unrealistically cold about this. They're my family—two of them produced me from the fire in their loins. One of them carried me for thirty-nine weeks and was forcibly sliced open so I could stick my gawky neck out into the world and breathe its foul and pestilent congregation of vapors.

And beautiful little Henny, whose mind has achieved more by age eight than I have in twice that plus.

But you're wrong. Because it's Saturday, and it's not even ten, and the activity wheel at the bottom of my steps states quite clearly that on Saturday, from nine thirty till lunch, I do not wish to be disturbed. Because I am embroidering.

"Lana." It's Henny, and her stocking feet are in my room now, probably standing in the middle of my sun rug, right in the center, because that's where she likes to stand. It's bright yellow there, nearly orange, and then it glides gently into yellow, and canary, and pale, and white, and sky, and then deeper and dark blues. It's handmade.

Not by me, mind you, though I think I'll copy it someday.

Henny likes to scrunch her toes on the orange-yellow middle. She says it's the softest part, but that's crazy, since it's all the same material. If it is the softest, it's only because she's been scrunching her toes on it for three years.

"You don't have to answer," she goes on, still scrunching; I can see the wiggling out of the corner of my eye, "but some flowers came for you."

"Shark attack!" I say, because the needle has gotten my finger, and there's a tiny bit of blood, so I drop my skirt to the floor and vow to kill whatever idiot has sent me flowers, because I'm going to have to tear out all the glimmering silver

136

thread and start that bit over. Then, an instant later, I'm out of my chair and halfway down the main stairs, because it occurs to me that these might be from Lesh.

Mom and Dad are flanking the half-moon side table just inside the entryway, at the bottom of the main stairs, and they're looking up with heavily smirked faces, their arms crossed, and I can't imagine what these amused glares can mean, except maybe *Is there something you're not telling us?* or *When do we get to meet this suitor?*

In the middle of the table, though, is what catches my interest, because it's a bouquet—it's lying there on its side, since there's no vase—and it's a perfect one. It's not twelve predictable roses. It's not a giant, flouncy show-offy bird-of-paradise or O'Keeffey iris. It's not a delicate and stunning orchid, daring you to get too close. This is a perfectly eclectic bunch of wildflowers. They're purple and orange and yellow and blue, with the tiniest, toughest little petals, and they're bound in a silver ribbon and a golden ribbon with little baby branches of pussy willow. I shove between my parents and grab them up, and then check the tiny cream-colored card hanging from the ribbons.

I think about you standing in the rain.

"Well?" says Mom. She's grinning at me, because if I'm honest, I don't get a lot of flowers. I've never gotten flowers.

"It doesn't say." And I tear the little card from the ribbon and hand it to her. She and Dad start theorizing, questioning, interrogating, and I'm not listening, because—trust me—I'm more confused than they are. "I'm going to bring these upstairs."

And I'm crossing the hall on the second floor, heading for my stairway, when my mom shouts after me, "I bet they're from Fry! Put them in water!"

They hit the bright orange sun in the center of my rug, and though they look pretty there, even perfect, I hate them, because she's probably right: these aren't the flowers a boy like Lesh would choose. These are the flowers a boy who's been at my heels for years would pick out.

A boy like Lesh would never pick out flowers at all. Maybe black ones made of iron.

"Yeah, I'd say you're right," says Roan on the phone. I'm never quite used to Roan on the phone. I can picture her, in her shared bedroom, shifting and fidgeting in the corner of her bed, maybe sitting on the couch in the sunken family room in her tiny Cape Cod, with her foot tucked up and under her. "I'd say those are from Fry."

I sigh. "I don't want him to send me flowers."

"I know," she says. "You told him so. I mean, you made it pretty clear."

I nod, though she can't see me, but she knows I nodded.

"Hey," she says, forcing some brightness into her voice. "Maybe they're from Abraham."

"Shut up," I say, and she laughs—louder and wilder a laugh has she than her little form would suggest. It is all the colors of fall. It is big orange maple leaves skittering along the sidewalk in front of a sudden strong wind. It suits her.

"He still likes you, you know," she says, and the brightness, though still in her voice, is just the tiniest trace now, a thin little membrane on a topic that doesn't want it.

"Maybe," I say, a mini admittance. I should have mentioned it earlier: Abraham and I have a certain failed history. He's quite tall (Lesh's height, I expect), and since high school began, four thousand years ago, I've spent more time with him (and Reggie and Cole and Roan) than anyone else, so it was bound to happen. Reggie is gay, after all, and very short, and didn't take me to the winter carnival freshman year. Abraham did.

He didn't bring me flowers, if you're wondering, but he did pass on dancing, and he did leave me to sit with Cole and Reggie while he went to play a ripping game of Magic: The Gathering with his brother and his brother's then-senior friends. They've gone on to college now, naturally, and I'd guess very good ones. They're probably studying engineering or math or prehistoric warrior cultures.

Don't get the impression I minded this. I didn't want to date Abraham. I never thought he wanted to date me. That night, I was happier sitting with Cole and Reggie than I would have been dragging Abraham onto the dance floor, or trying to figure out how to best look coupley with the boy anyone in our widest social circle would have expected me to be coupley with. But they'd be wrong. We're a terrible match, outside of tabletop gaming and heights relative to average.

"He does," Roan insists. Her voice shifts as she speaks, as she probably shifts on the couch or deeper into the corner of her bed. Maybe her sister came into the room. Roan's sister, Flannery, is ten, but she and Henny never hit it off as friends. They've also got the twin boys, now twenty, and still living at home and sharing a room.

The Garnets are not the type to say good-bye. Case in point: Roan, my own little barnacle. You should be so lucky.

"You know Abey," Roan goes on, using our cutesy, secret version of his name—the one he won't let us say because he finds it emasculating. "He's far too tough to let on. It would be just like him to make a gesture and not sign his name to it."

"I don't know," I say. "Wildflowers? Besides: 'I think about you standing in the rain.' What does that mean?"

"Hmm," Roan says.

I don't have to think about it: one boy likes me. One boy has recently been sent away, and one boy has spent time with me in the rain, probably thinking there was mutual flirting going on. Fry.

I can't talk about this anymore, because I'm wondering if this will mean another confrontation with the little trumpeter, so I ask Roan to tell me what's happening at the Garnet house, and even when you talk as fast as Roan, this will take awhile. I'll let my mind wander, daydream about Roan's little crowded house on the north edge of the city, filled with curly hair, laughter, and love.

CHAPTER 23

LESH TUNGSTEN
<ACCESSORY TO GANK>

My orc is a proud new member of Greg's guild, and on Saturday night, I'm making an appearance and squinting at the green text scrolling at light speed up the little chat window in the corner of my display. Trying to follow guild chat is like trying to read the writing on a spinning fan blade, with the fan set to medium, and with no grate in front of it so sometimes the fan clips your nose. I catch little more than the occasional word, because much of it is in acronym—acronyms that so far have no meaning—and the rest of it is emoticons, misspelled insults, and censored curses.

"You can turn the censor thing off," says Greg at my ear. I'd forgotten he was on the phone. I'm still grounded, but what's his excuse for being online tonight?

"How?" I ask, but quickly add, "Never mind. I don't care. I have no idea what anyone is talking about."

I'm leaning too close to my monitor, which is likely never

a problem for Greg. His display is probably twice as big as mine. The guild chat might even have its own little monitor, next to the main one. He has three, and hell if I've ever cared what the extra two did before. I just always figured they were for a triple-overhead porn experience. Or maybe that's just what I decided I'd use them for.

I'm digressing.

I lean back from the monitor, deciding to ignore guild chat until I get past the basics of the game itself, but then Greg is laughing.

"What?"

"Nothing," he says. "Just ganked an elf twice. I'm camping the corpse."

"I don't know the words that are coming out of your mouth," I say, and he invites me to group. "Where are you?"

"Check your map," he says, so I do, and there's his insufferable yellow dot, halfway across the world. I hop a giant bird thing, then head downstairs for a can of pop while my toon makes the trek without me. Mom's in the kitchen.

"Working on your homework up there, I hope?" she says.

"Yup," I say. Clearly this is a lie. But as I've been grounded a solid week, I think I'm entitled to some rebellion where I can get it.

She smirks at me as the fridge closes with its *thwack*. I've got a can of Mountain Dew in each pocket of my jeans.

"I heard you on the phone," she says.

"Just with Greg."

Her smirk goes smirkier.

"What?" I say, stopping in the kitchen doorway, and kind of enjoying the growing cold in my pockets. "Does grounding include the phone? Because if so, you need to say that in the rules to begin with."

"Just make sure you get your homework done," she says. "Show your dad that your work isn't suffering. Show your dad that your grades will be good this year." She takes a step toward me—it's enough to cover the entire kitchen—and puts a hand on my arm. "Show us both that you're doing your work, and we can probably convince him to end this punishment sooner."

"Okay, okay," I say, heading for the stairs.

"And two cans of pop, Lesh?" she calls after me. "Really?"

My ugly orc has landed now, and Greg's toon—an undead rogue (they can turn invisible, as we know; this strikes me as unfair)—is standing next to him, jumping up and down, spinning in circles, making fart sounds and slapping my avatar's face.

"Having fun?" I say after slipping my phone back between my ear and shoulder.

"Loads of fun," he says. "Where were you? Come kill this elf with me again."

"Where?" I say as he mounts his giant wolf thing. I don't have a giant wolf thing. I have to run everywhere on foot. I think this is why all the avatars are in such great shape in this game: constant marathoning will do that. Greg is as patient as he knows how to be in-game, and he rides his wolf around me in circles, sometimes darting off in front so I know where to go, until we reach the body of a dead elf.

She's beautiful, of course, and she's head-to-toe in drab

brown leather armor. She's probably a rogue or a hunter. It's hard to tell the difference when they're dead. I flick the mouse wheel to zoom in on her face. Her hair is cropped and dark blue, and across the bridge of her nose is a tattoo in the shape of two crossed daggers. A rogue, then.

"She's a higher level than you," says Greg at my ear. I realize he intends to wait for her to resurrect so he can kill her again. This must be camping. "You stand there in plain sight. I'll stay hidden."

"She'll kill me," I say. Hell, I'd kill me. You know it's a problem when you're rooting for your mortal enemy on the field of battle. I'm running the wrong avatar, but Greg doesn't know I'm leading this double in-game life, in more ways than one.

Still, I obey. I stand right next to the corpse. I watch Greg fade into the shadows and prowl around us. His toon is maxed—level fifty, the highest the game goes (for now; everyone knows they'll up the cap with the expansion, according to Greg)—so I figure this elf must be someplace in the middle: not as low as sad, ugly me, but not fully maxed. Otherwise, this wouldn't be so easy for Greg.

"What am I waiting for?" I say, and as if on cue, the beautiful corpse begins to fade, and then vanishes. The elf has been resurrected, and she's standing behind me.

The last place you want a rogue, by the way, is behind you.

I turn, but I'm far too slow—fat orcs being directed by unskilled noobs are bound to be slow—and she draws two blades, wraps them around my throat, and gives me a wicked slice. I can't move, and my health has dropped to less than twenty percent.

"Help!" I shout into the phone. Greg is, predictably, laughing, but as he does, I watch the screen and he appears behind her. His misshapen, undead form is as hunched at the shoulders and middle back as Greg is at his console, but despite the awkward gait and poor posture, he makes quick work of our stunning enemy. She falls at my feet with a shriek of pain and then a sigh of relief in the face of eternity . . . until she rezzes again.

All Greg has to say is, "Nice. How long do you think we can keep this up?"

I switch phone shoulders. "Is there any reason to do this?"

"You can get some honor points," he says, "but you'll have to attack her next time. You can't just stand there."

"She's, like, thirty levels higher than me," I say.

"Doesn't matter," he explains. "I'll do the killing. You'll just get the honor points."

This reminds me at once of my hunter and paladin friends, back in Svvetlana's world. Somehow, though, their help—taking her through dungeons, from quest to quest, helping her get better gear, helping her find and defeat the toughest monsters and the wickedest bad guys—felt good. It felt righteous and honorable and giving, despite the paladin's lewd comments and despite the hunter's near obsession with Svvetlana's pixelated backside.

In fact, I quite like Svvetlana's pixelated backside too.

But this—this was just torture. It was senseless, sadistic, antisocial behavior.

"This is lame," I finally say after the next cold-blooded murder. I wonder why this girl doesn't just log off, come back later. Go have a snack, take a walk, whatever. Certainly this murderous d-bag I call Greg Deel wouldn't stand here for that long, waiting for the resurrected elf to present herself for murder again.

Maybe she was enjoying it too.

"Don't be a homo, Tung," Greg says. "We're not actually murdering a girl repeatedly. We're messing with some faggoty noob who has no idea how to play his class. Any rogue should be able to rez, vanish, sprint the hell out of here without my killing him again."

"Her."

"Him," he says. "This is not a girl. I promise. There are no girls on the internet."

He's righter than he knows, I think. Just the same, if Svvetlana is a girl—and she is—then I don't see why this rogue elf can't be a girl too, even if the human fleshy thing controlling her isn't quite a hundred percent female.

"Well, whatever," I say, putting on the most exasperated voice I can muster. "I gotta go. My mom's on my ass about homework, and I've hardly done any all week."

"Peace," he says. And he's gone from the phone, and I'm gone from his world. But an instant later, I'm back in fantasyland, though this time the scene is green and lush, and my toon is breathtaking, and there's no green guild chat scrolling at breakneck speed up the little window in the bottom left corner of my screen.

There is, though, pink chat: whispers—private communiqués sent specifically to me, and by "me" I mean "Svvetlana."

In spite of myself, in spite of the equipment in my pants, I smile. They're happy to see me.

CHAPTER 24

SVVETLANA
<GOOD PEOPLE>

She wakes up at the inn. The fire is dying now, as is the light outside. But she feels rested, and she finds her robe on the floor beside the bed. She slips it on, then her sandals and slim metal crown. Her mace and talisman lean against the bare wood wall, near the door.

She stretches and collects them, runs a hand over the wood. "Hello, old tree," she says in her voice like a stream. The wood seems to hum in response—a slow, forever type of hum.

"Svvet!" It's a whisper, but a shout. The hunter Stebbins greets the refreshed priestess.

"Hi!" she says, and she is mindful of the brightness of her reply, and she wonders if it is bright enough, or too bright.

An instant later, the two have grouped, and they find each other in the wild. They are both level nineteen now, and both well geared with the spoils of many adventures in dungeons and the deepest, darkest caverns—holes of evil in the earth.

"Dewey and I are thinking about starting a guild," Stebbins says. The two elves run south together, into a new region. To Svvetlana, it is an entirely foreign, dark place, where at any moment the opposite faction might attack.

"I don't like this," she says as a cold breeze moves in from the shore and brushes the back of her neck.

The hunter moves closer. He'd like to put an arm around her thinly clothed shoulders, she thinks.

"Don't worry," he says. "Just keep moving. Soon we'll train in riding, too, and then we'll have mounts."

"Okay," Svvetlana says, but she can't shake the feeling—she imagines an undead rogue is riding on wolf-back beside them right now, watching them, laughing to himself, juggling his enchanted daggers, ready to kill them both in one fell swoop. He'll have the hunter bloody and dead in an instant, and his cat with him, and then he'll kneel on Svvetlana's chest, with his dirty blade against her long, white throat, and he'll say, "Lol. Fag."

"Let's get inside," she says, hurrying toward an elven building just off the path and stepping inside the wood-framed doorway. But Stebbins is in his own world, sending his pet in and out of the woods after small game. The hunter is kneeling over a fresh wolf corpse, carefully cutting away its hide, when from deeper in the woods flies a bolt of arcane fury. The hunter, with his skinning knife still in his hand, falls to the ground, quivering. His pet takes the second blast and collapses beside him, too dazed to join this fight and save his master.

"You got him!" comes a voice from the forest, and two orcs step into the clearing. They are both dark shamans, full of the elemental powers of earth and wind and fire. As the hunter comes to and climbs to his hands and knees, they both strike him again, knocking him back to the ground as they laugh in the guttural and half-witted way of their race. They'll kill him.

Svvetlana takes a deep breath. She's never faced these ugly, foul-smelling beasts from across the world before. They fight for the sake of fighting, and they thrive on the rush of blood and bone crashing against itself. They are more powerful than she and more willing and wanton in their violence. But if she does nothing, Stebbins will die.

The priestess closes her eyes and breathes in the dewy forest air. She encases herself in holy protection that, though temporary, will protect her completely, and then steps out of the elven building, her hands clasped before her chest. She focuses the light from within on the hunter and blasts holy power down from up on high. It cascades over him in a shimmering shower of light, like the stars themselves have rained down from the heavens for the sake of her friend. That is her power. That is her gift.

The hunter leaps to his feet, fully healed and protected by a holy force field of his own. Svvetlana quickly heals and protects the cat, too, and soon they're both on their feet, fighting the two orc shamans—and winning. When one shaman falls dead, his death-wail as vulgar as his laugh, the other runs off.

Honor must not mean much to that despicable race, Svvetlana thinks as she hurries to the hunter's side. "You're all right?"

He nods. "They came out of nowhere," he says, running his hand over his pet's back, checking for wounds as he scans the tree line in case the orcs return in greater numbers. "We better get inside."

Svvetlana, though, drops to one knee, grinning madly, still heady. "Did you see that, kitty?" she coos at the tiger, and it presses its forehead against her chin. "I was amazing, wasn't I?"

"Absolutely," Stebbins says, taking her elbow and pulling her to her feet. "But it'll take more than amazing if they come back with friends. Inside, right?"

The two elves and the cat hurry into the elven building and find a bench and some water. "I suppose we'd better get used to it," Stebbins says. "The player-versus-player aspect is about to get kicked into high gear. This entire zone is contested."

Svvetlana sits cross-legged on the bench, her back against the wall, and accepts the hunter's cat as it rubs against her knees. She stares at her wide-open palms-up hands, which glow and crackle, her holy spells still lingering on the skin. "We did all right," she says, barely there.

"I guess," Stebbins says. "I'm still jumpy. I don't like being ganked." He pulls some meat from his pouch and tosses it to the cat. "We'll be high level pretty soon, though. Then we'll gank them."

The priestess rolls her eyes. "Ganking," she groans. "It's not very noble." Outside, a battle is raging. Orcs and the bull-people of the opposite faction are attacking this elven strong-hold, launching flaming bolts from huge crossbows. "War. What is it good for?"

Svvetlana knows that the woman in charge here—she stands boldly on the balcony nearby, clad in heavy purple-and-green armor; she is the very model of elf pride and power—would like them to help. She will no doubt assign them their first quest in this dangerous new region. But Svvetlana is slow to approach her, to commit to this war fully. Her power to heal and to protect seem at odds with the battle raging across their world—yet it would be so valu-able to her people.

"So will you sign our guild charter?" Stebbins says. He'd been speaking, Svvetlana realizes, for several minutes. Her mind had wandered. She thinks maybe it tends to do that.

"Do I become a member of the new guild?" she asks.

"Of course!" says the hunter as he stands. "That's the whole point."

"Just me, you, and Dewey?"

"Well, for now," says Stebbins. "We'll get more people, don't worry." He walks to the warrior woman nearby and speaks to her. She's no doubt giving him instructions, telling him which orcs need killing, or what items need gather-ing. Stebbins will share these instructions with Svvetlana in a moment.

For now, she still rests, still leans against the living and breathing wood of the wall, and she lets herself smile, and she whispers to the cat next to her, licking its bloody paws, "We'll get good people."

LEVEL THIRTY

CHAPTER 25

SVVETLANA
<ONE KNIGHT STAND>

It's cool in the foothills outside the dwarven capital. It always is. In her thin robes, Svvetlana shivers and takes a long pull from her skin of spiced wine.

"Drunk yet, Svvet?" asks Stebbins, settling next to her on the dry grass. Any farther up the hill, and they'd both be sitting in snow.

She shakes her head, the skin still at her mouth.

"Lol, she'zh just getting shtarted," says Dewey. He's seated on his ram mount, fully clothed in Bavarian drinking garb. With his bold red beard and gleaming bald head, he is the quintessential dwarf at festival time.

The priestess pulls away the skin, and the deep, deep red wine drips from her lips, making them redder and darker. She pouts at Stebbins the hunter, and his jaw falls open.

The paladin laughs as he climbs down from his mount. He's had quite a few tankards of ale, and when he hits the ground, he stumbles his way into a traditional dwarven dance. It's not the most graceful rendition, though, and Svvetlana—fuzzy inside with spices and wine—giggles.

"Laugh now," says the dancing dwarf, "but shoon you'll be danshing too, I'd bet. Then we get to watch your—"

"Shut it, Dewey," says Stebbins. A gallant interruption, and the priestess beside him laughs and knocks his shoulder with hers, then swoons and lies back on the cold, dry grass.

"Whoa," she says, pressing her palm against her forehead. Her silver filament headdress slides back and off her head. "I don't feel so good."

"Lol," says Dewey, sitting on her other side. "How many of those did you drink?"

Stebbins stands and regards the sun. It's late. Even Svvetlana knows this, but the spinning in her head and the sloshing wine in her gut make it hard to care.

"We should get her to the inn," Stebbins says. "Help me get her up."

The dwarf stands as well, unsteadily at first. "Lol."

Each man takes an arm, and they manage to get her on her feet. Once she's standing, though, Dewey can't offer much help; he's half her height.

"How about thish?" he says, and he puts both his stout muscular hands on the elf woman's backside.

Svvetlana stiffens, and for an instant her head clears. She pulls her right arm free of the hunter's grasp, spins on the dwarf, and slaps him across the face.

As drunk as he is, he falls on his armored bottom. "Lol."

"Honestly, Dewey," the hunter admonishes, and the exertion has been too great for the priestess. She collapses again, this time a few feet up the slope toward the city, face-first in three inches of snow.

"I'll just rest here," she says. Her voice is muffled by the earth and snow, and in seconds, she is asleep.

There are moments of clarity. Svvetlana can't be sure how long it is between these spells, though, and remembers only being lifted from the ground, placed on her belly on Dewey's ram, quite a lot of bouncing, and quite a lot of laughter from her dwarven host. Stebbins must be with them, she knows, because he'd never leave the priestess so helpless with the paladin. Though it is an honorable class, this paladin cares naught for that trait.

These thoughts only fritter in her mind, foggy as it is, for the briefest moments, punctuating blackness and dreams, and always full of the smell of wet ram fur. When she comes fully to, she is lying with her knees pulled up, under a heavy wool blanket, and atop the white fur of a polar bear rug. She is quite warm, and soon aware of the fire in the hearth near her feet.

She squints against the new heat and dim lights. The sound of loud, jovial conversation and clinking tankards fills the air. It smells still of ram, but now the meat is roasting, not bouncing under her belly and breasts.

"She's waking up," someone says. It's not Dewey, and it's not

Stebbins, and the priestess is certain they've left her here to thaw and sober, among the practically heathen dwarfs who live and drink in the capital city. It's not a safe place for a beautiful elf priestess on her own, especially one who is only level thirty, and lacks the skills to defend herself.

A boot presses against her shoulder. It's gritty and cold, and she's sure it's left mud on her gown.

"Oi," says a voice close to her ear. "Get up, lass."

Her vision is blurry, but she can just make out the gruff, dark-bearded face of an iron dwarf. He's standing over her, a tankard in one hand and a leg of roast strider in the other. His friends recline—their chairs back on two legs, or their drunk forms slumped forward—at the table behind him. One chair, an empty one, is pushed back—his chair—as he's gotten up to harass her.

"Stebbins?" she says, but it comes out like a cough. Her head spins at the ragged sound of her own voice. Pain fires across her forehead, circles her crown like a bolt of lightning, striking hard against her temples.

The dwarf is squatting beside her now, leaning in close. The food and drink are gone; in one hand, he now holds a dagger by the blade, and he uses its hilt to push up the skirt of her dress, exposing her ankle, her calf, her knee, her thigh. She has almost no strength, but she bats at his hand and knocks the dagger to the floor. The dwarves—even the lecherous one beside her—laugh.

"What are you doing here, lass?" he says, and his breath is so strong with ale that Svvetlana's thoughts swim again, back to the festival outside. Did Stebbins bring her here? Did Dewey?

"Leave me alone," she says. "I'm very ill."

More laughter, and the dwarf's rough, thick hand is on her leg, squeezing it, playing with the fabric of her dress.

"Sap her," someone calls from the table. The place is filthy with laughter now, and the smell of alcohol is overwhelming. Svvetlana rolls onto her side and pushes herself into a sitting position, but it only makes her head scream in pain. She covers her eyes with both hands.

"You know what you need, lass?" says the dwarf beside her, and now his voice is right there, right at her ear. She can feel the heat of his breath on her skin, and it makes her shiver. "You need the hair of the dog that bit ya."

As the bar goes eerily silent, a flood of ale pours down from above her, running down her face and her dress and into her mouth and eyes. She gasps and coughs as tankard after tankard is emptied on top of her. The laughter in the room is deafening, and not far off a chorus of dwarven men bursts into song. She doesn't speak the language, and is glad of it, for the words are undoubtedly as sickening as the bath she's been given in ale and rum and the backwash of these disgusting cretins.

She gets to her feet and summons the energy to cast one spell—a protection spell, enveloping herself in a bubble of holy energy. The dwarves stand around her in a half circle, laughing and slapping their knees. "She looks like a wet rat!"

"A wet rabbit, you mean," says another, holding his fingers at the sides of his head like rabbit ears.

"Aye," says a third, barely able to speak through his laughter, "but a wet rabbit with tremendous tits!"

The place explodes with laughter, but it all cuts off when a great roar bellows from the entrance to the inn. The dwarves startle and turn, cowering. An arrow thwaps into the room and strikes their table.

"Ach!" says one, the drunkest one—the one who'd put his hands on her. "Yer boyfriend here to rescue you!"

The dwarves sulk and sit, pick up their empty mugs and thump the table, or else head to the bar for a refill.

The hunter—twice the height of every other man in the place, and accompanied by his great striped cat—steps toward Svvetlana. "I'm sorry," he says.

She looks up at him, her silver eyes shining, his golden eyes dull and faraway.

"I left you," he says. "I didn't mean to. I didn't mean to leave you here with these . . . these . . ."

"Jerks?" she offers.

"Worse," he says.

She nods. "A lot worse, actually."

"Come on," he says, and he wraps an arm and his cloak around her soaking-wet shoulders. "Let's find someplace a little safer and quieter."

"And free of dwarves?"

"Definitely," he says, and they both smile as they move

through the crowded streets of the dwarf capital. An inn near the fountain is friendlier to their kind, and they pause at the doorway. Svvetlana lets the hunter hold her by the shoulders. She lets him kiss her lips and her forehead as she looks down at the shimmer of magic in her slippers. Where was that magic a moment ago, when she quivered on the sticky inn floor, waiting to be rescued? Wasn't it there the whole time? "I have to go."

"Right now?" says Stebbins. His cat pushes between them, rubbing hard against her knees and thighs.

She nods and turns away, skips down the inn's front steps. "I'm sorry," she says. "I really have to go. But thanks. I mean, for rescuing me from that whole thing."

"Sure," says the hunter as he runs a hand across his cat's head and under its chin. "Bye."

And the priestess, just before she reaches the edge of the fountain, vanishes.

CHAPTER 26

SVETLANA ALLEGHENY
<BASEMENT KIDS>

The club is dead. I'm flipping through my summer's work and sitting at my sewing desk. My phone's speaker is on, and I'm listening to Roan. Well, I'm listening to her sister, Flannery, actually, I think. This happens a lot when I talk to Roan on the phone. The activity in the Garnet house takes over the line, her phone gets inevitably set down someplace, also with its speaker on, and I just listen to the bustling life of that giant clan of red-haired bons vivants. I really sort of love it. It's almost like being there.

"Lana!" says a voice, much louder, so someone's picked up the phone, but it sounds like . . .

"Reggie?" I say, lowering the papers onto my lap. "What are you doing over there?"

"Roan wasn't answering her phone, and I was desperate to get out of my house anyway," he says, which means he's still trying to take up smoking. He thinks it's hilarious and charming, but really it's revolting. I think he secretly likes it when I tell him so too, or when we're walking out of doors and he takes out a cigarette, so I ask for one too, and then he gives me one and I break it in half and ask for another. "Oops," I usually say. But he keeps giving them to me. He'll come around.

"So what's up?" I say, staring down at the open page of the campaign. It's a castle, or a palace, with dozens of tall, skinny spires that reach up into the top of the page. The tallest one, off center, is more slender than seems possible, like it's made of glass and spiderwebs.

"You need to run a game," he says. "Right now."

"The new campaign? Now?" I say. "Reggie, it's almost nine. My phone says so."

"Lana!" he says. He must have had a couple energy drinks on the way to Roan's too, because his voice is extra excited, like Reggie-plus. "We're seniors."

"Roan's not," I point out. Roan's our baby.

"Which is why I am here, and why you will be here soon, and why Abraham is already on his way: so Roan can stay in and still have an excellent Sunday night with her dearest and closest buds."

"This is okay with Roy and Ginger?" Those are Roan's parents, but Reggie's gone, and the phone's back on a table someplace—I'm beginning to think the kitchen counter, because I just heard Roy call out something about his missing Neapolitan ice cream, which—I suspect—one of the twins finished. I tap "end call," slip the phone into my tote with the stacks of campaign papers, and scurry down the steps and the hall. Mom and Dad's bedroom is open, and the light from the TV flickers through.

"Knock, knock," I say, poking my head in. "Um, I'm going to Roan's house for a couple hours."

Mom sits up and Dad sighs like I just asked him to pay for college this instant.

"It's Sunday night, Lana," Mom says. "And it's . . . nine. It's after nine."

"It's eight fifty-three," I point out, and she points at her clock, which shows 9:03. "Your clock is fast." Because it is.

"It's the clock with my alarm on it," she says, "and my alarm wakes me up, which means for me it's nine-oh-three, which is after nine."

"That has nothing to do with me," I explain.

"Ah, but we"—she thumbs at herself and Dad in rapid succession—"wake you up. So it has everything to do with you."

By now I'm actually in the room, which I'd hoped to avoid, and I sit on the edge of the bed. "Yeah, about that," I start, "you can stop waking me up anytime now. I have a clock too."

"When you start getting up on your own and showing up at the breakfast table for breakfast on your own," says Dad, "we'll stop waking you up."

"Fine, fine, fine," I say, closing my eyes to reset my brain, because this conversation has taken a severely wrong turn. "Listen. It's not late. I'll be awake up there past midnight anyway, sewing or drawing or chatting with Roan, because I always am." And I have to start talking louder now, because they won't shut up long enough for me to finish a sentence, putting in their little grievances like, "Why are you staying up so late?" and "If you can't maturely handle a room away from your parents, maybe we need to move you down to the second floor with us and Henny." I've heard it all before, and it's ridiculous, not to mention irrelevant to this conversation.

"The Gaming Club is finished because of Cole's departure, and I want to see my friends, and everyone is over at Roan's *right now* waiting for me," I say, talking fast and loud so I can finish my argument before they find more items to nitpick. I stand up. They cross arms, look at me—glare at me. Mom's mouth is so twisted I'm afraid she might spit venom the length of the bed and blind me in one eye.

"So?"

Nothing.

"I'm a *senior*," I try. "Honestly. I'll be getting, like, ten college acceptance letters any day now."

"So you think you can goof off?" Dad says, so . . . wrong tactic.

"I'm asking for your trust," I say, and Mom's twisted mouth settles down a little. We're onto something. "I'm seventeen. I've shown myself to be a good student"—moving on quickly before the issue of math comes up—"and a responsible person. I promise I will get ample rest for school tomorrow and be up on time. But this is very important to me. Please."

Another sigh from Dad, but this one is less "college tuition" and more "twenty bucks for gas."

They exchange a glance. They do that a lot. I think it means they have a good marriage, honestly, because they can say more to each other with just an exchanged glance—and whatever level of telepathy you happen to believe in—than most people I know can say with their mouths open and yammering.

"You can go," says Mom. "But you will be home at a reasonable hour, and you will not drink—"

"Mom."

"—or smoke! And you will be up on time tomorrow morning. And if I see you yawn even one time at breakfast, we are never trying this again. Is that clear?"

"Crystal," I say. I run to her side of the bed and give her a one-armed hug, and then blow Dad a kiss across the bed. "Enjoy *Everybody Loves Raymond*." And I'm out the door.

We haven't talked about my car. There's a very good reason for this, and I'm not proud of it, because I realize this is exactly the kind of problem that people like me—which is to say young white people of generally privileged upbringing—are typically accosted for complaining about. But I hate it. I hate my car.

The reasons are threefold, and I'm going to make a list while I walk downstairs and out the back door and across the backyard and into our garage, because it's easier than continuing to worry about whether Lesh is going to speak to me again after the weirdness at lunch on Friday.

1. It's huge. It's easily fifty feet long, and it's brown. It's got about eighteen corners somehow, and here I figured cars were supposed to be all smooth and sexy and aerodynamic. Not this car, which means this car is woefully inefficient. For such a huge car, you'd think a huge tank might mean lots of miles between trips to the gas station. Alas, it takes several gallons of fuel just to pull out of the garage. For this reason, and for reasons of my own personal well-being—spiritual, physical, and psychological—I nearly always ride my bike instead of take the car.

2. It's ugly. I covered some of this in 1, but here's more. It's still brown. On its rear are bumper stickers' sticky, stained, rectangular remnants, as the last owner (dear old Dad) was kind enough to remove the top layer of each sticker before bestowing the thing upon me. Its interior is tan, which is of course a type of brown, and in many places torn, knifed, burned, chewed, et cetera. Some of these cuts have been properly mended with tan duct tape. Did you know they make tan duct tape? Now you do. Since I inherited the behemoth on wheels, exactly four people have been in this car aside from me, and I'm going to see three of them in about ten minutes. The fourth, barring a surprise reconciliation of the romantic kind between himself and Reggie, I will probably never drive anywhere again. That is because I do not want to be seen in this car, and I do not want people about whom I care to be seen in this car either. This is not me being snobbish, by the way. I'll get to that in a minute. I simply appreciate things of a particular beauty, be they dragons,

palaces, embroidered skirts, exquisitely inked tattoos (I have none, but I can appreciate the creative art), electronic ballads from Iceland, or Romantic orchestral dream sequences. You'll notice "tan cars dying of rust and bigger than the *QE2*" was not on that list.

3. The car makes me feel like a snob. This makes very little sense, since if I just shut up, it won't be an issue. But my deep-seated loathing of this car sits in my brain like a walrus made of guilt. I know I should be happy that I have a car to use whenever I want, like late on a Sunday evening when I don't want to waste much of my precious and carefully argued time on traveling via bicycle. But the fact is, I'm not. If I must have a car—and the truth is, no one says I must—I'd prefer something very tiny and very quiet, or at least very good-looking. Hence, I feel like a snob.

But as it is, now I'm barreling up Lexington Avenue, across Summit and past the high school and across University Avenue, past where Lesh and I collided, over the train tracks and around the zoo, to Roan's house we go, and the monstrosity's engine is chugging and puffing like a steam locomotive, only louder. I forgot to mention the cassette player doesn't work, and I don't have any cassettes anyway besides Phil Collins's *Hits*, which has been in the glove compartment probably since my dad bought it the day it came out when I was four, when we lived in Como and my grandfather was still alive and owned the house in Crocus Hill.

"Finally," says Abraham when I reach the basement. "Where the fun have you been?"

I ignore him. It's easy, because I've just pushed through a gauntlet of Garnet hugs and grabs and a cheek kiss from Ginger and can now choose to acknowledge the smiling faces of Reggie and Roan. Reggie puts on his glasses and dumps his pouch of dice. Roan hops into her chair, tucks up her foot, and bounces.

"Yes," she says with the tiniest fist pump. "I can't believe we pulled this off. I never thought we'd all show up."

"Whose idea was it, anyway?" I say, and Roan thumbs at Reggie.

"What can I say?" says Reggie. "I need to see my people." Roan reaches over and gives him a one-armed shoulder squeeze, so I know he's been here awhile, probably crying over Cole. I am not in the breakup condolences loop. I make a mental note to reach out more, lest my already dwindling social circle dwindle even more, and then the lights pop and go black. Not just a bulb, mind you, but all the lights.

"What the truck?" says Abraham, and I really wish he'd cut it out, because I'm running out of words to use to replace the Queen Mum of swears here.

"Mom!" Roan shouts. Her chair legs vibrate on the indoor-outdoor, and in a minute her bare feet hit the steps and the door to the kitchen is open. A little flickering light gets in, and Abraham is looking at me. He quickly looks away, and turns in his chair and cranes his neck to watch Roan.

"What happened?" he asks.

I'm almost surprised he's surprised, but I guess he hasn't been to Roan's house as often as I have, or as often as Reggie has, because we both know.

"I'm sending Dad down!" Roan's mom calls back.

"It happens a lot," I tell Abraham. He keeps his eyes on the basement door.

The Garnets' house is a hundred years old, and the electrical system hasn't been updated since World War II or so. That means if someone's using the toaster, and someone is using a blow dryer, and then someone turns on the kitchen light: zap! A fuse blows. And since the box is older than your grandma, you can't just flip a switch. You have to remove a fuse and put in a new one. It's not complicated, but it is a pain in the butt. So Roy creaks down the steps, flashlight in hand. He's a tired man. He's always tired. His gray hair is extra bushy tonight and matted on one side. It was a big red bush when we were little. I hardly noticed it going gray, but there it is.

"Hello," he says, in this thick-voiced way he has, like he's always just eaten peanut butter. He goes right to the box, scans the fuses with his flashlight, and starts unscrewing one. "This old thing," he mutters for something to mutter, since we're all watching him, waiting for him to finish. "And there," he says, screwing in the new fuse, "we"—he's still screwing—"go!"

He turns and smiles at us, then calls up the steps, "Try it now!"

Two shoe thumps sound on the floor over our heads—a clear signal from Ginger that the lights and toaster and hair dryer are back on—and Roan hurries to the top of the steps and clicks on the basement lights.

"Thanks, Dad," she says, and she's back in her seat in a flash, before her dad even gets the box door closed.

"I swear," says Abraham.

Yes, you do.

"I don't know why I even bother with this," he finishes.

"What's that mean?" asks Reggie, because he feels like feeding the troll, I guess.

Abraham sighs. "Let's just start, okay?"

"Does everyone have character sheets?" I ask, and they say yes in their silent and variant ways: Roan's is a nod, but one of such speed that most of us would snap our necks. Reggie's is a quick succession of pats of his gaming folder, which for this campaign seems to be violently lime green. Abraham's is a nasty smirk and a wave of his stapled stats. They're the same characters they rolled at our unofficial meeting before school started—minus one party member.

And so we can begin, finally. I reach into my tote and produce the screen, and the maps, the monster manual of my own making, and a pair of big pedestal candles. "Now, I've had to make some last-minute adjustments," I say, "I mean, because Cole . . ." No one needs to finish that sentence. "Okay so, here, Reggie." I pull out a sealed envelope, which I antiqued by staining it with tea, burying it in the garden for a night, and then burning the edges just the tiniest bit, and hand it across the table to Reggie. "Don't open it yet."

Reggie's smile, full of sinister joy, makes my heart positively swell. "Roan, can you hit the lights?" I say.

"Hit the lights?" Abraham says. "We just got them working and now you want them off?"

He's getting on my nerves. I suspect he's getting on all our nerves, but Roan admirably ignores him and hurries to flick the switch just as I get the second candle lit. It's a big table—a folding buffet-type thing, over which Roan has laid a forest-green tablecloth—so their light is spread pretty thin, but the way it casts over each of our faces is perfect and séancelike. I unfold my screen and behind it set my notes and a portable iPod player. The playlist is already loaded, so I click play and begin their tale:

THUG, *you are a half-giant. Though your people have been enslaved in the wild jungle kingdoms to the far south, you escaped with your life—barely—and have been traveling alone for a month. You carry a broadsword and wear simple leather armor and boots. You were lucky to escape with that much. For the last two nights, you've noticed the road has been climbing steadily, and the temperature dropping quickly. Tonight, as the moon appears, you haven't eaten in two days and your leather armor isn't keeping you warm. When you spot the lights from a lamp and the glowing windows of an inn, you say a prayer of thanks and pick up your pace. A village isn't far.*

It's a small village, you discover before long, and the inn—the Sword and the Moth, according to the sign hanging over the door, written in the human tongue—is the first building you reach. From inside, you hear the voices and songs and laughter of cheer and strong drink, and you go in. All noises stop, and all heads turn to face you. Can the reputation of the half-giants have spread this far north, this far off the beaten path?

"He's a big one." It's a woman—maybe just a girl. She's at a table far from the door, near a fireplace along the north wall of the inn. And she's not alone. The table is crowded with men—dwarven men, elf men, and plenty of humans too. They're rough-looking and rowdy. And when she makes her crack about your size, they explode with laughter. The noise comes back, and the laughter and songs. You make your way to the bar and look for a drink.

MERIDEL, that girl—the one with the smart mouth and collection of male fans—is you, of course, and this time your lip might earn you a little trouble. As the half-giant passes your table, he sneers—growls, even. He's not much for words, but from his size and the girth of his arms—not to mention the sword strapped to his back—you know he's not someone even you want to mess with. You watch him at the bar a moment while your tablemates carry on, and then take a long drink from your mead, mainly for an excuse to head to the bar. You clank your empty onto the heavy table in front of you.

"Another, Meri?" says the dwarf at your right hand, and he's on his feet. He's an ugly one, poor thing, with a beard so thick and gnarly that it's nearly impossible to tell where it ends and the knot of hair on his head and the bush growing up out of the front of his shirt begin.

You grab his arm. "I'll get it myself," you say, to the protests of the other burly ruffians at the table. "I'll get it," you repeat, pulling your blade from its place, stuck in the table before you, "myself."

Hands go up, apologies are made, and the men sit if they were standing and stand up if they were sitting, like gentlemen getting up for a lady on her way to the powder room. You roll your eyes and slip your way along the sawdust-covered floor, between the sweaty, smelly bodies of warriors and rogues and hunters and thieves, and the perfume-and-powder stench of women hoping to sell their sordid wares. They sicken you—the fighters and the whores—but you don't mind, as you weave through them, help-ing yourself to a coin or two from their sacks, pockets, or bags. By the time you reach the bar, you've enough for a round.

"Another round for my table," you say, and you drop a pile of coins. The half-giant is next to you, and he grunts, so you say hi. "And one for the pituitary case."

He snarls.

"Kidding, kidding," you say, and quieting your voice and lean-ing toward him, you add, "What are you doing this far north, anyway?"

He looks at you sideways. The glance is easy to interpret: What do you know of my people?

You shrug. "I don't stay in one place for long," you say. "Whenever I've tried, they tend to want to arrest me, or beat me up, or cut off my head. It gets awkward. Suffice it to say, I've been everywhere, and you should be in shackles someplace, am I right?"

Despite your obvious charm and rough beauty, the half-giant isn't impressed with you, and since he now knows that you know he is an escaped slave, he grows defensive. In fact, you can feel his rage growing, and he balls his fists. When he turns, you're ready.

The two of you face off: Meridel wields a single dagger in her main hand, and has a length of strong leather wrapped around her off hand and wrist for blocking and punching. Thug hasn't drawn his sword, but his armor is stronger and his fists are weapons even bare. He is twice Meridel's height, but half as fast.

"Wait, whoa, whoa, whoa," says Abraham. "What the frog is this? I'm going to fight Meri?"

"No," says Reggie. "Thug is."

"Shut up," says Abraham, looking at me. "Seriously, Lana. She has a knife and I'm practically naked, and I haven't eaten in two days."

"Ooh," says Roan, jumping in her chair a little. "He totally has a penalty to health or strength, right?"

I don't answer. I just give them each a look, and then settle on Reggie. His avatar hasn't appeared yet, so I'm hoping he'll get my drift. He does.

"Guys," he says. "Just shut up. You're ruining the mood."

"We don't need to fight," says Meridel. She's bouncing lightly on her toes, ready to dodge, jump—she'll even use her daily ability shadowshift if she has to.

"True," says Thug, "but you have to die." And he raises his

right fist. Meridel is far too quick for a simple attack, though, and she—in the blink of his eyes—is on top of the bar, just out of his range.

"Come on," she says. "Let's just go our separate ways. I'll still pay for your drink."

He bellows with rage and swings both arms at her. This time the follow-through connects with her leg, and she falls behind the bar, landing against a stack of small ale barrels. A few of them collapse under her, pouring the frothy amber liquid across the floor. The bartender—and the other patrons—are not pleased, including the men at Meridel's own table. They jump to their feet and draw their weapons. Among them are swords, maces, axes, and flails.

And Thug, they're looking at you.

You've fought large groups before, but never so tired and hungry, and never so large a group at once. But you've busted their ale stores, and may have injured the obvious target of their affections at the same time. A quick retreat might be a good idea.

Meridel, you climb to your feet, shaking your head and stinking of beer, but you regain composure quickly, hurdle the bar, and stand in front of the half-giant with your back to him. "Lads," you say to your hirsute gang, "are you going to let this escaped slave get away with that?"

They grunt and sneer in reply. An escaped slave, after all, means a large bounty. After a brief pause, in which you can practically hear the gears slipping into place in their tiny little minds, one of them shouts, "Get him!" They charge.

Meridel, you drop to the floor on one knee, roll across the bar, and slip along the shadows against the wall back to your table. There, the bounty hunters, in their wild abandon in the face of battle and potential reward, have left their bags. As they encircle the poor half-giant, you quickly and deftly sack their sacks, coming away with a small fortune in gold, a necklace, and a skin of wine. Then, just as deftly, you make your way to the front door and slip outside. All in all, you decide it's been a good night's work.

Inside, Thug, you have been in better situations. These swarthy slavers—as far as you're concerned, that's all they are—have you in quite a spot. They're hesitant to make the first move, though, as they're drunk, disorganized, and badly outweighed. But with so many around you, you're not anxious to start this fight either. You take a challenging stomp toward one, and he flinches. You try again on another. He flinches too. All you're doing, it seems, is putting off the inevitable. So you take a deep breath, let loose a terrifying bellow, choose one, and charge him.

Your sizable head connects with his armored chest. To you, the armor is like balsa, and you hear the last breath he ever takes as it is forced from his lungs. He collapses against a table, probably breaking his back on the thick wood top, and then slumps to the floor. The rest of the men have been spurred to action, but you've made for yourself a nice gap in the circle, and rather than turn to face these men, you continue through it, toward the door.

"The girl," you mutter to yourself. "I will kill the girl."

The door, though, is not an option, because another figure in the bar has gotten to his feet. You didn't notice him before—no one did, truthfully, and that's how he wanted it. But like a veil has been lifted from the eyes of the world, he is very noticeable now. He is gleaming white, as though he produces his own light. His robe must be silk or something rarer, and the hood, which is up, completely prevents anyone from seeing his face—which is also what he wants.

AMBIENT, that figure is you, of course, and you say—no, you intone, "Be at peace," and you raise your hands, palms out, toward the half-giant. He stops. The men behind him stop, and they lower their weapons. The half-giant is of nimbler mind than you thought, though, Ambient, because after glancing over his shoulder at the pacified bounty hunters, he continues. He shoves you aside, opens the door, and goes out.

"Where did you go, girlie?" he bellows.

The peace has most definitely not been restored, so you follow. It's cold. You hadn't planned to go out again tonight, but this half-giant—and maybe even the thief he's pursuing—can help you. You'll have to save them from themselves first, though, and hopefully give them a reason to help you in the process.

Meridel, you didn't get far. You're a little impetuous, after all, and around the first corner under the light of a streetlamp, you've stopped to count your gold. Thug steps around a corner and spots you.

"Whoops," you say, cinching your sack and drawing your dagger. "Didn't my friends finish you off?"

The half-giant smirks and charges. You shadowshift and watch him collide with the lamppost. It's worse off than he.

"You are a strong one, aren't you?" you say, Meridel. "Look," you plead, backing away as he approaches slowly, "I wasn't going to turn you in. I knew you'd beat those morons. I just wanted a diversion. You can split everything I stole." You hold out the sack of coins. "See?"

He knocks it from your hand, sending gold and silver coins spilling into the cobblestone street.

"Oh, come on," you say. "Animosity is one thing, but can we have a little respect for the local currency?"

He raises his fist, and you're too worn out to shadowshift again tonight. You close your eyes and lift your arm to block the attack—it never comes.

Instead you open your eyes and find yourself floating above the street, encircled in a giant halo of light and warmth. The half-giant, too, is floating, only ten feet away. And below you both, down on the street, is an elf wizard in silk robes.

The wizard is you, Ambient, and you say, "Greetings," with both your arms out, and the holy power of light holding your captives aloft. "If you will both agree to cease and desist, I will let you down so we can talk."

The half-giant and the thief exchange a glare, but agree with a nod toward you on the cobblestones.

"Now let us down," says the half-giant, and you, with a flourish, oblige. The combatants slowly descend and land safely on their feet.

"You planning to tell us what that was all about?" the thief *asks as she sheathes her dagger.* "Or do I need to wrap your cloak around your throat and stick your staff of power where the sun don't shine?"

"My name is Ambient," you say. "You, Meridel, and you, Thug, have the skills and attributes I need to complete a mission of great importance."

The half-giant squints at the thief, and then glares at you, and says, "How do you know who we are?"

"There is much I can see," you say, "but much remains cloudy. Will you join me?"

"So?" I say, grinning like a moron and looking at each player in turn.

"Yes!" says Roan with a bounce.

Reggie nods vigorously. "Obviously, I mean, if I can join my own PC." That's player character.

Abraham, finally getting into the spirit of things, nods once and says, "Fork yeah."

"Excellent," I say. "In that case, Ambient, open the sealed envelope in your character packet and read it. It contains your quest's instructions. Your adventure is about to begin."

CHAPTER 27

LESH TUNGSTEN
\<LUSTY AT LUNCH\>

I'm sitting in my usual spot, watching the lunch line for Svetlana.

Svetlana. I'll say it one more time. Svetlana.

Sitting here, I sort of lip-synch it. Not quite a whisper—something quieter. And the cafeteria is bedlam, so there's no danger of anyone hearing me, except maybe the dreggy freshmen who still sit here at the start of week two, I guess not having found anyone they actually know to sit near, or anyone willing to sit near them.

But I do this anyway: mouth the word. I like the feel of my top teeth on my bottom lip when I struggle to find that seductive v at the beginning. I like the way my tongue taps the roof of my mouth and slides to the back of my teeth, gliding into the gorgeous l in the middle. And I like the way it bounces off the roof one more time, as the name settles into its finish with a gentle n.

When I speak to her—when she's sitting across from me in this lunchroom—I don't say her name out loud. At all. It's like how you're not supposed to say the name of God or something. And I know by now that her friends and family call her Lana. But I can't help thinking they're sorely missing out on feeling her real name in their mouths.

She's reached the cashier, and her tote is up on the runner where she can get at it. When she looks up—not at me, but at the cashier, and then into the cafeteria and still not at me, but at someone else—I realize I'm not the only guy at a table watching the line and waiting for Svetlana.

Fry is back. He's being more careful than I am. He's hunched over his lunch, with both elbows on the table and his chin close to his roast. Every few seconds, he risks a quick look up. This time, Svetlana is watching when he looks, and he quickly gets back to forking roast into his maw.

Forking roast, I think. It sounds like Svetlana, angry about dinner.

She's done now, and walking toward me. Fry's still watching, and for a moment I'm ready for anything, but he's back at his roast, and his shoulders are sagging and weak. He just ate a carrot circle. He grimaces and chases it with more forking roast.

Svetlana's tray is barely loaded: There's an apple, and she's watching it carefully, because it hasn't stayed on its butt and is now rolling around the tray with every step. There's the little ceramic bowl of vegetables, the ones they use just for the people who want veggies and don't want any forking roast.

But who cares about her food. I'm lucky that apple won't behave, because she's moving slow, in careful little steps, and watching it, so she's not watching me, so I can watch her. Forgive me for this:

Her skirt is heavy-looking and long. It usually is. This one is cream colored, and the design—in black and red thread, set along the front and left side—is a skull. A freaking skull! It's got one eye, bloodshot and wrecked, and a snake crawling out of its mouth. It's the most metal sewing I've ever seen. On top, she's wearing one of those button-up sweaters—this one is orange. But her hair—I saved it for last, because it's practically silver today as she stutter-steps past the big cafeteria windows and it catches the late-morning light.

She reaches me and puts down the tray. It takes ages, and she doesn't breathe. The apple survives.

"Hi," she says, half word, half sigh of relief. She takes off the sweater and drapes it over the back of the chair before sitting down. It's a terrible match: Svetlana's body and grace and homemade skirt, and the aluminum and plastic red lightweight chair.

"Your apple's okay?"

She nods, slow and serious.

"Fry was watching you," I say. I don't say, "too." I don't say, "I wasn't sure you'd sit with me." The french fries on my plate—I'd forgotten about them while watching her walk toward me—are ice-cold and limp.

185

This was the wrong thing to say. Her playful seriousness—concern over the apple—falls away, and she slumps, crosses her arms on the table in front of her, and leans on her elbows. Her hair drapes over her bare muscular shoulders: her shawl.

Silver Priestess Shawl of Sunlight (+10 spirit)

"He sent me flowers."

"Wow," I say, because I'm a genius at conversation.

It's good enough, and she nods, this time mournfully. "I'm not sure what to do about it. I mean, I was pretty clear, right?" She proceeds to tell me about his forlorn visit to her home and her bedroom—which makes me a bit queasy—and her in-no-uncertain-terms rebuff (her word). "Obviously I wasn't clear enough."

"Has he talked to you today?"

She shakes her head, just a little. Her shawl of sunlight is undisturbed. Her face shifts a bit as she sets her eyes on mine—I think for the first time since she sat down. Her mouth is twisted. Her eyes are suspicious slits.

"I'm not a hundred percent certain they were from him," she says.

I lean in for more, and then lean way back. "Whoa," I say. "They're not from me."

She cocks her head.

"That's what you meant, right?" I say. "You meant they could be from me?"

"It occurred to me," she says in a secret voice, an admittance. "But that would be ridiculous."

"Totally," I say. "I don't even know where you live." That's not entirely true.

"And you're not a creepy stalker."

Also not entirely true. Internet stalking is a type of stalking.

"And we don't have a history in the rain," she says.

"The rain?" I say, and she leans back. Her hair falls from her shoulders. This is a shame, because I was loving the silver shawl effect, but it's also quite nice, because her amazing shoulders are bare again, and they're nice too. She shivers.

"The card with the flowers," she says. "It wasn't signed, but it said something about us—the sender and me, I guess—in the rain."

"Ah."

"And Fry and I were in the rain the weekend before last," she goes on.

"Why?"

A glare. "I would rather not explain that," she says, and it'll have to be good enough, but my insides are twisting and I'd like to puke. Do these two have a real history? Did they have some kind of biblical hookup in the rain?

I'm thinking about Svetlana in the rain now, under the moon. Her hair is wet and clings to her bare shoulders. Her heavy skirt weighs a ton when it's soaked, so she pulls it off and lets him lower her to the grass. The grass is tall and emerald green, and they're under the canopy of a colossal tree, and not far off are the dandelion-colored pigs and sable young tigers of the starting zone.

I might have the wrong Svetlana. One *v*. Two *v*'s. My head swims. There's no more blood in it.

"It's nothing major," she says. "Just embarrassing."

She doesn't know embarrassing. Embarrassing is that I can't get up from this table because I've been fantasizing about a seven-foot-tall imaginary silver-haired priestess getting buck-wild with a senior boy whose name means "submerge in boiling oil."

CHAPTER 28

SVETLANA ALLEGHENY
<PST FOR INVITE>

What is wrong with me?

That's a rhetorical question for now. I'll put it to Roan eventually, once I tell her what's been going on. I don't know why I've been so slow to do that.

Of course I do. I know exactly why. I have lunch on my own this semester. I expected to spend the time sketching, writing encounters, developing new and more fearsome monsters and demons and warring enemies. Instead I've spent my lunches thus far sitting across from the very same boy in black who sent me tumbling from my bike only a handful of days ago, and at the same time sent my favorite gaming spiral notebook into the gutter.

And now I'm letting him believe some very horrible things. I'm implying that Fry and I have some kind of sordid past—which oh my gosh we very definitely do not—because . . . what? I want to make him jealous? Who have I become? If you'd asked me a week ago what I think about the miscreant across the table, I would have said just that: he's a miscreant. But this weekend—was it the flowers?—something shifted. I believed he had feelings for me, if only for an instant, and now they've grown in my heart, and flipped around, and here I am, doing my best not to stare, while his face goes red.

I once thought his face, too old for his age, was an affront. Now I find it adorable. I once thought his black gear and his sullen temperament were indicative of his outlook, a predetermined hatred of every situation and every person. Now I see them as a shield—a wall that is practically begging for a girl to tear it down, brick by brick. Is this the most nauseating thing you've ever heard?

Now I'm desperate to talk to Roan about this, though I know she'll have no great experience to draw upon, because she is one of those great observer types. You've no doubt met some, though you might not know it. These people see everything, and they record everything, and they have insight into the motives of people they've never spoken a word to. That is Roan's secret power. She hides it well, bouncing all over her chair, shuttling around the school's hallways, her tiny frame lost in the sea of taller, older students, only revealed as a beautiful Brillo of orange, sometimes accented with a handful of green barrettes.

I can only now imagine the goings-on inside Lesh's brain as he fumbles with the vagary I have just dropped in his lap. He doesn't speak. He can hardly look at me. He shrugs and stabs his plate of meatballs with a plastic fork.

"So," I say in as casual a manner as I can manage, "I want to ask a favor."

"Really?" he says, and he pops the little ball of pork and beef extra parts, sautéed in a creamy gravy and doused in something like berry sauce, into his mouth. He chews, one cheek much bigger than the other.

I nod once, and then launch into a speech that I might have prepared to some degree last night and then again this morning on the ride to school to the point of distraction. "There are a couple things I know to be true about metalheads."

"Careful," he says.

"They wear a lot of black," I say, which he cannot deny. "Also, they seem to be into skeletons and the undead generally, and on a related note, swordplay and dragons, et cetera."

"We could probably debate that as a generality," he says, "but go on." And he pops another meatball.

"And you didn't seem completely put off by the sundry scribblings in my notebook the other day."

"Right . . . ," he says, and I read the slightest hint of *Backing away slowly* in his tone.

I've gotten through the crux of my spiel without quite the vigorous reaction I'd counted on, so I skip ahead a bit in the face of his growing animosity and drop the favor: "Come to a Gaming Club meeting after school tomorrow."

"Gaming Club?" he says, leaning back in his chair, like it's some major affront to even be invited.

"Um, should I take your obvious offense as a no?" I say, and

I push my tray of cold steamed vegetables an inch or so away from me toward the middle of the table between us.

"I'm not offended," he says, and he gets all shuffley in his chair, a move I haven't seen him do before. He sweeps one of the two remaining meatballs across the plate in a vain attempt to scoop up as much of the remaining gravy and berry sauce as possible. He's not touching the fries, so I snag one and bite its head off. "I'm just a little surprised."

"Why?"

He cuts the last meatball in half, setting himself up to test Zeno's paradox: if he keeps cutting the remaining meatball quantity in half, he will never run out of meatball. "Because that's your thing."

"Right . . ."

"And I don't think I'd fit in with those . . ." He stops and chomps the half ball, then goes back and cuts the remaining half ball in half, as I predicted. We could be here a very long time, so I hope the mood improves.

"Those what?"

"People."

"Ah," I say, and I lean back and cross my arms. "You were going to say 'people.'"

"What did you think I was going to say?"

I look at the ceiling, like I have to think about it. "I don't know . . . nerds? Wonks? Geeks? Dweebs?"

"Come on, Svetlana," he says, and I think it's the first time he's said my name out loud, and the first time I've heard anyone say my full first name in forever, outside of the occasional teacher or sub on their first day meeting me. Those aren't exactly flutter-inducing. This is. "I don't think that about you. You have to know that."

And I do. "Okay, so what do you mean?"

"I mean they're probably smart," he says, slipping the tiny speck of meatball into his mouth and leaning over his plate, considering the remaining speck and its divisibility. "They're probably already your best friends. They're probably . . . happy."

I think of Roan—she is—and Reggie—he's not—and Abraham—he's just angry about something. Heaven knows what.

"Yeah, they're my friends," I admit. "But you are too."

He doesn't look up, but he does smile, and he does poke the last speck with one tine and he does eat it, abandoning Zeno like every decent philosopher since Zeno. "All right then."

"Yeah?" I say, no doubt visibly pleased. "I am so glad."

He nods one time, pleased to have pleased me, I think, and I—like a moron—add, "If we don't get a fifth member soon, we lose our club status."

"Ah," he says, dropping his fork on his plate.

"Oh no!" I say, doing my best to recover. "I would have invited you anyway! It's just that it's an emergency now."

"No, it's fine," he says with a little one-shoulder shrug and a smile that looks as real as the veneer on this cafeteria table. "I'll be there. I'll be the club savior, right?"

I smile back, and mine's real, but it's not the smile of pleasure

193

I had a moment ago. Instead I feel like I miss him, like he was with me a second ago, and now he's backed off again, behind his brick black wall. In a few minutes the bell will ring, and Lesh will nod at me as he gets up and pulls up his headphones, and I'll spend the night and the morning wondering again if he'll show up for lunch.

CHAPTER 29

LESH TUNGSTEN
<JUVENILE DELINQUENTS>

The last bell has rung, so I head for the exit to find Greg for the walk home. I step into the front hall, still obsessing over whether Svetlana wants me to join this club of hers or just needs any warm body to fill a chair, and when I look up from my shoes, Jelly's walking right at me.

The hall is nearly empty, and she's walking right at me, and her hips are amazing and her jeans are low and her hair is spiked and up. Her goddamn navel—pierced with a fang-shaped silver stud I've done my best not to stare at a hundred times—is exposed and amazing. And she's smiling at me . . . I think. I can't quite look at her directly, after a quick nod of acknowledgment, because it's like staring at the sun. She's the hottest girl offline and instead of nodding back, or waving, or saying "hey" and taking the first turn off the front hall that becomes available, she is still coming right at me.

This is something I've always wanted to see. We've never

been close, me and Jelly, though we have been hanging out in the same general circle for the last year and half. And god knows I've stared at her plenty. She's caught me more than once.

Maybe I'm taller now. Maybe looking eighteen at sixteen has its advantages, because this (in the movie in my head) slo-mo walk toward me, with hips swinging and hair bouncing and lips pouting and stomach bare, wouldn't have happened last year. I know this because it didn't happen last year.

"Lesh," she says, and she's running at me now, like a complete nut, with her booted feet slamming into the ground with each step, shaking the whole of the earth like a charging orc. "Lesh. Lesh. Lesh," she says, repeating my name with every thump of her boot on the hallway floor, and then she leaps and lands in front of me, claps a hand on each of my arms. "Lesh!"

"Hi, Jelly," I say, and she says it back in a super-low voice, like I'm Chef from *South Park*: *Hi, Jelly.* So I sneer at her, because licking her throat would probably not be okay. She spins halfway so she's next to me now, and she hooks her hand around the inside of my elbow.

"Walk and talk," she says. "Walk and talk."

"Where are we going?"

She shrugs. "Join me for a smoke in front?"

"I don't smoke."

"Doesn't matter."

She leads me the rest of the way down the hall and into the sunlight in front and down the hundred steps, and then around to the low wall that runs along the short steps down to the pool entrance. "Help me," she says, and she puts out her arms like she needs help getting her (amazing) butt up onto the wall, which is total bull, but I oblige, mainly because I don't hate the idea of slipping my hands between her arms and her chest, and also I'm a little afraid of her. "Thanks," she says when she's up there, and she swings her bag onto her lap and digs out a cigarette. "Want one?"

"No," I say, and she shrugs as she flicks a Bic and lights hers. She drags on it and blows the smoke out of the far corner of her mouth. There's something about the way she does that—she doesn't try for feminine; she doesn't let the smoke out through her nose while giving me a long look; she doesn't exhale in a narrow stream from puckered cherry-red lips. She does it without interest, without motive. She just does it, in the most natural, utilitarian way possible. It's as Jelly as Jelly gets. Unless she needs you for something, right now, she might as well be alone.

I hop up next to her and we sit there, watching cars pull up—some moms and dads of freshmen and sophomores, some seniors and older juniors; it's easy to tell the difference, most of the time, just by looking at the car. Here comes a Civic, all in black with tinted windows and a cheap kit job. The engine is loud, and the trim is red—looks hand painted. Before the door opens and a head pops up to call out to the gang of kids hanging around the steps, I know it's going to be a young guy, maybe just out of high school, maybe dropped out of high school, and probably Asian. Up comes the old gold Camry. That will be a

Somali mother, and as it pulls up, I spot her hijab through the windshield. She's got her cell phone tucked inside by her ear. It's the simplest hands-free device in the world. For some reason I find this ironic, though I don't think it actually is.

When Jelly drops her free hand on my knee—hard—I jump a little, and she laughs.

"What?" I say.

She nods toward the front steps, and down comes Svetlana, in her heavy skirt with the insane embroidery and white denim jacket buttoned over her orange sweater. She bounces down the steps in a syncopated hop, from one foot to the other, her hair bouncing the whole way, so she seems to be made of layers of cotton and snow, of sunlight and feathers from the wings of an angel. It occurs to me that Jelly and I are sitting about three feet from the bike racks. Svetlana's bike is there, chained up, and she's coming this way.

Jelly shakes her head as she lets out another drag. "My god, she's a walking arts-and-crafts fair," she says. "I can't believe that girl exists." She's looking at Svetlana, and probably noticed how intensely I was looking at Svetlana. I can't believe she exists either, and I can't believe that I'm about to consider possibly defending her to Jelly.

I should. But I don't. I keep my mouth shut. At least I don't laugh. I deserve a tiny bit of credit for that.

Svetlana rounds the corner and walks toward us, and her eyes meet mine and she actually smiles and hurries over to me. "Hi!" she says, and I know I should be careful with exclamation points, but she earns it for this one, because she's smiling—which is in and of itself worthy of an exclamation point—and she gives me a flutter in my chest.

Forgive me. I adore her. I admire her. I think about her all the time, in this world and that one. But I am also a tremendous failure at decency and composure, especially in daylight outside of the high school with Jelly's hand on my thigh. So I look down and mutter, "Hey," barely audibly. I can feel Jelly's eyes on me. I can't look back, but I can picture her cigarette dangling from her bottom lip, like she's stunned that this girl—this immaculate silver-haired beauty—and I are remotely associated.

Svetlana has stopped in front of us. I can see her feet. She's wearing high-top bright-blue Chuck Taylors, laced all the way up. "Lesh," she says, so I have to look up, and I do, and this skirt—it still makes me melt. It's the skull with the eye, and now I can get a closer look: the pupil and cornea, the pigment specks in red and black thread, and whatever else is in there, and it's bloodshot with red scraggly lines running from the edges into the white. It must have taken her hours. Days. It's amazing. Anyone could see that, but not anyone could say it out loud.

I can't. Maybe I'll be able to soon.

I finally lift my head and say hi when my eyes are just below her face. I'm focusing on her throat, I guess, which is long and white, except where there's a rubbed-red line on one side, probably where she's been absentmindedly scratching while doodling in her last class, or in the library since, or wherever she's been since last bell—maybe with her gaming friends.

Not doodling. That's obviously not the right word at all. I doodle, and all I come up with are stick figures playing guitar or shooting themselves in the head.

"Um," she says, because I'm an asshat and she's uncomfortable, and I can easily save her. I can hop down from the wall, smile, and walk with her the next ten feet to her bike. I can talk to her while she unlocks it, gets on. I can walk alongside her, even, as she pushes the bike toward her house. Why not?

But I don't.

"So, tomorrow afternoon, right?" she says.

"Yeah," I say. "Okay." I even shrug: *No big deal. I'll probably show up.*

"Bye, then," she says, and she's even giving me a look now, because I finally risk full eye contact, just for an instant. It's long enough to see her head cocked, like a kicked puppy. Sorry. There's nothing especially puppylike about her. She's tall, and strong-looking. She has the shoulders of a Russian-warrior-ice-princess, and probably the rest of one's body too.

"Later," I say, and while Svetlana is bent over and unlocking her chain, Jelly watches for an instant, then turns to me, her cigarette still dangling, and laughs. She throws back her head and laughs her (amazing) butt off.

I spot Deel coming down the big front steps. "There's Greg," I say, and I slide down from the wall. "I'm going to walk home with him."

"You and him dating?" she says.

"What?" I say. I can't even tell if she's kidding. Maybe she thinks I'm gay, and that's why she's hanging out with me. Maybe she can tell I'm half girl.

"Relax," she says, and she grabs my hand from the wall where it's resting. "I'm just messing with you. See you tomorrow, Tung." She bounces her eyebrows at the homonym that is my abbreviated family name. My face probably goes red. It definitely gets hot, and my mind is going places—parts of her body, to keep it general.

"Bye," I say, and pull away my hand. She gives it a last squeeze as my fingers slip out of hers.

"You still grounded?" Greg asks. We're walking along Lexington, past the gas stations at the I-94 overpass.

"Yup."

"Sucks."

"Does," I say. "Verily."

He looks at me sideways, and I smirk. It's a Svetlana word, and now it's a Svvetlana word and therefore a Lesh word. Greg has no idea how many people he's actually walking next to.

"Were you just smoking with Jelly?"

"Sitting," I say. "Just sitting."

He nods slow and groovy, like I'm getting some jelly from Jelly.

"Just sitting," I say again.

"She grabbed your hand when you were walking away,"

Greg says. "I want a giant pop." He veers left, into the gas station market, so I follow.

He heads for the pop machine, and I loiter in the grocery aisle. It's full of single-serving processed food items: microwaveable cans of soup, near-instant pasta meals, pouches of jerky and cheese. I have an appreciation for cheese that requires no refrigeration, but today it's making me woozy.

A woman who works at the market walks up the aisle toward me. I instinctively slip my hands into the deep pockets of my trench coat. She glares at me, then drops the big plastic box she's carrying. She flips open the top and starts restocking the cans of cheese dip. I slide past her and poke at the bags of pretzels, but I'm watching her. She's probably not long out of school. Maybe she's in college, probably at Saint Paul College or Metro State. She's not ugly. Her hair is blond, streaked with a slightly different blond. Her skin is a little zitty. But she's not bad-looking at all. The way she's squatting there, restocking cheese, the very top of her butt is showing. She's wearing a thong.

"Tung!" Greg calls from the door. He's pushing it open with his back, holding up his giant cup of green liquid. "We out!"

I head toward the door and glance at the gas-station woman. She stands up and grabs the belt of her pants. With a shimmy and a hop on each foot, she hikes them up, and for an instant gives herself a butt lift and a wedgie.

Mom's waiting for me at home. She's not doing something else, keeping half an eye on the door. She's not relaxing on the couch after a long day. She's sitting on the couch, on its edge, watching the door when I open it. As I come in, she stands up and waves something at me.

"What's this?" she says, but she knows, and I know too. It's about ten inches high, made of thin cardboard, and decorated in complex art in green, gold, and black.

"Um," I say, because what's the point? It says right on it what it is: it's the cardboard sleeve that the prepaid gaming card came attached to.

Did I mention the free trial ended and I spent some of my saved allowance on a sixty-day card? They sell them at Target.

"Do you know where I found this?" she asks.

"The recycling bag," I say, since that's where I put it.

"Right," she says, "and I wouldn't have known what it is, but I was looking for this exactly. Do you know why?"

"Why," I say as flat as I can manage. I'm pulling off my coat to hang up.

"Because one of the boys who works in the computer section," she says, and her voice shifts into extra serious, "at my store told me you were in buying a gaming card. He said, 'Aw gee, I didn't know your son played this game. What server is he on?'"

"Am I in trouble?"

"Are you in . . . ," she says, all out of breath and flustered. "Are you kidding? How much did you spend on this?"

"Thirty dollars," I say, and quickly add, "of my own money."

"Your own money," she says. "You don't have your own money."

I roll my eyes. This isn't a new conversation. Every time I spend more than a dollar, I hear about how my allowance isn't for whatever I want. It's for . . . well, I haven't figured that out yet.

"Do you know I spoke to Tom about this?" she goes on, though I have no idea who Tom is. "I made him tell me all about this game, and besides the fact that I feel like I don't even know who you are anymore because this game does not seem like something you'd be interested in—"

So true.

"—I cannot for the life of me understand where you are finding the time to play," she finishes.

"Um, I've been grounded, remember?"

"Yes, you have," she says, "which brings me to my next point. Did you think your father and I had *this*"—she waves that black card stock in my face again—"in mind when we grounded you?"

I shrug. I'm supposed to guess what they have in mind, and then remember what I guessed a week and a half later?

"So what did you have in mind?" is all I can think to say. I'm leaning on the wall near the steps now, itching to go upstairs— even itching to log on and run Svvetlana a little, despite what happened the last time I played. It's been a weird day, and I want to wind down in a predictable environment.

"First of all, a punishment," she says, "not some kind of gaming vacation."

"Gacation," I say, and I giggle.

"Shut up," she says. "Second of all, I thought you'd have a lot of extra time to catch up in math, to keep your grades up, to really focus on schoolwork, instead of on drinking and listening to that disgusting, despicable hate-fueled garbage—"

"Point made," I put in.

She takes a deep breath and puts her fist on her hip. "I'm not going to mention this to your father," she says, and she's waving the card stock again, "but I don't want to have to mention it to you again either. Do you get what I mean?"

"Not really."

"I mean homework," she says. "I mean your focus will be homework, not . . . orcs or elves or gnomes or whatever."

"Okay."

"Okay won't cut it," she says. "Not this time. I want to see the work you're doing, and you are not to play even one fraction of a second of that game until your work is done and I've seen it."

"Seriously?" I say. "Mom, I'm not a little kid."

She actually laughs. "When you stop playing little kid games, you can claim you're not a little kid."

I grunt a little. I must be channeling Kugnar this afternoon. "Can I go?" I head up the steps.

"I am not messing around about this, Lesh!" she shouts up at me.

"Yeah, I pretty much got that," I say. Door slam.

I fall into my desk chair, wake up my computer, and open the game launcher. Click, click, click, and there she is, bouncing and grinning, casting and wielding, ready to run. Click, click, click, and there's Kugnar, flexing and snarling, swiping and stabbing, ready to kill.

"If I'm about to dedicate a solid chunk of time each night to appeasing Mom," I mutter to myself, "one of you is about to get a lot less attention."

I'll give you one guess which.

CHAPTER 30

SVVETLANA
<LOITERERS>

The priestess and her dangerous cohorts lounge on the stone benches near the fountain in the grassy center of the human capital city. They're strangers here—not a drop of human blood in their three bodies—and they enjoy it. They're not out of place, exactly; elves and dwarves are welcome anywhere in the faction's territory. But when a young human mage, barely out of his linen robes and unable even to shield himself, happens by, he gives them a wide berth on his way into the bank.

"I'm bored," says Dewey. He's uncharacteristically still, lying on his back on the bench with his head in Svvetlana's lap.

Stebbins the hunter stands and draws his bow. He looses an arrow, and it strikes and picks an apple from a tree across the clearing.

"Nice shot," says Dewey, and Svvetlana giggles as Stebbins's cat darts away to fetch the fallen fruit.

"So what should we do?" says Stebbins. "We've run every

five-man a hundred times. I have more tokens of valor and emblems of honor than I know what to do with." He sits on the bench on Svvetlana's other side, and she takes his hand.

"We have to raid," Dewey says, rolling onto his side. "Seriously, I like you guys and everything, and even the other members of our guild are okay."

"But?" says Svvetlana. She looks down at his dirty, scarred, chubby face. It's nearly impossible to see through the thick knots of hair that grow from every inch of his body, but his eyes glimmer a bit, and it makes her smile.

"But," the dwarf paladin goes on, "if we don't get serious and start raiding and getting the really truly epic and heroic gear, I'm outta here."

"Aw, don't say that," says Svvetlana. She evens pats his head. He purrs and bounces his eyebrows.

"All right, all right," says Stebbins, batting her hand off the paladin's head. "She's taken, you dirty creeper."

"Am I?" says Svvetlana, but she's ignored.

"Look, the guild is the laughingstock of the realm," Dewey says, "because we have enough members, lots of us at fifty, and we just never raid. We're supposed to progress, you know?"

"We're not the laughingstock," says Stebbins. "There's no laughingstock."

"Well, we should be," says the dwarf.

Svvetlana shrugs. "So we'll start raiding," she says. She checks their faces. "Right?"

Dewey nods, somehow, on her lap. "Right."

"Okay then," says Stebbins. "I'll put the word out to the guild." His cat is back now, lying at his feet, gnawing at the bright red apple. Svvetlana can smell it, and it smells good—but it's nothing compared to the fruit of her homeland, so full of sugar and life that her mouth waters just thinking of it.

"Tell everyone to get Vent," says Dewey.

"Vent?" Svvetlana says. "What's Vent? Do I have it?"

"Lol," Dewey says. "I keep forgetting she's a noob."

"It lets us talk to each other," Stebbins says. "Like, in our real voices."

Svvetlana catches her breath and swallows hard.

"You need it to raid," the hunter goes on. "The fights are really complicated, and without talking to each other—like, if we just typed—we'd just wipe and wipe."

"And if you wipe too much," Dewey says, "you get hemorrhoids." The priestess looks across the field at the impossibly brown and green and red apple tree. The fruit the hunter shot is back, regrown, like everything does in this world.

"I have to go," she says.

"Aw," the hunter says. He kisses her cheek.

"Homework," the priestess says. "I'll see you later."

CHAPTER 31

LESH TUNGSTEN
<LYING LIARS>

"So," I say on Tuesday morning. My hands are deep in the pockets of my trench coat. My headphones are around my neck, the volume way up so I can still hear the blistering riffs of Coalesce. Greg strolls next to me. I haven't been looking forward to this conversation, though in a way, I have. My chest is swelling.

The morning is cold, the first truly cold morning of fall. The dry leaves on the sidewalk behind us as we walk are like the skittering feet of a giant spider, and I keep glancing over my shoulder, like I might have to cast a shield and defend myself. Finally, though, I finish my sentence that started with "so," like most of them do, and I can see my breath float toward Interstate 94. "I have to quit gaming."

"Oh, damn," says Greg. "Why?"

"Why do you think?" I say, shrugging, and we stop at the corner of Concordia Avenue to wait for the light. I tell him how some dink at Target reported to my mom about me buying that gaming card. "That and I'm supposed to be grounded. I guess virtual travel is not allowed."

"So that's it?" Greg says. "One strike, you're out?"

I cough a little. "I guess, when you're grounded already and your dad is a high school dropout"—I drop my voice an octave—"who wants better for you."

"Jesus, man," Greg says. "How much have you been playing? I don't see you on *that* often. You definitely play less than I do."

The little white-light man appears on the sign across the street, and we're walking again.

"I'm also not a natural at math," I say, figuring a little flattery might deflect this a little, "like you are. If I don't work a lot, it shows pretty quick."

He nods slowly, wisely, sagely, et cetera. "That's for sure," he says.

I cough, just to fill the silence and hear the dryness of my throat, as we reach the opposite curb. Central High looms from the hill in front of us as we walk around the high fence toward the main entrance. We don't speak for a while. We just listen to the music coming from my headphones and watch the cars at the corner, as they slowly take the turn onto Marshall, to see which will stop and let out classmates.

A girl on a lady's old-fashioned bike—with a basket on the handlebars and everything—rolls across Lexington as we reach the corner and the light changes. Her dress hangs down and flutters gently in the breeze. A few yards ahead, she drops her feet to stop, pulls off her helmet, and then twists to watch us approach.

CHAPTER 32

SVETLANA ALLEGHENY
<FOOLS IN LOVE>

This is a bad idea.

I watch Lesh and his baby-faced friend—the boys in black—approach.

Smile! I try, but it's weak and it freezes, and I feel like a moron. I'm standing over my bike, with one hand on the fork and the other on my helmet, waiting for Lesh, wishing I'd just waited till lunch, like a normal person, but I wanted to see him, to see what's on his mind and why he was so weird in front of that girl, and when I saw him loping up—he lopes; he doesn't walk, he doesn't stroll, and he doesn't stagger, except that one time—I couldn't resist. I should have. My smile isn't weak anymore, because his lope is amusing. He walks like an emperor penguin. I should buy him a white T-shirt to wear under his trench coat. That would make the disguise complete.

"Hey!" I call out, as if they haven't seen me already, standing here gaping at them.

Lesh raises his hand and maybe smiles. I'm probably imagining that, since he very rarely does, and the light at this hour can play tricks this late in the year. Also, my wool leggings are starting to itch, and I desperately want to get inside. Drop-off kids are pulling up and climbing out of SUVs and coupes by the dozen now, and they're all looking at me. I don't like it. But something on Lesh's face changes, just for an instant. I'm sure of it. His typical glower—a look he has in common with his short friend and probably seventy percent of the boys at Central—seems to vanish, and I am taking that to be his friendly face.

They're much closer now, and babyface's smile is plainly real, in that it is a physical smile and not a trick of the early-morning light, but not real, in that it is tighter, bigger, and obviously sarcastic, so I watch Lesh again instead.

"So," I say, patting my tote bag—full of notebooks, pencils, and my DM screen: all the goodness that awaits him this afternoon when we begin to chip away at his exoskeleton and bring out the gamer within—"still planning to join us today?"

He drops his head and his cheeks go a little pink. I wouldn't have thought him capable, and for this guy? For this mini baby Lesh at his side?

Yup, definitely a bad idea.

"For what?" the little one says. He looks at Lesh, and I know what he's thinking. I knew this was a bad idea, but I wasn't sure why until now. This boy has never heard of me. He doesn't know Lesh and I eat lunch together every day. He doesn't know his best friend—a no doubt lifelong boy in black—is friends with a freaky nerdgirl like me.

I wait, watching Lesh, seeing if maybe he'll speak up. I grip the fork a little tighter, swivel the post back and forth, desperately wanting to pedal off, right now. Lesh doesn't speak. He just finally lifts his head and looks at me. *You tell him,* he seems to say.

"Um," I say, but I know my face says more. Disbelief. Disappointment. Dysentery. My hair falls over my face, a thin yellow shield. "I'm a dungeon master," I say. "The tabletop Gaming Club meets after school today." I'm answering the little one, but I'm still watching Lesh. He could jump in any minute now.

The baby in black twists his pudgy face in judgment. "Tabletop . . . okay . . ."

Lesh coughs and elbows him, just a little. "Yeah, I think so," he says, never catching my eyes. "I mean, yeah, I think I'll try to make it."

I stand there and watch the boys in black for a too-long moment. I wish I'd never sat down with Lesh, never let him see my notebook over lunch, never wondered what his hands felt like, never imagined him lying next to me under the canopy over my bed. These aren't my friends, so Lesh isn't my friend. These were strangers—dark, cynical, judgmental strangers.

"Listen, don't worry about it," I say. "I gotta go. Just forget it."

"Okay," Lesh says quickly. It was the out he wanted, I realize, and I turn around and press hard on the pedals, and hope the boys in black will be in the school and far from the front doors by the time I get my bike chained up and make it inside. When I reach the bike rack around the side of the school, I shoulder my bag—it gets heavier every day—and lift out the cloth-wrapped heavy-duty chain at the bottom of the basket. I bend down to close the padlock, and as I stand I spot Roan's family car—a wine-colored Volvo sedan from before her parents were born—pulling up out front. A comrade in arms will do me good, so I dally a minute, and time my approach to the front doors to coincide with Roan's.

"Hi, Red," I say. Roan actually means "red." In fact, every given name in her family means "red." Even "garnet" means "red."

"Hey, Svet," she says, full of optimism. She slips a hand into the crook of my elbow and pulls me along, up the huge set of steps, at a good clip. We walk into the dry, hot light of the front hall of Central High.

"What are you doing at ten forty-five?" I say as we weave together through the morning crowds, chattering and touching and screaming and shoving in the wide entrance. "Wanna have lunch with me?"

"I can't," she says. "I'm meeting with Grimmish in the library today. It's Tuesday. Independent project."

Of course. Roan is doing her graduate thesis on the residual effects of Nordic and Welsh mythology on modern children through fairy tales, children's books, and blockbuster films, and the only exaggeration in that explanation is "graduate thesis." Anyway I nod, glumly, so she'll ask why I'm nodding glumly. Even so, when she does ask, I can hardly answer, because we both have to hurry off to our respective first classes.

"Get to room 3212 a little early, Svet," she says, backing quickly away as we move past the south stairwell, where we have to say good-bye. "Tell me before it starts."

"*If* it starts," I mutter, because it might not, because there's a good chance the fifth member I'd invited and who'd accepted, thereby guaranteeing our faculty adviser, meeting space, and credit, has just jumped at the chance for an out, which I might have just given him.

I'll be early to Gaming Club, I decide. Quite early, and I'll find Roan and catch her up completely. The dungeon master needs some help with this campaign.

CHAPTER 33

LESH TUNGSTEN
<THE LOSER TABLE>

I'm an asshole. I know this.

Lunch can't come quickly enough today, because I have to beg Svetlana to forgive me for acting like a tremendous douche to her this morning, with Greg standing there, letting her squirm. I only hope I can explain, but when I walk into the cafeteria as the bell to start skej A lunch sounds through the labyrinthine halls of Central High, I can't even explain it to myself.

She's not here yet, so I skip the line, grab a bag of corn chips and a little carton of chocolate milk, and fall into my usual seat to watch the line. From where I sit, I can also see that criminally obnoxious friend of hers, Fry. He's watching the line too, and he's watching me, and I can already see where this is going: I can't believe he still hasn't learned his lesson, after that whole brouhaha on Wednesday morning, but he looks ready to pick a fight.

I'm popping chips like mad, and I have to force myself not to stare at Fry or the line. She's not here. I'd see her come in, anyway. I'd probably smell her cucumber-strawberry essence mingling with the steam-table rankness. The mouth spout on the tiny chocolate milk doesn't open right; its glue is too strong and the paper or cardboard too wet and weak. I have to finagle a tiny hole and force a straw in before I can get a sip, and then it's gone. It's about five ounces to begin with. It was never going to last.

I stare down at the empty carton and the almost empty chips bag. This is what I'd dreaded, on the first day of school, and what she saved me from: sitting alone at the end of a table of assorted social rejects. Staring at my hands, at my meager lunch, feeling the weight of my coat on my shoulders and my headphones on my neck and my skin on my bones, on my own at the loser table. When I look up, the cafeteria is settled, the line is gone, and the little hand on the clock over the exit doors makes it pretty clear: She's not coming today. She saw me this morning, I was a dick, and she's done with me, probably for good.

Now Fry is stomping toward me from his little stakeout spot across the room. His jaw is set, his hair is too short to move, his little red eyes are slivered in threat.

"Why isn't Lana at lunch?" he asks, somehow without moving his mouth. I guess the laughing asshattery becomes scowling asshattery when the lovely Svetlana isn't around. There's no joking, no snickering, no hyena face. I have a feeling this is the real Fry, and I nod a little, slowly, to myself, because of course Svetlana would know that. Of course she wouldn't be the type of girl to fall for a generous and jovial facade with this douche nozzle underneath.

Anyway, I shrug. "I don't know. I haven't seen her today," which isn't one hundred percent true, I suppose, but I don't feel the need to let Fry in on the particular difficulties between Svetlana and me this morning.

"I saw you talking to her today," Fry says, and he steps a little closer to the table. He's across from me now, where Svetlana should be sitting, leaning just a little over the table, his belt pressed up against the back of her chair. I wish she were sitting there, so she could throw an elbow and knock him to the ground, where he could ball up with his hands over his groin, wailing.

"Oh yeah," I say, and I try to smile: Oops. "I forgot."

"Right."

"That's kind of creepy, anyway," I say, fiddling with my fingers in the empty chips bag. When I find nothing, I pull out my hand and lick my thumb, then crumple the bag and grab the empty milk as I stand up. "Are you spying on her?"

He leans farther and shoves me with both hands on my shoulders. I wasn't ready, and I tumble backward into a plastic chair and the freshman boy sitting in it. He's fine; I lose my footing and fall against the table and then onto my side on the floor. "Are you kidding?" I say as I get to my feet, pushing off the sticky tiles.

"I don't know who the hell you think you are," Fry says, stepping around the end of the table, "but you don't get to just step up here like you know her at all and start talking to me like I'm the weirdo. Like I'm the one who walks around here like the trench coat Mafia."

"What?"

"I've known Lana for a lot longer than you have," Fry goes on, and he gives me another shove. "So don't act like I'm just some guy who needs to back off. It's not like that."

"Okay," I say, not meekly, but with a sneer and a glance out the window, and it's obviously sarcastic and belligerent. I get a shove again. This time, I shove back—hard.

Fry's butt hits the table behind him and he stumbles, but he doesn't fall. Then he takes a heavy step toward me. Chairs scrape. Voices rise: "Fight." And he stops, which is a relief. I'm taller than him, but he's thickly built and could probably drive through me like a train through a garage wall. Mr. Andestic, the teacher on cafeteria duty, is on his feet and walking toward us. I slip back into my chair and Fry looks at the high ceiling.

"Everything all right, you two?" Andestic says.

"Sure," says Fry, his eyes still up, disinterested and guilty.

"Lesh?" Andestic says, looking at me.

"No problems," I say, and I grab my trash from the floor at my side and stand up. "I'm just heading out, actually."

"Straight to the library," Andestic says, and I nod.

"See ya, Fry," I add over my shoulder, and I can practically hear his teeth grinding. He wishes he had my carcass in his hands, and my femur in his jaw, crushing it to reach the sweet, sweet marrow.

CHAPTER 34

SVETLANA ALLEGHENY
<MEAN GIRLS>

Lunch alone. It's what I intended anyway, right? When this school year started—it was only recently, though it seems like an eternity of drama and Dannons and vasovagal episodes—I loved one thing about my schedule above all else, with the possible exception of Dr. Serrano's poetry class and Ms. McBee's drama elective: lunch by myself.

Schedule A lunch is early. No reasonable human being wants to eat lunch before eleven in the morning. It's really more like brunch, I guess, than lunch. But I was happy with it, because none of my friends were in it, and I could sit in the seat closest to the window and draw and write encounters and knit to my heart's content. Then Lesh came along—or actually I came along, seeing as the first time we ate together, I sat down across from him, rather than vice versa. The point is today I get my wish: thirty minutes on my own, in a quiet environment, with my notebooks, three pens, and a cast of PCs ready to exist on paper.

I'm filling in Meridel's torso, wondering how buxom Roan would like her to be, my mind with the thief on the page, only peripherally aware that I'm even in the library, when someone kicks my foot.

"Excuse me," I mumble, barely taking my eyes off Meridel, not even stopping my pen from moving. But the kick happens again. This time, I look up, and there's this black-haired girl—ripped tight jeans, belt made of I-kid-you-not iron spikes and leather, a T-shirt cut off above her belly to expose her piercing and emblazoned with a skeleton's face with its tongue hanging out. For an instant I have time to consider how a skeleton, whose skin and muscle has rotted away so fully that only clean bone remains, could possibly have a tongue. Then she talks.

"Who the hell are you?" she says.

"What?" I say, because I'm a bit shaken by the question.

"What?" she says back, her mouth all twisted, full-on metal mean girl, mocking me. And I recognize her now. This is the girl Lesh was sitting with yesterday after school, on the wall by the pool entrance, when he started this now-twenty-hour policy of treating me like a leper. He must like her. Not that I can't see why. She's like a walking advertisement for sex, drugs, and rock 'n' roll.

"What's your name?" she says, and she leans down, with her hand right on the table in front of me, and gets right in my face. I try to lean away; the smoky stench of her breath isn't pleasant. More than that, though, I'm getting fuzzy in the chest. I try to take a deep breath, and instead end up with a big whiff of tobacco and coffee and maybe even booze, but it's not even eleven and we're in school. I think it must be coming from her clothes. "Are you deaf or something?"

I shake my head.

"Hey, you can hear!" she says. She's keeping her voice super quiet, but every word snaps like a gunshot. My face is warm. Tingly sweat is forming in every crease on my body. "Here's the thing," she goes on, "whatever your name is: I don't like you. After today—after this very moment"—she presses her finger into the desk with each word, firmly, like a black-nailed hammer—"I would very much like to never see you again."

"Why?" I say. It's almost a whisper. The room is closing in like twilight.

"What?" she says. "Did you say something, you little precious butterfly?"

"I said why?"

"Have you been listening at all?" And she moves her face even closer. I can't lean back any more or I'll fall off this chair, and the heat and smell of her breath and her clothes, and her arm across the side of my body, holding her up, stiff-elbowed, so she can lean closer and closer to me, are making my vision fuzzy and dark. The sound in the library cuts out like someone's hit mute and is replaced with the tinny shriek of fear inside my head. "I don't like you."

I try to tighten my fists, pump my legs, keep my blood pressure up, but the strength is gone. The heavy tingle in my chest and my armpits and the sweat on my head all go cold and shimmery. It's like I'm bathed in light, and the mean girl's face waves and warps into a field of white, and then gray, and then black. She stands, her face now blank, and she swears and looks around. But she's out of my face now, and so I lean forward, too late, and I'm gone.

I am running along a narrow, thrashing river. My staff, slung on my back, bangs into the back of my legs, and the pebbles of the shore bounce under my feet and lodge in the ankles of my leather boots. The sun is low to my right, and the sky is already going red and purple and indigo from west to east. In the bushes to my left, a violent rustle follows me as I run. I reach a stream and ford it—in one, two steps—and as I do, I glance left and see the beast exit the undergrowth and bound across the stream.

I pull the staff from my back and hold it in both fists, then plant my feet on the opposite shore and stop. The beast reels to face me. It throws back its head, the fur there matted now with rainwater collected from the leaves and fronds in the forest. It roars, and I stumble, but only for a moment, and I raise my staff and roar back.

Beneath me, the ground rumbles. The trees tremble around us, and the stream begins to bubble like it's boiling. I can feel the power in my eyes and my lips. They both seem to fill with blood, and the beast is sent hurtling into the nearby stand of trees. It whimpers as its back slaps a thick tree trunk, and it slides to the wet grass. But I know it's down, not out, and I don't have much fight left in me. Without help, I can't beat this thing, and I have the feeling the beast knows that too. He's already recovering when I put my fingers to my lips and call my ride. The griffon lands beside me, and with one hand out and casting a shimmering shield of holy magic to hold the beast back, I manage to grip the griffon's leather rein tightly and get one leg over its back. We take off as the field flickers and drops. The beast plants a heavy paw on my calf and tears my boot to shreds.

I'm out of energy and bleeding, so I lower my head to the griffon's downy neck and begin to drift to sleep. She'll take me home, and there I can get help. The wind and cold air as we climb rush over my bare shoulders, and I shiver. Only my left hand, still gripping the rein, is warm. My palm and the strap of leather are damp with sweat. Soon we're diving; I hadn't realized how close we'd been to town. Why would the beast be prowling so close? I'm drifting away now as we descend from above the clouds. The cool mist presses against me, and then it's raining. Someone takes my hand, takes the reins from me, shakes me, and I can't get to my feet.

"Lana, dear," says a woman's voice—a familiar voice, a caring voice. "Can you sit up?"

I open my eyes and find Ms. Grimmish looking back at me. She smiles. "You'd better get to the nurse's office," she says. "I'll help you if you can't get there on your own."

The mean girl is gone, but I can't have been out for more

than a few seconds. It never takes long. The dreams, though, seem to last forever. My doctor once told me that if you don't have to actually do things—don't have to actually move within a physical space—time ceases to exist, and we can dream a lifetime in the most fleeting moment, like absorbing every frame of a whole movie as a single image. I admit I don't get it, but I do like it. I've never told my family, but sometimes I like my vasovagal episodes. Besides the dream and the feeling of weightless freedom, I usually end up in the nurse's office with a cookie.

Ms. Grimmish helps me stand and leads me out, Roan standing off to the side, watching. She's seen me like this before, of course, but I guess it never gets fun. As we pass through the media center doors and start down the steps toward the nurse, Lesh walks by on his way up.

"Svetlana," he says, but my voice is still not with me, and my tongue is thick and heavy and dry, so I grip Ms. Grimmish's arm a little tighter and do my best to just hold on.

CHAPTER 35

LESH TUNGSTEN
<CLOSED DOORS
AND OPEN WINDOWS>

"So you're actually going to do this?" Greg says. School's over, and we're standing out front, at the top of the ginormous set of steps that lead down to Marshall Avenue and, by extension, our homes. I'm looking over his shoulder at the white Pontiac Firebird idling in the drop-off/pickup spaces at the curb. It's Jelly's car, and I wonder who she's planning to pick up, and why she's already in the car and not just on her way out like the rest of us.

"Yup," I say. "I am."

"As long as you know what you're getting into here," Greg says. "I realize I'm not remotely the coolest guy in this high school, but you're talking about twenty-sided dice here."

I nod a little and say "Yup" again. Greg follows my gaze and finds the Firebird at the curb. "And you can forget that whole situation too," he says, "if Jelly hears you're hanging out with this Svetlana person and her deeply weird compadres."

"She knows," I admit, and briefly recount the happenings of the previous afternoon.

Greg shakes his head, disappointed as hell. I guess he figures if he doesn't have a chance with our resident metalhead hottie—and he doesn't—he'd at least like to hear about it from his lifelong best friend.

I put out my hand for a five, and he obliges, begrudgingly, head still shaking. I watch him hurry down the steps in a sideways quick descent. He goes straight to the Firebird and sticks his head in the passenger window. That Deel is kind of a brave little man. But I'm inside-bound, so I pull open the front door and find my way to room 3212, where I assume some kind of inaugural ritual is already being prepared.

CHAPTER 36

SVETLANA ALLEGHENY
<EARLY BIRDS>

Roan and I are walking laps around the basement before we head to Gaming Club.

"There's something you should know about the new possible member of the GC." We chose this area for a reason: it's so dead, you wouldn't be surprised to see tumbleweed fluttering up behind you. While much of the school at this hour is bustling with the rituals of departure, the basement is a dead zone. There are no after-school activities here. There are no lockers in this hallway. There are no exits—outside of a pair of emergency doors—and even the teachers have no reason to hang out down here. Only a handful of students, leaning on walls, and a pair of hall monitors at either end let on that this hallway is not in fact in some alternate dimension, where the apocalypse has begun, centered right here in the basement at Central High.

"Okay," she says, so I should go on, but I'm not ready to yet.

I start at the end. "He's very quiet."

"Okay."

"Also, he's a metal boy," I add. I'm choosing my words carefully, deftly avoiding such issues as my possibly blossoming affection for his person, and his person's central role in the destruction of the originals of our campaign, monster manual, and spell book, not to mention his ongoing crusade to distance himself from me and his female associate's apparent tendency to threaten me with bodily harm, even if not in so many words.

"Like, a robot?" Roan says, and I can't be sure at once if she's kidding, but obviously I haven't been choosing my words as deftly as I thought.

"Like, into metal," I say. "Heavy metal. A genre of music, such as it is."

"Ah," she says. "Is he, like, scary?"

"No," I say, and I try to remember if he ever was. I think so. I think he and his ilk were definitely scary, and one of them at least still is. I remember the pounding in my chest as I rode off on my dented bike that first night, and I can't be sure how much was anger, and how much was fear, and how much was the thrill of a violent collision in the small hours of the morning and the pair of eyes behind black bangs that came with it. "He's tall," I add, mostly for something to say.

"So are you," Roan says, so I nod. "Is that it?"

"What?"

"That's what you wanted to tell me about him?" she says. "He likes metal and he's tall?"

I take a deep breath and stop, and so Roan stops a step later and turns to face me. She waits.

I breathe.

She smiles.

"Roan," I say.

Her smile erupts. There's no other word for it, when Roan smiles and her mouth opens wide, so you can see her teeth and the pair of silver fillings in the back, and her freckles are like fireworks across her cheeks and forehead. When she throws out her arms and says, "You like him," I have to cover my face to hide the blush and grin.

But I do nod. "I think so."

Roan's arm's around my waist, and she's pulling me along the hallway. "Let's go," she says, hopping a bit as she pulls me along. "Now I'm even more excited to get to GC."

"Well, that's the other thing . . . ," I start, and I steel myself, because I'm about to admit that first of all he might not show, because this morning it sure seemed like he was taking his out, and second that the boy I might be falling for is in fact a cretin like the rest of them, and wouldn't be seen talking to me in public—twice now. I stop and stomp my foot and cover my eyes with my hand.

"Forget it," I say as we climb the steps toward the third floor. "Forget the whole thing."

But Roan isn't listening, because we've reached room 3212, and Roan is hugging my arm and whispering up at me, "Is that him?"

So I look, and it is.

CHAPTER 37

LESH TUNGSTEN
<NERDS AND NOOBS>

I'm sitting on the floor and leaning against the wall of 3212 when Svetlana rounds the corner from the stairwell. She's with a tiny freshman-looking girl with the craziest, curliest red hair I have ever seen. When they see me, they stop short. Svetlana's mouth literally hangs open.

"Hey," I say, standing up, shoving my hands into my pockets. I pull one out briefly to offer a halfhearted wave and glance at the redhead.

The girls continue toward me. "Um, I thought I should wait for you," I say. "I didn't know if those guys were expecting me or what."

"Um, okay," says Svetlana. "I didn't think you were coming. This is Roan."

"Hi."

"Hello," she says.

I face Svetlana and ask her quietly, "Are you okay? You looked . . . before."

"Oh, yeah," she says, even waving me off a little. "It was nothing. Let's just go in."

So we do. A teacher I recognize but don't know sits at the big desk at the front of the room. She looks up and says, "How are you feeling, Lana?" and Svetlana smiles and says, "Fine, thank you. I guess I was just so tired."

The teacher offers a weak and suspicious smile, but I'm not in on this, whatever it is, so I head toward the back, where two guys—one little and black and severely overdressed, the other taller and white and drumming his fingers on the table and his feet on the floor—are seated on the far side of a long table.

"Um, everyone," Svetlana says as Roan slips past us and grabs the empty seat next to the overdressed boy, "this is the new member I told you about. Lesh, you met Roan."

She waves again.

"Reggie."

The overdressed one tips his hat at me.

"And Abraham."

"Yeah, hi," says the last one. "Wait a minute. Did you say Lesh?"

"Um, that's me," I say, ready to once again deflect a childish comment about the uncommonness of my name. But it doesn't come. Instead comes this:

"Lesh the miscreant who knocked Lana off her bike?" Abraham jumps to his feet, like he's ready to fight me.

"Oh my gosh, Svet," says Roan, and I'm struck: Svet? I haven't heard this version before. It's so brusque and Russian. I hate it at once. "Why didn't you tell me?"

Svetlana takes a chair opposite the other three and says, "It's not a big deal."

I pull a chair a little way from the table and sit down. "We made up," I add.

"Made up?" says Abraham. He's still standing. How many guys are there who are so committed to ill-advised physical defense of this girl? "He destroyed your work and nearly our lives and you made up?"

"Shut up," says Svetlana, and she shoots him what must've been a pretty nasty glare, because he closes his eyes, puts up his hands, and sits down.

"Anyway yes, this is Lesh," she goes on, "and he is the boy who will help us maintain our official club status, and our firm grip on Ms. Grimmish." The teacher at the front of the room smiles and waves but doesn't look up from her book.

"Lesh," she says as she digs around in her bag, pulling out notebooks and pamphlets and a folded map, "we're already started on this campaign, so you can watch and kind of get the hang of what we do and how we play."

"He's never played?" Abraham says, barely containing his derisive laughter. "What the hell, Lana?"

"He'll learn," she says, taking her own seat again. She unfolds a screen—a big cardboard fold with lots of confusing things printed on the side facing her, and with drawings of dragons and elves and other such goodies on the side facing the players.

"Whatever, whatever," says Reggie. He pulls off his hat and

adjusts something and puts it back on. "Let's just get back to it, okay? Where were we?"

Abraham lets out a sigh to aggravate the dead. "We just stepped into the big chamber at the end of the tunnel under the inn."

"And it's cold," Roan adds. She shifts in her seat, pulls her foot under her butt like a booster seat. She's quite small. I can't understand how a girl who looks barely old enough for high school is hanging out with three seniors. "Svet said the temperature dropped by like thirty degrees."

"That's too much," Abraham says, crossing his arms.

"Who's the DM here?" says Svetlana.

Reggie pulls off his fedora again and puts it down on the papers in front of him on the table. "He has a point," he says. "I mean, if it's that much colder, our stats would . . . Oh."

Svetlana is grinning like a cat in a mousetrap factory. "Roll for a constitution check," she says, and her voice is sinister and frigid—icy enough that I almost feel the temperature in the classroom itself drop by thirty degrees. The three players each grab a die and toss it.

Svetlana examines the results. Only Abraham's roll is sufficient. "Meridel and Ambient, you both suffer a minus-three penalty to dexterity," Svetlana says. Then she reaches into her tote bag and pulls out a huge sheet of plastic. She lays it on the table between herself and the players, revealing it to be a map of the chamber on giant graph paper. She clicks a button on the iPod player behind the screen, and classical music starts.

"Ah!" says Ms. Grimmish from the front of the room. "Boito's *Mefistofele. Così bello!*"

"Here we go," says Reggie. He leans forward.

"Finally," says Roan, and she switches her booster foot with a youthful hop. Can she really be a high school student? She looks about thirteen.

"Finally is right," says Abraham. "Let's kill something."

"You can try," says Svetlana, and she lifts a cloth bag and dumps onto the giant graph paper thing a pile of little metal monsters. "It's going to be a tough fight. I hope none of you have any plans."

It is a tough fight. It's a long fight too, and it proves to be my first time ever listening to an entire opera. The opera is more tolerable than I would have guessed, but the game: I am a little disappointed at how little Svetlana gets to talk or do anything other than roll dice behind the screen and announce damage. The other three, meanwhile, are shouting orders at each other, calling each other by fantasy names, and getting visibly more and more nervous as the battle goes on. Finally the last monster falls. All the player characters are deeply wounded, even near death. If they rest, they will survive.

Ambient—Reggie's healing character—climbs to his feet, from what I can tell. "I'd like to investigate the chill in here," he says. "It must be related to the blue runic markings in the center of the chamber."

"Do you approach?" asks Svetlana.

"Dude," says Abraham. "Don't be a moron."

Reggie glares at his companion, and who could blame him. I already hate this guy Abraham, and I only met him about two hours ago. Reggie closes his eyes to push through the aggravation of listening to Abraham, and as he opens them says to Svetlana, "Perception check?"

"Sure."

Reggie rolls and calls out, "Fifteen."

"That's with your bonus?" Svetlana asks, and none of this makes sense to me, either, trust me.

Anyway, Reggie nods, and Svetlana leans back in her chair. She pulls her braid around front and holds it in both hands. "You identify several of the symbols glowing on the floor of the chamber, within the runic circle. They represent a minor demon, not of this dimension, but frequently worshipped by local shamanistic races and even some of the higher races— the humans, the dwarves—that live in the wild areas outside the main village."

Abraham sighs, and I glare at him. He doesn't notice.

"In the center of the runic circle, something is moving," Svetlana goes on. "You at once recognize it as a face of the demon himself."

"It's really him?" Reggie says. "Not an illusion?"

"You can't tell." Svetlana has a die in one hand now, and she's shaking it absentmindedly.

"Is it trapped?" Reggie asks. "Can it get out?"

"You can't tell that, either," Svetlana says. She puts the die down in front of her, then leans forward on her elbows and props her chin on her hands.

"Let's just get back to town," Abraham says. "We can come back and check on this in the morning, once we're rested."

"I think it's probably fine," Reggie says, and Abraham guffaws. "I use a healing salve on myself."

"Okay," says Svetlana.

"And I approach the rune."

"How close?"

"How far am I now?" asks Reggie, and he counts squares on the giant graph paper in the center of the table. "Thirty feet. I'll move in to . . . ten feet."

"Okay." Svetlana taps her pen. "Nothing happens."

"Boring!" You can probably guess who says that.

"Another perception check," Reggie says, grabbing his dice. He throws, and this time: "Twenty-three!"

"Your power to perceive this rune and all it means is . . ." She pauses, lowers her chin, thinking of the word. "Palpable."

"It is?" says Reggie.

Svetlana nods. "So palpable, in fact, that the demon trapped within the rune—"

"I knew it," says Abraham. "Moron."

"Shh."

"—bursts out," Svetlana finishes. "Fragments of the stone floor and of the rune itself—icy blue shards of elemental power—fly through the chamber like shrapnel."

"Whoa," I say. I can't help it.

"Much of it strikes your body and face," Svetlana says, her eyes still boring into Reggie's very soul.

"Crap."

"Fortitude check," Svetlana says, and Reggie rolls. I don't know much about this game, but I'm thinking a pair of threes is probably not a lot.

"The damage is severe," she says.

"Am I bloody?" Reggie asks.

"You were bloody before you walked over to the damn thing," Abraham points out. "Dammit." He throws down his pencil and crosses his arms.

"Language, Mr. Polsen," calls Ms. Grimmish.

"You're out cold, Ambient," Svetlana says. "You fall to the hard stone ground and black out."

"Ha," says Abraham. "Happy now, idiot?"

Reggie doesn't respond. Roan does: "Shut up, Abraham."

"Okay," he says, his voice thick and rich like sarcastic hot fudge.

"As you lie on the ground in a pool of your own blood"— wow—"the demon himself crawls out of the gaping hole the rune has left in the chamber floor."

"Oh, awesome," says Abraham.

"He stands at the edge of the elemental abyss, amidst a shimmery blue light—a clear sign of the great power within, no doubt leaking into your world from the demon's home dimension—and lets out a mighty roar."

"What's he look like?" Roan says, squinting.

Svetlana is glad to be asked, and she produces a drawing. He's pretty amazing: She did this one all in blue ink on the lined spiral notebook paper. He's huge—I guess; there's not really any scale—and muscular, and overall humanish. His face, though, is twisted and gnarly, inside out and grotesque, and on his head are two bent horns, one pointing up in a general spiral shape, the other curved and cracked and lower, aimed at his shoulder. Sprouted from his back are two enormous wings, like the wings of a bat, and they're torn and nearly skeletal. Strictly for looks, I guess—very imposing, the whole package.

Any feelings I've developed for this girl are entirely ridiculous. She is the most amazing person on earth, and I will withdraw any attempts to get closer to her.

"Nice," says Abraham, and he gives this groovy little nod, like Greg might upon listening to a song I play for him. It occurs to me that Abraham reminds me of Greg quite a bit—in-game Greg, to be specific.

"This is the demon," Svetlana says. "He is called Kor'Baela. The people of this village have worshipped him and prayed to him for centuries—they are a secret and secretive cult, and when they learn the rune has been shattered, they will undoubtedly come for you."

"This just gets better and better," says Abraham. "Jeez, Lana. Way to set us up for the worst wipe in the history of gaming."

She cocks her head at him. "Come on," she says. "Don't blame me for this."

Abraham sighs. "Initiative," he says, and he casts his dice.

Roan does too, and so does Svetlana. Reggie doesn't even reach for the bones, since his player character is lying in a pool of his own blood, dead to the world.

Abraham wins the roll. He leans forward and claps his hands together, shuffles his papers to check on his daily and encounter abilities. "This is the same encounter?" he confirms, and it is, per Svetlana's nod. "I still have my daily."

"Okay," Svetlana says.

There's a roll. Abraham's PC, Thug, charges at the demon, knocking it down and reducing its armor and attack power by half.

Roan cheers; her PC, Meridel, flashes through the chamber, appearing behind the demon, and then thrusts both her daggers into and under its rib cage. It shrieks in pain, doubles over, and spits up blood.

But it doesn't fall. Instead it lifts its head, and its eyes shine with blue light. It grabs Ambient, Reggie's PC, by the throat, lifts him over its head, and, after a chant in a language neither conscious character can understand, fires the poor wizard against the chamber wall.

"Fortitude check," Svetlana says, and she swallows. "I'm sorry, Reggie," she adds in a softer voice—a voice that's not in the chamber with them, underground and about to die, but up here, in room 3212.

Reggie grabs his fedora and puts it on, low on his head so it blocks us from seeing his eyes. He cups his hands around two of his polyhedral dice, raises them before his face, and gives them a dozen or so short and violent shakes. Then he releases the dice into the center of the table.

"Crap," he says. He lets his head fall forward onto his character sheet, and his fedora topples from his head and falls upside down on the table.

"Two?" Abraham says. "You rolled a goddamn two?"

"Is that bad?" I say quietly, smirking.

Svetlana narrows her eyes at me and says, "Shh."

"He's dead," Roan says.

"He's goddamn dead," Abraham confirms. He runs both his hands through his greasy hair. "Okay, how do we fix this?"

"We don't," Reggie says. His voice is muffled by the table his face is still on. "I'm the healer, and I can't cast revive on myself."

Svetlana shuffles her papers and lets out a long, "Well . . ."

Roan covers her face with both hands. "A potion," she says. Then she jumps in her chair onto her knees. "I loot the body."

Abraham snaps and points at her excitedly. "Yes! He has a potion. He got it from the fat ogre we killed in the woods on Sunday night."

Svetlana chews the inside of her cheek, then nods once. "Okay, roll for, um, agility."

"To loot a goddamn dead body?" Abraham snaps. "How much agility does that take?"

"The potion bottles are fragile glass and very tiny," Svetlana says. "Roll your twenty, and get"—she glances at Roan's character sheet—"a three or better. It's a formality."

"Fine, fine," Roan says. She grabs her die and tosses it: 19. "There."

"Congratulations," Svetlana says. She looks at Reggie's inventory list. "You loot five health potions, ten attack power potions, one vial of smoke bomb, one broken dagger, all his armor, his Staff of Rejuvenation, and three New Life potions."

"New Life potions!" Abraham says, leaning forward and thrusting his first finger at the dungeon master. "She feeds one to Reggie—I mean, to Ambient."

Roan nods with enthusiasm, but Svetlana shakes her head. "Sorry, he's dead. The potion dribbles down his chin and is absorbed into the floor of the cave. You now have two New Life potions left."

"What?!" Abraham says.

Ms. Grimmish calls from the front of the room, "Please, Abraham. Keep it down."

"Sorry," he calls back. Then he repeats—quietly this time, "What?"

Reggie rolls his head to face Abraham without picking it up from the table. "It's an auto-revive potion," he says.

"Like a soulstone," I say.

Abraham looks at me, eyes wide. "You game?"

I shrug. "Not really."

Svetlana squints at me. "You're going to explain this, you know."

"Not now," I say. "There's a man lying dead in a cave and you want to know my gaming history? Come on. Priorities."

I smile at her, and she smiles back and then turns to face Roan and Abraham.

"Reggie . . . Ambient had to drink it before he died, not after," she explains, though I think we all get it by this time.

"Which I did," Reggie says. "Six turns ago."

"But the potion only last five turns," Svetlana adds.

Abraham leans slowly in his chair and glares at the face-on-table Reggie. "So it is indeed Ambient's fault after all."

Reggie picks his head up and glares at Svetlana. "You could have warned me."

"Don't blame her," Roan says. She shifts in her seat and pulls one foot up under her butt. "Ambient messed up. We messed up."

"So now what?" Abraham says. He sits back in his chair and sulks.

"Now," Roan says, "you and I wait here, in the dark, and hope our lovely and brilliant and—"

"Easy with the flattery," Svetlana puts in.

"—um, dungeon master won't send any roaming kobolds after us," Roan finishes. "Reggie can roll a new character and join us."

Svetlana shrugs and smiles. She pats Reggie's head.

"But what about Ambient?" Reggie says. "I liked Ambient. And a new character will be, like, three levels behind."

"We don't have a goddamn choice, Reggie," Abraham says. His shoulders sag farther. "Just take a blank sheet and start rolling. We don't have all day."

"Um," I say. "What about me?"

"What about you?" Abraham says through a sneer.

Apparently he still doesn't like me.

"Remember? Newest member of the Central High Gaming Club?" I say. "Why don't I roll a character? I can catch up and rez your healer."

Svetlana winks at me and then turns to the others. "What do you think? Want to add a player to your party?"

"Another leader?" Abraham says. "What are we going to do with another goddamn leader?"

"There must be a class I can roll that can resurrect and do decent ranged DPS, right?" I say. I have to admit I'm getting kind of excited at the prospect. This tabletop gaming thing is more fun and exciting than I would have predicted. I glance at Svetlana, hoping I'm going about this the right way.

"DPS?" Reggie says, finally lifting his head. He eyes Svetlana. "He's a *video* gamer, Lana."

"Oh *god*," Roan says. She slumps onto the table. "Just kill me now."

"We can probably arrange that," Svetlana says. She shuffles her papers, as if to produce a band of roaming kobolds. "Let's see what's wandering the cave. . . ."

"Okay, okay," Abraham says, slapping the table. "Let it be known I find this course of action to go completely against the spirit of the campaign, the spirit of the game, and the spirit of role-playing in general. But if your new boyfriend wants to roll a cleric or paladin, fine."

I look at my shoes, then risk a glance at Svetlana—her face is pink, and her eyes are on her maps—and then back at my shoes. I can see Abraham's shoes under the table too. They're nearly identical to mine, and they're bouncing madly.

"Um," I say, "so, how do I start?"

"I'll walk you through it," Svetlana says, but the joy of the game—which had seemed to beam from her eyes and teeth moments ago—is gone. Her voice is quiet, as pale as the skin on her temples. She hands me a blank character sheet over her screen. "Use Reggie's dice for now. Next time, have your own."

I take the dice Reggie offers and mutter a timid "Thanks."

CHAPTER 38

SVETLANA ALLEGHENY
<SHOULD BE AT WORK>

My phone vibrates and sings "Alarm Call" the moment I reach my bedroom. "Did you see it yet?" It's Reggie. He sounds tired, depressed, and of generally foul mood.

"See what?" I still haven't fully caught my breath from the bike ride home and the climb up two flights of steps.

"Check your Facebook messages," Reggie says. "Abey must have gone straight from 3212 to the media center and typed like a madman."

I slip into my desk chair, drop my tote bag next to it, and wake up my laptop. After a few clicks, I'm staring at this message from Abraham to the rest of us Gaming Club members. His picture is there, beside the message. He's leaning in close to the camera, with his bangs long and over his eyes and his mouth open just the tiniest bit.

"Read it," says Reggie. "Read it out loud. I wanna hear it again." He's been crying, I realize, and he's outside, walking probably, shivering his way through Frogtown, the neighborhood where he lives.

Reggie, Roan, and Lana—

Please consider this email my official resignation from the Central High School Gaming Club. Due to recent events of a personal and financial nature, I have decided I no longer can—nor wish to—commit the time and energy required by this club or the interpersonal relationships and dramatic goings-on therein. That's to say nothing of the unethical gaming that went on this afternoon.

"What?"

"I know," says Reggie. He lights a cigarette and takes a drag. His exhale is decidedly loud. "Keep reading."

Furthermore, as I will be eighteen in just a few weeks, I have decided, in close collaborative discussion with my parents, that it's time for me to find a job. Of course, I will be attending the U in the fall, and I am looking forward to beginning my life as a new adult on the right foot, financially and socially.

"I think his lawyer wrote this for him," Reggie says.
I nod, though he can't see me, and continue.

Effective immediately, my priority after school, beginning the instant the final bell ends its dulcet tone,

will be finding employment. Once I have found a job, of
course my priority will become the job itself.

"Ugh."

"Mmhm," says Reggie. "You'll love what's next."

Please know I will always count you three among
my closest and dearest friends. (I cannot say the
same about Cole, whom I never liked, nor about that
sophomore dirtbag Lana brought into the club this
afternoon.) However, I think it would be best if we didn't
continue hanging out.

"What?!"

"Which part?"

I scan the passage again. "All of it!"

Reggie laughs. "He's jelly."

"Of Lesh?"

"Of course," says Reggie in his eye-roll voice. "Honestly,
Lana, if you and Lesh haven't made out, hooked up, and broke
up by New Year's, I'll eat my hat."

"Shut up," I say. "You love that hat."

"I really do."

"But whatever, Abey is way over me," I say.

"If you say so," says Reggie. "Look, whatever. I gotta get
home before the 'rentals. Love you."

"Bye, Reggie," I say. I tap the end button and drop my
phone on the bed. It looks like Gaming Club's pardon was
merely a reprieve.

* * *

Mom and Dad are in the kitchen, working on supper. Henny sits at the island with a sloppy pile of worksheets in front of her, Mom's iPad next to them, and a textbook opened to its middle, facedown.

"Lana," says Dad as I step into the fray. "How was school?" He doesn't look up from the carrot he's dicing, nor Mom from the butternut squash she's struggling with on the big wooden slab of a cutting board next to him.

"Miserable," I say, because it was. It started miserably, in a chilly wind, with me standing before the boys in black like a moron. Its middle was miserable, because though I planned to spend lunch on my own in the library with my spiral notebook and four-color pen, I would rather have spent it with Lesh in the cafeteria, and I could have done without the visit from Lesh's sociopath girlfriend. And its end was miserable, because even though yeah, Lesh showed up, Gaming Club was a nearly unbearable mess of death and failed romance and awkwardness betwixt the two, followed by Abraham's depressing missive.

"Abraham quit Gaming Club," I say. It's the only part I care to share, and Mom gasps. "Via email," I add. It occurs to me that I'll have to break this news to Lesh at lunch tomorrow. His membership in the Central High School Gaming Club will be the shortest club membership on record, at exactly three hours and fifteen minutes.

"That's cold," says Dad.

"It's worse than cold," I say, hopping up on the stool next to Henny. The worksheets are math, so she's struggling. It's a familial handicap, I suppose. "It's the end of the GC."

"Oh?" says Mom. I can't tell yet whether she can or cannot care less.

I tap the iPad, slide my finger around, and bring up a puzzle game I like. You have to stop a spider from eating a bunch of flies. While I cut spiderwebs, thereby eliminating the arachnid's route to the trapped flies, I explain to Mom the five-member minimum to secure a faculty adviser, a space in the school, and extracurricular and transcript credit for membership.

"Ouch," says Dad. He finally looks up. "There's something I've been wanting to talk to you about anyway, and now it's even more relevant."

"Oh, not now," says Mom quietly, like I'm not going to hear.

"Why not?" says Dad. He folds his flexible cutting board and dumps the diced carrots into the hot pot on the stove beside him. When they hit the oil, they pop and sizzle, and he grabs a celery stalk and starts in on that.

"Just say it." I shift in my stool and lean on the counter, pushing the iPad to the side. I can't finish this board anyway, and right now I can't bear to watch the spider devour the poor little fly.

"Your mother and I think you should get a job," says Dad.

Henny looks at me sideways an instant.

"Ah," I say, and I hop down from the stool. "I don't suppose you've been talking to the Polsens."

"Who?"

"Abraham's parents," Mom explains, because Dad, typically, cannot keep my friends' names straight. I don't find that insulting at all, why do you ask? "No, sweetie," Mom goes on.

"We've only been talking to each other."

"Well, not only," says Dad. "You know my friend Scott Hermann, right?"

"Yes," I say, and it hits me like the smell of yogurt-and-banana-stained pants that have sat on the floor of my bedroom overnight: Scott Hermann, my parents' friend by way of the Thunder fan club, is a franchisee. "The juice place?"

"That's right," says Dad.

"Honey," says Mom, even more quietly. "You didn't." She's holding the big chef's knife point up in front of her. The butternut squash sits half peeled on the cutting board.

He nods and adds the celery to the pot. "I did. He was very gracious."

"Dad!" I say. I actually stomp my stupid foot too.

He stops with an onion in his hand and turns around, leans against the counter. "It is not easy for a girl still in high school to find work, never mind work in a nice, clean environment in a good neighborhood."

"So am I supposed to be thanking you?" I say.

"Yes, frankly."

"I can't believe you," I say. "When were you going to drop this on me? It's like, Oh hey, you have to get a job, and by the way, you start Monday?"

"Tuesday."

"Dad!" I say, again with the foot stomp. "I have Gaming Club on Tuesday."

"You just said—"

"But you didn't know that at the time!"

Dad turns his head a little, like I'm speaking French, which I'm pretty sure I'm not, and then faces the counter again to start on the onion. Henny's eyes are about to pour with tears, not because she is overcome with emotion at watching yet another spat between myself and the parentals, but because her whole head—eyes, nose, throat, ears—is deeply susceptible to all irritants, including the microscopic onion fragments that Dad is about to unleash. It's almost like he's got me on the verge of tears, and he wants Henny to join me.

She must sense the burn starting, because she gathers her papers and textbook to move to the living room. I decide to follow, and I drop onto the stinky leather couch beside her. The pillows sigh with me as I sink into them.

"Do you think you'll get free juice?" Henny says as she works her eraser into problem seventeen like she's trying to skin a rhino with a rock. When she's done, the paper is thin and torn in spots. "I love their juice."

"How many times have you tried that one?" I ask, leaning over.

Henny shrugs. "A few times. Do you know how to do it?"

I take the paper from her. "Lemme see," I say, and she settles against my arm to watch.

CHAPTER 39

LESH TUNGSTEN
<FOOLS IN LOVE, REDUX>

Svetlana is all kinds of bummed for the rest of the week. She doesn't show at lunch, and it's only when I spot her in front of the school on Friday afternoon that she finally seems to see me and stops her bike.

"How's lunch been?" Before I can answer, though, as if I have an answer, she barrels on: "I've been in the library for days, I swear." She pats the tote bag in her bike's basket. "This whole campaign to rework." Apparently Abraham, my biggest fan in the Gaming Club, quit after my first meeting. I have the nagging feeling my presence had something to do with it. Svetlana doesn't say as much, but his "new boyfriend" crack was a dead giveaway.

Then she shrugs, kicks off, and heads toward Crocus Hill, disappearing in a swirl of hair and skirt.

I'm at home on Saturday, actively avoiding running Svvetlana, who I've been neglecting since the issue of Vent came up, and watching my mom go through the stack of mail that's been growing on the kitchen counter all week. Tonight will be different, though, because I don't plan to be standing here long. In fact, in a few minutes a busted-up 1991 POS will be pulling up to Greg's house down the block, and I intend to get in.

"So," I say. "I've done all my homework, and it's almost Saturday night."

"Mmhm," she says, because she isn't listening, and it's not like she's the one who's been paying close attention to the calendar, waiting for the sentence handed down by Dad—judge, jury, prosecuting attorney, and executioner—to end.

"There's a concert in Burnsville," I say as I open the fridge for a can of pop. "At the Warehouse." That's the teen center. It's square as hell, I know, but they get decent bands on the weekends sometimes. And this weekend, What Dwells Within is back in town. "Me and Greg are going."

"That's very funny," she says, "and 'Greg and I.'"

I crack open the can. "It's not a joke," I say, and nod toward the calendar as I take a long pull.

Mom smirks at me and cocks her hip, then, with her eyebrows up, finally checks the date. "What am I supposed to be seeing?"

I give up. "It's over, Mom," I say. With my thumb, I flick the tab on top of the can. It goes *boing!* "I'm not grounded anymore."

She faces me and lets her jaw drop open, but smiles, too.

"Has it been so long?" she says, and she comes at me with her arms out, like for a hug. "Oh, my little grounded boy is all grown up."

I deflect. "Okay, okay," I say, turning to the side and giving her my shoulder. I head for the door. "I'm just telling you. I'm going now." Like, right now, because even my dad, who works nearly every Saturday, has to come home eventually. For all I know he had a crap day and will end up extending my sentence. Better to get out while the getting's good.

"Don't be too late," she says.

"I know."

"How are you getting to Burnsville?"

"Three seniors are going," I say, and I struggle for a moment to try to remember a name, but I'm stuck on Jelly. It hits me: "Weiner!" I say. "Justin Weiner. You've met him."

"I have?"

"I think," I say, and I pretend like I'm trying to remember when, but I'm pretty sure she hasn't.

"Just keep your phone on."

I'm already stepping into my tennis shoes and pulling on my coat. "Always."

"And no drinking!"

Slam.

It's already nearly dark, and my eyes are playing tricks on me. Last summer, they redid the sidewalks and gutters in our quarter of the neighborhood—that's about four square blocks, and it took all of the summer and well into fall. Mom says they could have worked faster, but Dad tells her she doesn't know the work, she doesn't know the men, and she doesn't know anything, so she should shut up.

Whatever the reason, they had to hurry at the end, and they only replaced some squares of the sidewalks—the ones that were deeply cracked and in need of replacing, and the ones they damaged while they worked on the gutters and the boulevards. The rest of them, deemed okay, were left as is. This means that now our sidewalks seem randomly made up of old and new squares of cement—some pristine and freshly brushed and painted, some old and worn and a much darker gray.

Sometimes, when I'm walking down the block from our place to the Deels', as I step out of the light of the streetlamp and my foot falls from a new, clean cement square to an old, dirty one, I feel like the old one might fall away, like it isn't real, and in an instant I'll fall right through the world. I'll land in an abyss. Maybe I'll fall forever. Maybe I'll just die.

That's what I used to think. Tonight, though, I wish for it. I wish for my foot to find that empty old square, because I think at its bottom I'll find something magical and amazing, and I'll be Svvetlana, filled to bursting with love for the world.

I'm crammed against the door in the back of Weiner's Oldsmobile. Greg is on my left and practically in my lap. Past him is Fio, and then a pair of senior girls I hardly know. Cheese called out their names when they climbed in outside the Starbucks on Selby Avenue after we waited for them for, like, twenty minutes, but I couldn't hear him over the music blasting from the speakers. Weiner isn't worth much money, and his car even less, but he clearly sank a fair amount into the sound system in here. It's positively epic.

In front, Jelly is in the middle and smoking a cigarette, squashed between Weiner and Cheese. They're joking and passing a bowl, so the car is filling with two kinds of smoke. I only know they're joking around from the frequent guffaws and the movement of their mouths, but again, I can hear nothing over the music. Next to me, Deel has his phone out and is scrolling around. Fio's fly is open. The two girls on the end are talking—they manage over the din by speaking directly at the other's ear, and then switching for the reply, in a way that two guys would never do. After an especially thunderous guffaw from the front seat, Jelly turns her head and winks at me, very hammy, and I wonder what joke I'm the butt of.

The Warehouse is packed. It's five bucks a head, and if we came down here from the Cities, you can imagine what the kids in the suburbs are willing to do, and how far to travel, for a decent show that isn't a pop-singing dink or radio-friendly light metal at the Xcel Energy Center. We're streaming through the parking lot—all of us kids, I mean—forcing moms and dads in drop-off minivans to move slow and swervy around us. There's nothing they can do. They're so woefully outnumbered among us miscreants in black and blue and chains and studs and long hair and shaved heads. So they try to smile, some of them, and get sneers and backward Vs in response.

Jelly wiggles and slaps her butt at a dad in a Subaru.

"Jelly just made a deposit in the old man's spank bank," bellows Fio. Cheese and Weiner like that one. They clap and hoot and flip the dad the finger. Jelly accepts a couple high fives too.

At the door, we hand over our crumpled five-dollar bills and move into the main room, through a wall of heat into a mass of writhing, sweaty bodies. I'm being pushed from the back—at least three hands on my shoulders and arms—and we worm through the crowd of gyrating metal fans toward the stage. WDW is already on and ripping through "Canvas."

"I knew it," I said over my shoulder to Greg. "We missed the beginning 'cause we had to stop to pick up those two skanks."

"We definitely did," Greg says, and he's ogling one of them as she digs around in her bag and finds a bundle of singles.

I shake my head at him and push into the crowd, keeping my eyes on the stage. WDW are barely out of high school, which is definitely one of the reasons the bunch of us are such big fans. This song has an amazing blast beat after the intro, and they just hit it. The pit starts going absolutely mental, and I'm thrown into the deepest reaches of the crowd.

"Push through," says Jelly at my ear, so at least one of the hands on my back is hers. "Keep going."

Her breath makes my shoulder tingle, and my neck, so I can hardly disobey, and when we're past the thrashing mob, she edges me to the right side of the stage, near a fat column holding up the ceiling and away from the beefy security men who stand with their arms crossed in front of the stage, on the other side of the barrier. The stack of PA speakers is right next to us, and I can feel the bass drum and the whole bottom end in my gut and my chest. When I turn and face the band, Jelly presses up against me from behind. It's just us—just me and Jelly—behind the column. Greg and Fio and the rest are in the mass of bodies someplace.

Her arms come around my waist and she presses something into my hands. I look down at a leather-wrapped flask as she shouts at my ear, "Drink it." She has to shout. I can still barely hear her. I take the flask and get a chill from the scrape of the cap unscrewing—metal on metal. I sniff it: peppermint schnapps. It burns and cools and reminds me of my grand-mother at Christmas.

Jelly slides around me and takes back the flask, slips it into her pants, which is how she got it in here to begin with, and now she presses her back against me from the front. She's lean-ing on me, something like dancing, and I'm more than a little excited and a little afraid and kind of confused. This is Jelly—she's older than me, experienced, notorious even. It has to be some kind of joke, because there is no way Greg was right. No way Fio was right. There is no way Jelly is into me. There is no way she likes me, not like that. Not at all, probably.

I don't know what I'm supposed to do. I can hardly think, with my head still shivering from the schnapps, and my brain rattling around under the power of WDW's powerful bottom end, and every nerve in my body tingling from Jelly's bottom end. Jelly doesn't leave it up to me. She reaches back with both hands and takes my wrists, wraps my arms around her waist, and holds my hands against her stomach. I thank god it isn't bare, because I'm not sure I could handle that level of arousal in public, and then I curse god for the same reason. As if she can read my mind—oh lord, if she could—Jelly leads my hand under her T-shirt and against her skin. With her other hand she reaches up over her head and holds the back of my neck, pulls my head down, and whispers in my ear, "I'm drunk, Tung. Are you drunk, Tung?"

"No."

"You should be, Tung," she says. "It's more fun, Tung." She pushes the flask into my hands again, and I take another sip and hand it back. I look down over her shoulder to watch her stash it in the front of her jeans again.

"Why do you keep saying Tung?" I ask, but she can't hear me. She just dances, her hand on the back of my neck again, her butt still pressing against the front of my pants, my hand still flat under hers and on her stomach. The song ends, and Jelly turns to face me, barely letting an inch of space develop between our bodies. Both hands behind my neck now, she still writhes against me.

"The song's over," I say.

"Tung," she says, smiling up at me. She puts her hands on my chest and nudges me backward, past the big column, into the corner of the big black-and-blue room, far past the stage, away from the gyrating crowd and the surge of synthetic strings that's filling the room now, getting us ready for the next explosion of screams and blast beats and ear-piercing lead riffs, all good things. "Come on, Tung."

In the corner, in the deeper darkness on our own, she's at my throat. Her lips are on my skin. Her hands are on the back of my head, pulling at my hair, gripping my skull like she'd eat my whole head if she could. And my hands—my hands are on her back, my hands are under the back of her shirt, my hands are on her waist, and I don't know how far I can go. I know how far I want to go. It's taking every ounce of effort I have to control myself. My brain keeps spinning, swirling, looking for a clue—any hint to tell me how much I need to hold back, and how much I need to let go. But then we're kissing. The air rushes from my lungs, the sense flees from my mind, and I pull her against me harder. Her lips taste like cigarettes and peppermint schnapps and Dr. Pepper lip gloss—smoke and candy and sugar and flames. It's delicious and disgusting, just like Jelly.

There's no more blood in my brain. It's all rushed to my fingertips and my lips and tongue and other places it can be more useful. The music has become a violent white noise, a backdrop to the pounding of my heart and the humming in my mouth, from her tongue and her lips. My hands act on their own now, down her back, on her butt—just for an instant—and up and down her thighs. She pushes against me so I fall against the wall, and she wraps a foot around my ankle. Her lips never stop. She hums as we kiss, as our lips mash madly against each other, like the mouths of hungry wolves. I can't keep up. She's going to kill me. And suddenly she stops, she gasps for a deep breath, and she holds me by the collar of my coat.

"Let's go to the car," she says.

"What?"

"Just come on," she says, and she pulls me by the hand: the back exit—"No re-entry without a stamp," but we don't even pause—through the parking lot, and her hands are running up and down my arms, between parked cars, to the big baby-blue Oldsmobile with rust accents, where the doors are unlocked. Into the backseat, Jelly underneath me, and then next to me with her back against the seat backs. Then she's on top of me, crouched under the low roof of the car, her jet-black hair falling over my face and my neck. She leans down more and we kiss like we're hungry again. Her hands are everywhere. Mine are too. She's working on my belt. She's popping the button on my jeans. She pulls her face away and smiles down at me. Her lips and their edges are extra red, extra pink, extra alive. She looks beautiful. For the first time, I see her as she is: a beautiful girl, with an amazing smile. She's not so different from Svetlana, even. She's not the dark to her light. She's not the evil to her good. And she's . . .

"You're so beautiful," I say, and in the quiet of the car, with the only sounds till now our desperate breathing and kissing, and her hums and the tickle of the ends of her hair against my ears, my voice is too loud, too desperate and childish. She laughs and hits me. She actually forms her little black-finger-nailed hands into fists and pounds my shoulder.

263

"Tung," she says, "please tell me you're not some secretly sappy boy who is actually falling in love with me right now."

"What?" I say, because obviously it's all I should be allowed to say, ever, to this girl or any other. But my face goes hot, and probably red, and I'm not falling in love with her. I'm really not. But it's too late.

"Oh *god*," she says, and she awkwardly kind of sits up and looks at me, shaking her head. "Tung."

"It's not like that," I say, but by the sound of my voice—the desperation (can you blame me?), the breathlessness—I know she won't believe me. She pulls down her shirt, covering her stomach and the piercing, the belly I'll see over and over for the rest of the school year when she prowls the halls, and every time I'll wish I'd kept my stupid mouth shut.

"Sorry, Tung," she says. "We could have had some fun, but I do not need a little boy following me around like a lovesick puppy."

"Come on," I say. "I wouldn't do that."

She looks at me—a long look, like maybe she'll change her mind, but instead opens the door and backs out. "God, I need a cigarette," she says, and she's gone, sparking up as she walks away. I sit up in time to see her head in a puff of bluish smoke as she walks around the far side of the Warehouse. All I can do now is wait for the show to end, so I can get a ride home and get to my room, where for all I care my grounding can be extended until the end of high school, because I plan to never show my face around any of these people again.

LEVEL 50

CHAPTER 40

LESH TUNGSTEN
<GUYS IN REAL LIFE>

Greg shows up at our house the day after the WDW show. It's after noon, and Mom is at work and Dad is watching football. The Vikings are playing who the hell cares, so I bring Greg upstairs and let him have the seat at the desk. Then I fall face-first onto my bed.

"What's your problem?" he says. I hear my mouse clicking, but I don't have the energy to give a crap or even check what he's doing.

"I blew it with Jelly last night," I admit. On the ride home last night, I said nothing—not to Greg, not to Jelly, not to anyone. When Weiner dropped us at the corner, I didn't say good night or good-bye. I didn't glance at Jelly, and I didn't even slap five to Greg. I just hurried up the path and went inside, up the steps, and into bed. I've hardly moved since.

He lets out a low whistle, like it's big news, but the mouse is clicking, and now he's typing something. "What's your password?"

"What?"

"I'm logging you in," he says, and I finally lift my head. "That game card hasn't expired yet."

"Oh," I say, and I drop my head again, then mumble my password into the mattress. I hear the keys clacking away, and then I realize. "Wait!"

But it's too late.

"Whoa," he says. "What the hell?" I'm off the bed and trying to shove him out of the desk chair so I can hit escape before he jumps to any accurate conclusions. I'm way too late, and he shoves back, and he knocks my arms away. He slaps the enter key, and the load screen comes up.

I drop onto the bed and swear.

"A secret toon?" he says. Svvetlana appears, bouncing in the wild. The pink and green text scrolls up the chat window almost immediately. It's no surprise; none of them have seen me since they started talking about heroic gear, raiding, and Vent. "She's level fifty."

He leans in and slaps the C key. "And she's decked in epic gear. My god. She's better geared than your orc."

"Yup," I say, and I lean forward and try to reach the keyboard. "And now you know, so just log and get over it."

"An elf," he says, blocking my hand. "A freaking elf. And a priest? This is the gayest thing I've see—" He stops, his mouth still open.

"What?"

"Her name is Svvetlana?"

"So?"

"Isn't that the girl you've been having lunch with every day?" Greg says. He doesn't know I've hardly seen her all week. He also doesn't know that after last night, I'll keep avoiding her next week, too. "The girl who got you to join the D and D club?"

"It's not the D and D club," I point out, like it's relevant. Things are starting to come out now, and my stomach is flipping around like I've had too much vodka and banh mi.

"Okay, so you named your toon after her," he says, and I can't argue.

"Fine," I say, throwing up my arms like it's no big thing, and kind of hoping he'll let his guard down on blocking me from reaching the keyboard. It doesn't work. I lean back on the bed again. "So I have a crush on Svetlana. Big deal. She's hot." She is. It's true. And she's the reason I started playing. Sure, I was grounded too, but it's not like I've never had time on my hands before. Her drawings, her name, her body—that's what I was after in Greg's world.

"Well . . . ," says Greg, leaning in even closer, peering at the tiny green and pink text scrolling up the chat box in the corner, "some dude Stebbins says he's been wondering what happened to you."

"Please log out right now."

"He missed you."

"Deel, just log. Trust me and log."

"Tung," he says, and he finally looks away from the screen of my laptop and back at me, "this dude thinks you're a girl."

Sigh. I let myself fall back all the way and stare at the ceiling. My feet are still hanging off the edge of my bed, though, so Greg kicks my foot. Hard.

"Did you hear what I just said?"

"Yes."

"Are you going to answer me?"

"Probably not."

He hits a few keys—not enough that he could be replying to Stebbins, but enough that he's at least logging out. Finally. The laptop slams closed.

"It's not a big deal," I start.

"You're a G.I.R.L., Lesh," he says. "A guy in real life. It's a very big deal."

"It's not like that," I say, but I'm still not even sitting up. I don't want to look at him.

"Stebbins thinks it's like that," Greg says. "Jesus, from the crap he was typing, it sounds like you've cybered with him."

I lift my head. "What?"

"Cybersexed," he says, utterly exasperated.

"Oh, come on!" I say, throwing my head hard against the bed. "Fine, I pretended to be a girl. These guys gave me tons of free gear, free dungeon runs, free gold. And yeah, they treated me nice too, and sometimes talked to me like I was really a girl. So what?"

Greg is sighing and rubbing his face and sighing again. My whole body is tingling, and I can't tell if I'm thrilled this is finally out in the open, or if I'm scared out of my mind because

270

maybe it's a bigger deal than I thought—maybe I'm one of those guys who starts dressing up in women's clothes or gets breast implants or something. I mean, I expected Greg to laugh. I expected him to call me a fag. I thought he might even go in-game and out me as a fake and a perv, right then and there.

But none of that happens. Instead I get: "Are you serious?"

So I have to say yes, I am serious. And then I just get a head shake, and a very pale face—paler than usual—from Greg.

"I don't even know how to respond to this," he says. He's using a gentle voice, one I hardly even recognize. This is barely Greg. He gets up from the bed and moves to the door. It's an awkward dance, without eye contact, and he's extra careful to avoid brushing his jeans against my knees as he passes me, sitting on the edge of the bed. He opens the door and stands in the doorway, his backpack hanging from one hand. He looks like a little kid dragging a well-loved teddy bear.

"Why did you want to be a girl?" he says. At the last word, he screws up his face like he might puke.

I could say that I didn't want to, not really—that it had all been a slow-motion accident, gotten out of hand. But I don't say that. I just shrug.

"I don't really know."

So he pulls his hand down his face, turns around, and leaves. The sound of the Vikings game cheers up the steps and past Greg, into my room. I listen to his footsteps on the stairs. I hear the front door try to close. It always sticks.

CHAPTER 41

SVETLANA ALLEGHENY
<WORKING GIRLS>

I think everyone's avoiding me.

That's not entirely true. Roan makes herself available when she can, and she talks to me on the phone when she can. But I've been having lunch on my own—yes, in the library to work on the campaign. On Tuesday at ten forty-five, though, I showed up at the cafeteria, hoping to run into my favorite boy in black, but his seat at the Table of the Damned was empty. His brief club membership gave him and me a good excuse to exchange phone numbers, at least, so I feebly text him before unchaining my bike after school.

Me: <<Campaign is almost ready! Can you party soon? ;)>>

(There is no way he would get that pun. Texts need an unsend function.)

Lesh (an achingly long time later, and believe me that repeatedly checking one's phone for new texts is not among recommended behavior for a safe cyclist commute): <<idk keep me posted>>

I suppose what I'm trying to say is that Lesh has been avoiding me. I suppose I'm also trying to say that I might miss him. But if I'm honest with myself, maybe I've been avoiding him, for reasons entirely of my own making. And now it's Tuesday and school's over and I have to go to work.

The polo shirt is orange, emblazoned across the chest with a tiny logo of Mr. Hermann's juice shop. The bigger version is on the back, which means I don't have to see it, so I can at least pretend that this shirt is something approaching tasteful.

I'm sounding like a snob again, aren't I? Would it help if I admitted to driving to work on my first day because I didn't want to show up covered in sweat? I suppose I decided the brown behemoth was a better option than stinky Svetlana. As it turns out, I didn't think that through, because my shift started at four, and by six I'm so covered in all variety of fruity and powdery and active-culture gook that the natural smell of my postbike pits would be a welcome addition to my stench.

"Okay, Lana," Mr. Hermann says. "You seem to be getting settled in here." He's not in a polo shirt. He's in a pair of khakis and a tasteful, albeit pedestrian, blue collared shirt, much like my dad wears to his job at Target—the corporate building in Minneapolis, not one of the stores. At the stores, the employees wear outfits similar to the crisis I have on, except their polos are red.

"Yes," I say. "I'm getting the hang of it." As I say this, I'm scooping two balls of frozen yogurt into a giant blender, followed by three scoops of powder, a shot of apple juice, one cup of chopped frozen strawberries, and half a banana. I drop the blender top into its base, lower the splash guard, and flick the on switch. "That is one StrawNana Protein Blast."

"Excellent," says Mr. Hermann. He offers and I begrudgingly accept a high five. "And now I am going to leave you to it. If I'm not home in a few minutes, my wife will kill me." A wink.

"Okay," I say. "Sounds good. And we close at . . ."

"Nine on the dot," says Mr. Hermann. He's already got one hand on the door pull. "And you'll be in Kyle's capable hands for closing."

"Not literally," says Kyle, peeking in from the back room. He's the night manager—he's a short guy in his midtwenties with a shaved head and ears so full of piercings that I'm surprised he can keep a job in retail. I guess Scott Hermann isn't as bad a guy as I thought.

Mr. Hermann laughs and pulls open the door. "Okay, good luck, you two. Don't burn the place down." The door swings closed, and Kyle comes up from the back.

"It's a cold night," he says, and he comes up next to me at the front counter to lean on his elbows. "We won't be busy."

I nod slowly. *"C'est du gâteau."* He looks at me sideways, so I translate, "Piece of cake," and he smiles, but it's not a friendly smile. It's a Svetlana-is-a-crazy-person smile. I've seen it before, like in Dr. Serrano's class, or flashed across the face of the littler boy in black—even on my mom now and then. I've stopped showing her my embroidery projects.

"Dishes," I say, good and quiet and very much in English, and I vanish into the back room to tackle a sink full of blender pieces. Here's hoping it takes all night.

We get most of the cleanup done before the door is even locked, so once nine rolls around, it's a simple matter of closing out the register—actually not that simple, but believe me when I say it is a process not worth chronicling—and wiping down the counter. Kyle bags up the money, drops it into a slot in the back room, and then—and only then—unlocks the door so we can go home. It's nearly nine thirty when I park the monstrosity in the garage next to my mom's little Fiat, which I coveteth in a deeply sinful manner.

When I slip in through the kitchen door, Dad hurries out of the living room. He's got a glass of white wine, and a record's on. He's also beaming at me like I'm back from accepting my Nobel Prize in Embroidery.

"Hey," I say, keeping my manner as flat as I can.

"So?" he says, putting down his glass on the kitchen island. "How'd it go?"

I shrug: *C'est du gâteau.* "Fine. I'm pretty exhausted."

"I bet," he says, leaning on the counter. He's settling in for a chat, and in my mind I'm already standing under the high-pressure showerhead upstairs. "Was Scott there tonight to show you the ropes?"

I nod, slipping past Dad toward the steps. "Yup. Him and the night manager. It was a real thrill. I'm going to get cleaned up. I stink."

The shower, though desperately needed, proves a bad idea. By the time I step out and pull on my thick and wonderful robe, I'm practically asleep. I never thought blending yogurt drinks for a few hours could put a girl into a semicomatose state, but there it is. I consider sleeping in the spare bedroom if only to avoid climbing the steep steps to my room.

I suppose I'm not *that* tired, and I manage the trip. I step inside and there, on my bed, sitting on my folded pile of jammies, is a little box wrapped in brown paper and addressed to me. There is no return address. I scrape at the seams of tape and paper with my fingernail. Finally it comes off, and I flip open the box and slide out a small silver box. I actually gasp, because this is a little box of jewelry, and I have never been sent jewelry before, aside from the bracelet my grandmother in Reno sent up for my thirteenth birthday, and that doesn't count because it is the opposite of romantic, and if jewelry isn't romantic, then what is it?

I pull off the top, and sitting on the little square of cotton is a silver charm in the shape of a teardrop, and in its middle is a dark blue stone. When I pick it up—very gently, with the tips of my thumb and first finger—it's followed by a long whisper-thin silver chain, and I hold the charm up between my eyes and the lamp on my desk. "Wow."

Is it Fry? If so, he's got much better taste than I would've guessed—or else he's got an assistant with a very keen eye, like the gift-giver version of Cyrano de Bergerac. And if it's not Fry?

If it's not Fry, then my world has just become a whirling dervish of confusion, because if the necklace isn't from Fry, then were the flowers?

"Roan," I say aloud, and I grab my phone and dial, but Roan doesn't answer; Reggie does.

"Lana," he says. "Talk to me."

I close my fist over the charm, as if he might see it through the phone, or in the tone of my voice, and drop my fist to my lap. "How are you, Reggie?"

"I'm surviving," he says.

"Are you at the Garnets'," I say, "or is Roan at your place?"

"Ha, please," he says. "I'd not subject her to that miserable pit, particularly on a school night." The clock next to my bed says it's nearly ten.

"It's late," I say. "Ish. For a school night. For Roan."

"Yeah," he says. "I'm sleeping here. Slumber party in the basement! Woo-woo." His siren impersonation is flaccid and sad.

"Aw, Reggie," I say, and I settle back on the bed. "I'm sorry."

"For what?"

"For not being around much," I say. "I mean, since Cole. I should be."

"It's cool," he says. His voice is muffled, like he's in a tiny room, or even under a blanket. "You got your own stuff."

"You're my stuff too," I say.

"Darn right," he says, so I can smile, and then adds, "But I'm okay."

"Good." And I lean forward and drop the necklace into its box, close the lid, and knock it into my desk drawer. I flick off the lamp and Reggie talks about himself, and I close my eyes to listen, wishing I was across town with my friends on the floor in the Garnets' basement, and kick the drawer closed with my foot.

CHAPTER 42

LESH TUNGSTEN
<TESTING, TESTING>

It's Wednesday night. The self-imposed grounding is getting to me. Heck, it's gotten to me. And what's worse, with Greg having discovered Svvetlana and learned about that whole crisis, I'm not exactly amped to see him or any of the crew even at school. That leaves Svetlana herself, and thanks to my hormonal explosion on Saturday night with Jelly, I can hardly look at her without feeling like I've been cheating on her. How ridiculous is that? I've skipped lunch since Monday, offering excuses by text message when she's asked where I've been, just so I won't have to sit across from her in the cafeteria, wondering how much she can see on my face: Can she see my girl half? Can she see Jelly's lip prints, and the humiliation that followed?

Not literally, of course. But like I said, she's magical, and if anyone can see the aura of guilt and shame I'm exuding, I'd bet it's her. She even invited me to an unofficial meeting of the Gaming Club tomorrow, so I had to make up something about plans I already had. On a Thursday evening. Right. Not that I imagined for a second I'd be missed. And I'd once thought I'd be seen as the club savior. Even before Abraham's sudden departure, I didn't get quite the warm welcome I expected.

So I'm lonely, is what I'm getting at, and I'm even missing Stebbins and Dewey. But I know the instant I show up in the game, they'll bombard me with whispers, urging me to finally download and install Vent so we can raid—become a guild of note on the server, get our gear as good as it can be, and beat the bosses we've only watched YouTube videos of.

"Fine," I say, getting up from my bed, where I've spent the last twenty minutes—since dinner—staring at the darkening sky through the skylight over the bed. "Then I'll get Vent." I wake up the computer—which is a useless pile of junk when I'm not talking to my best friend and not gaming and can't concentrate on homework long enough to actually get it done. But instead of going right to the Vent download page, I make a quick detour at Google.

It takes a while to get everything set up as I want, or as close as I can get it. I've got my mic and headphones on. I've got Vent running. I've got the game open—not logged in as Svvetlana yet. And I've got one more important bit of software too: a voice changer.

Apparently it's a difficult trick to pull off. Any of the programs that seemed any good were all kinds of expensive, and the one I downloaded—free, of course—has a funny delay. I've tested it out, and whenever I say anything, it takes a second or so to hear through my headset. I can't even be sure it sounds anything like a girl. But it must be worth a try, because as it is I might as well never run my priestess again anyway.

I log in and check my friends list. It must be my lucky day: Stebbins and Dewey are both offline right now, so it's the perfect time to test this out. I find the guild's Vent room, go inside, and there are only two guys in there. I don't even know either of them, so they must be new members. I know Dewey has been spamming Trade chat lately, trying to recruit new members at any cost.

I can hear them in my headphones. They're talking about low-level gear: the best dagger set for a rogue in a PvP battleground at level nineteen. It's an unusually common conversation; I've seen it on Trade chat many times. I've seen it enough times, even, that I can add to the conversation somewhat intelligently. I decide it's now or never.

"Hello," I say into my mic. An instant later, I hear the modified voice in my ears. It's a little too muddy, like my throat is full of phlegm. But it could pass for a girl.

"What?" one of them says.

"The Dagger of Jil'Kallaer," I say. "Great agility." I can hardly get the words out; the echo at my ear makes me seasick, it's so off-kilter.

Silence.

"Hello?" I say. It's all wrong. It's so obvious now. The boys don't respond. But on the screen, the green guild text scrolls up from the bottom:

    <<lol that's a dude>>
    <<lol>>

I throw off my headset like it burns. Then I log my toon, quit Vent, and kick over my chair, mortified.

CHAPTER 43

KUGNAR
\<LOVE HURTS\>

The hulking warrior sits atop his canine mount as it tears across the red-dust fields of the orc homelands. He is in pursuit: an elf woman on a blue-and-gray-striped cat has been here. He can still smell her on the air as he makes chase. Her scent is life: it is cool like spearmint leaves, and humid like the air after a rain, and sweet like the honey he has licked from his hands after pulling it from a hive. When he catches her, he will tear her head from her body and spit down her throat.

But she is swift, and she is heading for a neutral town, where any belligerent behavior will not be tolerated by the guards. He must stop her and kill her before she gets there or his bloodlust will go unsatisfied.

Kugnar digs his heels into the wolf's haunches, and it howls and barks, increasing its speed. It's not enough. She is too far. He cannot charge from this distance, and he cannot slow her down. The neutral town is not far off now. She has escaped.

A new scent strikes his nose, and Kugnar looks to his right: he is not alone. It is a troll, a longtime ally of Kugnar's people. The troll is young and inexperienced, but it has an advantage that Kugnar does not: a long range. For this troll is a young mage.

"Stop her!" Kugnar shouts over the wind and the thundering paws of their mounts.

The troll cackles and raises his staff. A ball of ice shoots from its end, and it collapses over the elf woman. She falls to the dusty earth, frozen—helpless.

"Now she is mine," Kugnar says as he leaps from the hairy back of his mount. The troll stands back to watch; though he had one advantage, he has now used it, and this elf woman—as experienced as she is—will make short work of him if he gets too close.

The warrior, though, is without fear and without remorse and without mercy. He charges the elf woman, still slowed with cold, as she climbs to her feet. His shield connects with her weak body, sending her to the ground, stunned and dazed. Then he raises his powerful club, which gives him the strength of several oxen, and brings it down on her prone form.

"Now I will taste your blood, foul she-elf!"

But she is not without her own tricks, for she is close to the earth and its might—and she is a druid. And before the orc's club connects, she has become a cat. She darts off a short distance, and Kugnar finds himself bound by her power: the earth itself has climbed over and around him, locking him in a mound of clay and earth and the thickest roots of trees. He is immobile.

She is in her elf form again, and she is laughing. She calls upon the power of the natural world, and with two great bursts of sunlight sends the troll mage to his maker.

"And now, my noble adversary," she says, and her voice is like a melody; Kugnar almost doesn't mind his impending death, for he goes to his grave having heard her speak, "may you return to this plane someday so that you might see the evil in your ways and repent."

With her hands clasped and her eyes closed, she prays silently to her elf goddess. Kugnar's constraints are weakening, though, and he shrugs them and prepares to charge again.

His shield up, he rears back and attacks—but he is too late. The power of the sun and moon and the stars in the sky falls upon his head like cosmic bricks. He collapses. His health is low—too low. One blow will mean defeat.

The elf walks toward him, slowly, confidently. She is strong and beautiful, and he was a fool to chase her. He realizes now she was not running from him. She did not fear him. She only ran so that she might spare him this fate, this unnecessary death.

But now, with his health low, she does not leave him here to recuperate. She stands over him, so her face and front are shrouded in shadow, and she says a short prayer—one of respect for life and battle and the honor of Kugnar's race—and then brings down her staff. The world is black, and the orc is returned to the earth.

CHAPTER 44

SVETLANA ALLEGHENY
<HERMITS AND PARIAHS>

On Thursday morning, after working two closing shifts at the juice shop, my legs are sore and my hair, despite extra-long showers, smells vaguely of active cultures and banana. I'm cursing my father's name for making me take this job, and Mr. Hermann for offering it up so easily, as I pull up to the bike rack at Central, only a few steps from the wall of shame. This is what I call the short brick wall along the steps to the pool entrance—the wall where a particularly sullen Lesh talked to me like I had the plague while sitting with the girl I now know to be the scariest of my gender in all of the Twin Cities, grades K through twelve.

I'm pulling my chain from the bike basket when I spot a lanky figure, his black trench coat fluttering behind him like a superhero's cape, but his gait is less like Batman's and more like the Penguin's. I've hardly caught a glimpse of him since the Gaming Club meeting last week, so he's obviously avoiding me. But he's walking toward the big front steps alone—no little boy in black at his side. Is he avoiding everyone?

Quickly, I wrap the frame and wheels with the bike chain in a complex weave, click the padlock closed, and grab my tote. As I'm running for the steps to catch Lesh, though, a Volvo sedan chugs and coughs and screeches to the curb out front, and my favorite eleventh grader practically leaps from the thing before it even comes to a complete stop. She's in front of me, between me and the steps and the boy in black. "Svet," she says, hooking her hand into my elbow and leading me toward the steps, far too slowly.

"Hello," I say, but my eyes are on the steps far above us and the heavy black-and-glass doors at the top as Lesh pulls one open and slips inside.

"Was that Lesh?" Roan says.

"I think so," I say. "I haven't seen him in a week."

Roan's face, normally the most vivacious I know, falls, and she looks at her green tennies. I put my arm around her as we reach the doors and usher her inside, into the maelstrom of shouting and pushing and rushing to lockers and classrooms.

"It's not your fault," I say, and she shrugs. "It's really not." At least I don't think it is. I haven't been angry at her or Reggie at all since then. They gave Lesh a hard time, sure, but a little good-natured initiation is the norm in any small and exclusive group. Abraham, on the other hand, obviously had other resentment issues he was working out. "Maybe it's Abraham's."

Roan rolls her eyes at the very mention of his name. "He's

on my list too," she says as she pulls away from my one-armed hug to head to her first class. "What about you? Are you working tonight?"

I shake my head. "We're still on," I say, forcing a smile. "The three-member Gaming Club shall meet in the Garnet Dungeon in"—I check my watch—"ten hours." I don't know what we'll do, though. I haven't reshaped my campaign—yet again—for a party of two. I've only just finished working Lesh's new PC in, which was apparently a complete waste of my time.

Roan smiles back and disappears into the sea of bodies.

CHAPTER 45

LESH TUNGSTEN
<THE REAL DEEL>

On Saturday, late afternoon, I'm enjoying my self-imposed grounding. That's a total lie, but I am belly-down on my bed with Red Chord on the speakers, and I'm not actively wailing in agony. My door's been closed since after lunch, and I've been in and out of consciousness. When awake, my mind is on Svetlana—except when it wanders off to Jellytown. Both paths make my stomach twist in ways I can't begin to interpret, so I reach for my phone and stare at texts from Svetlana. I can't think of a thing to say.

That's not true. I can think of many things to say:

<<When will Gaming Club meet again? I'm ready when you are.>>
<<The cafeteria isn't the same without you.>>
<<So did you and Abraham have a thing or what?>>
<<I miss you.>>

But I'm a big wuss, so I toss the phone on the floor and go back to dozing till I'm woken by the banging and showering of Dad getting home from a job. I listen to him and Mom shout through the house about what movie they should watch for their stay-home-on-Saturday date night. I should have no problem enjoying my solitude for the rest of the weekend. The knock on my door before six, therefore, is a surprise.

"Yeah," I call out, and the door swings open. Standing in the doorway is my trench-coated friend, who I haven't spoken a word to since he left this bedroom last Sunday, head shaking and utterly disgusted by yours truly. I stand up.

"Okay," I say, arms crossed. "So what do you want?"

"I've decided to help you."

"Help me?"

He nods.

"I don't need help." Unless I need therapy. It's a distinct possibility I need therapy. But trust me when I say that will not be coming from Greg. An image flashes across my mind of Greg's psychotherapy office, with a shingle outside the door:

GREG DEEL, MSW
"JUST DEEL WITH IT"

"You need help, Tung old man, because you have a well-geared, fully leveled healing machine in that silver-haired beauty of yours." He sidles past me into my room and makes himself at home in front of the computer.

"So?"

"So it's a huge waste of spent time to let her wallow because you're such a huge freak and can no longer face the genuine and good people who helped get you this far." He clicks open the web browser and types in the address for the public database of every toon in the game. Then he enters her name. There are about ninety Svetlanas.

"Two V's," I say, leaning over him.

He makes the correction, and up she pops, all alone, the only one with two *v*'s. She's breathtaking. Even Greg says in a sacred whisper, "Wow."

"I know," I say back. "Isn't she amazing?" I'm looking at my priestess—and make no mistake, she's amazing—but I'm not thinking about her.

Greg gives me a look like I'm crazy, which like I said, I am. "Her gear," he says. "You'll be in full heroic epics if you deal with this problem."

"Oh," I say. "Right. But I can't get on Vent." I guess it's an unspoken understanding that admitting my lies to the guild is not an option I can live with. "And you need Vent to get the top gear. So I'm not getting the best gear. It's over." I drop onto the bed, pick up *Decibel*, and toss it across the room. "I'll roll a new one. I'll call her . . ."

"Him."

". . . Jelly."

That gets a laugh from the therapist. "Seriously, though," he says, closing the browser. "You're friends with Svetlana now, like, in real life, right?"

"Kind of," I say, or admit, or something. We haven't discussed my expanding and contracting social circle before, but he's obviously noticed. He's probably even mad about it, or hurt, or something. "Sure."

"So ask her to help."

Do I even need to respond to this? I try not responding.

"I'm serious," he goes on, and he swivels the desk chair to face me, leans way back, and crosses his legs. "Ask her to help. All she'd have to do is turn up on Vent one or two times. Hell, I bet she'd love this game anyway."

"I doubt it."

"I don't," he says. "It's not like I haven't seen what she's into, Tung. The girl has a sweater with a goddamn dragon stitched into the back."

I smile and he rolls his eyes.

"The point is, tell her. Ask her to help. She'd be psyched."

"About the game? Maybe," I say, leaning back to pick at a spot of dried poster putty on the wall next to the bed. "But you're skipping over the part where I admit to her that I'm so deeply obsessed with her that I've been pretending to freaking *be* her on the freaking internet."

He chews the inside of his cheek. "She might be flattered."

"She might."

"She might never speak to you again," he adds.

"Two in two weeks," I say, thinking of Jelly. My whole body tingles with the physical memory of her body on top of mine in the backseat of Weiner's car.

"Ah, Jelly will come around," Greg says. "Just be cool. I bet she'll give you another shot the next time she's rocking her hip flask."

I shrug, mainly because I don't believe him, but also because I'm not sure I want another shot. Do I want a shot with Svetlana? I can't even tell anymore which I want: to be with her, or to be her.

But he's right about one thing, even if he doesn't know it.

"Just talk to her," Greg says. He gets up, and the desk chair bounces and spins. "Feel out the situation. Don't spill everything at once."

"All right," I say, and I stand up, edging him out of the room. I think I'm just shutting him up and getting him out of my face. "I'll talk to her."

"Really?" he says, pulling his face in like a turtle. "Huh." He nods in approval. "I didn't think you'd have the stones for it, dude."

"Just get out," I say, this time physically shoving him.

"Hey, hey," he says, but he's grinning. "Just because you're a girl now doesn't mean you get to get bitchy with me."

"Get out!"

"I'm going," he says when he's got one foot out the door. "But show a little respect, huh? I think it was pretty big of me to even come over here and work on this problem with you."

"You're a gentleman and a scholar," I say, and he's in the hall now, so I shut the door in his face. And now I'm alone with my useless two-v's toon, self-imposed grounding, and the sickening urge to talk to Svetlana. I miss her, so it's been bubbling for days now, and with Greg's idea as a good excuse to get in touch, it's starting to erupt.

I grab my phone and start a new text, and then drop into my desk chair, staring at the blank screen, my fingers over the tiny keyboard, struggling for how to start this. I obviously can't explain the whole background to this catastrophe over a hundred text messages. It would take all night. Plus, I can't see how she's reacting. What if the moment I spill the major beans, she gets all disgusted with me physically? I'll want to know, so rather than wondering if she even got my texts or she got called to supper or went to the bathroom or something, I can just immediately cut off all contact with her. Imagine that. I might disturb the two most amazing girls I know, both of whom I've fantasized about in varying degrees of perversion, all in the space of about a fortnight.

I am just overflowing with these Sv(v)etlana words, aren't I?

Me: <<Hey. What r u doing?>>

It wasn't on the list, but it works.

She: <<Embroidery>>

Anyone else says that, I assume sarcasm.

Me: <<Of course. I have to talk to you about something.>>

Very dramatic, and predictably the text is followed by a nearly eternal silence, maybe three minutes.

She: <<OK. Wanna come over?>>

Now it's my turn to let the silence drag a little. I didn't expect such a quick appointment, so now I'm in full-on panic mode. I'm really about to confess to Svetlana that I've created an alternative fantasy eight-foot-tall alabaster version of her in an imaginary pixelated world?

Me: <<Right now?>>
She: <<Sure. Fam's out to movie and dinner. I had a fight w Mom and stayed home.>>

She texts her address—I had a vague notion already of where she lived: one of the nicest blocks in Saint Paul. Of course.

Me: <<OK. I'm walking, though. Might be awhile.>>
She: <<I'll be here all night :) >>

The walk from deep in the Hamline-Midway neighborhood to the southernmost edge of Crocus Hill is about forty-five minutes at a respectable but not hurried gait. Considering my intentions upon arriving at the Allegheny Estate (a slight exaggeration, I suppose), I know I'll need some firing up. I'll need to keep my stones at full strength, as Greg would probably put it, so I create a playlist special for this walk. The bpm's are right for the pace, and the aggression of the lyrics and the music will prepare me for this conversation, which will no doubt go very badly.

I should text back that I'm still grounded.

But I don't. I slip my phone into my pocket and drop my headphones around the back of my neck. It's not late, so when I pass Mom and Dad's room and call in, "I'm going out for a bit," I don't hear any protests—just one word: "Midnight."

I glance at the clock in the kitchen as I slip out the back door, and it's not even six. If I'm not home by midnight, it means the conversation went very badly and I jumped from the Smith Avenue High Bridge.

Or it means she was so supremely flattered by the situation I've gotten myself into out of the deepest admiration for her mind, body, and soul that she pulled me to bed for several hours of passionate lovemaking. This is where my mind is as I start walking south.

I'm never completely comfortable on the south side of Grand Avenue. Hell, I'm never completely comfortable south of 94, to be honest. There's just too much money down there, and too many little signs on too many front lawns with my dad's garage company printed cheaply on the front. He might build great garages, but he can't afford great signs, and I don't love that the name Tungsten is on display.

It's probably not that many lawns, I guess. If it were *that* many, we could probably afford to live down here. But when you're hoping not to see something, it feels like it shows up all over.

The farther you go past 94, heading south through Saint Paul, the more money you'll find, at least until you hit the hill that overlooks West Seventh—that's a neighborhood *and* a street, by the way. On that hill, with their cobblestone streets and sweeping vistas and architecturally exciting shapes, live families like Svetlana's, including, naturally, Svetlana's. These are very, very, very rich people.

One cobblestone street in particular has a steep curve as it reaches the summit. That's the Alleghenys' block. As I reach their house, the playlist I put together for the walk finishes and starts to repeat. I grin to myself, proud of the perfect length I made the playlist based on my best estimate on how long it would take to walk here, and switch off the player, then pull the headphones from my ears. I ring the bell. Nothing happens. I don't even hear the *ding-dong*, so either it didn't work (seems unlikely considering the immaculate condition of this house), or the house is so big and the ding-dong player so deep in its innards that I couldn't hear it out front. Still, no one comes to the door. I push it again.

Now, at my house, when someone's at the door—well, first of all, our bell doesn't work. It's painted over, and always has been, as far as I know. I think it was probably painted over at some point in the middle of the last century, long before it was our house. But anyway, the minute someone is on the porch, we all know about it. It's about twelve inches of house, from the front door to the back. Old joke: my family's so poor, the front door and the back door are on the same hinge.

Not so among the architect-designed behemoths that line the cobblestoned lanes on Crocus Hill. My point is, perhaps the maid is in one of the guest wings, maybe tending to the particular needs of a visiting dignitary, and it's taking her a very long time to traipse down the main hall to see what miscreant is at the door while the family is taking their tea in the south garden.

I'm reaching for the knocker—I first figured it was just for decoration, since it looks older than my dead great-grandma and might be made of pure silver—when I hear fast feet on the other side of the door. Sounds like they're hurrying down the steps. I pull my hand away and the door flies open. I say hey.

"Hi," she says, out of breath. "Sorry. I was upstairs." She steps back to let me in, and something's different. She doesn't seem like Svetlana, not the girl I know at school. Maybe it's the house, like I'm seeing the real, supercomfortable Svetlana for the first time.

Or maybe it's her hair. "What's different?" I say as I step inside. I duck a little, like there's a chance I'll bang my head on the doorway, which is ridiculous.

"About what?" she says, and she closes the door. It has a nice thick click. It's a good heavy door. Seems positively medieval, like she just closed behind me the front door to Dracula's castle. Of course that would make her Dracula—and me Harker, I guess. Or Lucy.

"Is your hair always like that?" I try. But it's not her hair.

"You haven't seen it braided before?" she says, tugging at the long, tight braid. She even pulls it around front, like to examine it, see if it's weird.

"I guess I have," I say, and she shrugs.

"Come on up to my room," she says, and she turns for the stairs. "Top floor!"

Then she's on her way up, and I'm dumbstruck, almost gasping for breath. I'm not trying to be melodramatic, but I've never see her like this before, and it occurs to me what's different.

"I figured it out," I say, slowly starting to follow her up the steps. "You're wearing jeans. You never wear jeans."

She's past the landing now—they're the kind of steps that have a break halfway up and then turn around for the second half of the trip—and leans over the banister to look at me. "I do on the weekends sometimes," she says. "Especially if I'm not going anywhere." Then she's gone again, on her way up, so I hurry and spin around the landing for another glance.

They're not Jelly jeans. They're not low in the hips and skinny and faded black and torn and so tight that every glance makes you feel like you should totally not be looking at this, but you cannot look away. But they are soft-looking and faded blue, and they're tight enough in the right places so that I'm quivering a little. She looks incredible. I'm nowhere near capable of telling her so, so I chase her—so to speak—up to the second floor and then up a narrow set of steps into the most obviously Svetlana bedroom in the history of bedrooms. It's like her, except it's a place, not a girl.

"This is awesome," I say. "It's like you have your own apartment."

"I know." She's already seated at a little desk under the half-circle window that looks out over the front of the house. "It's really the only thing about the house I like."

I laugh, but she's not kidding. "What? This house? What's not to like about this house? It's huge."

"True," she says, but she doesn't explain, so I just move a little farther into the room and take off my coat.

"Just throw it on the bed," she says, not even looking up from her laptop. "You wanted to talk?" She's got iTunes open and is scrolling through her music library. "What should we listen to?"

"I don't care," I say, "unless you secretly have a huge metal collection."

"You found me out!" she says, but she double-clicks something, and out comes . . . I don't even know. It's electronic and sounds completely random. If a throttling guitar riff blasted over it, it would have sounded cool, actually. A little like What Dwells Within sometimes, when the keyboard is at the top of the mix. But that's not what happens. Instead a snare drum—or an electronic duplication of a snare drum—starts this marching roll. Then a five-year-old girl with a funny accent starts singing. There are also violins.

"Björk," says Svetlana. "Is it okay?"

I shrug and toss my coat onto her bed, then sit down next to it.

"Sure," I say.

"I love her," she says, and she spins her chair so she's facing the bed. "She's who I always put on when I'm drawing or working on an encounter or even just sewing or whatever."

I smile. "This explains why your clothes are so weird."

Her mouth falls open, thankfully in a grin. "They are not!" she says, so I raise my eyebrows at her, because honestly, she has a dress with a giant eyeball stitched into the skirt. That's all kinds of weird.

"Fine, they're not *typical*," she says. She crosses her arms, obstinate. "I like them."

I throw up my hands. "So do I! I'm just saying they're weird."

"Yours too," she says, so I nod slowly.

The music has grown quite a bit. The vocals have become a confusing pile of voices, all Björk. They vibrate over and around each other. The strings are swelling at the top of the register and chopping along at the bottom. I can sort of imagine a metal band covering this, even. The rhythm of it is a lot like the blast-beat some of my favorite songs use.

"So is Björk your favorite?" I ask, mainly for something to say that isn't what I came over here to say, because Svetlana is just looking at me and smiling, and I know it's because she likes the song, not because she's in love with my stupid face.

She shrugs. "I guess so," she says. "Not yours, huh?"

"I don't hate it," I say, "but it's not something I'd probably put on."

"Sure, because you're obsessed with death and Satan," she says, and her voice gets louder and more urgent and kind of growly, and she stands up from her chair and thrusts a fist into the air, "and charging armies of the undead!"

"You got it," I say, and I tap my nose. "That's what heavy metal is all about. You got it in one."

"You seem to be implying it's not all about that," she says, and she drops down on the bed next to me. She wasn't aiming to sit too close, I don't think, but beds are soft and tricky, and the bed itself bends just enough so that we end up practically thigh to thigh.

I lean back on my outstretched hands, so we're at least not shoulder to shoulder. "It's not," I say, and I take a deep breath because I'm nervous as hell and I have a fair amount to say on the subject of heavy metal's relevance as a genre, but I take this deep breath through my nose and quickly realize something: if Svetlana on her own, even among the foul stench of Central High School's cafeteria, emits a scent so intoxicating that my head spins, then her bedroom—full not only of her but of her clothes and bedsheets and blankets and fluttery silver curtains and pens and pencils and a towel hanging over the back of her chair and a hairbrush on her nightstand and a pair of satin pajama pants folded on her pillow and her pillows and their cases and the gossamer canopy hanging over her bed—is atmospherically a Lesh drug.

I might hyperventilate, so I lean forward again and wipe my nose with my sleeve. It proves clarifying. "Heavy metal," I say, now that I have my breath and mind under control, "is the most challenging, progressive, difficult, and exciting music currently being produced."

"You practice that speech?" she says.

"I don't have to," I say with a shrug. "I'm called upon to defend metal often enough that it comes pretty naturally at this point. But it's true. These guys—the great ones, anyway—are super talented, really proficient at their instruments, and willing to try things and experiment with music and scales and tempos and stuff more than any other musicians out there."

She shakes her head slowly, like she can't believe what she's hearing. "I don't see how you can say that with a straight face"—she gestures toward the laptop—"with this coming out of my speakers."

I have to admit it, the Icelandic banana is doing some pretty insane stuff at this point. Crackling like speakers lit on fire. Clicks and whirls. Synthetic voices arpeggiating all over the place. "But just being weird for its own sake isn't breaking ground," I say. "It's just, like, getting attention."

"'For its own sake'?" she snaps, turning on the bed, her shoulders high and arms stiff at her sides. "This is gorgeous." Her head goes back as she says "gorgeous," and she draws the word out for several seconds. She closes her eyes, like the insanity is the ocean crashing on her naked body.

I'm sorry, but that's what it looks like to me. And the music has gotten even more insane. Björk is screaming. The music has devolved into nothing but echoing clicks. She wails and shrieks and screeches. I wonder if Björk recorded this track—I can't call this a song at this point—while naked, with the ocean crashing on her.

When it ends, Svetlana opens her eyes and smiles at me, maybe expecting me to say, "You win. She's the best!" But I don't. I just smirk.

"Fine," she says. "Fine. I'll put on something else."

"I didn't say—"

"No, no!" She's messing around. *We're* messing around. I decide then and there to never play the dumb video game again. I'm giving up any and all future chances to pretend to be her, because I much prefer actually being near her. "You want groundbreaking? You want challenging? You want technical musicianship? Here it is."

A tympani roll appears, quietly and gently, like it snuck into the room. There are soft horns with it, sneaking around like an elephant on its toes. But then it stops with one thunderous pound, and it retreats, and the music is strings and one little horn. The violins mourn, maybe, and the horns blast a warning.

"What is it?" I say. "I don't know anything about classical."

"Romantic," she says. "It's '*Marche au supplice*,' by Hector Berlioz."

I start to say, "Who?" and she cuts me off and stands up. She raises her hands like a conductor as the music builds and falls and builds and falls. It's fast. It's bright and a little frightening,

304

too. Then it blasts. The horns are proud and sort of amazing. And Svetlana. She's the most amazing of all, because her hands start moving, and then the rest of her, like she's on a podium, and she's facing the laptop like her orchestra, conducting—her arms all a flurry, and I just wish I could see her face, because I know she must be beaming.

After the flurry is over, the music settles back down, and Svetlana catches her breath and drops onto the bed again. "I love it so much."

"You don't say."

She nods. "I want to tell you about it."

"Okay."

"So it's from his *Symphonie fantastique*," she says, grabbing her braid. It's all messy now, and she runs her palms over it like it needs soothing. "That means—"

"Let me guess."

"Okay, okay," she says. "But the full name is *An Episode in the Life of an Artist*, and it's about this artist. He's madly in love, and in this part he can't take it anymore. She doesn't love him back. So he poisons himself."

I groan audibly.

"It gets better," she says. "Honestly, you're such a boy."

Ha.

She settles back in, with the caressing of the braid. "The poison isn't enough to kill him. It just makes him hallucinate, and in his visions he believes he has murdered the woman he loves. He cries and wails and begs for forgiveness, but he's captured and sentenced to death. Then he's marched to the scaffold—that's what the name of this part means, '*Marche au supplice*'—and it's where they cut the heads off murderers."

The music swells again, for the march. Svetlana sits up a little taller, and her hands start to work again on the music, and she speaks louder. "And now at the very end—" She points at the room, like the music is there to see, not just hear, and it blasts horn after horn, in very big and grandiose classical style, with the crashing of cymbals and blowing of trumpets, and Svetlana has to shout over it: "His head bounces—daDUM! daDUM! daDUM!—down the steps!"

She sags again and shakes her braid back around back where it goes and leans back on her stiff arms. Out of breath, she turns to me and smiles.

"I like it," I say. How could I not? Honestly, if the sound of a rock scraping against a metal file cabinet made Svetlana react like that, I'd buy the boxed set in Dolby Surround.

"Good," she says. "I think the Romantic era and heavy metal have a lot in common."

"Really?"

She shrugs. "I think I read that online once."

"So is this guy—"

"Berlioz."

"—your favorite?"

She chews her cheek. "Maybe? I always put that symphony on for encounters. I swear, if Reggie even hears the opening strains of '*Rêverie*,' he starts sweating." She gets the tiniest

French accent when she says "*Rêverie*," and though in anyone else I would think it pretentious and it would make me want to laugh or roll my eyes and then walk out, with her . . .

I say it back: "*Rêverie*," and I try for the accent.

"Don't make fun of me," she says.

"I wasn't," I say, and it's true. "You say it nice. I was seeing if I could too."

She isn't sure whether to believe me, and I feel my face going red—it reminds me of why I came over here tonight—so I stand up and lean over the laptop. "Let's see what else you have."

"You can put on whatever you want."

"You know the real test?" I say. "The real way to figure out what your favorite is?"

"What?" she says, all slow and suspicious, which is just what I was going for.

"You sort by the 'plays' column," I say, and I scroll to the top and click said column. She's on her feet and trying to push me aside at the same instant. "Uh-oh," I say, blocking her and double-clicking the top song.

"Don't!" she says. But it's too late, and a very fat, very 1970s, and very cheesy keyboard line bounces from her speakers. Svetlana falls backward onto the bed and covers her face with her hands.

"*Love. Love will keep us together.*"

I'm watching her and laughing. "Don't be embarrassed," I say. "My mom totally loves this song too. Like, totally."

"Shut up," she says, and I check the music player again.

"Wow," I say, shaking my head in mock mourning. "Over three hundred plays. That's like two hundred fifty more than the next highest."

"I swear," she says. "I am going to punch your face."

So I crank up the volume.

"Oh my gosh!" she says. "Stop!"

And then we both laugh, because she said "Stop!" at the exact time Tennille did. And I wasn't kidding. My mom really does love this song, and has probably played it three hundred times on her music player too, so I know every word, and I'm feeling a little odd—maybe a little drunk on the scent of cucumbers and strawberries, and the physical memory of her thigh against mine, and the mental image of Svetlana with her head back and chest out, with waves of the Björk Ocean crashing over her.

So I finish from there. I pick it up at her *"Stop!"* and I sing, *"'Cause I really love you!"* and on and on. And it works, because she uncovers her face, and now she's smiling, and she pushes herself into sitting position, and I reach for her and she takes my hand. Now she's singing too, and we're holding hands face-to-face, both hands up and our fingers laced together, full-on disco.

When *"Stop!"* comes around again, we're laughing and dancing and singing, and Svetlana's braid is bouncing, and by the time *"Da da da da"* comes around I can hardly breathe and my face hurts from smiling. Svetlana is flushed, and I'm warm all over, and then she pulls me back onto the bed as the next song starts. It's Björk again, but I can hardly hear it, because I'm lying on top of her, and her arms are around me, and my hands are on her face, though I don't remember putting them there, but I don't pull them away. She's looking up at me, her lips just a little bit open. She says hey.

"Hi," I say. "You're the most beautiful girl in the world."

She rolls her eyes, but she smiles too, and if her face weren't already flushed from the Captain and Tennille, I think she would've blushed too. But she doesn't laugh. She doesn't kick me out of her house and prowl a parking lot puffing madly at a cigarette. Instead her hands on my back are moving slowly up and down. I don't want to take my hands off her face. They're like a plain pine frame on a perfect Renaissance painting. So still holding her, still with her amazing being in my hands, I let my head move closer, just a little, and she raises her head, just a little, and my breaths are short and coming from somewhere other than my lungs. And my lips are already tingling, and hers have the slightest hint of a smile, and I just hope it's happiness and not laughter.

"What are you doing?"

Svetlana's eyes go wide. For an instant I think it was her voice, but her lips—her lips that are shining with strawberry-scented (and I wonder now if flavored, and will I ever know?) lip gloss—didn't move, except for the bottom one to tuck in and under her front teeth an instant later. So I look to the left, and there, standing just inside the doorway from the stairs, is a tiny Svetlana.

"Hi," I say.

"Hello," she says.

"You should probably get off me now," says Svetlana, so I do, and it's as awkward and difficult as you'd imagine. I push off the mattress, because I can't push off Svetlana's body, because I would crush her, probably, and would molest her in the process. But the bed, being supersoft as we already covered, has a tremendous amount of give, and so for an instant my body presses more firmly against her, and my cheek grazes hers, and she turns her face to the side, and my lips brush her ear. She gasps, and by now I've gotten some leverage and am able to get onto all fours and off the bed.

"Hen," says Svetlana as she gets up onto her elbows and then palms on stiff arms, "when did you get home?"

"One minute ago," says the girl, who I guess is a chicken? "Mom sent me up to tell you to turn down the music."

"Of course she did," says Svetlana. She looks at me. "This is my sister, Henrietta."

"Hi," I say, and the little girl—I swear, a spitting image of Svetlana, only much tinier—says, "You said that already." She doesn't smile. She doesn't even blink. I'm beginning to wonder if she's actually some kind of bionic clone of Svetlana, missing her emotional chip.

Svetlana, meanwhile, has gotten up and is leaning over her laptop. Björk's shrieking is suddenly much quieter. It sounds even sillier at lower volumes, oddly enough. "There," says Svetlana, standing upright again and next to me. "It's turned down."

"Don't get mad at me," says Henrietta. "I didn't do anything wrong."

"Get," says Svetlana. "Out."

The little Allegheny shrugs and departs.

"She's . . . ," I start.

Svetlana puts up her hands at me and shakes her head.

"I was going to say 'creepy,'" I say. "Maybe 'stoic.'"

Svetlana laughs and drops her head. She covers her eyes with one hand. "I'm sorry," she says. "She's totally telling on me right now, by the way."

"Oh." I grab my coat and start pulling it on. "I should go, I guess."

She nods as I turn for the door. "Look, sorry I got you in trouble," I say, and she grabs my wrist from behind me and half turns me and I half turn around myself. She rushes me, grabs my face—now the frame is alabaster and the art is rough and primitive—and is up on her toes. My arms move of their own volition and are around her, pulling her against me. Her mouth is on mine, her lips still parted, just a little, and I'm at once afraid and excited and thinking about where my hands should be and where I want hers to be, and before I can process any of this it's over, and I'm out of breath and my mouth is open and her lips are shining and red, like ripe fruit, and she's grinning at my stupid face.

"Wow," I say.

"Uh-huh," she says. "Bye." And she nearly shoves me down the steps, into the cold and sterile air of her family and the rest of her house. Though I couldn't before, I now see just why she hates it. It is too big, and it is too clean and too calm and too full of itself. I make a mental note to ask her about that, if that's what she hates, and then run into Mr. Allegheny at the bottom of the steps.

"Hello," he says, taken aback. His wife zips past me, barely taking the time to shoot me a disapproving and loathing glance. I try to smile at her and nod at Svetlana's dad, sort of at the same time. With the remnants of that kiss still on my lips and probably the rest of my face as well, it's quite a stunt to try to manipulate my expression in such a way. It doesn't work. He adds, "Nice shirt," because my coat is still open—Svetlana attacked before I got a chance to zip it up—and Eddie (the Iron Maiden skeletal mascot) is waving the British flag in his face, the undead trooper.

"Oh, thanks," I say. Her dad, then, is not mad—or he's very crafty. I'm trying not to strain to listen to what Mom and Svetlana are discussing two flights up. It's getting difficult as their voices get louder. "You like Maiden?"

He shrugs and puts aside the short stack of mail he'd been flipping through. "I was never a big fan," he says, "but that doesn't mean I can't appreciate a cool shirt from the era of music when music was at its best."

Don't feed the troll. Look, I love 1970s metal as much as the next guy, and these guys clearly laid the groundwork for the whole thrash scene, but to suggest that Maiden was doing anything that remotely compares to what's been done in the last five years? It's ridiculous. But I wasn't about to argue with Svetlana's dad on the subject.

Svetlana's voice fires down the steps like two cannonballs: "Nothing! Happened!"

"Well, that's not what your sister said," her mom shoots back.

"Frogging lace, Mom!"

"Lana!"

This is awkward. Mr. Allegheny's face falls and bounces back, and he says, "Hey," in a very slow drawl, like it is the 1970s, to distract me, I guess, from the goings-on two stories up. Now I can smell wine on his breath. "You'll like this. Come here." He gives me a pat on the upper arm, just below my shoulder, and heads out of the entryway into the next room, through a set of double doors that stand open. Inside, it's a living room, but it's a living room bigger not only than our living room, but probably bigger than our entire house. I wish I were exaggerating. The rug that covers the center of the wood floor is big enough to carpet our first story. The couches that sit face-to-face on either side of the rug and the antique-looking coffee table on its middle are rich brown leather. There are two big windows in the far wall, and along the wall to our right is a deep bookcase full of hundreds—maybe thousands—of books. I don't think my parents have read a book between them in the last fifteen years.

"I guess that explains Svetlana's love of English class," I say, nodding at the shelves.

He glances and chuckles. "Maybe," he says. "I sure haven't read any of them." He walks toward the bookshelves, though, and squats. The bottom shelf, it turns out, is full not of books, but of vinyl records. He flips through them for a few long seconds, and then says, "Ah! Here it is." And he pulls one out and hands it to me. "How about that?"

It's the craziest thing I've ever seen. I don't mean the vinylness of it. I'm a big fan of vinyl art. It's big and worn on the edges and I have, as I explained, raided my dad's vinyl collection on more than one occasion. But this vinyl art in particular: it's got a beach, and in the foreground there's a woman in a red dress standing on an iceberg out in the water. She's wearing a fox mask. I squint at the band's name in its weird font.

"Genesis!" says Mr. Allegheny. "Don't tell me you've never heard of Genesis."

I shrug. "Sure," I say, and I have, but I'm not sure I'd know them if I heard them or anything.

"This album is a classic," he says, taking the jacket back from me. "It's got their masterpiece, in my opinion. 'Supper's Ready.'"

"That's what it's called?"

He nods as he slips out the vinyl and carefully drops it onto the player. "It's the last track, and it's, like, twenty minutes long," he says, gingerly picking up the needle and even more gingerly putting it down. He finds the sweet spot on the second try, after a click and hiss, a blast of music for a split second, and another click. The track starts with a simple metal-ballady acoustic riff. It's not bad. The lyrics are kind of simple, the music is dark and ominous enough.

"This goes on for twenty minutes?" I ask.

"No, no," he says. "It's not like that. It's like, you know, a symphony. It has all these different sections and movements."

Mr. Allegheny drops into one of the leather couches and slouches with one elbow on the big armrest. He just sits there grinning, kind of waving his hands around, like Svetlana had done for Berlioz, but mellower and with his eyes closed. He hasn't invited me to sit, though, and I don't want to sit here for the next twenty minutes anyway, listening to seventies prog.

I clear my throat and shuffle my feet. His attitude doesn't seem to be affected. "It could use a guitar solo," I try.

"Mmhm," he says without opening his eyes. "Ten-minute mark. Steve Hackett tears it up."

I nod, faking enthusiasm, but with his eyes closed anyway, I don't know why I bother. "Well," I say, "I guess I'll head out now."

He sits up and leans forward and gives me a little fingers-splayed wave, so I wave back and turn for the front door.

"Hey, by the way," he says, hurrying toward me. "Don't worry about that." He rolls his eyes toward the ceiling, like I shouldn't worry about the fight between Svetlana and her mom, which is still about me, as far as I can tell. ("I don't even know who that boy was!" "So? You know who Fry is, and he's a moronic *jerk*!" "Lana!")

"Yeah?" I say. "It doesn't sound good."

Her dad shrugs and offers a lazy smile. "You know how daughters and mothers are when they get to be this age," he says, but I don't. How the hell would I? "Something like fathers and sons, I'd bet."

"Ah." Yes, I know what that's like, for sure.

He gives my not-quite-shoulder another firm double pat. "Anyway, good to meet you," he says. "What's your name, by the way?"

"Um, Lesh," I say.

His eyes go wide. "Like Phil?" he says. Now he's a five-year-old boy who just heard Barney would be at his birthday party, so he's an overgrown child, into drinking and the music he loved at sixteen—just like my dad. I guess millionaire corporate-heads aren't playing role model either.

"My mom was a pretty serious Deadhead back in the day. She named me after him."

"Wow," he says, nodding in his groovy chin-thrust way. "Not really a chip off the old block then, are you?"

"My dad's into metal," I say. "I mean, not much of the new stuff. But he saw Maiden five times in the eighties."

Footsteps tumble down the stairs. They're Svetlana's; I know instinctively. When she hits the bottom—and nearly collides with me and her father—I smile before I even look up.

She looks at me, quizzical, and then at her dad, and then back at me, her eyes going wide. "Here," she says in a feminine bark, and she's holding out a book.

"Um," I say, taking it.

"It's why you came over, right?" she says, her eyes wide.

"Oh, right," I say, finally looking at the cover: poetry and other writings by Longfellow. "Thanks."

She'd made up a story to appease her mother, apparently. "To borrow a book," she'd probably said. "For school," she might have added.

"I'll see you in school," she says. "Um, on *Monday*."

"Right," I say. I glance at her dad. "Bye." He smiles at me, and I give Svetlana a quick look, and the wink I get in response is enough that I nearly trip as I cross the threshold and head out into the world, thinking about that wink and her crooked smile when she shot it at me. Then I'm thinking about the kiss, and her body under me on her bed beneath the canopy.

The moon is high and small. I fumble with my phone, find my playlist, and start it, then turn it right off. It's not the right feeling now. On the way down here, it got me fired up. Now, with strawberry lip gloss on my tongue and "Supper's Ready" in my head, it's completely wrong, so I pull down my headphones and let them hang around my neck, and instead listen to the traffic and music and Saturday-night conversation rolling toward me from Grand Avenue.

CHAPTER 46

SVETLANA ALLEGHENY
<THE BLACK SHEEP>

"Lana!"

We've been over this. There is an activity wheel at the bottom of the steps. It is in plain sight. My father is as capable of referring to this activity wheel as anyone else in the house. I can say with the utmost certainty that upon coming in from my Sunday morning shift at the juice shop, I scrubbed the stench of old yogurt and bananas off my body and hair, and then set the activity wheel to "Naptime! ☺." There should be no confusion. So why, as I am drifting toward sleep on a gentle lioness with the wings of an eagle and a melodic voice as deep and rich as gold made of chocolate, can I also hear my father's most irritating, pseudo-joyful bellowing of my name?

"Svetlana!"

And again, I can hear, and it's followed quickly by Tiny Henrietta Thunderfeet, my darling sister.

"Lana."

"Go away," I say, and I still haven't moved, because if I do, I'm sure I will fall off this golden-voiced lion and never find her again.

"Can't," she says. "We're leaving in two minutes. Mom says she told you, like, five times, including when you got home from work."

"*We're* not going anywhere," I say into my pillow. The lion is losing patience with me now. "I don't know where you're going, but I'm staying right here. Tired."

"Yes, you do," Henny says. "Play-offs. Remember?"

The lion is gone. She vanished in a puff of Fry's hair and the fluttering belch of his tiniest trumpet. "I forgot."

"We know," she says. I peek out from under my duvet to see her kneeling in the middle of my sun rug.

"I don't want to go."

"We know." She lowers her head, then her body, until she is curled over on herself like a potato bug. "Mom and Dad will be mad."

I swing my legs off and scan the room for something to put on.

"I have other plans, though," I say, though it's not one hundred-dred percent true. I plan to have plans, though. I plan to text Lesh and pick him up and drive him out to Elm Creek Park. He doesn't know it yet, though, because I just decided it this very minute.

Henny jumps to her feet, pulls open my jeans drawer, and tosses a pair at me. "Here," she says. It's the brightest she gets.

Maybe the sun energy from the middle of my rug seeped up through her knees and butt into her heart.

"Thanks," I say, and when I'm dressed, I let her lead me downstairs. She still thinks I'm going with them, and I feel kind of bad about it, but she'll forgive me and I cannot bear the Dannons, maybe not ever again.

Henny takes the main steps in two big jumps: from the top to the landing, and from the landing to the entryway. I used to do that. I can't remember when I stopped. Today, though, I get as far as the landing and stand there and face my parents. They've both got their coats on already—official Thunder merchandise, I'd point out—and a cooler of various meat and beer is strategically placed by the door. There will be much parking-lot grilling and drinking this afternoon before the game officially begins at seven.

"All right, we're all here," says Dad. He claps three times as he tells me to put on my coat.

"I'm not going," I say, and I do my best to keep my voice even, mature, and most of all not belligerent. It's wasted effort, though, because of course it doesn't end there. It doesn't end with, "Oh, all right. We're disappointed, but you're almost eighteen, and if you want to stay home instead of going to a soccer game, we understand. Have a nice evening!"

"Lana," says Mom, "you've known about this game for too long to back out now. This is a family fun night, and it is not optional." How fun. It's fascistic recreation.

Henny sits on the little cushioned stool near the door.

I think it's actually a footstool, but she keeps sitting on it, so I guess it's a normal stool, too.

I shift my weight from one foot to the other and cross my arms. Too belligerent, so I uncross them and let them hang at my sides. That feels weird, so I put my hands on my hips, and then I just feel like Wonder Woman or something, so I cross them again. "I don't want to see Fry."

"Well, his parents are some of our best friends," says Dad.

"Oh, please," I put in, because they never even see them except at Thunder games.

"And," Dad says over me, "that means you're going to have to be adult about this and learn to get along with their son, even if you're not in love with him like he's in love with you."

"Have to?" I say. "Did it occur to you that I don't want to go sit on the bleachers in the crazy section as the sun goes down and it starts to get freezing and all I can do is watch the cheese in Henny's nacho tray congeal?"

Mom mirrors my pose. I don't know if she means to or what, but it's striking. Behind her, hanging over Henny's little stool, is a family portrait. It was taken at the Wisconsin Dells—the water park capital of the world. Their words, not mine. Anyway, it was fun then—probably less than three years ago—being an Allegheny. So when did it stop being fun? When did I pull away?

Mom huffs. "Did it occur to you that you might try enjoying yourself?"

"Have we met?" I say. "Hi, I'm Svetlana. I don't like soccer." But I'm still staring at my smiling face, my drenched hair, hugging a towel around myself, with littler Henny hardly up to my waist and in the same state. Dad's got his arm around both of us, and Mom is leaning down so her cheek is against mine.

"Lana," says my dad. It's some kind of correction. I guess I got the teensiest bit too snarky.

"It doesn't matter anyway," I say, "because I have other plans." I make a mental note to text Lesh to let him know we have plans I just invented. "With Lesh."

"That disgusting boy who was here last night?" Mom says. "You must be kidding."

"Honey," says Dad quietly to Mom. His idea of defending Lesh and me, maybe? What exactly did they talk about while I was exchanging shrieks with Mom upstairs?

"What?" Mom snaps back. "He looked like a druggie!"

I roll my eyes and stomp back upstairs. I have to grab my phone and my keys.

"Lana!" Dad calls after me. "Get back down here n—"

By the time he's done barking orders, though, I'm already on my way. But I don't even look at them. I just grab my coat from the rack near the back door, and without another word I'm gone. I can hear Mom screaming from inside, and then I hear the back door open and my father's protestations. But I slam the garage door behind me and climb into my big brown beast. I'm Midway bound.

I don't usually text while I drive. It's a very dangerous habit. But I risk it and fire off <<I'm coming to get you>>, then toss the phone onto the seat next to me. The beast coughs and belches as I head up Lexington Avenue. I might have taken my bike—and probably should have; it would help to work off some of the negative residual energy still coursing through me after that run-in on the steps—but I couldn't afford a slow departure. That would've led to another showdown in front of the house. Better to slip out quickly and through the garage. Besides, I have a wild idea, and it is not a short distance away.

I cross Grand Avenue and Summit Avenue. The car bounces along the divided section of Lexington, where it becomes Lexington Parkway, just for a flash, before it reaches the high school. When I show up there tomorrow morning, either on foot or on my bike, I'll be Svetlana Allegheny who kissed Lesh Tungsten. Maybe I'll be Lana who takes Lesh by the hand during lunch and hides with him at the end of the hall past the music room to kiss some more. It makes me a little dizzy, and then I reach University.

While Grand and Summit were hushed and classy, University is dizzy with noise and confusion. While Grand and Summit were tree-lined and serene, University is dirty and crowded.

A team of men from some utility or other have closed off the right lane at the intersection, and traffic is backed up nearly to the interstate. When I reach the light, it's red. The car stops with a lurch. To my right is a check-cashing place and a Chinese restaurant. Past that, a line's formed outside the plasma center across from the KFC. I hope the sellers of blood haven't just eaten there. It doesn't seem right to include extra cholesterol. Someone's going to need that blood.

It's quieter once you cross, and I nearly forget where I'm going. I'm halfway or more to Roan's house, and if not for that text, it might be the easier destination. Maybe I could convince her and Reggie to hold an emergency gaming session. But the campaign is on what feels like permanent hiatus—unless we commit to adding Lesh, and I'm not even sure what those two think about him. I imagine nothing good.

So I turn left off Lex and into Lesh's neighborhood, and I find his house and park. I grab my phone, expecting to see a flashing little green LED, but there's none. Lesh hasn't written back. He might not even be home. His dad's truck is parked in front, the words TUNGSTEN GARAGES emblazoned rather messily on the driver's-side door. I check my phone again. Still no reply. But I can see through the front window, even from my car, that someone's in there and watching TV. It might just be his dad—Lesh could be out listening to metal or something—but he met my dad, so I should be allowed to meet his.

It's awkward right away. The little bungalow has a three-season porch with its own glass door, and there's no bell, so I'm stuck wondering: Do I knock on this door, or do I step onto the porch and knock on the heavy wood door beyond? Standing here, they might never know I exist. But going onto the porch might be imposing. I decide to try the porch door first, and I lightly knock on the glass, and then on the door's aluminum frame. I try again, and this time I see someone get up in front of the TV. He peeks through the windows and waves me inside. As I step in, the wood door opens.

"Hiya," he says. "Something I can do for ya?"

He's taller than Lesh, but not by much, and he's young— younger than my parents for sure. He's tan, too, almost leather in the face.

"Hi," I say. "Is Lesh home? I'm a friend of his from school."

"Oh yeah?" he says, and he steps back a little. "He's upstairs. He might have fallen asleep. He does that on Sunday after- noons pretty regularly. Come on in and have a seat. I'll see if I can rouse him."

"Thanks," I say, and I step inside. There's no entryway, nothing but the door and then the living room. Lesh's dad waves toward a chair for me, so I sit.

He heads toward the back of the house. "Is he expecting you?" he asks over his shoulder as he starts up the stairs.

"I'm not sure," I say, and start to add, "I texted him but he never got back," but by the time I'm halfway through the inane explanation, he's long gone and probably can't hear me. So I lean back and watch a grown man in a purple jersey slam his plastic-covered head into the chest of another grown man, this one in a rich and vibrant red, the color of strawberry chewing gum.

CHAPTER 47

LESH TUNGSTEN
<WE PVP IN REAL LIFE>

It's Sunday afternoon, and I've been on air since last night's kiss. I'm lying faceup on my bed with my hands behind my head, listening to an online grindcore radio station. I tried listening to something else—a classical station, a Björk station, anything that seemed vaguely Svetlanish—but it's going to have to grow on me. I don't mind. Dad's got the day off, as he occasionally does on Sunday, and Mom's less than a mile away at Target. I hope she's on the floor today; she prefers it to cashiering.

It's a few minutes after five when there's a knock on my bedroom door and Dad pokes his head in. He draws his finger across his throat—his macabre signal for *Turn off the music a second*. I lean over and slap the mute button on my keyboard.

"Yeah?"

He's smiling, which isn't as rare as I've made it sound, I guess, but has sure seemed so the first few weeks of school.

He sits on the edge of my bed, so I have to scoot up a little and lean against the back wall. I prop up a pillow. He's still smiling, looking at me.

"What?" I say.

"You have a visitor," he says. "She's downstairs."

My eyes must go wide. I must tense up. Something. Because Dad laughs.

"Um." I start to get up, but he stops me with a hand, eyes closed, smile narrow and gentle.

"Just a second, just a second," he says. "Why don't you tell me who this girl is?"

"I don't know who she is," I say. "What does she look like?"

He laughs at that, too. "Okay, I'll play along," he says, and he leans back and looks at my ceiling, still coated with the glow-in-the-dark stars and planets I stuck up there when I was eight. "She's a hippie, for one thing."

"What?" I say, grinning.

"And she's a blonde," Dad goes on. "Intensely a blonde."

"Okay."

"Tall as me, I think."

"Dad, I get it," I say, and I stand up, but he blocks me with his leg and ignores my cues to shut up.

"She's good-looking too," he says.

"Shut up," I say.

"And definitely not a sophomore."

I groan. "She's a senior. Can I go now before she thinks we both died up here and just leaves?"

"In a second," he insists. "Is there anything going on here I should know about?"

"You should know about?" I say, scratching my chin. "Not that you should know about, no."

"All right, just don't be stupid," he says. "You know what I'm saying?"

He's saying don't get Svetlana pregnant. For some reason this makes me want to punch him. "Yes."

"Okay," he says. Then he nods once, his jaw set like stone, as though we've had a major talk. He leans back, smiles again, as relaxed as when he came in. "You're not the first metalhead to fall for a hippie."

"You and Mom," I say, because I've heard this before. "I know."

"Let me just say one thing about it, and then you can go down and show—what's her name?"

I can't tell him. It's not that it's a secret. It's more that it's mine—that word: the sibilance, the top teeth on the bottom lip, the tip of my tongue on the roof of my mouth twice, once a peck, once a glide. So instead I say, "Lana."

"Show Lana the time of her life," he finishes. "And here's the one thing: don't worry about the idiot dirtbags you normally hang out with. I hung out with the same dirtbags, and believe me, they had plenty to say about your mom."

"Like what?"

"Like she's a hippie and flake and stuff I won't repeat to you," he says, "but you're going to hear the same stuff if you keep hanging out with Lana, so you'll be familiar with it all soon enough."

I nod, because I've already heard a little from Greg and Jelly.

Dad slaps my back. "All right, go ahead," he says. "She has a car. It's an old American POS and I approve, if you're wondering."

"I'm not," I say. I didn't even know she had a car, but I head down the stairs, leaving my dad behind me on my bed, and Svetlana comes out of the TV room slowly at the sound of my feet on the steps. She peeks her head around, smiles up at me, and grabs my hand.

"Can you go out for a bit?"

"Sure," I say. "Where we going?"

"I want to show you something," she says.

There's hardly a word between us as we head west on the interstate, through Minneapolis and north into the suburbs. When she finally exits, the sun is low to our left and we're past Brooklyn Center. Sometimes she puts her hand on top of mine between the seats.

I have no idea where we're going, except that it seems like the middle of nowhere, and it seems like we're heading for the sunset, on our own, in a car with very large seats.

"You're going to love this," she says, and we're rumbling up an empty road, with fields and farms on either side, and a forest ahead. She stops in a little gravel lot and turns off the car.

I am not ashamed to reveal that I'm at this point a virgin.

I mean, first of all, I'm sixteen, and I'm pretty sure the latest statistical information shows the average person loses their virginity when he's sixteen. That gives me till my birthday in July. And second of all, Jelly—the hottest girl I have ever known and am ever likely to know—recently demonstrated with great clarity that she would like to jump my bones. That is, if I would keep my mouth shut.

All that said and out there, this is Svetlana.

"Listen," I say. I'm fidgety as hell too, picking at the seam of the leg of my jeans, examining my thumbnail—it's dirty. My palms are sweaty, my mouth is dry—probably too dry to even kiss properly. I haven't showered.

But she's already opening the door. She looks over her shoulder at me. "Come on," she says, grinning. "You have to see this. And stay quiet."

"Okay . . ." Then we're not parking. I climb out and close the door. It's a heavy door. This act is inherently loud, but she shushes me anyway. "Sorry."

"Follow," she whispers, so I do, to the edge of the gravel lot and the entrance to the woods. They're thick, and it's cold and dark in there. It seems like Svetlana has been here before, though, and she walks crouched and quiet across the dead leaves and brown needles, her feet stirring low plants and whispering themselves. The smell here is decay and earth, and mixed with Svetlana's scent of berries and vanilla, it's intoxicating. "Wait."

I stand there at the edge of the woods, just watching her.

She's really Svvetlana—two *v*'s—just for that moment, as she creeps deeper into the woods and crouches behind a big old silver maple. Thing must be a hundred years old. But she creeps behind it with her hands on the rough bark, and I realize she's in jeans again, and the thrill of being behind her returns. Somehow she's as magical as ever, though, and in combination with the woods in front of her, and how she's crouched at that tree, it's as if she really is an elf priestess of the forest. In the dim orange light of the sunset, her hair shimmers like gold.

I feel almost faint from the image, and then she quickly turns her head and sees me standing there, like an unshowered, ill-rested doof.

"Come on," she whispers loudly at me. And she beckons me with a curved finger and a smirk. Then she looks back into the woods. "They're starting. You have to see this."

As coolly as I can manage, and still stinging a little at having been caught staring, I crouch through the weeds and low-hanging branches and stoop beside her. "What am I seeing?"

"Shh," she says. "Look," and she points—her arm touches my elbow and sends a tingle across my skin—at a thick area in the underbrush, maybe fifty yards into the woods. As she does, the brush shakes violently. I barely have time to focus on the area before—and I kid you not—a human mage leaps from the undergrowth, brandishing his staff (ahem), and he holds the knotty and bejeweled length of worn wood over his head, spreads his sandaled feet, and throws out his free arm.

"Magic missile!" he shrieks. "Magic missile!"

You can't make this stuff up.

"My god," I whisper. "What is he doing?"

"He's LARPing," she hisses back. "Live-action role-playing. Amazing, isn't it?"

I nod dumbly and watch as the mage's target—probably a fighter class of some kind; the guy wields an immense wooden sword with both hands and wears a heavy-looking helmet, complete with full visor in front and feathered pouf on top—charges the poor caster.

"Why doesn't he bubble or something?" I say to Svetlana, maybe a little too loud, because she shushes me again.

"Watch."

From the bushes, behind the mage, dive two more LARPers, one with a shield and giant hammer, the other with two small swords, one in each hand. They both charge the solo warrior, and then the melee begins in earnest. The mage was just pulling, I guess, and now these two take the brunt of the foe's attack.

It looks like slow motion, with parried thrusts, dodged swings, and ridiculous pratfalls, and the mage—still hovering by the edge of the clearing, and still shouting "Magic missile!" Finally the warrior doesn't get up. He rolls onto his belly, his arms and legs stretched out, and the mage approaches, plants his foot on his back, and holds his staff up to the setting sun.

"Our enemy is defeated!" he shouts.

"Was that a boss fight?" I whisper.

"I guess," Svetlana says. "Pretty lame boss. I've seen three guys dressed like a dragon as a boss before." She sighs and stands up straight. "Still, wasn't that amazing?"

"You've come out here before?" I ask. "Just to watch?"

She's grinning like crazy, watching the guys in the woods, and she nods. "They're a group from the U," she says. "I don't really want to join, but it's pretty cool to watch."

"Do they know we're here?"

"No way," she says. "It would entirely ruin the drama, if they knew they had an audience."

"Seems kind of creepy," I say.

"Hey, it's a free park," she says in what I hope is fake defensiveness. "If they want to LARP, I'm going to watch from the bushes like a weirdo."

"Fair enough."

And so we watch—still huddled close to the ground and each other—as the lame boss, now dead, gets to his feet and pulls off his helmet to reveal his sweaty, greasy, acne-riddled face.

"What," Svetlana whispers. She stands up. "What," she says again, louder now, and I stand up next to her.

"Shh . . . ," I say. "They're going to see us!"

"What?!" she says again, this time very loud, distinctly ignoring me, and she pushes through our cover and into the clearing.

The LARPers turn to watch her approach, and as silly as they looked in the heat of battle, they look even sillier with their shoulders sagging. She stomps toward them—toward the boss in particular, it looks like—and I decide I should probably hurry to catch up, in case this is Svetlana's way of starting a role-players brawl.

Turns out I'm not far off: the acne-ridden warrior is my favorite former member of the Central High Gaming Club.

Svetlana strides right up to him and stands there, arms akimbo—it's one of her words, I know—her face inches from his. It nearly makes me jealous. I jog up next to her as she snaps his name like an accusation: "Abraham!"

She's angry, and who could blame her. He was a member of the party fighting its way through Svetlana's semiannual campaign, a campaign she sweated and slaved over all summer, apparently, and which was, in my opinion, evidence of nothing less than her overarching creative and intellectual genius.

The same member who dropped out of the club—thereby reducing its membership below the school's threshold for formal extracurricular status—with the excuse that he'd be finding a job to start saving money for college and establish himself as a true adult, and pressure from his parents had gotten too thick. I related at first, when Svetlana told me that he'd quit and why; after all, I'd had to cut down drastically on my own gaming when my mom put her foot down about homework. But this—this is evidence that Abraham didn't need the extra time at all. He'd simply shifted his role-playing from the big back table in room 3212 to the woods in Elm Creek Park.

"That's pretty cold, man," I say, shaking my head.

"Stay out of this, interloper!" he spits at me, so I throw up my hands, but I don't walk off. Meanwhile the other three

LARPers—the party of one mage, one warrior, and one rogue, who just bested the fearsome boss—step up behind Abraham.

"I can't believe you," Svetlana says. "You knew this would be the end of the club, and you—you—"

"Don't be so high and mighty," Abraham says, but he doesn't look her in the eye. "You're the one who brought in this guy"— he nods toward me—"thereby destroying any camaraderie that had developed within the game over the last three years. Besides, these guys are freshmen at the U. This is relevant to my college career."

"Oh come on," Svetlana and I say at nearly the same instant.

She glances at me and says like a secret, "Jinx-you-owe-me-a-Coke."

"Jesus, Lana!" Abraham says at that little display. "Why did you even come here? Just to show off your new boyfriend and make me feel even crappier?"

"Wait," I say to Svetlana. "Did you guys used to date?"

"One time!" she says, furious, not looking at me, but red in the face and looking ready to claw out Abraham's eyes. "We went to one stupid dance. We didn't even dance!"

Abraham sticks out his lower jaw and narrows his eyes. "I liked you." His voice is eerily calm and deep, devoid of all the rage and fiery emotion it had possessed only seconds ago. "I liked you so much."

Svetlana crosses her arms and looks into the woods. "This is why you quit the GC."

Abraham shrugs and adjusts his tunic.

The sun is mostly down now. It's dark. Svetlana shakes once with a chill. "I didn't know."

"Now you do." Then he bends over and picks up his wooden sword.

"Whoa," I say, backing up a little. But he's not attacking. He just storms off into the woods. His vanquishers hurry after him, their robes and tabards fluttering behind them.

Svetlana stomps the earth once and kind of grunts. I stand beside her for a minute, thinking of offering her my coat, before she lifts her chin and calls into the woods, "Enjoy being the lamest boss in all of role-playing!" Then she turns around and stomps back toward the parking lot and her car.

The ride back starts quiet again, but this time there's no hand on mine, and I assume the quiet is letting her dwell on that scene in the woods. We're chugging along 94, approaching the junction for 694, when she seems to snap out of it. She jerks the wheel hard, moving the car into the slow lane and onto the shoulder—right there on the interstate, she stops and puts the thing in park.

"Question," she says, and her voice is urgent, desperate, kind of insane. It's not a Svetlana I've ever seen. I'm not sure how I feel about it.

"I don't think you're supposed to pull over here," I say. "I mean, unless it's an emergency."

"This is an emergency," she says, "because that is 694, and I think we should go that way."

"Why?"

She takes a deep breath, shifts on the bench seat so she's facing me, and scoots a little closer. "Do you like soccer?"

"What?"

She doesn't repeat it, but I heard her, so I say, "No, I don't like soccer."

"Good," she says. Then she takes my hand and leans close to me, and I put my hand on ours and lean close to her. She exhales gently. I cough. She puts her hand on my cheek, and she presses her lips—so gently—against mine. As she pulls away, she whispers, "Do you like me?"

"Obviously," I whisper back.

"Okay," she says. "Then we're going to the play-offs."

CHAPTER 48

SVETLANA ALLEGHENY
<BIRDS OF A FEATHER>

I pull into the sports complex's big parking lot a little after seven. The pregame cookout is over. The coolers of meat and beer have been packed up and stashed in trunks. A handful of grills sit out in the lot, being allowed to cool before storage. It's nice to see the Thunder fanatics have the good sense to do that. I am angry at Abraham, though, not the Dark Clouds, so I take a deep cleansing breath and turn off the car.

"We're here," I say, but I don't get out. I don't even pull the key from the ignition.

"Yes, we are," says Lesh. "Why are we here?"

Another deep breath and I drop my head onto the steering wheel, because my skin is starting to tingle. I am not prepared for this. The good news is my anger toward Abraham, which was so palpable only moments ago, has faded, flooded from my system by a rush of anxiety and deep loathing for the embarrassment that is my parents.

Forget it. It's not worth passing out in the NSC parking lot. I reach up, grab the key, and turn it. The car roars back to life.

"And we're leaving?" Lesh says.

I sigh again and turn off the car.

"That's probably not good for the car," says Lesh. I glance at him, and he's smiling kind of adorably. He hardly ever does that. Today he does. Last night he did. It's because of me, I think, and I pull the key from its stupid keyhole. I'm okay.

"Okay, let's go," I say. "I'm paying for your ticket."

"Ticket to what, exactly?" he says as he climbs out. I look over the car at him after I get out, and he's leaning on the top. "I mean, the play-offs. You said that part."

"Soccer," I say.

"Ah," he says. "You also said that part."

I turn to face the stadium, so he does too. "The Minnesota Thunder are in the play-offs."

"I wouldn't have guessed you were a soccer fan," Lesh says, and he walks along the length of the car's hood. I grumpily do too, and we meet at the car's nose. He puts out his hand and I accept it.

"I'm not," I say, "but my family . . . is. Are. They are. They're fanatics."

"Wow," he says. "I wouldn't have guessed that about your parents either. Or what's her name. Chicken."

"Hen," I say, and I smile a little.

He shrugs. "Chicken suits her too," he says. "Like Chicken Little."

"Pff," I say as we walk. "If the sky were falling, she'd be the last to panic. Trust me."

The parking lot and the path to the ticket booth have never felt longer. The game's already started. I can hear it now. The announcer is shouting—as unintelligible as ever—but louder and far more upsetting are the Dark Clouds. Fry's little trumpet is blaring early, and the chants of "Minnesota, go!" and "Crack, crack, *BOOM!*" jump up and out of the stadium like baby demons crawling out of a chasm in the earth, a gateway to a dimension of pain and suffering and humiliation and blue-and-yellow face paint.

When we reach the ticket taker, the girl smiles at me and waves from behind the glass. I recognize her, though I don't know her name. The place is staffed mostly with students who go to the nearby high school. I don't know if they even get paid. They do have to wear some very ill-fitting baby-blue polo shirts, though. I know that much, so I sympathize.

"Your family is already inside," she says. "They left your ticket with me. They said you might have a change of heart."

I glance at Lesh and say, "I guess I did," and, "But we need another ticket. I've never even bought one. Are they a lot?"

"Look, I can pay for my own ticket," Lesh says, and he reaches for the wallet at the end of the chain at his hip, but I elbow him, pull a wad of bills from my pocket, and hand them through the window.

"I insist," I say as I lead him away from the ticket booth and through the turnstile. "Believe me when I say you are giving me a huge and generous gift by even coming here. If you are a

340

firm believer in the hereditary nature of personality traits such as soccer fanaticism and the tendency to drink and act like an oaf in public, you will very likely never want to see me again after tonight."

"I doubt that."

I raise my eyebrows and lead him by the hand past two souvenir stands and one food stand, across the concourse, and into the middle of the stadium. It's more crowded than usual, since this is the play-offs. Under the lights, the field is like two great circles of preternatural green. The men's uniforms are still gleaming in white and red and blue and yellow. They won't be for long; it's a rough game, this small-stakes professional soccer. Directly across the field from us is a set of bleachers disconnected from the rest. It looks like it would fold up and roll away if only there weren't about thirty people—stomping, singing, chanting, and playing a tiny trumpet—standing on it right now.

"There they are," I say. "Right in the front."

"Where?" Lesh says, and he's looking too close. He's looking at the saner people sitting in the front row only thirty feet away, on this side of the semicircular stadium.

"No," I say, tugging his hand and then pointing. I find Henny's little bright-white head. Everything else is a maddening rush of yellow and blue and beer and waving arms. Only Henny, sitting on the bottom-most bench of the bleachers with a plastic clamshell of nachos on her knees, really stands out.

"I see Hen—" Lesh says. Then he rolls back his head in a tragic nod. "Oh."

"See them?"

"I do. I see them."

He puts an arm around my shoulder. "It's not that bad."

"Now you've seen them," I say, and I pull away from his half embrace. "Let's go."

"We're not going to watch the game?" He sounds genuinely upset about this.

"Not from here."

We walk around half the stadium through the cement concourse, passing ads for beer and souvenirs and Totino's and Kohl's. The last exit is a set of steps down to the field behind the visiting goal. Target Field this isn't. In fact, to get to the fanatic bleachers, one has to walk on the grass itself—the carefully manicured playing surface, albeit out of bounds—behind the goal, around the side of the field, in plain sight of everyone watching the game and very likely to the distraction of the men playing too.

Halfway to the fanatics section is the children's playground. It's tucked away behind a little section of six-foot wooden privacy fencing. I can imagine someone deciding to install a playground here at the stadium to entertain children otherwise disinterested in sports; I don't know who thought it was a good idea to put said playground behind the visitors' goal of a professional soccer field. Maybe little kids use it sometimes when I'm not around, but tonight, as usual, it sits alone, its individual parts looking fairly brand-new in the low light. Under sunshine, I'd probably see the faded bits, from sunshine and little butts, and maybe a length of rubber-coated chain where the rubber has cracked or fallen away. But right now it looks pristine.

"Wait." I take Lesh's hand. It's cold and a little damp, and as I sit down on a swing, I pull him down too, to the next swing over. He sits and grabs the chains and stares straight ahead toward the Dark Clouds while I watch him.

"You don't have to worry about them," he says. The action is off at the Thunder's goal, which I can see a bit of around the fence. It seems like it's miles away. "I mean, it's pretty hilarious."

I nod and even smile. "It is. It really is. And I wouldn't mind it so much if they didn't drag me down here every week all summer."

He shrugs one shoulder. He does that a lot, I'm realizing. "Doesn't seem too bad. I bet they have pizza rolls."

Fine, so I laugh. "I just don't want you to think I'm like them," I say, and I hate the sound of my own voice. It's rude. It's hateful and rude. "I don't want you to think I'm some weirdo who thinks this stuff is important or fun."

"Do you?"

I admit I give it a moment's thought, but still: "No. No, I don't."

"Then there's no problem," he says. "Besides, your parents seem fine to me. They're just like mine."

"Really?" I say, squinting toward the bleachers. "'Cause I met your dad this afternoon, and I don't see him over there with my parents and his face painted blue, halfway to drunky town."

He lifts a shoulder again. "I think both our moms are

decent ladies who work hard, and both our dads work hard and also like to drink and listen to the same music they liked in high school. So my dad likes American football and yours like European football."

I kick at the scraped-up dirt under my swing and watch my parents. They're both turned around now, facing the rest of the Dark Clouds, leading them in a cheer—bullhorn and all. I never thought to ask whose idea it was to show up at these games to begin with, Mom's or Dad's. I have a feeling Mom's a pretty great lady. So I get up from the swing and offer Lesh my hand with my eyes closed, like I have to prepare myself physically and mentally and spiritually for the walk and experience we are about to attempt, and he takes it. I start to pull him away, to finish the march around the field to my seat in the back row of the fanatics' section, but he gives my arm a little tug.

"Ow," I say, and his arms fall around my waist. "Oh."

And he gives me a kiss. It's a nice kiss. It's not desperate. It's not hormonal. It's a nice kiss. It's a soft kiss, and a kiss that ends with a smile instead of a sigh or a groan or a moan.

"Okay, I'm ready," he says, and then we walk the rest of the way side by side and hand in hand. When we climb the steps to the top of the bleachers, we pass my mom and dad, both in painted faces and both shouting and cheering and chewing something bready and fried. Dad's got a blue beer in one hand. Mom's got a bottle of water bigger than my left leg slung over her arm, and when we pass her, she gives me a wink and smile and wave. She even smiles at Lesh. Dad's less subtle. He

344

doesn't notice us at once, but when he does, his eyes go wide and his big plastic cup of beer is held high as he cheers our arrival. Only a few drops land on Mom.

Lesh and I sit side by side on the top bench, and he takes my hand in his lap and keeps his eyes on the field. Below us, Henny shouts at Mom's ear to be heard over the crowd, and a moment later, she and her clamshell of nachos are cuddled next to me. She pops open the plastic and holds them out to us. "Thanks," Lesh says, and he takes a satisfying-sounding chomp from a cold-cheese-laden tortilla chip.

CHAPTER 49

SVETLANA ALLEGHENY
<THE DOUBLE BERRY
RAZZMAJAZZ>

The week is a long one. I'm working at Mr. Hermann's juice shop four days a week after school, and that's just the school days. That added to the end of the official Central High School Gaming Club and that I spend too much class time thinking about a boy in black and when I can get my lips on his again means every red-second-handed minute seems to last for an eternity.

On Wednesday, Lesh promises to drop by the shop while I'm working. It's after five when he shows up. He's alone, in his black trench coat and with his heaviest headphones hanging from his neck. "I can't believe you're working," he says. "It's honestly melting my brain a little."

"What?" I say. "Is it so hard to believe I have a work ethic?"

He puts up his hands and flashes an open-mouth smile. "Oh, I know you have that," he says. "But for stuff you actually want to do, not for chopping bananas and blending them with carrots and wheatgrass."

"I don't actually think anyone's ordered that yet," I say, chewing my cheek.

"So are you alone here?"

Kyle peeks out from the back. "No."

"Hi," Lesh says, extra perky with a little wave. Kyle rolls his eyes and vanishes. "So you gonna get me a job here? My mom wants me working before I turn seventeen."

"When is that, anyway?" I say, grabbing a rag to wipe a spot in front of the blenders that doesn't need wiping. "I just realized I'm dating a child."

"Dating?" he says.

"Shut up," I say. "When's your birthday?"

"July."

"That means," I say, now wiping the counter next to the register right between us, "that for well over three months I will be an eighteen-year-old woman dating a sixteen-year-old boy."

"Hey."

"This cannot stand," I say, and give my head a mournful shake. Then I slap both hands on the counter and declare, "We're going to have to get married."

His eyes go wide and so does his grin, but he's also shaking his head and backing away. As he does, the bell over the door dings. A customer.

"Did you want something?" I say. "It's on me."

"Damn right it is," calls Kyle. "No free drinks."

I roll my eyes and smile at Lesh. "No, it's really on me."

He looks past me at the menu. It makes him extra adorable, because his big eyelashes flutter a little against his eyelids, and the whites in his eyes south of the pupil get extra big. I actually read someplace that women find that particularly attractive. Turns out it's true.

"You'll really be eighteen in the spring?" he says as he browses. The man behind him is getting impatient. "How's that feel?"

I have to give that some thought. "Scary?"

He nods, then shuffles to the side and turns to the new guy. "I haven't made up my mind," he says. "You go ahead."

"Thank you," says the customer. He's almost thirty, I'd say, and he doesn't look like he just got off work anywhere. He steps close to the counter and looks at my name tag. The name tags at the juice shop are pretty distinct. They're not printed. Instead, first thing on my first day, Mr. Hermann handed me a bucket of crayons and markers and a blank tag and told me to label it how I liked, fill it with personality. So I did. It took about twenty minutes, which I don't think he was expecting, but it says "Lana" in beautiful, intricate script. I'm thinking of doing the rest of the alphabet and turning it into a whole font.

"Is that short for anything?" the customer asks.

"Yes, actually," I say. "Svetlana."

He grins at me. "That's a beautiful name."

"Thanks," I say, and shoot a glance at Lesh. He's standing right there, listening, and he shrugs one shoulder. "Do you know what you'd like?"

"Yes," the customer says, looking up at the menu. It doesn't do much for him. "I'll have a Double Berry Razzmajazz."

I poke at the keys on the register, ringing it up, and he's giggling. "Why do they have to give them such ridiculous names? It's so embarrassing to order."

I've been working at the shop for a little bit more than a week now, and I have heard that comment no fewer than fifty times. So I'm starting to wonder myself, but I flash my practiced What-can-you-do? smile and say, "You get used to it. I think they're kind of fun." That's what Mr. Hermann coached me to say.

Lesh sticks around for about half my shift. I make him a Berry Blast and a Rabbit Punch. He likes the first one; the second gets poor marks for tasting like grass. "It's Rabbit Punch, Lesh," I say. "Were you expecting something other than grass?"

He leaves in time to be home for supper, and I miss him immediately, especially when seven thirty rolls around and Kyle implies unsubtly that I should mop the back room.

CHAPTER 50

LESH TUNGSTEN
\<MEN WORKING\>

It's a long week. When Saturday finally rolls around, I just want to be back under Svetlana's canopy, but she's working from lunch till close. I drop by for a juice around three, but I know I won't be able to spend any quality time with her until after she closes at nine. It's a nice afternoon for October in Minnesota, so I sip my twenty-two-ounce AppleBerry Slush—it's the best one I've tried so far—and instead of taking the bus, I walk home. I cut across Summit Avenue and head up on Griggs, toward the pedestrian bridge over the interstate. As I cross Selby, though, I hear a familiar sound: the *thwap* of a nail gun in bursts of three. I'm not surprised when I spot Dad's beat-up Ford pickup and a Tungsten Garages lawn sign a block up. And there's Dad, up on a frame, nailing in the triangles to hold up the roof.

I reach the truck and lean on the curb side—right against the big magnet Dad had printed to slap on the driver's-side door: TUNGSTEN GARAGES, and his cell phone number. He's an advertising genius.

I don't say anything. When he's working on a garage, he's strictly in the zone. Interruptions that don't start with things like "Mom is on fire!" or "Guns N' Roses original lineup are going on tour!" are not welcome. So I just watch. He wouldn't have heard me anyway. His old boom box that lives in his pickup is in the flatbed, right behind me and much louder than I would probably shout, if I didn't want to embarrass both of us. It's blasting . . . *And Justice for All*. I'm shocked the neighbors haven't been out here to ask him to turn it down.

He's in the middle stages of construction, and despite the slight chill, he's worked up enough of a sweat that he's going at it in just his wife-beater. The frame is up, except for the long triangles that make up the roof, and that's the best part, really. It looks like a two-man job. Maybe three, even. But Dad's got a system.

He's got a length of blue string—special sturdy stuff they make for contractors, I guess. He marks it up so everywhere a roof beam needs to go has a bright yellow line. High contrast. That way he doesn't have to stop to measure every time a new beam is going up. Once the beams on the front and back of the garage are on—which he does in a way you wouldn't have thought of and I'll explain in a minute—he connects them at their peaks with that string.

Then he grabs one of those preassembled triangles that are the beams. He leans it against one wall. He climbs the ladder, uses the slope of the top of the beam to slide it up so it's hanging—upside down—between the two walls. Then comes the fun part: he swings the thing, back and forth, back and forth, like, ten times, getting the momentum up, until it just flips—swoosh. And now it's point-up, like it's supposed to be. Then he just has to make sure it's lined up with the yellow mark on the string, nail-gun the joints, and move on to the next beam.

It's slow work, and it looks hard as hell, but at least he doesn't have to pay a team. If he did, trust me, we wouldn't eat.

This afternoon I watch him swing up two of those triangles before he finally sees me—the CD ends, and he glances at the truck. He doesn't wave, doesn't smile. He shouts, "Put on *Piece of Mind*."

That's an Iron Maiden album—an oldie even for Dad. It's pretty good, though. I turn around and dig through the cracked cases till I see Eddie—chained and in a padded room—and pop in the disc. I know enough to get . . . *And Justice for All* into its case too. As I lean on the truck, the familiar opening drum fill of "Where Eagles Dare" blasts across my back. Halfway through the dual-lead guitar solo, I start walking again.

Then I'm home and in my room, and it's still hours before Svetlana finishes work. I look at my desk, where my computer sits, untouched for days. Before I know what I'm doing, I've fired it up. It's been a long time; maybe I'll just peek in and see how Svvetlana's getting on.

CHAPTER 51

SVVETLANA
<SECRET ADMIRERS>

The elf priestess kneels at the base of the tree. It is not one of the old ones, but it is still their child. She presses her palm against it, feeling its strength and love and the life force coursing through it.

"I could fall asleep right here," she says. Her eyes are closed, but her connection to the earth and all its inhabitants is strong. She knows instinctively that her companion Stebbins the hunter is seated not far off, and his big striped cat beside him. He is drinking wine. He is so often drinking wine.

Dewey, too, the stocky paladin, is nearby, but it doesn't take a connection to creation to know it. He is laughing and riding his ram in circles around her. Every so often as he passes, he calls out "Nice butt" and "Nice tits," depending on where along his circular route he happens to be.

"I'm ignoring you, Dewey," says the priestess, but she smiles too, because though his behavior and comments once irked her, she has come to find them amusing, like one finds amusing the irritating quirks of an old house—a loose doorknob, a squeak in the floor, a sticking drawer. She and Dewey and the hunter have been through a lot together—they've gathered experience and gold on the seas, at the tops of snowy mountain peaks, in great caverns hidden in the farthest reaches of the driest deserts. They've slain demons and dragons in dungeons and woods. Dewey has been a troublesome, annoying dwarf through all of it, but he's also saved her life more times than she could count.

She's done the same for him. In spite of herself and her caution in the spring of her adventures, now in their winter she's grown to care for them, even to love them.

"I'm heading to the inn," says the paladin. "Get Vent!" And without waiting for good-byes, he gallops off. It is his way, and Svvetlana is not offended. She simply smiles and waits, her eyes still closed, knowing the hunter will be beside her in a moment. He always is, and when Dewey leaves, he moves closer still.

"Just us again," he says. He sits beside her, facing the tree. It took him a few days to get used to her tendency to sit, rather than leaning on trees, facing them, like they were part of the circle of conversation. He puts a hand on hers, and her smile grows.

"I've been wanting to ask you," he says. His cat is far off now, released to play and prowl in the tall grass. They've chosen the finest spot for this little repose: a wide rolling field dotted with tall silver trees, little ponds of the clear, bright water elves tend to favor, and sparkling wisps—the spirits of lost elves, come back to the woods to play. It is a corner of the elven old world, where their ancestors once walked among great cities, today only ruins and ghosts. "You never mentioned the gifts I sent."

"Gifts?" she says. Her mind is still with the tree, with the grass, with the dew seeping through her dress.

"Mmhm," he says, moving closer. He kisses her neck, and she shivers. "I sent you flowers."

"Did you?" she says, and it sounds coy, but she doesn't recall. She didn't get flowers.

"Mmhm," he says again. She shivers again. "And a necklace."

She'd remember a necklace. She loves necklaces, particularly ones with blue gems, like the one she's wearing: a long silver chain, dangling a charm, at its center a blue stone. She fingers the charm and opens her eyes. Stebbins's face is right there—his eyes so golden and bright, she lets him kiss her.

"Not this necklace," she says. "I'm sure I fought for this necklace."

He smiles and kisses her cheek. "The demon boss Gal'kaelin. I was there."

"Of course you were," she says with a smirk. "Then what?"

The hunter leans back on his hands. "I'll seriously kill someone if the necklace didn't arrive."

"Arrive?" Her heart seems to freeze in her chest, and the cold skitters across the surface of her body in a rush of frost. She turns away from him and gets to her feet. "You sent the flowers."

"You did get them!" he says, and he jumps up as well. "Good."

"I didn't know they were from you," she says. "I thought they were . . . I thought they were from someone else."

"Someone else?" says the hunter. He backs away, puts his face in his hand. She's broken his heart, it seems. "Who else has kissed you in the rain?"

"Kissed me in the rain . . ." She is falling now. She wants to run from him, run from this world. It's all gone wrong. "How did you find me?"

The hunter shrugs. "It wasn't hard," he says. "You have a rare and beautiful name, and you live in Saint Paul, and you're in high school."

"My god," she says, and her mind reels, frantically searching her memory for any inkling she might have given him: she's in high school, she's in Minnesota, she's in the Gaming Club. It's all out there. It's all out there and he found it all. The hunter moves toward her, and she pushes him away. "I have to go. I have to go right now."

"Have I upset you?" he says. "I didn't want to upset you. I thought you'd like the flowers."

"You shouldn't have sent them," she says. "Everything is messed up now."

"I'm sorry," he says. "Let me make it up to you."

"No."

"I'm insisting," he says. He whistles for the cat, and it gallops toward them. In a moment, he's mounted his riding tiger. "I'll see you soon. I'm going to make it up to you."

"No," she says. "I'm not coming back. I'm leaving and I'm not coming back."

"No," he says from fifty yards away. His voice carries across the field like one of his arrows. "I'm going to see you IRL."

"No," she says. She runs after him, grabbing at his feet and his robe. "Do not do that."

"Why?" he says. "Don't act like you're afraid of me now. I'm still Stebbins."

"Please," she says, thinking quickly. "I have to work tonight. I'm working."

"Good," he says. "I love juice, especially the Double Berry Razzmajazz."

"Wait, what?" says the priestess. She feels cold and light: a cocoon of ice crawls over her skin and if she falls, she'll shatter. "That was you. The other day. That was you."

The hunter flashes a smile and kicks his steed. It breaks into a gallop. "I'll see you there, Lana."

He rides off, and before he reaches the horizon, he vanishes into the shimmering mist at the edge of the sea.

"Stebbins," she calls. She shouts it. "Stebbins!"

<<There is no player online with that name.>>

CHAPTER 52

LESH TUNGSTEN
<EMERGENCY RESPONDERS>

Mom's working. Dad's got at least five beers in him and a sixth one in his hand. Short of calling Weiner or Jelly for a ride—not going to happen—I'm stuck waiting for a bus or riding my bike.

I'd run if I had to.

The garage door has no opener—aside from me, I mean. Dad's got old gear in there—ladders he doesn't touch, a lawn mower that spends two-thirds of the year plugged in to get ready for the six times I have to push it around the yard. And hanging from one wall on a red-rubber-coated hook is my mountain bike. It was my thirteenth birthday present. Deel got a BMX thing, and we rode them like crazy for about twelve seconds. The tires are low on air and I don't care. I think I heard flattish tires are better in the rain anyway. Did I mention the rain?

As I ride through our back alley and then onto Griggs Street, the rain is pouring over me in sheets. I'm soaked to the skin in seconds and University Avenue is like a blur of color, like a runny painting, the red-and-white lights of the cars and the streetlamps and the red and green and yellow of the traffic signals reflecting in the deep running puddles along the curbs. It's Saturday night, and the drivers don't see the brainless boy in all black as he struggles to cross. Finally I have to dismount and run across, pushing my bike beside me.

Over the interstate, the wind picks up. I feel like it might blow me over the high fence and down to the road, where a semi doing seventy can flatten me. I don't want to die, but at least I wouldn't have to explain this to Svetlana.

Past the high school and the park next door, the world is greener, the houses cleaner, the cars newer. It's quiet, aside from the sound of the rain in the trees and hitting my back and the street around me. It's almost beautiful. Svetlana would think it was beautiful. Svvetlana would too.

I push up Summit Avenue and take a dangerous left from the bike lane, across two lanes of car traffic, and down a side street. The juice shop is close now. I just hope Stebbins had a longer way to go, because I don't want him to beat me there. Please don't let him beat me there.

CHAPTER 53

SVETLANA ALLEGHENY
<THE CLOSERS>

I've got both elbows on the counter next to the registers and am leaning on my fists, watching my closing coworker/boss and well-regarded night manager Kyle sweep the front of the store. It's very small, and I don't think he quite trusts my skills with a broom just yet, so he's doing the sweeping. I've already done the part where my arms are bicep-deep in alternating tubs of scalding soapy water and then ice-cold water and bleach to wash all the myriad of funny-looking pieces of equipment we use here at the juice shop.

I'm also wearing a green-and-orange baseball cap with my braid pulled through the hole in the back.

"Any big plans after work tonight?" Kyle says as he pushes the broom. "Say, why don't you fill the mop bucket?"

"Nope," I say, "and okay," and I go into the back and turn the tap marked "scalding," then slip the big yellow wheely bucket under the flow and add a squirt of soap. Then I resume my leaning, except now it's on the edge of the sink instead of the counter.

"Lana!" calls Kyle from the front. "You've got a customer."

I peek out from the back and there's this guy in a suit and holding a bunch of flowers. He's looking around the place, examining the flyers on the wall next to the register, looking at the posters in the window, flipping through the nutritional information notebook tied to the counter. "Just a second," I call out to him, and he jumps at my voice. I hurry back to turn off the sink, then head to the counter, drying off my hands as I go.

"And that's nine," says Kyle. He pulls his extendable key from the ring on his belt, bends down, and locks the door so no one else can come in. The man in the suit will be our last customer. I hope his order is simple, because, like I said, the dishes are done. Kyle heads to the back, probably to grab the full mop bucket and get started on the last job of the night.

"Can I help you?" I say. He's at the counter now, grinning like crazy.

"Hi," he says.

"Hi," I say. "Have you decided what you'll have?" I ask.

"Not yet, Svetlana," he says. He licks his lips and grins as he scans the menu hanging on the wall over my head.

"Oh!" I say. "You were in the other day. You asked if Lana was short for anything."

"That's right," he says, squinting at me.

"Um, those are nice flowers," I say, because they are. "Are

361

they for your wife or girlfriend or something?" It's a wild bouquet of tiny-petal flowers in every color. If not for the professional paper wrapping and baby's breath, I'd think this man had just been in a field someplace, gathering exactly the right samples for this bouquet.

"I'm glad you like them," he says, and he holds them out, sneaking a glance over my shoulder toward the back. "They're for you."

"For—" My stomach twists a little, and I take a step back. I'm still smiling, but now it's a frozen thing, stuck to my face, and I can't break it. My forehead goes cold, and the icy tingle under my arms starts its crawl across my body. Behind me, the water is running. I can't figure why. The bucket was full. Why isn't Kyle up front yet? Why is he still back there? Who is this man?

"I'm sorry," says the man across the counter. He lays down the flowers between us and reaches out for me, as if to comfort me, like I'm a frightened cat who might hide under the couch. My forehead tingles and starts to go cold. "I didn't mean to upset you."

"Who are you?" I say, and he stands up straight and his smile comes back and he says, "I'm Stebbins."

The water running behind is so loud. It fills my ears, so my voice sounds like it's not my own, like it's coming from far away, deep in a cave on the other side of the world. I shake my head and step back a little farther. "I don't know you."

"Sure you do," he says, pulling in his chin. "I'm sure it's weird. You can take some time."

Someone's trying to get in. Someone's tugging on the locked door, over and over, but we're closed. It's dark outside, and through the glass, with the ultrabright juice shop lights on and pounding down on me, I can't see a thing. My polo shirt is clinging to the cold sweat on my back.

The man in the suit—Stebbins—leans one hand on the counter and puts the other on his hip. "You're just how I pictured you," he says. "You're just exactly how I pictured you." He's shaking his head, so impressed with me, and the water is still running behind me like a torrent.

"Kyle," I call to the back, because I wish he'd turn off the water, and Stebbins seems to come to life—his face flashes and his smile is gone, and his hand shoots from his waist and grabs my wrist, pulls me closer to him, down across the counter. I tug back, but it's no good.

"You're hurting me!" I snap, and the tugging on the door is back, like it might burst from the hinge, and then there's pounding on the glass, and a voice—a voice is shouting from the darkness, calling my name: "Svetlana! Open the door!"

I shriek for Kyle and the water finally switches off. He comes from the back now, drying his hands, and he's angry— he's angry at me. I pull the key from his belt and run around the counter for the door. Stebbins gets there first, though, and he's pleading now with his hands up. He takes my shoulders and tries to hold me there. What is he saying? My ears ring, an echo of the water's white noise, and pound along with my pulse.

"Lana, don't freak out," he says. "It's me. You know me. You're just having a hard time. But it's me."

I shake my head and raise my shoulders, try to pull away. Kyle is shouting now too, reaching over the counter. He's got Stebbins's suit coat by the sleeve, pulling. It's going to rip.

"Let go of her!"

The banging on the door is so loud. The glass will break. "Stebbins!" says the voice outside. "It's me!" It's Lesh. He's screaming. He's screaming and crying. "That's not her!" His throat will tear and bleed. "It's me!"

Stebbins stops. He lets go of my shoulders. And I can breathe, and I can see, and I thrust my knee and connect with his crotch. His breath catches and he says, "Uf," and he falls to his knees in front of me. I drop beside him and unlock the door, and Lesh throws it open. He pulls Stebbins by the lapel onto the sidewalk, and I shove the door closed and lean on it. Kyle is beside me in an instant, with his arm around my shoulders, and I'm crying.

CHAPTER 54

LESH TUNGSTEN
<USELESS SAVIORS>

It's raining and cold, and in no time we're drenched. Stebbins gets to his feet and faces me.

"What the hell is this?" he says. He's coughing, too, holding his stomach. His face is red, and I can't tell if he's crying or if his cheeks and the corners of his eyes are just holding on to raindrops. "Who are you?"

I stand there, letting the rainwater flood over my face. "I'm her. I'm Svvetlana."

He stares at me.

"Not her," I say. "She has no idea. I'm Svvetlana. I'm the one you're looking for."

He looks back through the glass door. Svetlana has her back to us, sitting against the door next to her boss. Her shoulders are shaking, and I know it's my fault.

Stebbins turns, like he's done, like he's heading back to his car, but he only gets one step and turns back, and he pulls back and throws a punch. His fist connects with the side of my face just under my eye, and I go down. I lie there, watching Svetlana's shoulders shake only inches away on the other side of the door, and I'm listening to his heavy wet footsteps and then the roar of his engine, and letting the rain fall down over me.

The water coats my face, and I can't tell if I'm bleeding, but while I watch her, Svetlana looks over her shoulder at me, her face still wet and tired. I know what it means: it means disappointment, scorn, confusion. I'm going to have to explain, but for now I just sit up, stand up, and start walking.

ACCOUNT DELETED

CHAPTER 55

LESH TUNGSTEN
<PATHETIC AND SAD>

She eats lunch in the library now, I guess, every day. I've hardly seen her. I've only caught a glimpse here and there of a white-blond head above the crowd in the entrance of the school, or bouncing down the stairs on the east side, or even coasting south on Lexington at two thirty. I haven't tried talking to her, not since I sent a long message—a rambling thing I read and reread and wrote and rewrote fifty times, all that Sunday, knowing it was pointless, knowing I didn't deserve to be forgiven.

I'd said I was sorry, though. I'd said I hadn't meant to hurt anyone, or scare anyone. I'd tried to tell her I admired her, that I adored her, that I saw something in her that was so special, so beautiful, so powerful, that it had seemed so natural to me at the time, and every time, that this magical, strong, silver-haired elf would be her. She couldn't be me, I tried to explain. I'm not beautiful. I'm not powerful. I'm not special. I'd made an orc, I even thought of saying, and that was me: smelly and mindless and wielding a single heavy sword like—well, it's obvious, I guess.

But I couldn't get any of that to sound right, so instead I typed this:

There's a scarecrow stuck to the top of my neighbor's chain-link fence. She's just a little one, like something you buy at a craft store to decorate around Thanksgiving. She's been there for a couple years now, and she's faded and bent, and looks a little sad, but all told she's holding up pretty well. Don't worry; I'm not about to compare you to a world-weary scarecrow. But here's the thing: I don't know why I call that thing "she." It could just as well be a he. I suppose it's the apron, a little square of once-red, now-pink tied around her waist. Pink means she, I guess, in my little pea brain. I'm watching her from my bedroom window right now. She's fluttering a lot. It's windy.

I don't know if it's like this for everyone, or even for every boy, but when I was little, it was pretty simple: boys have a thing; girls don't. Obviously there's more to it, but that was enough as a kindergartener, I guess. I'm older now, and I'm realizing that's bull, and here's why: because the difference between boys and girls and men and women isn't about what men have and women don't. It's about what women have, and men don't.

Svetlana, you have grace and beauty and strength

and confidence and purpose and talent and love for the world and your friends. I have none of those things, and when I grow up, I'd much rather be like you than be another giant boy with a beer in one hand and a remote control in the other. I hope you can forgive me.

Then I explained about the game, and I explained about Stebbins, and I hit send. A week later, I haven't heard back, and I kind of hope I never do. I'm finished with lunch quickly, and I head for my eleven-fifteen class, Olsen's English class. It's up on the third floor, so I take the main steps past the library—I still hope to catch a glimpse, now and then, if I can—and settle down on the floor outside room 3217 and pull out the reading. I've read it—I'm not gaming anymore, and I can't bear to even talk to Greg these days, much less hang out with him, so I have more than enough time to get my homework done; I'm sure Mom's happy. But I pull out the reading anyway because it's something to put in front of my face.

I don't think Svetlana went around telling anyone what happened. I don't think Deel spread my elf priestess's existence around either. Even so—I know it's out there now, out of my head and my body and in the world. That means it's on my face, and it's part of who I really am, who I've really been. So I sit, with the book in front of my face so no one can see me, no one can see the word printed across my face: G.I.R.L. Maybe it doesn't even need the periods anymore.

Someone's standing over me. But my headphones are on,

and the book shield is up, so I ignore the shadow falling over me and keep pretending to read. But whoever it is won't have any of my crap and kicks my foot. I look up.

You already guessed, I suppose, and I jump to my feet and pull off my headphones, so panicked and afraid that they miss my neck and hit the wall behind me and fall to the floor. She laughs and I apologize.

"Do you want to take a walk?" she says, and I look at my feet and hers and mumble something about class and Mr. Olsen. She points out we have twenty minutes.

"I ate faster than I meant to," I say, and then add, "I don't like being down there anymore, by myself."

She swallows and looks at the stairs. "Come on," she says, and she walks and I gather my books into my bag and follow. She's carrying her tote over one shoulder, so I walk on that side of her, a little behind, and she leads me down the steps—two flights down, to the drama rooms and the music classes and the pool, and we meander down the long, wide halls without lockers. She doesn't speak, so I don't, and instead we listen to the orchestra instruments tuning and playing and tuning in a random and wild—I'm searching for the Svetlana word for it, and it doesn't come. I miss her. I want to tell her it sounds like Björk, and that Björk reminds me of her, and of the afternoon in her bedroom when she grabbed me and kissed me after the little hen ran downstairs. But I don't.

"I wanted to ask you something," she says.

"Okay."

"You like me," she says, and it's not a question, so I stay silent and wait for the rest. It's twenty-five paces before it comes. "But there's a lot I don't get."

"Me too."

She looks at me sideways and keeps walking. "Your message has been on my mind," she goes on, "like, all the time since I read it."

"Really?"

A little nod. "I've read it over and over, too. I'm trying to wrap my head around it, but I'm not sure I can."

"That's because I'm a mental patient."

A smile. "I doubt it."

I don't.

"But I don't really get one thing, and it's kind of the important thing," Svetlana says, and here she finally stops and turns to face me. "Do you want to be *with* me, or do you want to *be* me?"

That's the million-dollar question.

Her face is only inches from mine. I feel like I haven't seen it, this close and this well, in so long. I've been parched for it, maybe, and glimpses in the hall—fleeting ones—and glimpses of her online profile haven't been terribly fulfilling. Now here she is, with me, and I would do anything to not have this conversation, to go back ten days, three weeks, to that night at the corner of Thomas Avenue and Hamline, to do this right, to bury down deep whatever inkling in my messed-up brain of rocks told me to climb into a silver dress of spirit and a pair of leporine ears.

"I . . ."

The buzzer sounds. We have to go. But Svetlana shakes her head and crosses her arms. "Uh-uh," she says. "Answer me."

But . . . "I can't."

She takes a deep breath through her nose and sighs. Strawberries and honey and maybe the tiniest bit of garlic and soy sauce. The tiniest bit. "We're going to try meeting in Roan's basement tonight," she says. "Gaming Club, I mean. You're still a member, right?"

"I am?"

She puts a hand on my wrist and smiles, and then she's off, leaving me standing here outside the orchestra room as the place starts to empty, students streaming past me, around me on both sides, like I'm a rock in a stream, each of them carrying a hard black case, boats in the stream, full of potential music.

Roan's house isn't far from mine, really just a straight shot north across the train yard. Mom's driving me up there. It feels weird. I can't remember the last time I asked my mom for a ride some-place. Normally if I'm going anywhere, it's with Greg, and if we're going beyond his house off the bus route or far enough away that we'd have to transfer a bunch, we're going with Cheese or Weiner or one of those guys. No mom ride necessary. Anyway, tonight I'd be happy to walk, but it's really getting to be winter here, and winter in Saint Paul is no joke.

We turn left onto Horton—the road I generally just think of as the one we take to the zoo and little amusement park.

Mom's feeling wistful. "I used to take you up here, jeez, three times a week sometimes," she says, nodding to the right as we pass the turnoff to the zoo parking lot. "Sometimes we walked. Or anyway I walked. You rode in the stroller. It was the only exercise I got, I swear."

I'm leaning against the passenger window, breathing on it so it fogs up around my nose. Then the fog recedes when I inhale, like it knows. I get that it fogs when I exhale, but the inhale part really weirds me out for some reason.

Roan lives just a few blocks from the zoo, so in no time we're pulled up in front. I'm relieved to see a plain old Como bungalow, sort of like ours, but sideways, and not one of the giant Victorian things that line Midway Parkway.

"Thanks," I say.

"Let me know when you want to be picked up," she says. "Give me a little warning, too, okay? And you won't be too late?"

"I doubt it," I say, and I'm secretly hoping I won't call for a ride, since Svetlana probably drove. Maybe she'll offer, and maybe that'll mean I'm getting another real shot at—at something. Don't make me say friendship, because we both know that's not all I want. Now if I could just figure out what I do want.

Roan's little house is crowded with red-haired Garnets. Her father, the only gray-mane, lets me in, shakes my hand, tells me his name and his wife's name—she's standing behind him about twenty paces, in the kitchen, and she waves. She's got a towel over her shoulder, and a girl with pin-straight bright orange hair is leaning against her leg, watching me come in.

"Let me hang up your coat," says Mr. Garnet, and I let him peel it off me, then watch as he tosses it over the back of the couch.

"Thanks."

He slaps me on the back and then grabs a magazine from the little table near the door. It has a painting of Mars on the cover. He heads into the bathroom, leaving me standing near the front door.

"Um," I say, not to anyone in particular, but kind of hoping someone will figure out that I don't know where the basement is, and a moment later a door in the kitchen flies open and Roan's freckled face pops out at floor level.

"Down here, miscreant!" she shouts. I hear Svetlana's admonition and Reggie's exaggerated guffaw from behind her and decide to take it as good-natured ribbing instead of ongoing distaste for my person.

The basement is done up—it feels at once like Svetlana's handiwork, like she's done her best to cover the Garnets' basement in a thick coating of her brain. That sounds grosser than it looks. The walls are partially covered with whisper-thin hangings—a few just fields of abstract color, one of a red dragon, twisting and turning, and one of a black jungle cat, peering out of the art at me. The dragon seems to breathe and cavort as the slight draft from the open basement door flutters the silk. The cat prowls, its yellow eyes nearly demonic; it threatens to pounce from the fabric and knock me to the floor at the bottom of the steps.

"Saved you a seat," says Reggie, patting the folding chair beside him. The three of them are at the table already, and the screen is up and the dice are out, and metal figurines stand boldly on the empty middle of the table, between short, fat, flickering candles.

"Get the light," Roan adds. She does a seat hop—I can't remember when she's ever sat still—and nods at me. The light switch is next to my shoulder, so I hit it and go downstairs.

As I sit next to Reggie, right across from Svetlana, I try a smile. It doesn't quite take, but I say, "Hi." She smiles back, and she's a lot better at it.

"Okay," she says, and she does a two-handed ear-hair tuck. "We're going to have to start from scratch."

"Again," says Reggie, and he winks at me.

"Again," Svetlana allows, "and I don't mind at all. I've tweaked the campaign a tiny bit, and Lesh, let's get you set up to take over as a fighter for our deceased companion."

"Deceased?" I say.

Roan and Reggie close their eyes and hold hands. They look down, like they're praying. "Poor Abey," says Roan, shaking her head. The frizzy collection of hair bounces and wiggles.

"I heard they found him on his back in the woods with a pair of daggers in his chest," says Reggie.

Svetlana leans forward and whispers, "In the suburbs." She winks. They're kidding.

"I'm going to take that as a warning," I say. "Don't cross the Gaming Club."

"Again," Svetlana mouths at me. She hasn't told these two about what happened, and I can hardly bear to have such faith from this girl. "So, where were we? Rolling a new PC for the miscreant?"

"Right," I say, pulling my chair in. I reach into my jeans pocket and pull out a little wooden box and pop off its cover, dump a set of dice onto the table. "I'm ready."

"Hey, look who finally got a set," Reggie says, and I don't know if he intended the double meaning, but I'm hearing it, and it's fair enough.

So I roll a PC—a big, tough human who can stand at the front and take the brunt of damage while my companions Meridel and Ambient tear our opponents to shreds and keep me alive. My PC is a warrior, clad in heavy armor and wielding a shield and sword. When we're done filling in the stats, Svetlana grins over the top of her screen.

"Everyone ready?" Her finger is poised over her iPod's play button.

We nod. Her finger drops.

And then . . .

CHAPTER 56

SVETLANA ALLEGHENY
<THE NEW STARTS>

It's before sunrise in the weird little village at the base of Frozen Flame Mountain in the far north. You, MAEVE, *stand in the doorway of the Sword and the Moth and scan the big, dark room. A human girl and a robed elf—obviously a wizard—are seated in a booth along the wall farthest from the door, out of the flickering orange light of the potbelly stove in the center of the room. It's a slow night—or morning, actually—at the inn. The few customers still there, who haven't found a bed to sleep in or a hole to crawl into, are slumped across the tops of their tables or necking in the corners of the room. The barkeep is dozing himself in a high-backed chair behind the bar. The girl and wizard are awake, though, and she is counting glittering coins on the table in front of her. She takes a big swig of her ale and catches you checking her out. She nods toward you, and the wizard turns to see.*

They both stand. It's clear now that the girl, clad in leather and with a dagger sheath on each hip, is a thief. Your right hand goes instinctively to the leather pouch on your belt, Maeve, but there isn't much there to protect. You haven't found work in days, and if this village doesn't provide some, you'll go hungry before too long.

The thief and wizard move toward you. When they're close, the wizard raises one hand in a show of peace. "We are not your enemies," he says.

"Not yet," you say back. It's nearly a whisper, giving you a threatening and mysterious air. The thief smiles. The wizard does not.

"I can see you're a powerful warrior," he says, "and we are in need of protection."

You scan both their faces for any sign of ill will. Finding none, you nod. "Go on."

The wizard goes on to tell you of their quest, and of their fallen companion, who died in a way so gruesome and painful and humiliating that I shall not repeat it here.

"Does it pay?" you ask.

The thief snickers and turns around.

"There will be treasure and loot along the way," the wizard explains. "As to your portion of the booty, you'll have to deal with Meridel about that. I only seek the completion of my quest for the good of all creatures."

You squint at the thief, and she looks back and shrugs. "We'll work something out," she says. "If you're good protection, you'll make a fortune. Deal?"

"Deal," you say, and you put out your hand to shake. They both accept. "What's your name?" you ask the wizard.

"I am Ambient," he says, and he pulls up his hood. "The sun will be up soon. We should get started."

"Don't you want to know my name?" you say, but the wizard slides past you, through the inn's door, and into the street.

"Don't worry," says the thief, clapping your shoulder. "He already knows."

"Maeve?" Reggie says. "You know that's a girl's name?"

Lesh glances at me an instant, and then back at Reggie. "Yeah," he says. "My warrior is a woman."

Roan shifts in her seat, changing her booster foot from right to left. "I rolled a male PC in our last campaign," she says, looking down at her character sheet. Then she looks up at me. "Remember that, Svet? He was hot."

"He was," I admit, and Reggie nods vigorously.

"What about you, Maeve?" Roan says. She leans far across the table on her elbows and knees. "Are you hot?"

Lesh smiles. In better light, we'd probably see his face go red. "Of course," he says.

"Of course," Reggie mocks, and as Roan slips backward into her chair, the draft blows out the candles in the middle of the table. Reggie runs for the light switch, and when he does: *pop!* The fuse blows.

Reggie opens the door to the kitchen. "Sorry, Ms. G!" he calls out.

"I'm making microwave popcorn," she shouts back. "Or I was."

"Hand me a flashlight," Roan calls up, and she hurries to the top of the steps and grabs it from her mom through the slightly open door. Then she hurries to the fuse box.

"Popcorn. Now I'm hungry," Reggie says. "Are there snacks? Because we should probably have snacks."

"I skipped dinner," Lesh says. He's found the lighter and sparked one of the big candles. "I'm that committed to this club." His face is lit only slightly. The flickering candlelight sends shadows like moths under his chin and across his cheeks. When he blinks, his eyelashes are long-legged spiders.

"How noble," I say.

Roan is still at the box. "I'm going to make pizza rolls," she says. "I have it all planned."

"And I," says Reggie, getting to his feet, "am going to help."

They hurry up the steps, not even hitting the light switch on the way up. "Guys!" I call after them, because I know their mischievous little brains. I didn't give them details about that night at the shop, and no one knows about Lesh's note, but anyone could sense there's something going on. Still, I'm not ready for another try with Lesh, and I'm sure he's not either. I get up from the table and feel my way through the dark to the ratty old couch. Because maybe he and I can talk. It'll be easier to say whatever we have to say with the lights off.

"Sorry," I say once I've sat down. "They think they're cute."

"They are kinda," he says. The feet of his chair rub on the flattened carpet as he gets up. He blows out the candle before approaching, and I'm glad.

"Sit here," I say into the darkness. I find the throw on the arm beside me—it's musty and old and smells like a Garnet and my youth and generally like brown and red. Maybe in the dark, colors and smells are kind of the same thing.

As I'm covering up, the couch gives on my left. He's leaning forward, his elbows on his knees. He's running a hand through his hair. He's cracking his knuckles. I only know for sure about the last one, but I can guess the rest. I didn't realize how much time we'd spent together. I didn't think I'd miss him. I didn't think I'd want to find him in the dark. But I do, and he's here, and I have to think of something to say.

CHAPTER 57

LESH TUNGSTEN
<THE CHEESY MIDDLES>

"You never gave me an answer," she says. She's right next to me and holding out the corner of her blanket to me, and she's whispering, I guess so Roan and Reggie won't hear us—won't know we're huddled together against the dark and the cold under a musty blanket on this decrepit couch. "About me, I mean."

"About what I want?"

She nods. I know even though I can't see her, by the way the air moves between us, and the change in her breathing, and the brush of her hair—a few escaped strands at her forehead or temple kiss my cheek like butterflies.

"Because I still don't know," I say.

She shifts a little, moves away the tiniest bit on the couch. There's a draft on my neck I hadn't felt a moment ago.

"None of it's true, you know," she says. "That stuff about women and men."

"Seems true to me," I say, and she kind of grunts, slaps the pillow of the couch. "What?"

"Then fine," she says, all kinds of grumpy. "Then be a woman. Who cares?"

This is not where I expected this conversation to go. I can hear Roan and Reggie's feet on the floor over my head. They're in the kitchen, I guess, and through the floor we can sometimes hear them laugh or talk, when their voices get a bit louder and animated.

"Are you serious?" I say.

"Sure," she says, and she's standing. I'm not sure when she got up, but she's moved across the room a bit.

"Don't turn the light on yet," I say.

"I don't want to be a woman," I say. "I mean, I don't want to, you know, wear a dress and grow breasts and all that."

"So what do you want?" She's standing in front of the couch now, facing me. Being blind feels good. I'm feeling connected to her now, connected to the air in the room and the breath in her lungs. Every inch of my skin seems to be reaching out, grasping for stimuli in the space around me and between us. It's late, and my tiredness is getting the better of me. While we're silent, the music changes, and in a moment a familiar tympani roll appears. In this darkness, with my new blind vision, it is a new experience. Svetlana isn't conducting. It's just our bodies in the dark space of the basement, the calling horns, the pounding drums, the mournful strings, and the heavy feet of the condemned man climbing the scaffold to his death.

"Lesh?" she says. I've been silent too long.

"I'm just listening," I say, and it comes out in a whisper.

She sits next to me, right up against me, and leans on my shoulder. "Me too."

As the horns finish their second fanfare, I see more clearly than I have before, so I start talking. It's less than a whisper; I can hardly be sure I'm talking out loud. I can't be sure that she hears me. But maybe it doesn't matter. I have to say it.

"I just want grace. I want passion and heart and beauty and a sense of connection to the world. I also want to feel your breath on my neck like I can right now, and the heat coming off your hands and leg. I want to walk down the halls of the high school and instead of feeling nearly crushed by the bricks and tiles and masses of other bodies, pressing against me, pushing me deeper into myself, I want to smash the walls and people away so I can breathe under a wide-open sky, with grass under my feet and the sun on my hair, and when I imagine that—when I sit here in the dark where I can see everything and imagine myself doing that—you're with me, and you're smiling, and I don't think I could have done it without you."

When the oboe cries and the snare rolls, followed by the bouncing head down the scaffold steps, I'm sad only that it's such a short piece. The basement door flies open, and the lights flash on. Svetlana jumps to her feet, and her eyes are red and she's smiling down at me.

Roan calls from the top of the stairs, "Pizza rolls!"

ACKNOWLEDGMENTS

Thanks first and foremost to Beth and Sam. I could not and would not do a thing worth doing without you two.

Thanks to Edward, for sticking with me through some weird-ass books. Thanks also to Jordan, who helped shape this particular weirdness into the best book it could be.

Thank you to my family all over the country, blood and otherwise: my mother and her ilk back east; my brother and his brood out west; and my in-laws here in the middle. You've all always been nothing but supportive and have also given of yourselves in the form of free babysitting.

The Minnesota children's and YA literature scene is not to be believed. It's huge, for one thing, and its people are impossibly supportive of one another. Thanks, then, to the entire MN KidLit crew, and to the Loft for existing, and in particular to the Black Sheep—Jeremy Anderson, Kelly Barnhill, Jodi Chromey, Karlyn Coleman, Christopher Lincoln, and Kurtis

Scaletta—for everything, to Anne Ursu for talking me up, and to Pete Hautman for not giving me a hard time about the head-bonk thing. Jaclyn Dolamore is a writer not from Minnesota, but her sketches and notes from her days creating RPGs were invaluable; thanks to her as well.

Thanks also to local dungeon master Anthony Strafaccia for letting me observe, and to the brave adventurers on his campaign: Marc Carey, Nicholas Henkes, Erik Hoskins, Abigail Kooiker, and Stu Wester. It was educational and thoroughly entertaining every time.

I wouldn't have gotten a good peek inside Central High School in Saint Paul without the help of teacher Andrew Andestic, and I wouldn't have had any deep insight into cafeteria and hallway idiosyncrasies without some help from his students; thanks to them.

What Dwells Within was a real band from Omaha, Nebraska, and they were gracious enough to let me use their band name and a few song titles herein. They've since changed their name to A Sound in Sight and can be found at www.asisofficial.com. They kick ass. I'd be remiss also if I didn't mention Laurine from Green at Heart Rugs Etsy shop, who created the rug that sits on my office floor and in the middle of Svetlana's bedroom.

I wrote nearly every word of this book at the best coffee shop in Saint Paul, Groundswell, right in Hamline-Midway—where Lesh and Greg live. They've expanded a bit since my day, two years ago, and have become quite the talk of the town, but they're still as friendly and comfortable as ever. You should go if you're in town.

I must acknowledge the Dark Clouds, a very real and very excellent group of pro soccer supporters here in Minnesota, and Minnesota United FC, our professional soccer team. (They used to be known as the Stars, and before that, yes, the Thunder.) If you're in the neighborhood, get out to a game and sit in the east stands. Thanks, by the way, to Kristen and Charlie Martilla for dragging my wife and me to our first game. I don't think I could have ever imagined Henny and her congealing nachos otherwise.

Finally, though I haven't seen Sooz in a very long time, I know she'd like to send her thanks to guildies Antosiak, Kenisfis, and Vigilannie.